Tales from
HIGH
HALLACK

the collected short stories of
ANDRE NORTON

Volume 1

TALES FROM HIGH HALLACK, VOLUME 1

Print ISBN: 978-1-62467-189-0

eISBN: 978-1-62467-188-3

Published by Premier Digital Publishing
www.premierdigitalpublishing.com
Follow us on Twitter @PDigitalPub
Follow us on Facebook: Premier Digital Publishing

FROM THE SWORD OF UNBELIEF

Its weapon was terror, not any sword. As I stiffened and drew deeply upon my power, I realized it for what it was—a thoughtform born out of ancient fear and hatred. So did it continue to feed upon such emotions, drawing into it at each feeding a greater substance. My fear, my anger, must have both summoned and fed it. But it was real. That I could swear to, as much as if I laid hand upon that outstretched arm of bone. And Fallon's wide-eyed terror was meat to it also. While it trailed behind it, like a cloak, a deep depression of the spirit.

Fallon reared, screamed. That mount of bone opened wide its jaws in answer. I struggled with the panic-mad horse under me, glad for a moment that I had this to fight, for it awoke my mind from the blast of fear the spectre brought with it.

FOR BILL FAWCETT

CONTENTS

ACKNOWLEDGMENTS

After Andre Norton moved into my Tennessee home in mid-2004, she often spoke of wanting all of her short stories gathered in a special collection . . . all in one place so she could have easy access to read them. Unfortunately, circumstances beyond our control got in the way of her dream while she was alive.

Andre's estate has come a long way. Lots of good things are happening with careful and strategic planning. I am pleased to finally make available to you, Andre's special-edition short story collection. I never lost sight of my dear friend's project; it was important that I followed through to make it happen.

On behalf of Andre's estate and myself, I extend heartfelt thanks to Jay Watts, who was so dedicated and loyal to our Lady. Jay put in countless hours gathering and copying her stories, which paved the way for this collection. This could not have happened without him. He also devoted a lot of effort to Andre's estate-authorized website. Please show him your support by visiting that website at andre-norton-books.com.

I would also like to thank Jody Lynn Nye, who happily accepted my request to write the introduction. Thanks to Jean Rabe, who lovingly agreed to edit these books. Thanks to Ethan Ellenberg, Evan Gregory, and Premier Digital Publishing, all instrumental in getting Andre's works into your hands.

Above all of that—many, many thanks to Andre Norton, for sharing her stories with the world, and sharing a part of her life with me. Rest in peace, my dear friend.

Sue Stewart, the Andre Norton Estate

INTRODUCTION

I wasn't looking for Andre Norton when I found her.

I'd just had a terrible shock, literarywise. I had asked a couple of my high school teachers, "What is this thing called science fiction?"

In all kindness, they lent me books that they felt really represented the genre, a book each from Kurt Vonnegut and Ray Bradbury. With no disrespect meant to the grand masters themselves, those were not the books to hand to an impressionable and sensitive fourteen-year-old girl who was having personal issues. Those books were products of the Cold War era, during which everyone thought that nuclear war was imminent, and the Armageddon-heavy fiction reflected that bleak time. The writing was compelling, of course; full of futuristic ideas, yes; but in particular, early on in *The Martian Chronicles*, they blow up the Earth.

That was a concept I was not prepared to handle. After all, I live here, and if my home was going to be destroyed with no possibility of survival, I had nowhere else to go. Reading those books terrified me. Our future was to be burned alive! I felt trapped. "If that is science fiction," my past self said with the dogmatic conviction only possible in people that young, "I will never read it again."

Cue the cackling of the Fates.

Being the kind of reader who must pass words before her eyes as many hours as possible during the day, I still needed books.

I read *The Lord of the Rings* and the *Chronicles of Narnia*. I wanted more. So, I browsed through the three floors of my high school library, picking up things that looked interesting to me, careful to avoid anything that had a spaceship on the cover or anything science-y in the title. I read a good deal of nonfiction. I loved biographies, although they usually ended the same way, with the main character dying.

The library was well-stocked with fantasies.

In this way, I came to pick up a book that looked good to me: *The Crystal Gryphon*, by Andre Norton. Its cover featured a young woman, not much more than my age, and a young male whose pupils in his golden eyes were slitted horizontally. Good start.

The story, one of the first I had ever read written in first person, sounded like a grand tale of high fantasy. I was sucked in immediately by Norton's writing. She drew pictures in my mind of a hardscrabble, ancient landscape, with feuds, fears, and magic. The narrator, Kerovan himself, with his hooved feet and goat's eyes, was descended from the Old Ones who had once populated High Hallack. I was too inexperienced to pick up on the clues that would have told me what I was dealing with. So it was not really until close to the end, when Kerovan and his lady Joisan came upon a metal contraption that said "Hot" on one side and "Cold" on the other that I realized that this was yet another piece of post-apocalyptic fiction set on Earth. The difference was that humanity, however altered, had survived. I had been tricked into reading a piece of science fiction, and I liked it.

From then on, Andre Norton's books became my safe place.

With her to retreat to, I ventured forth into other SF writer's realms, always knowing that if they scared me too much, I could go back again to her. But she gave me confidence in the genre. Not every book or story pictured a bleak and terrible future. In fact, there were broad, exciting ideas aplenty to discover and ponder. I have always been grateful to Norton for giving me that second chance. Think of how much I would have missed, if I had not found her in my library!

Apart from that aha! moment, I just plain enjoyed Norton's writing. I cared deeply for her characters. Many of them were as young as I was, but they fought to survive, always coming up with ingenious ways to defeat the menace they faced. Where they had no allies, they stood fast. Norton provided many of them with lovers, rescuers, mentors, and friends, just as well drawn, and just as interesting to know.

Images and moments, described so vividly that I felt them, have ingrained themselves in my memory from each of the books I read. I was delighted to learn how many books there were yet to read. Like anyone else who has been frustrated to fall for an author who wrote just a few books, or perhaps only one book of note, I was so pleased to find a writer who had produced so much literature that I could wallow in it.

Since there was no biography at the end of *The Crystal Gryphon*, it wasn't until later that I discovered that Andre was *Alice* Andre Norton. As an aspiring writer myself, I always looked for role models.

To find a woman writing science fiction with such skill and style was a joy. Her heroines never waited limply for someone to save them. She could have coined the term "self-rescuing princess." Just reading her work taught me a great deal about my chosen craft.

Norton blazed a trail that I followed humbly. To this day, every time I read something of hers, I learn something new. I am as freshly impressed and surprised as was that girl in her high school library long ago.

If this is your first experience with Andre Norton, you're in for a treat. Her short fiction appeared in magazines, many of which have long crumbled to yellowed fragments, (damn that acid-treated paper!), or in out-of-print anthologies. Jean Rabe and Sue Stewart have put together these collections so Norton-lovers have those lost pieces all together at their fingertips.

Enjoy them! I certainly will.

Jody Lynn Nye
www.jodynye.com

THE LAST SPELL
Ancient Enchantresses (1995) DAW

She had somehow gotten him here—to this, his own well-guarded shrine where the ancient wisdom had been so many times called upon. Some of its power *must* cling to these rough rock walls. How long had it been—two days, three—she could not remember with any certainty. Her mind had been too occupied with hope and what she could recall of the knowledge which had been his gift to her.

They had this place as their goal when the first pangs struck him and he had near fallen from his mount. Only his iron will had kept him in the saddle. And they had both known at once what darkness had struck at him. Her lips thinned over her teeth in a vixen's snarl, as the she fox might lift lip to show teeth when her den and cubs were in danger.

She had brought him here, and by the time they had stumbled within he was nearly past her handling. He was a tall man and though not full-fleshed, she was well overtopped by him. Since that coming she had fought—by the Lady—how she had fought!

It was twilight dim in the cave except where a spear thrust of sunlight struck through a high wall crevice to reveal clearly the bed and that wasted figure lying under the covers. So quiet now. The watcher edged her stool closer. Fear arose in her, making her firmly call upon the controls she had

1

learned so well.

The air was thick with scents of herbs—herbs steeped, herbs charred, herbs crushed by impatient hands. And there was sound as ever present as those odors. Breathing, slow, which seemed now and then to pause. Then she who crouched on the stool would lean yet farther over that shrouded body, listening with a catch of her own breath.

Not yet—not yet was her battle lost! He must not leave for whatever waited outside, even though she knew—the hurt deep in her—that might be his choice. The last spell—she must have the last, otherwise all she had labored for was nothing more than a broken sword left lying on a field of dire defeat, useless even as a trophy.

Her eyes smarted. She rubbed at them impatiently, fearful of losing some small sign. Now she leaned still farther over—his breathing sounded more regular. Would there be another short period when he would rouse—would know her—be able to listen and respond?

She slipped her arm under the folded cloth which served him as a pillow. His gray head rolled a little toward her. By the Lady, he was old—old!

Memory broke through her absorption—a man in the full of his strength, a man who drew all eyes when he strode in company, who had sought out a girl-child braiding buttercups into a wreath beside the mirroring lake. The summer sun had lain warm on her hair, as brightly yellow as the flowers she twisted to suit her will.

Even as she had reflected the sun, so had that stranger cloaked himself in a kind of shadow. Still she had no warning of any ill intent when she looked upon his straight body, his ordered hair, the subtle richness of his cloak. However, he had been a stranger—and when her eyes had been caught and held by his, she had been slightly troubled.

This man, who had said he was sworn in service to a great lord and knew the court, had somehow changed her life even with his first greeting. He had settled himself on the ground a little away from her, but he had continued to talk or, rather, to subtly question. He had drawn from her much more than she had learned from him.

The hair against her arm, now wet with death sweat, had not been ash colored then but black, with a gloss under the sun's touch. And from the beginning his gray eyes had held a fire such as she had never seen in another's.

Though how limited had been her chance of knowledge of the outer world, cloistered and curtained as she had been in the Lady's lake hall. King's daughter she might once have been, but when her father impatiently brought her to the refuge, honoring as he said a promise to his wife lately dead, she became no more, no less, than any new sister in learning. There was no hint of rank or old blood among them.

Having chanced upon her that day, the stranger had not left her. Oh, no. He had schemed and sworn oaths until she was bonded to him as pupil to teacher, for he had revealed himself at last to her guardians as Merlin, he who stood in the High King's shadow but whose own shadow lay over king and land alike.

She knew the rules of the Old Learning—it passed from man to woman, woman to man. Thus he had awakened her quick interest, fed her hopes, brought to life ambition, held before her promises which had finally led them to this place, this hour of fast speeding time.

Quick of mind, swift of hand, she had served him very willingly. In his own place she had read lore supposedly long lost to the world, the lore of the drowned western lands. She had watched while he wrought with forces strong enough to claw them both into shreds had he not known the bindings.

Ah, yes, she had learned, drinking in what he offered as water sinks into sand, always eager for more and more. While he tantalized her with hints and half promises of greater power to come.

She knew what others had whispered behind their hands at the court when she had journeyed there with him at the High King's asking—that she warmed his bed and fed his man's appetites. But that was not so, for such lusts were no part of the kind of bond which tied them. Other men there had eyed her and had striven to make her aware of their interest. But to her they meant nothing. She was too thirsty for what her service would bring her in the end.

In the end! The girl who was Nimuë, King's daughter, seer's chosen vessel of knowledge, stared down now at the man half resting against her shoulder. He had sworn to her that time itself could be tamed, brought to a halt even as one would break an unridden mount. Time was the last of the great talents to be mastered. And here and now time was her enemy—as if it were a being that sensed what she wished to do.

"Lord!" Her voice was imperative as she thought she saw that twitch of the eyelids which signaled another small moment of consciousness, of being aware of where he was and why. Surely hate for the one who had set this doom on him must burn hot enough to give him strength—Morgause—King's sister, Queen now to stern Lot, Mistress of dark weavings.

That one had broken the pattern Merlin had woven for the safety of Britain, enticing the young High King to her bed, he unknowing of their shared parentage. Thus that one—Nimuë's lips moved now as if she gathered moisture to spit—had thought to hold Arthur under her rule in secret because she carried and birthed a child of forbidden union—an act which could blacken his name among all men.

But Morgause had failed in her schemes, even as Merlin had failed in his plans partly because of her. When he had earlier tossed and turned here on this bed, he had often muttered in delirium, reckoning up all that had gone awry.

To bring Arthur to birth Merlin had wrought one of the first high magics, delivering the Lady Ygraine to Uther Pendragon who wore, through Merlin's powers, the seeming of her rightful Lord, Galoris. So it had been set by the ancient rule which was older even than Britain itself—that a woman of the noble blood of the Drowned Lands was to lie with Pendragon, born of the very stuff of Britain, and so bring forth in secret a son to hold fast the old order against the chaos of the new. But death had spread a red hand across that planning—Galoris' death, which had set the first besmirching of the bright future Merlin strove to bring.

And Arthur himself had failed him then—twice—once when he fell victim to Morgause and again when he had chosen Guinevere, the wrong wife.

Nimuë frowned at the thought of Guinevere—the beautiful, the light of mind, the traitor at heart. Perhaps even yet Merlin's cause could be served if someone kept close guard on Guinevere. While Merlin was still at court that one had feared him. Without him—was that one reason for what Morgause had done? For truly it was her poison which ate at him now.

Some said the Queen was barren, for she had not quickened though the High King showed her all favor and shared her bed. But others looked from Arthur to Morgause and spoke of a sin which could smite a man so. Perhaps it was both—who knew what moved the Great Powers to grant or deny?

The man Nimuë half supported sighed as if he shared that dread thought of hers. His eyes opened and for a moment he again showed that strength which had drawn her to him from the beginning.

"Master—" she said softly.

His features seemed to change under her very eyes, become firmer, younger. For a breath or two she even hoped that her potions had turned the tide, routed what Morgause had secretly sent to slay him.

"Bright one—" Even his voice was stronger, closer to that half-teasing one he had always used when they were private together. Then his mouth worked as if something sour had been dribbled into it. She felt his body stiffen in her hold and knew that once more the pain of his coming death was sharp. He must tell her—he must!

Did he not realize that his sharing of that last knowledge might perhaps save his life—if she were strong enough to try?

"The Time Spell!" Her words were sharp, a command. "The Time Spell— as you promised, Master."

He was still staring at her; he had not slipped back into that place of inner hiding. She hunched around a little and caught up from the floor the cup of the last of her brewing, the most potent she had ever mixed.

Nimuë held the cup to his lips and he drank, drank as if it were spring water, such as he had once drunk from her cupped hands beside the lake among the earliest flowers of a year.

Visibly he swallowed.

"Tell me—" She was not ordering now, she was pleading. "The last spell— teach me the bending of time itself, Master."

There was a shadow smile on his lips. "So is it ever," his words came more briskly than she had expected. "They frowned when my choice fell upon you, child of light. But when I first looked at your face, I was certain. The last spell—what would you do with it?"

She spoke fiercely now. "I will use it to save you!"

Slowly his head turned on her arm. The smile had vanished. "For me the end comes. Three times I have tried to make safe the future, yet each time there was a flaw. The old order changes. One cannot stand forever against change."

The weariness in his voice caught at her, her grasp on him tightened. This was not the Merlin she had known—strong to stand in strange battles. Had that she-devil leached the manhood out of him?

"Our reckoning with that woman is yet to come," she said between gritted teeth. "Death has not gotten you yet. I shall seek the answer to what she willed on you. But I must not let you go before I can do this. Master, give me the last spell. Aid me and yourself!"

Again he held her eye to eye with that strength of will he could use to bring any man or woman to his service.

"You shall indeed serve a purpose, even if it is not the one you seek, my child. But the grand design has failed, and you can only hold off the coming night for a little while."

"The last spell!" Now she feared—was he choosing not to give it?

Again he stretched that shadow smile. "The last spell. If you use it as you

5

think to do, my heart's daughter, you will be reviled by men until their curses become tattered legends."

Nimuë eyed him narrowly. "I ask this not for any foreseeing, Master, but only that my knowledge will be complete even as you promised it must."

Again his head moved slightly, this time in a nod.

"True. Full knowledge I promised when I chose you—so will it be. In your own time, Nimuë, you may find one fit to pass it to in turn." He stopped almost in mid-word and then his eyelids closed, making her heart give an extra beat before they reopened.

"No, great in the Old Learning you shall be, heart's daughter. But the magic drains and will not last forever. Only faint gleams of it will light men's memories. This, then, is the spell." There were words. They came slowly, emphatically, and she shaped each herself as it was spoken. He gave a dry cough and his body once more quivered in her hold, yet he continued to look at her.

She had had the old training which took into memory and rooted there forever whatever of import was given her. The words were hers for all time.

"Go to the High King." He moved, slid away from her support to lie flat once more. "In time there will be services at his need."

Nimuë arose and stood looking down at him.

"You have taught me great things, Lord Merlin. Now this I swear—perhaps there is more than one kind of knowledge in the world. If so, I shall seek it out and bring you back to life and strength again. As you awakened my mind, so shall I awaken your body—but I shall keep you safe until that hour."

Her hands moved, her lips shaped, she wrought with all the force which was in her. The last spell of all.

She saw his eyes blaze and knew that he realized what she had said and meant. He raised one shaking hand as if to pull at her robe.

It fell limply back again. His eyes closed. But not in death—no, not in death! Tears gathered in her eyes, trickled unnoticed down her cheeks. He would sleep, and sleep, and sleep—even as she would search. If she was not successful, the Lady would send some greater mage to come to his aid.

Yet he would sleep until at the appointed time, time itself would release the bonds she had set upon it and him. He had given her life in a way when he had plucked her out of the stultifying bonds of the cloister; now she would do what she could in return by giving him another chance against the tyranny of time.

A shimmer appeared over his now-motionless body. That darkened, hardened, until it took on the appearance of a trunk of a mighty tree felled in its prime. Nimuë looked around the cave; there was very little here to be taken with her. She set about gathering what she must.

Already the burden of foresight was closing upon her. At the lake cloister she who had ruled there so long was dead. It was now set upon her, Nimuë, to become in turn the leader there. "Lady of the Lake" men would call her. Then she must go to the High King's court, to pick up that flawed weaving left by her master and see what might be done with it—what still might be saved. His own words warned of dark rising. But the dark always rose and still the light flooded about it. She must believe it would happen now.

Foresight also told her what would be her name among men—traitor, even as Morgause, one who had betrayed her master—her commonly named "lover"—for gain. But truth often went awry in the world. She straightened her shoulders as one who would take on a burden. Strong he had found her when he tested her, strong she would be to carry also such infamy while still she followed the path on which he had set her feet. She was Nimuë, the chosen, and that she would hold in her heart.

She knelt for the last time beside what looked to be a tree trunk, her hand going out to touch its rough surface as she might touch the cheek of a sleeper. Foresight again—she would not be the one to wake him. No, she would have long since ceased to walk the earth when he roused. What deeds he would do in that far time were not for her viewing.

So she would leave him, the true guardian of a land which would enfold him until that last spell was tattered and gone. Once more she touched the seeming shell of wood and then she turned to leave—Lady of the Lake—one and alone.

SWORD OF UNBELIEF
Swords Against Darkness #2 (1977)
Zebra, Wizards' Worlds (1989) TOR

1: FURY DRIVEN

My eyes ached as I forced them to study the hard ground. From them a dull pain spread into the bony sockets that were their frames. The tough, mountain-bred mount I had saved from our desperate encounter with the wolf-ravagers stumbled. I caught at the saddle horn as vertigo struck with the sharp thrust of an unparried sword.

I could taste death, death and old blood, as I ran my tongue over lips where the salt of my own sweat plastered the dull gray dust of this land to my unwashed skin. Again I wavered. But this time my pony's stumble was greater. Strong as he was, and war-trained, he had come near to the end of endurance.

Before me the Waste was a long tongue of gray rock, giving rootage only to sparse and twisted brush, so misshapen in its growing that it might well have been attacked by some creeping evil. For there was evil in this country, every sense of mine warned that, as I urged Fallen on at a slow walk.

That wind which whipped at my cloak was bitter, carrying the breath of the Ice Dragon, it raised fine grains of gray sand to scour my face beneath the half shading of my helm. I must find some shelter, and soon, or the fury of a Dune-Moving Storm would catch me and provide a grave place which might exist for a day, a week, or centuries—depending upon the caprice of that same wind and sand.

An outcrop of angular rock stood to my left. Towards that I sent Fallen, his head hanging low as he went. In the lee of that tall fang I slipped from the saddle, keeping my feet only by a quick grasp of the rock itself. The ache in my head struck downwards through my shoulders and back.

I loosed my cloak a little and, crouching by the pony, flung it over both his head and mine. Little enough shelter against the drive of the punishing grains, but it was the best I had. Another fear gnawed at me. This flurry would wipe out the trail I had followed these two days past. With that gone, I must depend upon myself, and in myself I had lesser confidence.

Had I been fully trained as those of my Talent and blood had always been—then I could have accomplished what must be done with far less effort. But, though my mother was a Witch of Estcarp, and I was learned in the powers of a Wise Woman (and had indeed done battle using those powers in the past), yet at this moment I knew fear as an ever-present pain within me, stronger than any ache of body or fatigue of mind.

As I crouched beside Fallen, this dread arose like a flood of bile into my throat, which I would have vomited forth had I could. Yet, it was too great a part of me to allow itself to be so sundered. Feverishly I drew upon those lesser arts I had learned, striving so to still the fast beating of my heart, the clouding of my thoughts by panic. I must think rather of him whom I sought, and of those who had taken him, for what purpose I could not imagine. For it is the way of them to kill; torment, yes, if they were undisturbed, but kill at the end of their play. Yet they had drawn back into this forbidden and forbidding land taking with them a prisoner, one worth no ransom. And the reason for that taking I could not guess.

I set a bridle of calmness upon my thoughts. Only so might I use that other Talent which was mine from birth. So now I set my mind picture upon him whom I sought— Jervon, fighting man, and more, far more to me.

I could see him, yes, even as I had sighted him last by the fire of our small camp, his hands stretched out to warm themselves at the flames. If only I had not—! No, regret was only weakening. I must not think of what I had not done, but what I must now be prepared to do.

There had been blood on the snow-shifted ground when I had returned, the fire stamped into cold charred brands. Two outlaws' bodies hideously ripped—but Jervon ... no. So they had taken him for some purpose I could not understand.

The dead wellheads I left to the woods beasts. Fallen I had discovered, shivering and wet with sweat, within the brush and brought him to me by the summoning power. I had waited no longer, knowing that my desire to look upon the shrine of the Old Ones, which I had turned aside to do, might well mean Jervon's death, and no pleasant death either.

Now, crouching here, I cupped one hand across my closed eyes. "Jervon!" My mind call went out even as I had brought Fallen to me. But I failed. There arose a cloud between me and the man I would find. Yet I was as certain that behind that shadow he still lived. For when one's life is entwined with another's and death comes, the knowledge of that passing through the Last Gate is also clear—to one trained in even the simplest of the Great Mysteries.

This Waste was a grim and much-hated place. Many were the remains of the Old Ones here, and men of true human blood did not enter it willingly. I am not of High Hallack, though I was born in the Dales. My parents came from storied Estcarp overseas, a land where much of the Old Knowledge has been preserved. And my mother was one of those who used that knowledge— even though she had wed, and so, by their laws, put herself apart. What I knew I had of Aufrica out of Wark, a mistress of minor magic and a Wise Woman. Herbs I knew, both harmful and healing, and 1 could call upon certain lesser powers—even upon a great one, as once I had done to save him who was born at the same birth with me. But there were powers beyond powers here that I knew not. Only I must take this way and do what I could for Jervon who was more to me than Elyn, my brother, had ever been, and who had once, without any of the Talent to aid him, come with me into battle with a very ancient and strong evil, which battle we had mercifully won.

"Jervon!" I called his name aloud, but my voice was only a faint whisper. For the wind shrieked like a legion of disembodied demons around me. Fallen near jerked his head from my hold on his bridle, and I speedily set myself to calming him, setting over his beast mind a safeguard against panic.

It seemed to last for hours, that perilous sheltering by the fang rock. Then the wind died and we pulled out of sand drifted near to my knees. I took one of my precious flasks of water and wet the corner of my cloak, using that to wash out Fallen's nostrils, the sand away from his eyes. He nudged at my shoulder, stretching his head towards the water bottle in a voiceless plea for a drink. But that I did not dare give him until I knew what manner of country we would cross and whether there would be any streams or tarns along the way.

Night was very near. But that strangeness of the Waste banished some of the dark. For here and there were scattered rock spires which gave off a flickering radiance, enough to travel by.

I did not mount as yet, knowing that Fallen must have a rest from carrying a rider. Though I am slender of body, I am no light weight with mail about me, a sword and helm. So I plowed through the sand, leading Fallen. And heard him snort and blow his dislike of what I would have him do—venture farther into this desolation.

Again, I sent forth a searching thought. I could not reach Jervon. No— that muddling cloud still hung between us. But I could tell in what direction they had gone. Though the constant concentration to hold that thread made my head throb with renewed pain.

Also there were strange shadows in this place. It would seem that nothing threw across the land a clear dark definition of itself, as was normal. Rather those shadows took on shapes which made the imagination quicken with vague hints of things invisible which still could be seen in this way, monstrous forms and unnatural blendings. And, if one allowed fear the upper hand, those appeared ripely ready to detach themselves and move unfettered by any trick of light or dark.

I wondered at those I followed. War had been the harsh life of this land now for so many years it was hard to remember what peace had been like. High Hallack had been overrun by invaders whose superior arms and organization had devastated more than half the Dales before men were able to erect their defense. There had been no central overlord among us; it was not the custom of the men of High Hallack to give deference beyond the lord in whose holding they had been born and bred. So, until the Four of the North had sunk their differences and made a pact, there had been no rallying point. Men had fought separately for their own lands, and died, to lie in the earth there.

Then came the final effort. Not only did the Dale lords unite for the first time in history to make a common cause, but they had also treated with others—out of this same Waste—the Wereriders of legend. And together what was left of High Hallack arose with all the might it could summon to smash the Hounds of Alizon, driving them back to the sea, mainly to their own deaths therein. But a land so rent produces in turn those with a natural bent towards evil, scavengers and outlaws, ready to plunder both sides if the chance offered. Now such were the bane of our exhausted and warworn country.

These were such that I followed. And it could well be that, since they were hardy enough to lair within the Waste, they might not be wholly human either. Rather be possessed by some emanation of the Dark which had long lurked here.

For the Old Ones, when they withdrew from the Daleland, had left behind them pools of energy. Some of these granted peace and well being, so that one could enter therein timorously, to come forth again renewed in spirit and body. But others were wholly of the Dark. And if he was destroyed at once the intruder was lucky. It was worse, far worse, to live as a creature of a shadow's bidding.

The ghostly light streamed on before me. I lifted my head, turned this way and that, as might a hound seeking scent. All traces of trail had been wiped away by the wind. However, I was sure that I followed the right path. So we came to two stelae which fronted each other as if they might once have formed part of an ancient gate. Yet there was no wall, just these pillars, from the tip of which streamed cloudwards thin ribbons of a greenish light. And they had been formed by men, or some agency with intelligence, for they had the likenesses of heavy bladed sabers. Yet on their sides I could see, half eroded by time, pits and hollows which, when the eye fastened straightly upon them, took on the semblance of faces—strange faces—long and narrow, with large noses overhanging pointed chins. Also it seemed that the eyes (which were pits) turned upon me, not in interest or in warning, but as if in deep, age-old despair.

Though I felt no emanation of evil, neither did I like to pass between those sword pillars. Still it was that way my road ran. Quickly I sketched with my hand certain symbols before I stepped forward, drawing Fallon on reinhold behind me.

These pillars stood at the entrance of a narrow gash of valley which led downwards, the steep sides rising ever higher. Here the dark had full sway, for there were no more of the luminous stones. So that I went with that slow caution I had learned in the years I had ridden to war. I listened. Outside this valley I had heard the murmur of the wind, but here was a deep quiet. Until my straining ears caught a sound which could only be that of running water.

And there was a dampness now in the air, for which I was momentarily grateful. Fallon pushed against me, eager to slake his thirst. But where there was water in this desert land there could also well be a camp of those I pursued. So I did not hasten, and I held back the pony. He snorted and the sound echoed hollowly. I froze, listening for any answer which might mean my coming was marked. But if the wolves I followed were human, certainly their sight here would be no better than mine, even more limited for they did not have—or so I hoped—the Talent to aid it.

On we went step by hesitant step. Then my boot, slipping across the ground, struck against some obstruction. I stooped, to feel about with my hands. Here was a cluster of small rocks, and beyond that, not too far, the water. I felt a path as clear as I could. As far as I could tell, a spring broke ground on my left, some way up the wall of the valley, and the water poured from that into a basin which in turn must have some outlet on the other side.

I scooped up a handful of the liquid, smelled it. There was no stench of minerals or of other deadliness. I splashed it over my face below the edge of my helm, washing away storm grit. Then I drank from my cupped hands, and squeezed aside to let Fallon have his way. The noise of his gulping was loud enough, but I no longer feared detection.

Those I sought had come this way, yes. My refreshed mind assured me of that. But there was no camp hereabout.

"Jervon!" I pressed both hands over my eyes, pushing back my helm, reaching out in mind search again. For a moment it was as if my touch found a weakness in that mist I had encountered before. I touched—he was alive, mauled yet not badly injured! But when I tried to deepen contact, that I might read through him the numbers and nature of the force which held him, there was once more a cutting off of communication, as suddenly as a sword might descend between us.

The nature of that interference I could judge. There was that ahead which was aware of me, but only when I tried to reach Jervon. For as I hunkered there, my mind barrier up, I did not sense any testing of that. In me now fear was lessened; instead another emotion woke to life. Once before I had fought against very ancient evil—with love—for the body and soul of a man. Then I had sought my brother Elyn trapped in a cursed place.

What I felt for Elyn, though we were of one blood and birth, was but a pale shadow to that which filled me when Jervon looked upon me. I am not one who speaks easily of what she thinks the deepest upon, but in that moment I knew how completely Jervon's fate and mine were rooted together. And 1 experienced fury against that which had cut the cord between us.

Recognizing that fury, I drew deep upon it, used the hot emotion to fill me with new strength. For, even as fear weakened that which was my own, so could anger give it sword and shield . . . providing I might control that anger. And there in the dark, by that unseen pool, I fashioned my invisible armor, sharpened those weapons which no one but myself could ever wield. For they were forged out of my wit and my emotion even as a smith beats a true-edged sword out of clean metal.

2: THE SHADOW HUNTER

It was folly to advance farther into the dark. I dared not risk a fall and perhaps a broken bone for me or for Fallon. Though every surge of emotion urged me on, I held to logic and reason. Here dark was so thick it was as if the ground about generated some blackness. Above hung clouds to veil even the stars.

I fumbled in my saddlebag and brought out a handspan of journey bread, hard enough perhaps to crack teeth gnawing it unwarily. This I soaked in water and fed the greatest portion to Fallon, whose lips nuzzled my hand to search out the smallest crumb. Then I used my will and forced upon his mind the order that he was not to stray, before I settled in between two rocks and drew my cloak about me as poor protection against this damp chill.

Though I had not thought to sleep, the fatigue of my body overcame the discipline of my mind and I dropped into a dark even deeper than that which enfolded me here. In that dark, presences moved and I was aware of them, only not clearly enough to draw any meaning from such fleetings.

I woke suddenly into the gray of early dawn. And I awoke because I had been summoned as if someone had clearly called my name, or a battle trumpet had blown nearby. Now I could see the dim pool with the runnel of water leaping down the rocks to feed it. On the other side of that Fallon grazed on clumps of tough grass, which were not green but sickly ashen, withered by the chill of the season.

There was indeed an outlet for the pool basin, a kind of trough which ran on into the morning fog beyond. I moved stiffly, but, now that my mind was once more alert, I cast ahead for that blankness which hid Jervon and his captors.

It was there, and this time I did not make the mistake of trying to pierce it, and so alert whatever I had touched the night before. At any rate, for the present, there was only one road, that walled by rises of stone on which I could not even see finger holds. Yet there were markings there— eroded and time-worn as those upon the stelae guardians —too regular to be nature's work, too strange to be read by me. Save that I misliked the general outlines of some of those symbols, for with their very shape they aroused misgivings.

As I broke my fast with another small portion of water-soaked bread, I kept my eyes resolutely turned away from those shadowy scrawls. Rather did I strive to see into the mist which filled this cut in the earth. And again I listened—but there was nothing to hear save the water.

Having filled my two saddle bottles I mounted, but I let Fallon for the moment take his own pace. For the way was much cluttered with rocks, with here and there a landslip over or around which we crept with care.

The sense of new danger crept slowly upon me, so intent was I on keeping contact with that peculiar blankness which I believed imprisoned Jervon. This was first like a foul smell which is but a suggestion of rottenness, but which gradually grows the stronger as one approaches the source of corruption. Fallon snorted, tossing his head, only kept to the path by my will.

Oddly enough I could not sense any of the ancient evil in this thing, though I bent my mind and my Talent to test it by all which I had learned from Aufrica and the use of my own power. It was not of any source I knew— for the taint was that of human not of the Old Ones. Yet also during our hunting of the Waste outlaws this I had not met either.

Now my flesh roughed as if more than the chill of the fog struck at me. Fear battled for release from the iron guard I had set upon my emotions. With that fear came a disgust and anger—I found myself riding with hand upon sword hilt. Listening—ever listening—but my ears caught nothing but the thud of Fallon's hooves, now and again the ring of an iron shoe against an edge of rock.

The fog closed about, beads of moisture dripped from my helm, shone oily wet upon my mail, dampened Fallon's heavier winter coat into points.

Then—

Movement!

Fallon threw up his head to voice a shrill squeal of fear. At the same instant that which I had sensed struck and lapped me round. For, through the rim of the fog, came horror unleashed. The thing was mounted even as I, and some trick of the fog made it loom larger than it was. But that which it rode was no horse of flesh and blood—rather a rack of bones held together by a lacing of rotted and dried flesh. And it was as its mount, a thing long dead and yet given a terrible life.

Its weapon was terror, not any sword. As I stiffened and drew deeply upon my power I realized it for what it was—a thoughtform born out of ancient fear and hatred. So did it continue to feed upon such emotions, drawing into it at each feeding a greater substance. My fear, my anger, must have both summoned and fed it. But it was real. That I could swear to, as much as if I laid hand upon that outstretched arm of bone. And Fallon's wide-eyed terror was meat to it also. While it trailed behind it, like a cloak, a deep depression of the spirit.

Fallon reared, screamed. That mount of bone opened wide its jaws in answer. I struggled with the panic-mad horse under me, glad for a moment

15

that I had this to fight, for it awoke my mind from the blast of fear the spectre brought with it.

I raised my voice and shouted, as I would a battle cry, certain Words. Yet the rider did not waver, nor did the mount. And I summoned my will to master my own senses. This thing needed terror and despair to live, let me clamp tight upon my own and it would have no power—

Fallon sweated so that the smell was rank in the narrow defile of that way. My will had clamped upon him also, held him steady. He no longer screamed, but from his throat issued a sound not unlike the moaning of a man stricken close to death.

It was a thing fashioned of fear, and, without fear ... I made myself into a bulwark, once more spoke my defiance. But I did not shout this time; rather I schooled my voice into obedience, even as I held Fallen.

The thing was within arm's length, the stench of it thick in my nostrils, the glare of its eyeless skull turned upon me. Then ... it faded into the mist. Fallen still gave forth that unanimal-like moaning and great shudders ran through his body. 1 urged him forward, and he went one unsteady step at a time, while the fog coiled and spun around as if to entrap us.

It was enough for a moment that the horror had been vanquished. I hoped dimly that what I knew of such was the truth, that they were tied to certain places on earth where raw emotions had first given them birth.

As we paced along beside the small stream I heard sounds, not from ahead, but from behind. Faint they were at first, but growing stronger—there was the beat of hooves in such a loud tattoo that I thought some rider came at a speed far too reckless for the stony way. I heard also voices calling with the mist, though never could I make out the words, for the sounds came muffled and distorted. Still there reached me the impression of a hunt behind. And a strange picture flashed into my mind of one crouched low on a wild-eyed horse, behind him, unseen, the terror which drove him.

So keen and clear was this picture that I swung around when I reached a pile of rocks against which I could set my back. And I drew my sword. There was a rushing past where I crouched, my left hand tangled within Fallon's reins, for he was like to bolt. But nothing material cleared the mist. Again ancient shadows had deceived me. Though I waited tensely for whatever pursued that lone rider of the distant past, there was nothing. Nothing save the uneasy sense that here were remnants of ancient terror caught forever in the mist. Then, ashamed at my own lack of self-control, I started on again, this time leading Fallen, stroking his head and talking softly to him, urging into his mind a confidence I did not wholly feel.

The walls about us began to widen out. Also that mist was tattered and driven by a wind which whistled down the valley, buffeting us with the frost it carried. But also it brought me something else, the scent of wood smoke, of a fire which has been recently dampened out.

We came to a curve in the near wall which served as a guide through the now disappearing mist. 1 dropped Fallon's reins and ordered him to stand so, cautiously crept forward; though the probe of my Talent picked up no whisper of a human mind.

Still so strange was the Waste that I could believe those who harbored here might well have some defense against my power. There had been a camp there right enough. A drowned fire still gave off a strong odor. And there were horse droppings along one side. I could see tracks crossing and recrossing each other, though the sand and gravel did not hold them clearly. But plainest of all was what had been painted on one massive rock which jutted forth from the wall. And that was no work of years before; the symbols must have been freshly drawn, for they were hardly weathered or scoured by sand.

One was a crudely drawn head of some animal—a wolf or hound—it could have been either. It interlaced the edge of the other, a far more complex and better executed symbol. I found myself standing before that, my forefinger almost of itself following its curves by tracing the air.

When I realized what I was doing I snatched my hand back to my side, my fingers baited into a fist. This was not of my learning, though it was a potent thing. And dangerous... There was an unpleasant otherness about the symbol which aroused wariness. However, 1 believed, though I did not understand its complete meaning, I did pick up the reason for those mated drawings. For among the Dales there was an old custom that, when a lasting truce or alliance was made, the lords of both parties chose a place on the boundaries of their domains and there carved the Signs of their two Houses so twined in just the same fashion.

So here I had come upon a notice that the outlaws I hunted had indeed made common cause with some dweller of the Waste who was not of their blood or kind. And, though I had suspected no less, having trailed them through the haunted valley, yet I could wish it otherwise.

To have some knowledge but not enough is a thing which eats upon one. If I might have read that other symbol I could be warned as to what—or who—I had to face. As I began a careful search about the deserted camp I alerted the Talent to sniff out any clue to the nonhuman. But the impressions my mind gathered were only of the same wolfish breed as we had hunted—desperate and dangerous enough.

Jervon had been there and he still lived. I had half steeled my mind to find him dead, for the Waste wolves did not take captives. What did they want with him? Or were they but the servants and hands of another force? The impression grew on me that the latter was so. That they had some purpose in bringing him hither could not be denied.

My years with Aufrica had taught me well that there are two kinds of what the untalented term "magic" or "witchery." It was contagious magic which I used to track Jervon, for about my throat I wore the amulet of a strange stone shaped not unlike an eye, which he had found and carried for a luck piece since he was a boy, and then had put into my keeping upon our handfasting, having in those years of war no other bride-jewel to offer.

But there was also sympathic magic, which works according to the laws of correspondence, and now I prepared to call upon that. From my healer's bag I brought forth a length of ash stick, peeled, blessed by the moon, bound with a small ring of silver wire, which is moon metal. Now I faced that symbol on the rock, pointed to it with ash rod which was no longer than my palm and fingers together.

Immediately the wand came to life in my hold, not to trace the characters, rather turning and twisting in a manner to suggest it would leap from my grasp rather than face what was so carven there. So I knew what I suspected was true and that this was a thing of the Dark from which the Light recoiled.

Now I touched the wand with the eye-stone which I drew forth from beneath my mail, rubbing the stone down one side and up the other. Then I held out my hand with the lightest hold upon the ash. Again it twisted, pointing ahead.

My battle with fear in the mist had drawn too heavily upon my inner resources; I could no longer depend upon mind search to follow those whom I sought. However, with the wand I had a sure pointer, in which I could trust. So I continued to hold it as I mounted Fallen and rode out of that camp, turning my back upon the entwined symbols of an unholy alliance.

The valley widened even farther, as if it had been but a narrow throat to open country beyond. I saw trees now, as misshapen as the brush, and monoliths, as well as tumbles of stone, which suggested ruins so old they could not be dated by my own species.

There were tracks again. But within a very short time we came to a place where those turned to the right at an abrupt swing. Only, in my hand, the wand did not alter course, but still pointed straight ahead. There was only one solution to accept: Jervon was no longer with the wolf pack which had pulled him down.

Had there been some monstrous meeting beneath those symbols and he whom I sought been given to that Other whose sign was set boldly on the rock? I dismounted to search the ground with a scout's patience. And was rewarded with faint traces at last.

The main body I hunted had indeed turned here. But two mounts had kept to the straight track. One of those must carry Jervon.

If he rode with only one outlaw as guard—I drew a sharp swift breath ... This might well herald a chance for rescue with the odds much in my favor. I mounted again and urged Fallen to a faster pace than he had kept during that day's travel, watching keenly the country ahead.

3: THE FROZEN FLAME

Here in the open the mist was tattered by the wind and one could see farther. So my eyes caught a flash of light. Yet it was plain that this did not rise from any fire but rather sparked into the sky, perhaps as a beacon.

Now the stones of the forgotten ruins drew together, formed tumbled walls, with here or there some uprise of worked rock which might have once been a statue. But these were now so worn away by erosion that such shapes remained only vaguely unpleasant ones, hinting of ancient monstrous beings. Gods or guardians? What man now living could say?

The sun broke through, yet here it had not even the pallid light of mid-winter, rather a drained, bespoiled radiance, with nothing to warm either body or heart. And still shadows clung to the rocks, though I resolutely refused more than to glance at them. I knew the power of illusion, for much of that lies within the Talent.

Before me rose a wall, massive in its blocks, some larger than myself, even when mounted on Fallen. This time had not used so harshly. The pale sun struck points of icy fire from gray-white crystals embedded in its surface. The way I followed led to the single break in that wall, a gateway so narrow that it would seem no more than one had ever been meant to pass therein at a time.

Now the wand in my hand flipped so that I barely prevented it from slipping through my fingers. Its silver-bound tip pointed to a dark stain smeared on that wall near the height of my thigh, riding as I was. Blood—

and that of him whom I now sought!

I could only draw hope because the smear was so small a one. Jervon had not been overborne without a fight, that I was already sure of. He was too seasoned in war to be easily taken, and the bodies I found at our last camp had testified to his skill in defense. Yet this was the first sign that he had been wounded. Now I glanced at the pavement underfoot, expecting to sight more splotches thereon.

The wall was the first of three such. And they varied in color, for the outer one, in spite of its clusters of crystals, was a gray as the rest of this Waste. The second, some twenty places beyond, was dull green. Yet it was not any growing thing which had clothed it, but part of the blocks themselves. While the third was the rusty-brown-red of dried blood and in it the stones were smaller.

The entrance through to it was still narrower, so that, despite my misgivings, I was forced to dismount, and essay that on foot.

If there were any blood smears here to mark Jervon's passing, those were cloaked by the natural coloring of the stone. Before me stood a squat building, only a fraction higher than the wall, windowless and dour, the stone of its making a lusterless, thick black, as if it had been fashioned from shadows themselves. From the roof of this issued, straight up to defy the sullen sun, the beam of light that shone across the land.

Now that I drew nearer I could see that beam pulsated in waves, almost like the ever-changing and moving flames of a fire. Yet I was sure it was not born from any honest burning of wood.

Windowless the place might be, but there existed a deeply recessed doorway; so deep and dark a portal I could not be sure if any barrier stood within. I paused, using my senses to test what lay about me, for to go blindly into danger would not serve either Jervon's cause or my own.

Hearing? There was no sound, not even the sigh of wind across twisted shrub and sliding sand. Smell? I could not pick up any of the faint rottenness which had alerted me to the coming of the phantom in the valley. Sight? The deep door, the pulsing flame, unmarked ground between me and that doorway. Touch?

I held up my hand, the wand lying across the palm. That moved again, wavering from side to side with a growing speed until it had switched around and the wire-wound tip pointed to me or to the wall entrance through what I had just squeezed. There was warning enough in that. What lay ahead was highly inimical to such forces as I dared call upon. And I was somehow certain if I took these last few strides, passed within that portal, I would be facing danger worse than any wolf blade or phantom hunter.

If only I knew more! Once before I had gone to battle with one of the evil Old Ones, in ignorance and using only my few poor weapons. And Jervon, at that hour (having far more to fear than I, for he possessed none of the safeguards of the Talent), had come with me, trusting only in the power of cold iron and his own courage.

Could I do less now? As I stood there, the fluttering wand in my hand, I thought of what Jervon was to me. First an unwanted road companion through a hostile land, one who made me impatient for I feared that he might in some way turn me from my purpose. Then—my life was bound to Jervon's. I could not deny that. Whatever force had brought him; it was for no purpose except his destruction—and perhaps also mine. Yet I accepted that and walked toward the doorway.

There was no door to face me. Once I had stepped under the shadow of that overhang, there was a cloud of darkness so thick it seemed one might gather together folds of it in one's fingers as one could a curtain woven on a Dale loom. I raised the hand I could no longer see until I thought the wand was level with my lips. Then I breathed upon that and spoke three words.

So tiny a light, as if a candle no thicker than my own little finger, shone feebly. But as that sparked into being I drew a deep breath. There was not yet any pressure on me. In so little had I won a token victory.

That other time I had had an advantage because what dwelt anciently in such a place had been all-powerful for so long that it had not seen in me a worthy opponent. Therefore it had not unleashed its full strength against me until too late. I did not know that lay ahead, nor could I hold any hope that it would be the same here.

Time is often distorted and altered in those places of the Old Ones. All human memory is filled with legends of men who consorted with Those of Power for what seemed a day or year, and returned to find that their own world had swept on far faster. Now it appeared otherwise to me.

The very darkness, which was hardly troubled by the light on which ray spirit fed, was like a flood of sticky clay or quicksand catching at my feet, so that it was a physical effort to fight against that to advance. As yet there had been no other assault upon me. Slowly, I gained the impression that what intelligence had raised this place for its shell of protection was otherwise occupied, so intent upon that concentration that it was not yet aware of me.

Even as the pinpoint of flame I held before me, that thought strengthened my courage. Yet I dared not depend upon such concentration holding. At any moment it might be broken, by some unknown, unseen system of alarm, to turn the force of its interest in my direction.

I fought against the sticky dark, one step, two. It seemed to me that this journey had consumed hours of time. My body ached once more with the effort I must exert. One more stride—

Thus I passed from complete dark into light so suddenly that for two breaths, three, I was blinded. Then, blinking, I was able to see. The space in which I stood was round, with two great chairs, by their dimensions made for bodies larger than humankind, facing each other across a dazzling pillar which formed the innermost core. Then I saw that it was not really a pillar, but rather a rounded shaft of ceaseless rolling radiance. No heat radiated from it, only an inner flickering suggested the flames it mimicked.

My inner warning sounded an alarm. Instantly I averted my eyes. There stood the force and purpose of this place. I had come out behind the nearer chair, its back a barrier, but I could see the other. Something had fallen from its wide seat to lie like a pile of wrung out rags on the floor.

Jervon—?

But even as I took a step toward that body, for dead that man must be by the very limpness of his form, I saw more clearly the face turned toward the light, the eyes wide in horror. And a stubby beard pointed outward from the chin. One of the outlaws!

Then Jervon—?

Carefully averting my gaze from that challenging, beckoning fire, I edged around the chair before me. Yes, he whom I sought sat there. There were bonds about his arms, loops bringing together his booted ankles. His helm was gone and there was a gash on his forehead which had been only roughly bandaged so that congealed red drops lay on the cheek beneath.

He was—alive?

I reached forth my hand. The wand trembled. Yes, there still was a spark of life in him, held so by the stubbornness of his own will and courage. But his eyes were locked on the pillar of fire.

I could do two things. Recklessly, I first tried mind seek. No, his consciousness was too depleted to respond. If I attempted to break the binding of the flame I could overturn the result of his own courage, loose him and lose him. There was a great strength in Jervon. I had seen it in action many times over during the seasons we had ridden together as comrades and lovers (seldom can those two be made one, but so it was with us).

So—I must follow him—into the flame. Front that Power on its own ground.

If only I knew more! I beat my hands together in my impotent frustration. This was a great force, and one I had no knowledge of. I did not know if I could face it with any Talent of my own. It might be invincible in its own stronghold.

I moved slowly to look at the dead outlaw. He had been emptied of life force, easier prey by far than Jervon. The way he had fallen made it seem he had been contemptuously thrown aside. But I knew Jervon. And upon that knowledge I could build now. It would do me no good to take his body from this place, even if the flame power would allow that. For then he could never regain what he had already lost—what must be returned to him . . .

Returned—how?

Desperate I was, for I might lose all, his life, mine, and perhaps more than just the lives of our bodies. But I could see no other way.

Deliberately I went to that other throne, careful not to touch the wasted body as I stepped over it. I am glad I did not hesitate now, that my inner strength carried me up unflinchingly to where that dead man had sat. I settled myself within the curve of the arms, under the shadow of the high back. My wand I took in both hands, forcing it up against the power which tried to forestall me, until the point was aimed at Jervon's breast.

I did not believe that the power I would confront was of my plane of existence. Rather I thought that the frozen flames were but a small manifestation visible to our world. I must seek it on its own ground if I were to have a chance.

The outlaw had been its creature already. Doubtless he had lain under its spell even before he had entered here, perhaps sent by it to find such strong meat as Jervon. And Jervon it had not completely taken. Also it might never have tried to absorb one learned in the Talent.

Such a hope was very thin; I could count on nothing save my own small learning and my determination. But it was not in me to leave this place without Jervon. We would win or lose together.

So—the battlefield lay within the flame—

My grip on the wand was iron tight. Now I deliberately raised my eyes, stared straight into that play of curbed fire. I need only release my will for a very little.

4: ELSEWHERE AND ELSEWHEN

I was—elsewhere. How can one summon words to describe what is so wholly alien to all one's experience? Colors rippled here that had no name I knew, sensations wrenched at the inner core of my determination and Talent as if they would pull me apart while I yet lived. Or did I live now? I was aware of nobody in this place; five senses no longer served me, for I realized I did not "see" but rather depended upon a different form of perception. Only seconds, breaths long, was I given. Then a compelling force swept up the consciousness which was all that remained of my identity and drew me forward across a fantastic and awesome country.

For country it was—! Though it was subtly wrong, my human instinct told me. There were growing things, which did not in the least resemble any I had ever seen, of eye searing yellow, threatening red. These writhed and beat upon the air as if they fought against their rooting, would be free to do their will, and yet were anchored by another's ordering. Branches tip-clawed the earth or swept high into the air in ceaseless movement.

Then I was beyond them, carried so by the force which I had momentarily surrendered to. And I put aside my preoccupation with the strangeness of this place, to fasten inwardly, nurse my Talent with all my strength.

Yet must I also conceal that hard core of defiance within me. For I was sure that I must not dissipate that before I fronted the Power which ruled here.

I had heard legends through Aufrica (though from whom she had gained them she never said) that when the Old Ones held the Dales they had meddled with the very stuff of life itself. And that the adepts among them had opened "gates" to other dominions in which the human was as unnatural as that which passed swiftly below me now. That this might be such a "gate" I have begun to believe. But its guardianship was alien.

Here was a stretch of yellow ground unbroken by any of the monstrous growths. Patterned deeply on its surface were many tracks and trails, some deer-worn as well-used roads. Yet my own feet, if I still possessed those appendages, did not seek to tread there. Rather I had the sensation of being wafted well above that broken surface.

Those tracks and ways converged, angling toward some point ahead. And, as I passed on, I began to see moving figures, ones which pressed forward step by reluctant step. Yet none was clear, but rather cloaked in ever-shifting color so that one could not define their true outlines. Some were dully gray, one or two a deep black that reminded me of the dark through which I had passed to reach the chamber of the flame. Others showed as sickly green, or a sullen, blood/rust red. As I swept over them I longed to shriek aloud my pain, for it seemed that from each there came some thrust of despair and horror which was like the cut of a sword one could not guard against. Thus I realized that these were victims of this place even as I might be.

Why I winged my way rather than trode theirs I could not guess. Unless that which ruled here knew me for what I was and would have me quickly within its grasp! And it was not good to think of that. But I had made my choice, and must hold firmly to my resolution. Thicker became the figures plodding so slowly. Now I began to believe that their doom was deliberately prolonged by purpose, that their helpless suffering was meat and drink to something—

Was Jervon one of those?

I tried to delay my own passage, hover above those misty lights which were still substantial enough to leave tracks on the plain. But then a second thought came to me, that in allowing myself to show interest in any of those tormented wayfarers I could in turn betray the more plainly what I was and why I had come.

So I turned my new sense of perception from those travelers, and allowed the compulsion full rein to draw me in. I came at last to where that yellow plain gave way abruptly to a chasm.

The walls of that were dull red and in shape it was round. Down its sides the lights which tracked the plain made a painful descent, now so thronged together that their colors seemed to blend and mingle.

Though I thought in truth no entity was aware of its fellows, but only of its own sore fate.

Down I was drawn, past those toiling victims. Once more into a pool of dead blackness and loss of all perception. Here I began to exercise those safeguards I had learned, seeds of which had been mine from birth. I was myself, me, Elys—a woman, a seer, a fighter. And I must remain me and not allow That Other to take away my oneness with myself and my past.

Still I raised no opposition save that belief in myself which I kept within me. At this meant I must put even Jervon from my conscious mind and concentrate on my own personality. Instinct told me this, and for a Wise Woman such instinct is a command.

The dark began to thin and I could see light again. But in that sickly yellowish glow there was nothing to be marked, save directly under me, or that part of me which had come seeking this grim venture, a throne.

It was fashioned of the black, the dark itself, and on it there wavered a ruddy mist in which whirled gemlike particles.

"Welcome—"

It was not sound which reached me, rather a vibration which shuddered through whatever form I now wore.

Slowly I settled down, until I fronted that towering throne and the unstable form it contained. Very small was I, so that this was like looking up at the face of some high Dale hill."Good—"

Again the word vibrated through me, bringing with it both pain and—may the Power I serve forgive me—also a kind of pleasure which defiled that which I held to be the innermost core of my being.

"It has been long and long since this happened—"

The glittering mist of the throne was melting, developing more of a form.

"Are there then again those to summon for the Gate?"

That form leaned forward on its throne. The glitter points flowed together, formed two discs which might serve the alien for eyes. Now those centered upon me.

"Where is the gift then, servant of—" The name the thing mouthed was like a flame lapping about me, so strong was the Power that carried, even though I was no follower.

Before I could frame an answer, its shadowy head bobbed in what might be a nod.

"So the gift comes—yet I think it not of your devising. Think you I can be so easily deceived?" And the form shook with what might be silent and horrible laughter. The contempt in which it held me and all my species was Hire a loathsome stench in the air of that place.

"Your kind has served me," the vibration which was speech continued. "Long and well have they served me. Nor have I ever withheld their rewards. For when I feed, those feed—Behold!"

It stretched forth an extension of the upper body which might well serve it for arm, and then I could perceive indeed that all it had fed upon was a part of it. But not in peace. For the torment of those it consumed and yet nourished within its own substance was that they were conscious of what had happened to them, and that consciousness lasted throughout ages without respite. While as a part of this Thing they were also forced to feed in turn, damning themselves to further endless torture.

Even as I watched one of those long appendages flickered even farther out and returned, grasped in it a writhing core of grayness which was one with those shapes I had watched on the plain above. This it clasped to its body so that the gray sank into its mass and another life force was sentenced to an existence of terror and despair.

Seeing that, my mind stirred. Even as that rider I had seen in the valley was a thoughtform fed into life by the terror of those whose emotions strengthened it, so was this Thing a product of similar forces. I had heard it said that men are apt to make their gods in their own images, attributing to those gods their own emotions, save that those emotions are deemed far greater than any human mind and heart can generate. Thus this Thing might once have been born—to serve a people whose god it was, who fed it for generations. So that at last it was no longer dependent upon their willingly brought sacrifices, but could indeed control mankind, and so its dominion.

But if that were indeed the truth, then the weapon against it was . . . unbelief. And, in spite of the evidence of my senses, here I must bring that weapon into being.

The glittering eyes that were set so on me did not change, and the despair and horror which it exuded in waves wrapped me around with all the force long generations of worship could generate within it.

"Small creature—" again it shook with that unvoiced demonic laughter. "I am, I exist—no matter from what small seed of thought I was born. Look upon me!"

Now its substance grew even thicker and it indeed formed a body. This unclothed body was godlike in its beauty—its tainted beauty—brazenly male. And the eyes shrank, to become normal-sized in a face whose features were those truly of some super being without a flaw.

Except the flaw of knowledge of what it was and from what it had come. And that knowledge I clung to. It did not show bones and rotting flesh, but that was its true state.

"Look upon me!" Once more the command rang out. "Females of your kind found me good to look upon in the old days before I grew tired of your world, and that which closed Gates swept across the land. Look—and come!"

And that vile pleasure, which had troubled me before, again assailed me. Against that I set the training of my Talent—the austerity in which we learn to master all that which is of the body. Though I felt myself waver a little forward, yet my determination held me fast.

Then those perfect lips smiled—evilly.

"You are more than I have tasted for a long time. This shall be a dainty feasting—" Now it raised a fine muscled arm, beckoned to me with its long fingers.

"Come—you cannot withstand me. Come willingly and the reward will be very great indeed—"

My thought arose in answer and I shaped the name it had given me, and with that name certain words. It was a forlorn hope. And, as that head tossed back and it laughed openly, I knew how vain that hope was.

"Names! You think that you can lay upon me your will by names? Ah, but that which I gave you is but the name men—some men—called me. It is not the name by which I know myself. And without that—you have no weapon. However, this is exciting—that you dare to stand against me! I have fed, and I have gathered strength, and I have waited for those who closed the Gates perhaps to hunt me. But they have not come, and you, worm thing who dares to face me—you are of such as they would not trouble themselves to look upon, far less do you stand equal to them.

"Only you shall give me sport, and that will be pleasant. You have come seeking one, have you not? Others have been led by pride and kinship to do so. They were fitly rewarded as you shall see when you join them. But name me no names which have not power!"

This time I did not try to answer. But feverishly I went seeking in my memory for the smallest trace of knowledge I had. Aufrica's learning had been shared with me to the best of her ability. We had visited certain forgotten shrines in the old days and sometimes dared to summon influences, long weakened by the years, which had once been dwelling in them. Spells I knew, but before this creature such were as the rhyming games small children play.

No—I would not allow room to that despair which insidiously nibbled at my mind! What I could do I would—!

The creature on the throne laughed for the third time.

"Very well. Struggle if you wish, worm one. It amuses me. Now—look what comes—" It pointed to the left and I dared to look. There had come, very slowly, plainly fighting the compulsion which drew it, one of those columns of light. This one was not black, not gray, nor yet red, but a yellow which was clear and bright. And in that moment I knew that this was what this world would see of Jervon.

Nor did it crawl abjectly as the one the false god had claimed in my sight, but stood erect, as it fought against the power of the thing on the throne.

"Jervon!" I dared at that moment to send forth a thought call. And instantly and valiantly was it answered:

"Elys!"

But the thing who commanded here looked from one of us to the other and smiled its evil smile.

5: TOGETHER WE STAND

So sweet a feasting —a tongue tip appeared between the lips of the handsome face, swept back and forth as if indeed savoring some pleasant taste. "You give me much, small ones — much!"

"But not all!" I made answer. And that yellow flame which was Jervon no longer advanced, but stood with me, as we had stood together through the years when there was a blooding of swords and a need for defense. I knew that this was not all of Jervon, that still in his ensorceled body he held stubbornly to his identity even as I went armed behind the wall of mine.

That which sat enthroned leaned forward a little, its beautiful and vile face turned to us.

"I hunger — and I feed — so simple is it."

It stretched out one of those seeming arms to an unnatural length, gathering to its bosom another crawling blob. In my mind there was a shriek of despair.

"You see how easy it is?"

Rather did I in turn reach with the Power for Jervon. And it was as if we now stood hand-linked before this thing that should never have been. All the clean strength of Jervon was at war with what abode here. And to that I joined my Power, limited as it might be. I formed symbols and perceived them glow in the air, as if written in fire.

But the Thing laughed and stretched out a hand of mist to sweep those easily away.

"Small are your gifts, female. Do you think I cannot wipe them from sight? So and so and so—" That hand of mist moved back and forth.

"Jervon," I sent my own message, "it feeds upon fear—"

"Yes, Elys, and upon the souls of men also." And it seemed to me that his reply was so steady. It was as if I had indeed found an anchorage which I needed.

Twice more the creature fed upon those blobs which crawled about the base of its throne. But always its eyes were on us. For what it waited, save that it must have our greater fear to season its feasting, I could not guess.

But that pause gave me time to draw in all which I knew, suspected, or hoped might aid us. How does one kill a god? With unbelief, my logic told me. But here and now unbelief was nigh impossible to summon.

We who have been burdened with the Talent must believe, yes. For we know well that there are presences beyond our comprehension, both good and evil, who may be summoned by man. Though we cannot begin to understand their true nature, limited as we are by the instincts and emotions of our corporal bodies. I seek certain of these intangible presences every time I exercise the Power which is mine, small that it is. And in Jervon also there is belief. We do not all walk the same roads, though in the end those roads must meet at a certain Gate which is the greatest of all, and beyond which lies what we cannot begin to imagine with our earthbound minds and hearts.

Only to this Thing I owed no belief. I was not one who had bowed in the courts of its temple nor sought its evil aid in any undertaking. Therefore—for me—it was no god!

"So do you think, female," flashed its thought back in answer. "Yet you are of a like kind to those who gave me creation. Therefore in you lie certain matters which I can touch—"

It was as if a slimy, rotting finger sleeked across my shrinking flesh. And in its wake—yes—there was that in me ready to respond to that nauseating touch. I have weaknesses as inborn as my Talent, those it could summon into battle against me. Once more it laughed.

"Elys—" The thought that was Jervon's overrang that laughter. "Elys!"

It was no more than my name, but it broke through that feeling of abasement that anything in me could respond to this horror. I drew once more upon logic. No man or woman is perfect. There is much lying within us that we must look upon with cold, measuring eyes and hate. But if we do not yield to that hatred, nor to what gave it birth, but stand aside to let one balance the other, then we do what those trained in the Way can do to fight that which is base. Yes, I had in me that which could quicken from this thing of the utter dark. But it was how I met that weakness, not the weakness itself which counted.

I was Elys, a Wise woman, even as Jervon had reminded me by the speaking of my name. Therefore I was no tool of that which had led me to this throne. I had come of my own free will to face it, not been dragged by dark forces overcoming my spirit.

"Elys—" It was the enthroned creature that uttered my name now, and there was enticement in that naming.

But I stood fast, summoning up all which was born of my long training to armor me. And the beautiful head so far above me shifted a little. Now, though keeping me still in its gaze, it also could see Jervon. It raised its hand to beckon.

The yellow flame which was my fulfillment in this life wavered toward the throne. Yet it was not muddied as were those others which crawled about us. Nor did Jervon ask aught of me in that moment, but made the struggle his own. I knew, without his telling, that he feared I would be depleted should I undertake his defense as well as mine. Then I moved whatever form this world had left me, standing between Jervon and the thing which reached with its shadow hand to grasp him.

Once more I pronounced the name men had given him in their fear and horror of this baneful worship. But I sent no symbols into the air for him to sweep aside. Rather I did send a thought picture, and this was of an empty throne crumbling in long decay.

Fear I fought, and anger I reined in, making both feed and serve me in what I would do. This was—not!

I held valiantly to the small weapon I had. I did not worship, I did not believe, nor did Jervon. Therefore: this thing was NOT!

Yet it was growing more and more solid even as I so denied it. Beckoning—BEING!

The imagination of countless generations of men had fashioned it, how could I hope to dismantle it with only a denial?

An empty throne—a nonbeing—!

I threw all that was me, all which I sensed I drew now from Jervon with his willing consent, into that picture. This was no god of mine. I did not feed it—it could not exist!

Torment indeed was that denial; ever it called to a part of me, to force homage and worship. Yet that I held out against. No god of mine! There must be faith to bring a god alive, to perform deeds in his name—without faith there was no existence.

I knew better than to summon the Powers I did kneel before. In this place all worship the enthroned thing would take to itself, whether given in its filthy name or not. No, this was the bareness of my spirit and my belief in myself, and Jervon's belief in himself that mattered. I did not accept, and I refused homage because it was—NOT!

The thing lost its lazy assurance, its evil smile and laughter, even the quasi-human form it had assumed to tempt me. There was nothing in the throne place now but a ravening flame touched with the deep black of its evil. That swept back and forth as might the head of a great serpent elevated above a coiled body, waiting to strike.

Its rage was that of madness. The long years it had existed had not prepared it for this. It was here, it could seize my kind, absorb into it their spirits—

But could it?

Humans are composed of many layers of consciousness, many emotions. Any who deal with the Talent—and many who do not—knew this. The throned thing fed upon fear and those viler parts of us. The miserable blobs it drew to it, which were now packed tightly around me, swaying in time to the swaying of that flame on the throne, were dominated by the worst that had lain in the humanity they had once been, not the best. They had been held prisoner by their fears and their belief, until they had been summoned here to be delivered helplessly to their master.

A master who could in turn not hold them unless they surrendered, whom they had created and could now destroy—if they so willed it!

I threw that thought afield as I might whirl about me an unsheathed sword. If they were all lost in the depths of their foul belief then it would avail me nothing. But if only a few could join us—only a few!

The thing on the throne was quick. It lapped out and down, and took with that lapping the first row of the blob things, swelling in power as it absorbed their energy.

"Elys—Elys—"

Only my name, but into it Jervon put all he could to hearten and sustain me. I was aware of a brighter burst of the clear golden flame to my left.

Again the false god pounced to feast. There was something too hasty in its movements, as if time was no longer its servant, but might speedily be its enemy. It wanted to cram itself with life force, swell its power.

But it could not feed on unbelief. That logic I held to as one holds to a rope which is one's only hope of aid.

An empty throne—

Now that rusted and diseased flame uttered a kind of shriek, or perhaps that was not any cry but a vibration meant to shake me, loose me from my rope of hope. It flickered out and out toward me, towards the light which was Jervon.

We did not believe, therefore we could not be its prey.

I was in the dark; my perception was totally gone. I was—in ... No, I could not be within something which did not exist. I was me, Elys, and Jervon. We were no meat for a false god whose creators were long since dust, its temple forgotten.

It was as if my bare body was seared by a cold so intense that it had the same effect as fire. I was one with—no, I was not! I was Elys. And Jervon was Jervon! I would feel him through the torture of the cold, holding as I did to his own identity. We were ourselves and no servants—victims—of this thing which had no place in the world. We had no fear for it to batten on now, and those parts of us which it could awaken, those we could control. There was an empty throne—there was nothingness—nothingness but Elys and Jervon who did not believe—

Pain, cold, pain, and still I held. And now Jervon called to me and somehow I found the strength to give to him even as earlier he had loosed his for me. Together we stood, and because of that both of us were the stronger, for in our union was the best part of us both—mind and spirit.

Darkness, cold, pain, and then a sense of change, of being lost. But I would not allow fear to stir. A god who was naught could not slay—

I opened my eyes—for I saw with them now and not with that special sense I had in that other place. Before me was a column of light, but it was wan, sinking, growing paler even in the space of a blink or two. I moved; my body was stiff, cold, my hands and feet had no feeling in them as I slid forward on the wide seat where I had awakened, looking about me for something familiar and known.

This—this was the round chamber where I had found Jervon—

Jervon!

Stumbling, weaving, I staggered to that other chair, fumbling with my dagger so that I might cut the ropes which bound his stiff body. His eyes were closed, but he had not tumbled flaccidly down as had the outlaw who had been drained. I sawed at his bonds with my numb and fumbling hands, twice dropping the blade so I had to grope for it in the half light. For the flaming pillar in the center gave forth but little radiance now—more like the dread glow which sometimes gathers on dead bodies.

"Jervon!" I called to him, shook him as best I could with those blockish hands. His body fell forward so his head rested on my shoulder and his weight nearly bore me tumbling backward. "Jervon!"

It seemed in that moment that I had lost. For if I alone had won out of that evil place then there was no further hope for me.

"Jervon!"

There was a breath against my cheek, expelled by a moan. I gathered him to me in a hold, which even the false god could not have broken, until his voice came, low and with a stammering catch in it:

"My dear lady, would you break my ribs—" and there was a thread of weak laughter in that which set me laughing too, until I near shook with the force of that reaction. I almost could not believe our battle won. But before us, where we crouched together on the wide seat of that throne, the last glimmer of light died. There was no gateway now into elsewhere. Outside the outlaws of the Waste might be waiting, but we two had battled something greater than any malice of theirs, and for the moment we were content.

EARTHBORN:
A WITCH WORLD STORY
Masters of Fantasy (2004) BAEN

Mereth drew a deep breath. Breezes here were still ice-kissed, though this cup of land was well beneath the mountain walls which formed its confines. She pulled her heavy cloak closer and secured its throatlatch before freeing Mage Ruther's experimental distance see-all. Mereth never ceased to wonder at its ability to draw into her vision things that lay far away.

If this tool had only been available in the days of the invasion. It seemed, she thought, that nowadays minds were proving sharper. Knowledge, either long forgotten or newly discovered, advanced steadily from one sunrise to another. It was almost as if the constant alerts--necessary before the Warding—having now vanished, had been opened for the flourishing of learning. Mereth did not, of course, accept the suggestion that a Golden Age had come to Estcarp and her own High Hallack. No, when the Gates, known or secret, had drawn captives from many far sources to people this long-mixed world—Estcarp, Arvon, High Hallack, Karstan, Escore—evil had come, nonetheless, twinned with good.

Gone were the Gates, yes. But though the Dark might not feed its forces here now, it had not yet shrunk to nothingness. Behind her now, within the near-repaired walls of Lormt, more than a score of scholars engaged in research, eager to recover any hint of what might rise to threaten again. Towers, brought low by the Dance of the Mountains, were now near restored. However, beneath the ancient floors of those venerable storehouses of knowledge, long-hidden rooms had burst open to be explored by the then few, reclusive inhabitants. Newcomers, sages of high learning, had flocked in. The efforts of at least three quarters of the Lormt dwellers were now bent toward this exploration and were being repaid.

She lifted again the far-seer, held it to her right eye and turned it down slope. There appeared movement now, which in this near-deserted country might herald a visitor, one of those seeking to trace war-tossed kin, raider scout, or homeless wanderer.

Peering so through her new tool, Mereth saw straightly enough. What leaped into instant view was a gaunt villager garbed in rags. It was the shepherdess she had observed warding a tiny flock of bedraggled sheep a day gone. To the woman's eye, skilled through years in merchanting, the pitifully thin mottled creatures rated of the poorest quality. Such faded, ragged wool would bring scarcely half a glance in the past from the factors at Ferndale Warehouse.

The distant village girl rounded a rock and then half stumbled against the stone as if unable to stand erect. Mereth gained her feet with the aid of her long staff, thrust the far-seer into a belt loop and headed down the hill. She had made no mistake in reading the expression of abject horror that had grimaced that narrow face. Being a mute, Mereth could not call out, nor did she appear to possess any of the Old Talent of mind-touch. Suddenly her feet struck something slick in the sprouting grass and she dug in her staff just in time to prevent herself from falling.

The shepherdess's head jerked up and she looked directly at Mereth, terror still etched on her features. She screamed and lurched away from the rock, running, not toward Mereth, but away.

Mereth was not close enough to bar the girl's way with her staff and had to steady herself, once more unsure of her own footing. Just as she reached the upstanding spur of rock, the girl had reached the far side, no chance to stop her now.

Leaning heavily on her staff for support, the woman of Lormt doggedly followed the frightened girl; however, now a strange awareness broke upon her so sharply that she almost staggered. Clutching the rod of polished wood with all her might, she met such an odor that she held her breath for a moment. Death's foul stench, Death with the sickening effluvia of an ancient evil.

A battleground might well poison the rising wind so, but even during the years of the war, Mereth had only once met with such a stomach-twisting smell. It filled the nostrils, but it also reached deep within her and awakened a nameless fear. Perhaps the loss of one ability, that of speech, stirred and sharpened all her senses. It posed a question for the likes of Maid Mouse, whose visits she cherished. Mouse was renowned for her magic talent and the gift of discerning the balance of things.

As the woman continued to plod persistently along the track the girl had taken, her thoughts were rudely interrupted.

Looking down, she was met with a strange sight indeed. At her feet in the spring-green meadow grass was a fleece, rent and be-splotched with great gouts of blood. Among the young blades of recently nibbled grass there showed rough patches of blood-soaked mud.

Mereth carefully inserted the ground tip of her staff under the edge of the hide and flipped back a part of it to examine the flesh side. With so much blood about, this must be a fresh kill, but how could this be with no sign of paw-, claw- or footprint?

Furthermore, there was not one scrap of flesh adhering to the underside of the sheepskin. No animal could kill and clean its prey and leave the hide thus. And where were the bones? There was no sign of any remains, nothing but blood and hide!

There were feral hunters in plenty in these mountains, borse-bear, vallops, snow cats. But sites of their feasting bore no resemblance to this. The very look and feel here shouted danger in the Lormt woman's mind.

Wessel, he might know. Lormt and its grounds had been his charge for years. He was truly both Lord Duratan's right and left hand and the first to be queried about land or towers. She had seen him an hour earlier supervising the finishing of the crenellations of a new tower in the outer wall. But, the herder . . . Mereth turned slowly to scan the reaches of the meadow. Of course there was no sight of the girl. She might have traced the child by the sound of her running, but the sight of the strange kill had lost her that advantage and she probably could not have kept pace long enough to catch her. Many heavy boulders thrust up along the fringes of the pasturage like ill-socketed teeth. Any one of them offered an ample hiding place.

Perhaps later she might borrow one of the tough little ponies and ride down to the village to inquire about the girl, though the prospect of success was dim. There was no great friendship between the village and Lormt, for many of those living there now were Karsten survivors of the Mountain Dance and deeply bitter against those with Talents.

No, to learn what she could from Wessel was her best move at present. Again planting her sturdy staff with care, Mereth turned to retrace her steps.

She found Wessel leaning on an overturned cart, happily engulfing, with obvious hunger, a huge round of herb bread wrapped about a fat chunk of cheese. The filling looked about to escape his hold, but he adroitly stuffed the last of it into his generous mouth. Mereth hesitated; to call a man from his midday meats simply to observe a puzzle lying down-mountain was hardly fair. But, time was crucial. The evidence must be seen immediately or be of no value.

The bailiff swallowed again as she came up.

"Trouble, M'Lady?"

Mereth steadied her slate and carefully printed, the easier for him to read.

"Down slope, look, something curious to see."

He rolled what remained of his meal into a square of coarse linen and tucked it into the front of his jerkin. Then he hesitated for a moment and looked closely at her.

Instinctively catching his unspoken question, she shook her head and he forbore to pick up the only possible weapon at hand, a mattock that leaned against the wall behind him.

This time she took more careful account of her footing. At the nooning it was warmer now and her hearing, always acute, caught the drone of buzzing insects. As they approached the site of the kill, it seemed that the stench had intensified; however, the near-palpable evil she had sensed clouding the spot was now dissipated. Wessel practically vaulted the last few paces down to stand beside the blood-clotted fleece and after a moment squatted, his hand over his nose.

"'Pears something took one o' Fuser's ewes," he had half advanced a hand near but not quite touching the befouled wool.

Again Mereth's writing tool was busy. "Mot-wolf, bear, Snow cat?"

He shook his head in response to her list. "Not as any mountain hunter was this done, M'Lady. Where be the paw prints, bones and the like? Best we put Lord Duratan on this, he was ranger trained. Now," Wessel rose to his feet, "I'll just go and tell him."

Mereth withdrew. The cloud of blue flies and the pervasive stench were more than she could bear. Even when she reached Lormt again, she avoided visiting the buttery for a while. Instead she went to the tiny chamber that opened off her well-appointed living space and sat down at her desk, which was thickly spread with documents and a couple of wood-covered books so heavily fashioned to protect the ancient parchment pages.

There was the Larweeth case, this was her duty at Lormt; she must keep to it. The great war behind them, the massacres of the old race in Karsten, the Moving of the Mountains had stirred up her entire world as one stirs the stiff batter for a feast cake. Families and clans had been brutally rent apart.

Now Lormt was devoted to gathering and cataloging of news of such losses, ready to offer aid to any who came seeking news of kin. Sometimes one had to sift through very old records for needed clues. Accustomed to keeping accounts of business on land and sea for her trading family, Mereth had found this a suitable occupation in her old age, one she could ply with skill.

She closed her eyes for a moment and saw only bloody wool. Clapping her hand to her lips, she swallowed firmly and reached for a book of armorial bearings. This she opened with determination and forced herself to locate a particular mark.

At last able for a time to push the disturbing scene out of her mind and settle down to pursue her research, Mereth became shortly so engrossed that it almost startled her when a messenger from Lord Duratan arrived to ask, if it were no trouble, could she attend upon him?

It was near twilight when Mereth trudged through the halls, aided by her staff in making cautious descent into the bowels of Lormt. There she knocked on the door of Lord Duratan's quarters from whence he ordered the affairs governing the safety of the ancient seat of knowledge. Once of the Borderers, he kept his chamber well lighted, and when the woman knocked and entered at his invitation, she immediately caught a sound that betrayed his mood, a random clicking.

He had swept a space clear of paper, pens, and folios on the ancient wood surface of the table before him. Above this his hands rose and fell as his fingers gathered a partial palmful of colored crystals, only to toss them in a scattered pattern, which he studied after each throw. So he gauged this matter serious indeed! Mereth stared in turn at the results of his last pitch, one shaped by chance and his particular Talent. The crystals lay about the cleared place in a discernible array.

Most of the darker colors had fallen well away from the central core, where appeared different shades of green—from that of new spring grass to the darkest bramble leaf hue. However, these were lightened by a sprinkling of pale yellow, lying randomly. After one long stare, the Marshal of Lormt raised his head to look directly at Mereth and began to recite as if reading from some report drawn from Wessel's account book, ending:

"Lady Mereth, in the days before the Warding the ships of your house sailed far. Have you ever heard report of such a foulness as you discovered today?"

The woman's slate and stylus were at the ready. "No." A terse enough answer, but none further was needed.

"There are beasts enough in these heights to be feared." He was sweeping up the crystals to pour them back into a double bag of lizard skin. "At this season of the year such are well hungered from the sparseness of winter game. Yet none known to be at large hereabouts gorges to the point of leaving naught but an empty hide. Wessel is now asking questions."

Duratan's next word was drowned by a sound, which instantly brought them both to their feet and swinging toward one of the narrow windows in the guardian's chamber. The man reached it in two strides, but Mereth was not about to be left behind and crowded against him to see.

The last vestiges of twilight dimmed the slope that walled the valley. Some distance below small blazes bobbed up and down, torches, by the look, Mereth opined. These seemed not to be approaching Lormt, rather milling around.

Duratan pushed the woman aside as he strode across the room, pausing only to snatch a cloak draped over a chair back. Uncaring that she was many passages away from her own covering, Mereth followed him through the door, though he was running now. Even with the aid of her staff, she could not keep pace, and by the time she reached the center court, a small company of armed guards was assembling, while two at the gate were grunting as they opened the massive portal with straining muscles. They carefully limited the space to just enough to let a single armsman pass.

Though the torches were not visible from this level, a shout came from a wall sentry two levels above.

"Still there!"

"M'Lady, this be a cold night! Here, get you into this." Mistress Bethelie, housekeeper for Lormt, had whipped off her own cloak to wrap it around Mereth's shoulders. Mage Lights swayed above them, brighter than any torch. Clearly Lady Nalor's powers were at work.

Mereth gave hasty thanks, for Duratan had, by then, slipped through the narrow opening of the gate and the porter was preparing to shut it when she squeezed by. He made as if to stop her, but she paid no heed. Only, as the darkness closed around her outside, did she pause. The mage globes did not extend to this place. A misstep would surely mean a painful fall. Ahead came the sounds of the armsmen, and she bit her lip in irritation. She had no choice but to stumble along at a crawling pace, exerting her waning strength to dig in her staff for support at each step. Cries rose from the huddle of torchbearers and there came a shrill scream, suddenly cut off, as if by a blow. When Mereth finally reached the point of action, the flickering torchlight, though poor, was enough to reveal much of the struggle that surrounded her.

No armsman had drawn steel, but all were fighting with short, thick wooden staffs, not unlike her own longer one. Their opponents were men from the village who shouted raucously as they fought.

Mereth could make out raw oaths mingled with cries of "Ye Dark Ones! Be gone! Leave us be!" Historically the researchers of ancient lore in Lormt had little contact with the villagers, save for the troublous times when they had opened the great depository of knowledge to shelter those fleeing for their lives. The landsmen and their families had been grateful enough then, but after the vast disaster of the Turning, distrust had arisen and communication was limited to dealing for supplies. However, she had never heard of such trouble as she now witnessed.

Mereth had scarce time to ponder the matter, for as she pivoted about her staff, she barely escaped a killing blow aimed at her head. As it was, it landed crookedly and painfully against her shoulder.

Rober! Why, only that morning the carter's son had greeted her civilly with proper respect, but now his reddened face was drawn into a twisted mask like a blood-mad raider. Mereth shuddered. It was as if the old days had come again. Instinctively she retaliated, swinging her stout staff with practiced force and caught the youth at knee level. He screeched and went down.

Holding his knee, he rolled over. He had not landed on bare ground but on another body. Naked flesh revealed by torchlight writhed frantically. The shepherdess, so small and withered-seeming without her rags, had been roped into a bundle. Raw marks across her arms gave evidence of earlier abuse.

Mereth moved to stand over her, ready to defend the pitiful girl and herself, but Rober had dragged himself away, still clutching his knee and howling continuously. The core of conflict had moved away from them and shadows enclosed the two females as torches were either snuffed or carried distant. However, there was just enough light for a few moments for Mereth to spy a refuge of sorts, another of the upstanding rocks. She could not carry the girl but she might perhaps roll her. She leaned over and grasped the girl's hair, greasy and dust clotted.

She could tell by a brief gleam that the shepherdess's eyes were upon her. The older woman made a hand motion to indicate rolling and pointed toward the stone, hoping the girl would understand.

There was no answer, but push Mereth did with what strength she had left, and the small body did seem to undulate into a roll until together they came up against the harsh surface of the boulder. The woman dropped to the ground, near exhausted, with the helpless girl lying against her. Mereth was shivering. No, rather what she felt was wrenching shudders that shook the girl's so-thin body. Mereth had no blade with her to cut the small captive's bindings, but loosing the throatlatch of Bethelie's cloak, the woman drew the trembling girl into her arms and did what she could to pull the sturdy length of tightly woven wool about them both.

As she attempted to draw the girl higher in her grasp, the edge of her cloak tangled about one of the thin arms so strictly bound. The villager lurched forward as best she could, but was unable to free herself. Twisting in Mereth's tightened hold, she screamed again and managed to near face her captor squarely.

"Evil, Make kill, quick!"

Mereth was in no position to write either question or answer. But at that moment one of the torchbearers, a supporter on either side, retreated near enough that the woman saw. Across the shepherdess's tightly bound arm, stretching as a ghastly fringe along the shoulder was rough, raw flesh, lacking any skin. Immediately Mereth swung the girl from close contact, the better to see the bony back riddled with more vicious patches of exposed flesh, in which was embedded bits of torn leaf or dark broken stem.

There was evidence of not a heavy flogging, but something far more frightening. Mereth shuddered. She must get the victim to Lormt, where Nalor could employ her healer's skill to ease the child's torment.

The girl writhed, trying to pull herself away from Mereth, though even the slightest movement brought harsh cries of pain. The woman's attempts to hold her closer to prevent further self-inflicted torture only made her screech louder. Without the ability to communicate, Mereth was near as helpless as the bound one. No! No! NO!

Her mind battled against the gag nature had laid upon her, as she had once before in her life when her younger sister had been cut down before her eyes by an Alisonian during the Kolder War.

"M'Lady!"

The light was stronger. Wessel stood nursing his left arm against his chest as Master Forbie, with whom she had exchanged greetings that morning, lowered closer a torch.

"What have we here?" Duratan joined them. "Lady Mereth, how came you here?"

She looked down at the trembling girl, who seemed to have suddenly shrunk to little more than a tiny armful of abraded flesh. As Mereth leaned back against the rock, the torchlight pitilessly revealed more of the blood-oozing body. Wessel uttered a blistering oath while the commander of Lormt's garrison turned to shout, "AID!" over the field where the battling guards and villagers could no longer be seen.

Back at last at Lormt, a gesture from Nalor, two of the elderly scholars pushed a table closer to the high blazing fire of the chamber where dried herbs swung on cords anchored well above. Mereth crouched on a stool within close reach of the flames' warmth, nursing a mug of cordial hot enough to be a blessing to her frosted hands. She watched Nalor whisk a length of bed sheet across the table and Duratan, aided by a guard, stretch the village girl thereupon, face down, the herb mistress at the last moment turning the youngling's head gently to one side. A low swung lamp chained to a beam above the table revealed the child's abused flesh.

To Mereth's astonishment, the ghastly skinless wounds did not continue clear across the back as would signs of a severe lashing. Instead they could be seen on left shoulder, left arm, and left hip; the rest of the skin was bruised but untorn.

Mistress Bethelie, bringing with her a small steaming kettle, folded cloths in a pack under one arm, appeared beside Lady Nalor as the men left.

Her face was contorted, flushed with anger. "What manner of brutes are these village louts?" she demanded.

Lady Nalor made no answer, but she opened one of her medicine pouches to take out slender tweezers. Mereth guessed her intention, pulled herself up, setting aside her drink, and twitched one of the cloths from the housekeeper's grasp.

Stretching this flat on her palms, Mereth pushed Bethelie aside to stand at the Herb Mistress's side as, with obvious care, Nalor began to free the wounds of the bits of stem, matted leaves, and portions of blossoms, which clung so tightly to the raw flesh that they seemed to be embedded.

Once she had cleared these all away, she nodded to Mereth, who had immediately clapped one side of the waiting cloth over the other, that nothing escape.

"Feel it?" Nalor asked.

Mereth nodded, the cloth pressed tightly between her hands. Feel it, she did. Perhaps not as strongly as did Nalor, who was of the Old Race and had some of the Talent: rage, blistering, concentrated rage, such an emotion as might drive a man into battle with no thought of himself, simply to slay and slay until he, in turn, would be slain.

And, though there was no possible physical cause, the emotion was rooted in the folded cloth she held.

She must continue to hold; she could not reach for her slate to write any of the questions churning in her mind. Thus Mereth stood and watched Nalor go about her healing work, while keeping half her attention on the wadded cloth into which her nails burrowed.

At length Mistress Bethelie supervised two of her own staff as they carried away the girl, heavily swathed in bandages. But there was no time, even then, for questions and answers. Either Mereth had become accustomed to the burning of the strange rage, or else much of that had subsided. She still clasped the cloth tightly, however as cudgel-battered men began to be either carried in or aided by comrades. There came both defenders of Lormt and villagers, bloody, bruised, and somehow scarcely aware of their surroundings. Lady Nalor paused to snatch up a glass bowl and curl a summoning finger at Mereth.

"In." She opened a hinged lid. Mereth pushed in the crumpled fabric and the Herb Mistress snapped the lid back down instantly and made it secure.

The housekeeper appeared, holding Mereth's staff, and drew the cramped and wrinkled hand of the older woman into the crook of her sturdy elbow. "Come, M'Lady, 'tis near sunup. We do not wish any fever, now do we? Bed for you now."

Nalor had not only relieved her of that burden that had hammered against her strength, but it seemed that she had drawn on Mereth's energy, draining her as well. She allowed herself to be half guided, half carried to her own chamber and the soft comfort of her waiting bed.

It was light again, and the clear gloss of very early sunlight touched the undrawn curtain of the bed as she roused. Mereth sat up among the pillows and drew her hand across her forehead, a gesture which brought no relief to her aching head. She looked around twice to reassure herself that no evil shadow had followed her out of the dreams that had imprisoned and tormented her. Slowly she washed in the tepid water she found in her bowl. Its warmth suggested that someone had looked in at her not long before. Shivering, she drew a heavy gown of quiet violet from her chest and a gray shawl formed into lace by knitting. Mereth continued to battle the pain, which had established itself behind her eyes and, leaning on her staff much more heavily than usual, she sought out company.

This she found in one of the common rooms. The chamber was more crowded than she had ever seen it, and voices rose more loudly than usual. As Mereth entered, partly unnoticed, she was near deafened by fragments of news that were being passed around the room.

Lord Duratan had sent for the nearest Wise Woman. No, he had ridden off to seek her, he was going to appeal to Lord Koris who ruled in Es these days. The villagers had been dabbling in ancient and forbidden things, they had actually brought a girl child as a sacrifice to some devilish thing, and on it went!

Mereth lingered near the door, wanting to escape the din. If she could only cover her ears, but she dared not lose the support of her staff and perhaps end up on the floor for her trouble.

"Lady Mereth!"

Mage Faggold, one of the oldest scholars, suddenly appeared beside her. Though he had counted a vast tally of years, he had not retired as far from the world of the present time, as most of his age group. He was credited with being perhaps the finest historian of those now at Lormt.

He raised his voice more strongly to overcome the din. "This is indeed fortunate, finding you so. We are about to sit in council." He offered her his arm with the grace of a courtier. Thus those, who might be considered the new defenders of their world, gathered. Lord Duratan was not present. In his place sat Nalor, his lady, and lying before her on the table, around which their chairs had been gathered, was the cloth Mereth knew well. There sat Wessel and another former Borderer, three of the sages, and Faggold.

When Mereth was comfortably seated, her slate to hand, Lady Nalor, using the point of a pen as an indicator, raised the edge of the cloth and flipped it out flat. Next she pointed to indicate brown splotches, sticking to its length, which was now far from white.

"You have seen what lies here as it appears beneath the enlarging glass. You have felt," she paused, looking from one face to another.

From the moment her eyes had touched that cloth, Mereth's head moved from side to side. She strove to repel what had followed her out of her feverish dreams. Without her conscious mind's order, she was writing on her slate.

"It lives, it eats, eats the living." The horror of that thought shook her write-stick from her hand. Faggold caught it before it fell to the floor. Lady Nalor nodded.

"Yes." Tapping her pen on the table, as if to center their attention to her, the healer separated one of the dark twigs. "This is not a thing of the sun or of the Light. It lives beneath. Though it seems a plant, yet it is not as we know plants, for its food is flesh and blood." She gazed from one to another of the council members.

Mereth picked up her writing stick from beside her slate where Faggold had placed it. She had regained her control and shaped her words firmly. "Is this one of the ancient evils awakened again? Or, is there a gate undiscovered, unsealed? Do we dig to tear it up by the roots?" She lingered a moment, supplied a final sentence, her memory awake. Of course there in the past the crew had been fighting a lesser peril on the strange island to the far south, however their improvised weapon had worked very well. "There is fire to cleanse, weed killing potions to poison," she listed on her slate.

Faggold and Lady Nalor had both been following her writing closely.

"Acid of Safall," Nalor nodded vigorously.

"Hot coals held tongs of bale iron," the Mage added his suggestion as quickly. "We must make the villagers aid."

Mereth leaned back a little. Those in the council were all talking at once again. She felt as if a cloud hung above her head. This was all too simple somehow. She picked up the slate and stick to stow them into the bag fastened to her girdle. Those about her were planning now; sometimes they seemed of two minds as to what method to use, but all were united on the fact that the task must be done with all possible haste, before the monstrous ground-creeping scourge could spread farther.

Mereth chewed her lower lip. There was more, of that she was sure. Was a villager, one with some Dark learning, backing this?

With the aid of her staff she got to her feet. Lady Nalor looked up and Mereth made a small gesture with her right hand. Over the years she had been at Lormt she had developed hand signals, easily understood by her daily companions. Now she also gave a slight nod.

However, Mereth did not return to her chamber when she left the council, rather she went but a short distance down the hall, into a small side room. A kitchen maid sat nodding in a chair beside an occupied bed. She quickly slipped out of the chair, rubbing her eyes and yawning. Mereth smiled and gestured to the door. The maid disappeared gratefully, leaving the chair for the old woman.

Mereth settled gingerly, her attention all for the occupant of the bed. She was entirely alert now, as more and more her suspicions grew firm. The village girl lay with her well-padded back up-turned, the bandages giving forth an herbal scent. However, her head was turned toward the elderly woman and now her eyes opened abruptly.

Mereth's head jerked. It was as if she had heard sly laughter.

"What would you have of me, old woman?"

This creature could surely not be one with the Power Women. "Right," the word struck into Mereth's aching head like the point of a spear. "Power sweeps in both ways. All things balance. What would you have of me, I ask it again. And I am not patient. Think what you would ask, scraping around on a slate wastes time. If we deal together, something must be done about that."

Mereth clasped her hands tightly together. She had walked daily with fear in the war days, but this was something else, she might be chained in some cell while a flood of filth rose about her. Only she must force herself to discover what monster had been brought into Lormt.

"Who are you?" She shaped the thought with difficulty, painfully.

"I am Vorsla, Starqua, Deden, Karn." Smooth flow of thought paused. Mereth's eyes were on her own tightly clasped hands. She refused to meet those other gray ones.

The voice spoke again in her mind. "Ufora."

Involuntarily a short guttural sound escaped Mereth's throat. "Yes, oh, yes! When you were little did your dam never strive to threaten you with that name? Ufora of the darkest woods, she could make you one with a tree chosen by a logger, or with a jumper already entangled with the Skinner, the Eater."

Mereth forced herself upright in the chair. Could this creature read more thought than that intended for communication? Quickly she readied another question.

"What do I do here?" The woods demon continued, "Well, I emerged from the Long Sleep as you see me, a small one easily abused by others, a throw-away of the war. It has taken me too long to become truly myself." The girl touched the crushed linen covering her breast. "Only now after the letting of blood do I fully remember. These dolts of upper dwellers believe they won the ancient war at last by closing the Gates to the worlds of another level. We remain, we who were sleeping away the flooding of endless years. So again we were free to fold time. There have been openings left for those unguessed, in which to build their nests anew. So will Ufora do!"

The slight body on the bed moved, pulled up to its knees and slewed around. It plucked at the thick, odorous bandages until it was free. Smooth skin, shown much more darkly against the bedclothes, covered a body in which bones were no longer visible.

Mereth fought desperately against the pain in her head, throbbing as if words were beating a drum within her skull.

The seeming girl snatched up the uppermost sheet and was winding it about herself. She tied two ends together and knotted them, patting the knot when finished.

"Now," She had spoken only the one word aloud. Standing with her head tilted a little to one side, as if listening, she remained quiet for a moment. Then her face twisted into a mask of rage. "So," she spoke at last. "They would." She started toward the door but her bulky covering slowed her.

Mereth made a determined effort. Her staff, wielded as a spear, thudded home on the other's ribs. The girl screamed, caught at the bed for support, then collapsed to the floor. At once the door flew open with such force it crashed against the wall. Mistress Bethelie gave one glance at Mereth and then centered her attention on the girl, who was snarling at the old woman and visibly working her fingers in a pattern between them.

Bethelie caught at the heavy bunch of keys swinging from her own girdle, snapped it loose and crashed the jangling ball against the girl's hands with good aim. Mereth sat back weakly in her chair. She was finding it very difficult to breathe and her head pain seemed to draw a veil, clouding her vision. However, she could still hear Mistress Bethelie's precise voice:

"Iron, cold iron, to you, evil slut, iron!"

The ringing words followed Mereth into darkness.

Never, since her venture with the Magestone, had Mereth felt herself so removed from real and daily life. There was no sense of transition from the small room, of rising from the chair and making her way through the halls and the great courtyard into the open. A will, which she did not claim as her own, possessed her. Nor did she see anyone on that misty journey. In the huge edifice of Lormt, she might have been totally alone.

Then, with no warning, the walls and restored towers vanished. Mereth was no longer alone, though those about her had a tenuous look. Before her now stretched the sharply sloping, rock-studded land where the skirmish with the villagers had been fought. The sod had been torn away and, not too far away, more of it was yielding to rakes not meant for a farm laborer's cultivation. They were larger than customary and the prongs wider, scratching up clods of earth with vicious points more like weapons than farming implements.

It was near to this activity that the major part of a large assembly was to be found.

Mereth blinked once and again, trying to rid her eyes of the cloying mist. Lord Duratan stood there with Wessel and two other one-time Borderers whom she knew to be expert archers. A step or so beyond stood Lady Nalor holding a drawn sword whose weight was obviously burdening her.

And, that force, which had brought Mereth here, thrust her forward at a quicker pace. Fear like one of the sudden mountain ice showers, struck her full faced. A bundle, resting on the ground between Nalor and the yet undisturbed turf, stirred. She who claimed to be Ufora got to her feet. Her face was like a mask carved from greenish ice of the higher mountain slopes. She tried hard to raise her arms, but her wrists were drawn tightly together. Though there was no strong light, the day being gray, yet flashes glittered.

The captive was in irons, iron, cold iron, Nalor was chanting. Now and again Duratan tossed at Ufora a fistful of crushed herbs.

Once, twice Ufora tried again to raise her hands. The lips of her masklike face twisted. She might have been seeking to utter words of some dark ritual of her own.

Then, the seeming girl lifted her head a fraction and the dark eyes in her oddly green face fastened on Mereth, meeting those of the elder woman. Ufora was instantly before her, fettered arms inching out to her. She could see them, impossibly reflected in the creature's eyes. If one pressed there, and there, the bonds would loosen. Mereth knew what the other strained to force her to do.

Three times her own hands came up and out toward the iron-encircled wrists. Three times her own will prevailed and they fell again, but she grew weaker, her head filled with such pain as she was sure would overcome her.

There was no hesitation in Nalor's chant. Her words held no meaning for Mereth. Only there were others!

"Anchor's up, ye sons of Gry, To the sails, let us fly!"

A man's voice, deep from the throat, armed with courage, about to sail on a final voyage.

Deep in her resonated the words she could not voice,

"Wind and sail

Cannot fail

Men with the Light.

Not even,"

The song she could not voice aloud was fading within her. Rolf, she shut away that memory fiercely. But, but, he had freed her! The staff, her ever-ready companion, lifted. She could no longer sense those dark eyes holding her in thrall. They were light, oddly flat.

Nalor's words were lifting upward in a single, final trumpet-voiced phrase.

The strange girl retreated, still facing Mereth and Nalor. Her foot caught as a noose of roots suddenly snaked out. She screamed, stooping to batter thin green stems ending in yellow flowers with petals that had the shape of sword blades.

Before the watchers could move, the land did so. A great crevice gaped and from it arose a thin netting of fine roots to close ominously about the girl. Again the ground shook, preparing to close its doom-crack. Nalor moved; into that heaving growth she tossed a ball, only to snatch a second one, then a third, which Duratan held out to her.

Close, the earth did at last! Mereth shuddered as shrill screams slowly faded away, death cries of that which should never have lived.

Thus passed the Latter Battle of Lormt, fought and won, and though the sages housed there sought often to find record of its like in the chronicles they prized, they did so in vain. However, Mereth related the tale to Maid Mouse of the Learned Ones and what she heard in reply, she never told, save that talk by thought became a gift to which she fiercely clung, so dearly was it won.

THAT WHICH OVERFLOWETH
Grails: Quests, Visitations and Other Occurrences (1992)
Unnameable Press, Grails: Quests of the Dawn (2004) Penguin/Roc

There are many tales, legends, and stories misshapen by years of mistelling, generations of adding to—or subtracting from. Once there was a man who fled with a handful of followers overseas to the farthermost known portion of the great empire. He took with him, it is said, two things of Power, a staff and another possession, which he guarded so jealously that even those who shared his exile seldom saw it.

In the far country he set the staff into the ground in a place which was already known to Power, where older Presences than those the voyager worshiped, had long held steady. And that staff, cut and dried for years, rooted and brought forth blossom so that the man believed he had found that place where the seeds he and his carried could flourish. But his other treasure was hidden away—though in plain sight—and so remained through the rise and fall of kings and empires and the passing of uncounted centuries, even into the final years when the world itself grew sick, promising death's coming.

They came just after dawn, the dire wolves. Since Jan had broken his leg there was no trained sentry on the High Hill. Guran was very young, but he had the horn and he sounded it, before he was picked off by a sky bolt. Thus he bought those at the shrine village a small measure of time.

Not enough.

She Who Spoke had already reached the inner shrine when the alarm sounded. For a single breath she stood tense and still, and then she beckoned to those two who had lingered by the entrance in awe of this sacred place.

"There." She pointed to the dressed stone on which stood the unlit candles of sheep fat, alongside the faded flowers of yesterday's offering. Then, in demonstration of what must be done, she set her hands to the edge of the stone, feeling frantically for what was a key.

There were screams from beyond now, the cries of a village put to pillage. Death cries. Cassia, as she stooped to obey the Voice, shuddered. She heaved with all her strength as Lana was doing to match her at the other end of the stone. Reluctantly it began to move.

"In with you," the Voice's fingers bit painfully at Cassia's shoulder as she pushed the girl-child toward the black hole they had half uncovered. There was no way to protest that order. Terrified, not only of the dark gap before her but at the sounds which reached them, she pushed into that opening, and, a moment later, felt Lana's weight shoving her yet farther in and down. Then, before she could protest, the stone was swinging back, to leave their thin childish bodies pressed tightly together.

"Lana." There was no answer from the other—she was only a heavy weight against Cassia's shoulder and arm. "Lana? Voice?" she whimpered once again and then was silent.

Her sight adjusted a little. There was a measure of light here, cramped as their quarters were. Now the sounds from outside. . . . Cassia cowered and tried to put her hands over her ears to blot out those cries and yet could not because of Lana's weight.

"Voice?" her lips shaped a whisper, "Voice?"

She scrunched herself forward and found that she could look out—but only at the level of the rough flooring. The edge of a dull green robe swung, blinding her peephole. She could guess that the Voice had not tried to run any more than she had tried to squeeze into this too small place, but was standing at the altar, even as when she called upon the High One.

Lana stirred now, and then shrilled a cry which nearby Cassia viciously stifled, finding the other girl's mouth quickly enough to muffle that. She bumped her head against Lana's and whispered fiercely: "Be quiet!"

The outside clamor was growing stronger, and there was a last piercing scream from just without the shrine. Then they came—Cassia could only see boots cobbled from badly dried skins, the point of a stained blade which still dribbled thick red drops to the pavement.

"Calling down your Word-Wrath, slut?" That voice spoke words so oddly accented that Cassia found them hard to understand. She felt Lana strain and jerk beside her.

"You have come to *her*, what would you?" That was the Voice and she spoke with such calm that Cassia could almost believe the woman's wits had been rift from her and she did not see these crowding in—three of them, counting by the boots she could see.

"In that, Spar. They keep their goodies in that!" A different voice, puzzling because Cassia had heard it before—when? Who could be evil enough to betray the secrets of the shrine?

"Goodies, eh? Well, let us see these goodies you would guard, slut. We've found precious little worth the taking elsewhere in this swine's pen."

"Spar, the slut's got a knife." There was a roil of movement among those tramping feet, the green robe edge swirled away, freeing Cassia's line of vision the more. There was a choking cry, a hand slipped slowly down over the peephole and was gone.

"Get that ring from her, Harve. You say their stuff's in here?"

Cassia shuddered and Lana twisted in her hold as there came a blow which vibrated through the altar stone above them.

"Oh, so you weren't talking out of the wrong side of your jaw after all, Vacom. Well, well. And here we were thinking that all the good stuff had been combed out of these pens long ago. Black, yes, but that's silver. And this is something better!"

Cassia could understand now what was happening. They had opened the top of the altar stone and were dragging out those very precious things which only the Voice might touch, and then only after purification. Vacom? Her lips formed a vixen's rage snarl—that trader whose ship had come to grief on the outer reef a season ago and who had been given refuge in the village afterwards until he could join with a band of traders who had come through in the fall. He had been here at Midsummer.

Again Cassia snarled. So that was how he knew about the Precious Things! Sneaking spy—Let the High One smite him with the sloughing of skin and the blindness of eye so that he would take a long time in dying!

"Old," that was the first voice, "this is damn old. And I'd wager on it that those are real stones! We've more'n enough paid for this raid!"

"Hey—you broke it!" There was a sharp protest.

"No. It just comes apart. What's this inside? Some stinking clay pot thing—we can do without that."

It struck the floor straight in the line of Cassia's sight, a round brown cup just such a one as Farllen the potter made and fired from riverbank clay. Oddly enough, the rough handling it received did not break it; through all her fear Cassia wondered at that.

"That's it. Get this slut's cloak and bag it up." The one who gave orders was already turning away from the altar. He toed the cup and it spun around, out of Cassia's sight.

Cassia waited, her ears straining for the slightest sound. All screams and cries had ceased, the feet she had watched had tramped out. Still . . .

"Voice?" she whispered through dry lips and knew somehow she could expect no answer to that call.

Lana squirmed around against her. Their heads were now so close she could feel the younger girl's fast puff of breath against her cheek.

"Wait." Cassia dared to whisper again, this time to her fellow prisoner.

How long did they wait? Cassia felt the sore cramp beginning in her arms and legs. If they did not move soon they might be too stiff to try at all. She loosened a hand and groped into the dark over her head, feeling along the inner side of the altar. She found that deep groove she sought and settled her fingers well in.

"Lana," she breathed, "find the other turn point."

"They will kill," the other girl protested.

"They must be gone—at least from the shrine." Cassia held on to her patience. "We cannot stay here any longer." Though, of course, Lana might also be right and they would be simply betraying themselves. However, there was little choice.

She felt the movements of the other girl, knew that she was indeed in search of that second hold which would give them a door to freedom.

"Ready? Then move." Cassia felt her nails break, the skin of her fingertips abrade, as she obeyed her own order. Slowly the stone walling them in answered, and there was enough light to set them blinking.

Cassia squeezed through that opening. She pulled herself up by a grip on the altar itself and nearly lost her hold when there came a faint moaning from very near at hand. Then she was out, to crouch by the Voice. The woman's robe was rent at the breast, and over that she was pressing tight her hands, as if she could so stem the blood which oozed between her fingers. Her eyes were open and she looked at Cassia with understanding and knowledge.

"Voice—let me see!" The girl tried to pull away those binding hands.

The woman opened her mouth, and a trickle of blood rolled down her chin.

"This is an end blow, my daughter-in-light. There is no heal-craft which will answer."

Lana had crept to her other side, shaking, white faced. "Voice—Voice, what—what shall we do?"

"That which is willed for you. First," she turned her eyes, not her head, as if all the strength she had left would not allow more, to Cassia, "give—give me to drink—from the Blessed pool."

Cassia scrambled on hands and knees toward the entrance to the shrine. In going, her hand struck against something which rattled across the floor, and, catching at it, she found what she held was that earthen cup. Clutching it, she moved out. There was the stench of death here. Already carrion birds dropped out of the sky, their blackness an offense in the daylight. Cassia tried not to look at the two hacked bodies which lay most plainly in sight. Old Kazar, who had lost an arm three seasons ago, yet must have come to the shrine's defense, sprawled half into the pool. The red from the gash, which had hewn him near in two, swirled out in the once clean, sweet water.

Cassia stood helplessly looking at the befoulment, the cup in her shaking hand. She could not dip out—that. . . .

She edged about the basin in the opposite direction from that body, seeking some place which was still clear. There was nothing—and farther on. . . . She caught her lower lip between her teeth to cut back a scream. A child, Rowna's babe, staring sightlessly upward.

Cassia broke and ran back toward the shrine. Alive—why was she alive when all else were dead, dead befouled—lost.

As she entered the shrine she strove for control. She was a Chosen—she must remember that always.

"Voice," she knelt beside the woman whose head Lana now supported against her own thin shoulder. "The water—it cannot . . ."

"Dip the cup, daughter-in-service, and bring it to me!"

All the old command was in the Voice's words. Cassia could only obey. She returned, found a place at the pool farthest from these two bodies, and dipped her cup into the water which was ever thickening with the red stain. She filled it near to the brim and started back, nursing the cup against her breast lest she spill some of its contents. But as she moved—surely that could not be true—the water was clearing with each step she took.

"Voice," she cried breathlessly, "the water—it holds no more the stain of death—it is pure."

Swiftly she put it to those lips between which blood still welled a little. The Voice drank.

"How . . . ?" Cassia marveled.

"Drink," commanded the Voice. And Cassia, raising the cup carefully with both her hands, took a mouthful. Not just pure water—this had the richness of the first fruits—she could feel the warmth of it in her throat, and then through her, driving out the death chill, the ragged tatters of fear which had been a binding on her.

"Lana," commanded the Voice for a second time, "drink also!"

Cassia passed the cup to the younger girl and watched her drink. Yet when Lana handed back that small rough bowl it was as full as it had been after the dipping at the spring.

"The cup that overfloweth," the woman's voice was thinner, as if she tired after some great task. "It cleanses evil—brings fresh life again. Things of power exist for our comfort, my daughters. Such may be lost from time, yet always they rise again. This much is true, that those who serve are themselves served in a different way. Now. . . ."

She closed her eyes for a moment. When she opened them again they seemed to Cassia to be seeking, as if they could no longer find her face.

"My time has passed, daughter-of-the-heart. Take you that Power and go forth from this place of death to find what may be healed or cherished under the wide arms of the High One. You shall be led, and when you find the place meant for you there shall be a sign. For a thing of Power knows well where it must shelter. Go with the blessing of sun and moon, earth and sky, fire and water, all that sustains life."

There had been a feast long ago, in a far county. And a cup passed which held the promise of life. Things of Power are never lost, though they may pass from the sight of men for a time—yet always they shall come again.

BY A HAIR

Phantom Magazine (July 1958), Wizards' Worlds, TOR (1989)

You say, friend, that witchcraft at its strongest is but a crude knowledge of psychology, a use of a man's own fear of the unknown to destroy him? Perhaps it may be so in modern lands. But me, I have seen what I have seen. More than fear destroyed Dagmar Kark and Colonel Andrei Veroff.

There were four of them, strong and passionate: Ivor and Dagmar Kark, Andrei Varoff and the Countess Ana. What they desired they gained by the aid of something not to be seen nor felt nor sensed tangibly, something not in the experience of modern man.

Ivor was an idealist who held to a cause and the woman he thought Dagmar to be. Dagmar, she wanted power—power over the kind of man who could give her all her heart desired. And so she wanted Colonel Andrei Varoff.

And Varoff, his wish was a common one, though odd for one of his creed. When a man has been nourished on the belief that the state is all, the individual nothing, it is queer to want a son to the point of obsession. And, though Varoff had taken many women, none had produced a child he could be sure was his.

The Countess Ana, she wanted justice—and love.

The four people had faith in themselves, strong faith. Besides, they had it in other things—Ivor in his cause and his wife, Varoff in a creed. And Dagmar and Ana in something very old and enduring.

It could not have happened in this new land of yours, to that I agree; but in my birth country it is different. All this came to be in a narrow knife slash of a valley running from mountains to the gray salt sweep of the Baltic. It is true that the shadow of the true cross has lain over that valley since the Teutonic knights planted it on the castle they built in the crags almost a thousand years ago. But before the white Christ came, other, grimmer gods were worshipped in that land. In the fir forest where the valley walls are steep, there is still a stone altar set in a grove. That was tended, openly at first, and later in secret, for long after the priests of Rome chanted masses in the church.

In that country the valley is reckoned rich. Life there was good until the Nazis came. Then the Count was shot in his own courtyard, since he was not the type of man to suffer the arrogance of others calmly, and with him Hudun, the head gamekeeper, and the heads of three valley households. Afterwards they took away the young Countess Ana. But Ivor Kark fled to the hills and our young men joined him. During two years, perhaps a little more, they carried on guerrilla warfare with the invader, just as it happened in those days in all the countries stamped by the iron heel.

But to my country there came no liberation. Where the Nazi had strutted in his pride, the Bear of the north shambled, and stamped into red dust those who defied him. Some fled and some stayed to fight, believing in their innocence that the nations among the free would rise in their behalf.

Ivor Kark and his men, not yet realizing fully the doom come upon us, ventured out of the mountains. For a time it appeared that the valley, being so small a community, might indeed be overlooked. In those few days of freedom Ivor found Dagmar Llov.

Who can describe such a woman as Dagmar with words? She was not beautiful; no, seldom is it that great beauty brings men to their knees. Look at the portraits of your historical charmers, or read what has been written of Cleopatra, of Theodora and the rest. They have something other than beauty, these fateful ones: a flame within them which kindles an answer in all men who look upon them. But their own hearts remain cold.

Dagmar walked with a grace which tore at you, and when she looked at one sidewise. . . . But who can describe such a woman? I can say she had silver, fair hair which reached to her knees, a face with a frost white skin, but I cannot so make you see the Dagmar Llov that was.

Because of his leadership in the underground, Ivor was a hero to us. In addition, he was good to look upon: a tall whip of a man, brown, thin, narrow of waist and loins, and broad of shoulder. He had been a huntsman of the Count's, and walked with a forester's smooth glide. Above his widely set eyes his hair grew in a sharp peak, giving his face a disturbingly wolfish cast. But in his eyes and mouth there was the dedication of a priest.

Being what she was, Dagmar looked upon those eyes and that mouth, and desired to trouble the mold, to see there a difference she had wrought. In some ways Ivor was an innocent, but Dagmar was one who had known much from her cradle.

Also, Ivor was now the great man among us. With the Count gone, the men of the valley looked to him for leadership. Dagmar went to him willingly and we sang her bride song.

It was a good time, such as we had not known for years.

Others came back to the valley during those days. Out of the black horror of a Nazi extermination camp crawled a pale, twisted creature, warped in body, perhaps also in mind. She who had once been the Countess Ana came quietly, almost secretly, among us again. One day she had not been there, and the next she was settled in the half-ruinous gate house of the castle with old Maid, who had been with her family long before her own birth. The Countess Ana had been a woman of education before they had taken her away, and she had not forgotten all she had learned. There was no doctor in the valley; twenty families could not have supported one. But the Countess was versed in the growing of herbs and their healing uses, and Maid was a midwife. So together they became the wise women of our people. After a while we forgot the Countess Ana's deformed body and ravaged face, and accepted her as we accepted the crooked firs growing close to the timberline. Not one of us remembered that she was yet in years a young woman, with a young woman's dreams and desires, encased in a hag's body.

It was late October when our fate came upon us, up river in a power boat. The new masters would set in our hills a station from which their machines could spy upon the outer world they feared and hated. To make safe the building of that station they sent ahead a conqueror's party. They surprised us and something had drained out of the valley. So many of our youth were long since bleached bones that, save for a handful, perhaps only the number of the fingers on my two hands, there was no defiance; there was only a dumb beast's endurance. Within three days Colonel Andrei Varoff ruled from the castle as if he had been Count, lord of a tired, cowed people.

Three men they hauled from their homes and shot on the first night, but Ivor was not one. He had been warned and, with the core of his men, had taken again to the mountains. But he left Dagmar behind, by her own will.

Maid and the Countess were warned, too. When Varoff marched his pocket army into the castle, the gate house was deserted; and those who thereafter sought the wise women's aid took another path, up into the black-green of the fir forest and close to a long stone partly buried in the ground within a circle of very old 'oaks, which had not grown so by chance. There in a game-station hut, those in need could find what they wanted, perhaps more.

Father Hansel had been one of the three Varoff shot out of hand, and there was no longer an open church in the valley. What went on in the oak glade was another matter.

First our women drifted there, half ashamed, half defiant, and later they were followed by their men. I do not think the Countess Ana was their priestess. But she knew and condoned. For she had learned many things.

The wise women began to offer more than just comfort of body. It was a queer wild time when men in their despair turned from old belief to older ones, from a god of love and peace, to a god of wrath and vengeance. Old knowledge passed by word of mouth from mother to daughter was recalled by such as Maid, and keenly evaluated by the sharper and better-trained brain of the Countess Ana. I will not say that they called upon Odin and Freya (or those behind those Nordic spirits) or lighted the Beltane Fire. But there was a stirring, as if something long sleeping turned and stretched in its supposed grave.

Dagmar, for all her shrewd egotism (and egotism such as hers is dangerous, for it leads a man or woman to believe that what they wish is right), was a daughter of the valley. She was moved by the old beliefs; and because she had her price, she was convinced that all others had theirs. So at night she went alone to the hut. There she watched until the Countess Ana left. It was she who carried news and a few desperately gained supplies to those in hiding, especially Ivor.

Seeing the hunched figure creep off, Dagmar laughed spitefully, making a secret promise to herself that even a man she might choose to throw away would go to no other woman. But since at present she needed aid and not ill-will, she put that aside.

When the Countess was out of sight, Dagmar went in to Maid and stood in the half-light of the fire, proud and tall, exulting over the other woman in all the sensual strength and grace of her body, as she had over the Countess Ana in her mind.

"I would have what I desire most, Andrei Varoff," she said boldly, speaking with the arrogance of a woman who rules men by their lusts.

"Let him but look on you. You need no help here," returned Maid.

"I cannot come to him easily; he is not one to be met by chance. Give me that which will bring him to me by his own choice."

"You are a wedded wife."

Dagmar laughed shrilly. "What good does a man who must hide ever in a mountain cave do me, Old One? I have slept too long in a cold bed. Let me draw Varoff, and you and the valley will have kin within the enemy's gate."

Maid studied her for a long moment, and Dagmar grew uneasy, for those eyes in age carved pits seemed to read far too deeply. But, without making any answer in words, Maid began certain preparations. There was a strange chanting, low and soft but long, that night. The words were almost as old as the hills around them, and the air of the hut was thick with the scent of burning herbs.

When it was done Dagmar stood again by the fire, and in her hands she turned and twisted a shining, silken belt. She looped it about her arm beneath her cloak and tugged at the heavy coronet of her braids. The long locks Maid had shorn were not missed. Her teeth showed in white points against her lip as she brought out of her pocket some of those creased slips of paper our conquerors used for money.

Maid shook her head. "Not for coin did I do this," she said harshly. "But if you come to rule here as you desire, remember you are kin."

Dagmar laughed again, more than ever sure of herself. "Be sure that I will, Old One."

Within two days the silken belt was in Varoff's hands, and within five Dagmar was installed in the castle. But in the Colonel she had met her match, for Varoff found her no great novelty. She could not bend him to her will as she had Ivor, who was more sensitive and less guarded. But, being shrewd, Dagmar accepted the situation with surface grace and made no demands.

As for the valley women, they spat after her, and there was hate in their hearts. Who told Ivor I do not know, though it was not the Countess Ana. (She could not wound where she would die to defend.) But somehow he managed to get a message to Dagmar, entreating her to come to him, for he believed she had gone to Varoff to protect him.

What that message aroused in Dagmar was contempt and fear: contempt for the man who would call her to share his harsh exile and fear that he might break the slender bond she had with Varoff. She was determined that Ivor must go. It was very simple, that betrayal, for Ivor believed in her. He went to his death as easily as a bullock led to the butcher, in spite of warnings from the Countess Ana and his men.

He slipped down by night to where Dagmar promised to wait and walked into the hands of the Colonel's guard. They say he was a long time dying, for Andrei Varoff had a taste for such treatment for prisoners when he could safely indulge it. Dagmar watched him die; that, too, was part of the Colonel's pleasure. Afterward there was a strange shadow in her eyes, although she walked with pride.

It was two months later that she made her second visit to Maid. But this time there were two to receive her. Yet in neither look, word, nor deed, did either show emotion at that meeting; it was as if they waited. They remained silent, forcing her to declare her purpose.

"I would bear a son." She began as one giving an order. Only—confronted by those unchanging faces she faltered and lost some of her assurance. She might even have turned and gone had the Countess Ana not spoken in a cool and even voice.

"It is well known that Varoff desires a son."

Dagmar responded to that faint encouragement. "True! Let me be the one to bear the child and my influence over him will be complete. Then I can repay—it is true, you frozen faces!" She was aroused by the masks they wore. "You believe that I betrayed Ivor, not knowing the whole of the story. I have very little power over Varoff now. But let me give him a son; then there will be no limit on what I can demand of him—none at all!"

"You shall bear a son. Certainly you shall bear a son," replied the Countess Ana. In the security of that promise Dagmar rejoiced, not attending to the finer shades of meaning in the voice which uttered it.

"But what you ask of us takes preparation. You must wait and return when the moon once more waxes. Then we shall do what is to be done!" Reassured, Dagmar left. As the door of the hut swung shut behind her, the Countess Ana came to stand before the fire, her crooked shape making a blot upon the wall with its shadow.

"She shall have a son, Maid, even as I promised, only whether thereafter she will discover it profitable—"

From within the folds of her coarse peasant blouse, she brought out a packet wrapped in a scrap of fine but brown-stained linen. Unfolding the cloth, she revealed what it guarded: a lock of black hair, stiff and matted with something more than mud. Maid, seeing that and guessing the purpose for which it would be used, laughed. The Countess did not so much as smile.

"There shall be a son, Maid," she repeated, but her promise was no threat. There was a more subtle note, and in the firelight her eyes gleamed with an eagerness to belie the ruin of her face.

Within two days came the night she had appointed, Dagmar with it. Again there was chanting and things done in secret. When Dagmar left at dawn she smiled a thin smile.

Let her but bear a child and they would see, all would see, how she would deal with those who now dared to look crosswise after her and spit upon her footprints! Let such fools take heed!

Shortly thereafter it became known that Dagmar was with child. Varoff could not conceal his joy. During the months which followed he made plans to send her out of the valley, that his son might be born with the best medical care; and he loaded her with gifts. But the inner caution of an often-disappointed man made him keep her prisoner.

Dagmar did not leave the valley. She could not make the rough trip by river and sea. The road over the mountain was but a narrow track, and just before Varoff prepared to leave with her there was such a storm as is seldom seen at that time of year. A landslide blotted out the road. The Colonel cursed and drove his own soldiers and the valley men to dig a way through, but even he realized it could not be cleared in time.

So he was forced to summon Maid. His threats to her were cold and deadly, for he had no illusions concerning the depth of the valley's hatred. But the old woman bore his raving meekly, and he came to believe her broken enough in spirit to be harmless.

Thus, though he still suspected her, he brought her to Dagmar and bade her use her skill.

For a night and a day Dagmar lay in labor, and what she suffered must have been very great. But greater still was her determination to be the one to place a living son in the arms of Andrei Varoff. In the evening the child was born, its thin cry echoing from the walls of the ancient room like the wail of a tormented soul. Dagmar clawed herself up.

"Is it a boy?" she demanded hoarsely.

Maid nodded her white head. "A boy."

"Give him to me and call—"

But there was no need to complete that order for Andrei Varoff was already within the chamber and Dagmar greeted him proudly, the baby in the curve of her arm. As he strode to the bedside she thrust away the swaddling blanket and displayed the tiny body fully. But her eyes were for Varoff rather than for the child she had schemed to make a weapon in her hand.

"Your son—" she began. Then something in VarofTs eyes as he stared down upon the child chilled her as if naked steel, ice cold, had been plunged into her sweating body.

For the first time she looked upon the baby. This was her key, a son for Varoff.

Her scream, thin and high, tore through the storm wind moaning outside the narrow window. Andrei loomed over her as she cowered away from what she read in his eyes, in the twist of his thick lips.

It was Maid who snatched the baby and sped from that room, at a greater speed than her years might warrant, to be joined by another within a secret way of the castle. The twisted, limping figure took the child eagerly into long empty arms, to hold it tenderly as a long-desired gift.

But neither of the two Maid left were aware of her flight. What was done there cannot be told, but before the coming of dawn Varoff shot himself.

Where is the magic in all this, besides the muttering of old woman? Just this: when Dagmar demanded a son from the Countess Ana, she indeed obtained her desire. But the child she bore had fine black hair growing in a sharp peak above a wolf cub's face—a face which Andrei Varoff and Dagmar Kark had excellent reason to know well. Who fathered Dagmar's child, a man nigh twelve months dead? And who was its true mother? Think carefully, my friend.

Not a pretty story, eh? But, you see, old gods do not tend to be mild when called on to render justice.

THE GIFTS OF ASTI
Fantasy Book Vol. 1, No. 3 (1948)

Even here, on the black terrace before the forgotten mountain retreat of Asti, it was possible to smell the dank stench of burning Memphir, to imagine that the dawn wind bore upward from the pillaged city the faint tortured cries of those whom the barbarians of Klem hunted to their prolonged death. Indeed it was time to leave—

Varta, last of the virgin Maidens of Asti, shivered. Lur, the scaled and wattled creature crouching beside her, turned his reptilian head so that his golden eyes met her aquamarine ones set slantingly at a provocative angle on her smooth ivory face.

"We go—?"

She nodded in answer to that question Lur had sent into her brain, and turned toward the dark cavern which was the mouth of Asti's last dwelling place. Once, more than a thousand years before when the walls of Memphir were young, Asti had lived among men below. But in the richness and softness which was trading Memphir, empire of empires, Asti found no place. So He— and those who served Him—had withdrawn to this mountain outcrop. And she, Varta, was the last, the very last, to bow knee at Asti's shrine and raise her voice in the dawn hymn, for Lur, as was all of his race, mute.

Even the loot of Memphir would not sate the shaggy headed warriors who had stormed her gates this day. The stairway to Asti's Temple was plain enough to see, and there would be those to essay the steep climb hoping to find a treasure which did not exist. For Asti was an austere God, delighting in plain walls and bare altars. His last priest had lain in the grave niches these three years; there would be none to hold that gate against intruders.

Varta passed between tall, uncarved pillars, Lur padding beside her, his spine-mane erect, the talons on his forefeet clicking on the stone in steady rhythm. So they came into the innermost shrine of Asti, and there Varta made graceful obeisance to the great cowled and robed figure which sat enthroned, its hidden eyes focused upon its own outstretched hand.

And above the flattened palm of that wide hand hung suspended in space the round orange-red sun ball which was twin to the sun that lighted Erb. Around the miniature sun swung in their orbits the four worlds of the system, each obeying the laws of space, even as did the planets they represented.

"Memphir has fallen." Varta's voice sounded rusty in her own ears. She had spoken so seldom during the past lonely months. "Evil has risen to overwhelm our world, even as it was prophesied in Your Revelations, O Ruler of Worlds and Maker of Destiny. Therefore, obeying the order given of old, I would depart from this, Thy house. Suffer me now to fulfill the Law—"

Three times she prostrated her slim body on the stones at the foot of Asti's judgment chair. Then she arose and, with the confidence of a child in its father, she laid her hand palm upward upon the outstretched hand of Asti. Beneath her flesh the stone was not cold and hard, but seemed to have an inner heat, even as might a human hand. For a long moment she stood so and then she raised her hand slowly, carefully, as if within its slight hollow she cupped something precious.

And, as she drew her hand away from the grasp of Asti, the tiny sun and its planets followed, spinning now above her palm as they had above the statue's. But out of the cowled figure some virtue had departed with the going of the miniature solar system; it was now but a carving of stone. And Varta did not look at it again as she passed behind its bulk to seek a certain place in the temple wall, known to her from much reading of the old records.

Having found the stone she sought, she moved her hand in a certain pattern before it so that the faint radiance streaming from the tiny sun gleamed on the grayness of the wall. There was a grating, as from metal long unused, and a block fell back, opening a narrow door to them.

Before she stepped within, the priestess lifted her hand above her head, and when she withdrew it, the sun and planets remained to form a diadem just above the intricate braiding of her dull red hair. As she moved into the secret way, the five orbs swung with her, and in the darkness there the sun glowed richly, sending out a light to guide their feet.

They were at the top of a stairway, and the hollow clang of the stone as it moved back into place behind them echoed through a gulf which seemed endless. But that too was as the chronicles had said, and Varta knew no fear.

How long they journeyed down into the maw of the mountain and, beyond that, into the womb of Erb itself, Varta never knew. But by the time her feet were weary and she knew the bite of real hunger, they came into a passageway which ended in a room hollowed of solid rock. And there, preserved in the chest in which men born in the youth of Memphir had laid them, Varta found that which would keep her safe on the path she must take. She put aside the fine silks, the jeweled cincture, which had been the badge of Asti's service, and drew on over her naked body a suit of scaled skin, gemmed and glistening in the rays of the small sun. There was a hood to cover the entire head, taloned gloves for the hands, webbed, clawed coverings for the feet—as if the skin of a giant, man-like lizard had been tanned and fashioned into this suit. And Varta suspected that indeed might be so—the world of Erb had not always been held by the human-kind alone.

There were supplies here too, lying untouched in ageless containers within a lizard-skin pouch. Varta touched her tongue without fear to a powdered restorative, sharing it with Lur, whose own mailed skin would protect him through the dangers to come.

She folded the regalia she had stripped off and laid it in the chest, smoothing it regretfully before she dropped the lid upon its shimmering color. Never again would Asti's servant wear the soft stuff of His Livery. But she was resolute enough when she picked up the food pouch and strode forward, passing out of the robing chamber into a narrow way which was a natural fault in the rock unsmoothed by the tools of man.

But when this rocky road ended upon the lip of a gorge, Varta hesitated, plucking at the throat latch of her hood-like helmet. Through the unclouded crystal of its eye-holes she could see the sprouts of yellow vapor which puffed from crannies in the rock wall down which she must climb. If the records of the Temple spoke true, these curls of gas were death to all lunged creatures of the upper world. She could only trust that the cunning of the scaled hood would not fail her.

The long talons fitted to the fingertips of the gloves, the claws of the webbed foot coverings clamped fast to every hand- and foothold, but the way down was long, and she caught a message of weariness from Lur before they reached the piled rocks at the foot of the cliff. The puffs of steamy gas had become a fog through which they groped their way slowly, following a trace of path along the base of the cliff.

Time did not exist in the underworld of Erb. Varta did not know whether it was still today, or whether she had passed into tomorrow when they came to a crossroads. She felt Lur press against her, forcing her back against a rock.

"There is a thing coming—" his message was clear.

And in a moment she saw a dark hulk nosing through the vapor. It moved slowly, seeming to balance at each step as if travel was a painful act. But it bore steadily to the meeting of the two paths.

"It is no enemy—" But she did not need that reassurance from Lur. Unearthly as the thing looked it had no menace.

With a last twist of ungainly body the creature squatted on a rock and clawed the clumsy covering it wore about its bone-thin shoulders and domed-skull head. The visage it revealed was long and gray, with dark pits for eyes and a gaping, fang-studded, lipless mouth.

"Who are you who dare to tread the forgotten ways and rouse from slumber the Guardian of the Chasms?"

The question was a shrill whine in her brain, her hands half arose to cover her ears—

"I am Varta, Maiden of Asti. Memphir has fallen to the barbarians of the Outer Lands and now I go, as Asti once ordered—"

The Guardian considered her answer gravely. In one skeleton claw it fumbled a rod and with this it traced certain symbols in the dust before Varta's webbed feet. When it had done, the girl stooped and altered two of the lines with a swift stroke from one of her talons. The creature of the Chasm nodded its misshapen head.

"Asti does not rule here. But long and long and long ago there was a pact made with us in His Name. Pass free from us, woman of the Light. There are two paths before you—"

The Guardian paused for so long that Varta dared to prompt it.

"Where do they lead, Guardian of the Dark?"

"This will take you down into my country." It jerked the rod to the right. "And that way is death for creatures from the surface world. The other—in our old legends it is said to bring a traveler out into the upper world. Of the truth of that I have no proof."

"But that one I must take," she made slight obeisance to the huddle of bones and dank cloak on the rock and it inclined its head in grave courtesy.

With Lur pushing a little ahead, she took the road which ran straight into the flume-veiled darkness. Nor did she turn to look again at the Thing from the Chasm world.

They began to climb again, across slimed rock where there were evil trails of other things which lived in this haunted darkness. But the sun of Asti lighted their way, and perhaps some virtue in the rays from it kept away the makers of such trails.

When they pulled themselves up onto a wide ledge, the talons on Varta's gloves were worn to splintered stubs and there was a bright girdle of pain about her aching body. Lur lay panting beside her, his red-forked tongue protruding from his foam-ringed mouth.

"We walk again the ways of men." Lur was the first to note the tool marks on the stone where they lay. "By the Will of Asti, we may win out of this maze after all."

Since there were no signs of the deadly steam, Varta dared to push off her hood and share with her companion the sustaining power she carried in her pouch. There was a freshness to the air they breathed, damp and cold though it was, which hinted of the upper world.

The ledge sloped upward, at a steep angle at first, and then more gently. Lur slipped past her and thrust head and shoulders through a break in the rock. Grasping his neck spines she allowed him to pull her through that narrow slit into the soft blackness of a surface night. They tumbled down together, Varta's head pillowed on Lur's smooth side, and so they slept as the sun and worlds of Asti whirled protectively above them.

A whir of wings in the air above awakened Varta. One of the small, jewel bright flying lizard creatures of the deep jungle poised and dipped to investigate more closely. But at Varta's upflung arm it uttered a rasping cry and planed down into the mass of vegetation below. By the glint of sunlight on the stone around them the day was already well advanced. Varta tugged at Lur's mane until he roused.

There was a regularity to the rocks piled about their sleeping place, which hinted that they had lain among the ruins left by man. But of this side of the mountains, both were ignorant, for Memphir's rule had not run here.

"Many dead things in times past." Lur's scarlet nostril pits were extended to their widest. "But that was long ago. This land is no longer held by men."

Varta laughed cheerfully. "If here there are no men, then there will rise up no barbarian hordes to dispute our rule. Asti has led us to safety. Let us see more of the land He gives us."

There was a road leading down from the ruins, a road still to be followed in spite of the lash of landslip and the crack of time. And it brought them into a cup of green fertility where the lavishness of Asti's sowing was unchecked by man. Varta seized eagerly upon globes of blood red fruit which she recognized as delicacies which had been cultivated in the Temple gardens. Lur went hunting into the fringes of the jungle, there dining on prey so easily caught as to be judged devoid of fear.

The jungle choked highway curved, and they were suddenly fronted by a desert of sere desolation, a desert floored by glassy slag which sent back the sunbeams in a furnace glare. Varta shaded her eyes and tried to see the end of this, but if there was a distant rim of green beyond, the heat distortions in the air concealed it.

Lur put out a front paw to test the slag, but withdrew it instantly.

"It cooks the flesh, we cannot walk here," was his verdict.

Varta pointed with her chin to the left where, some distance away, the mountain wall paralleled their course.

"Then let us keep to the jungle over there and see if it does not bring around to the far side. But what made this—?" She leaned out over the glassy stuff, not daring to touch the slick surface.

"War." Lur's tongue shot out to impale a questing beetle. "These forgotten people fought with fearsome weapons."

"But what weapon could do this? Memphir knew not such—"

"Memphir was old. But mayhap there were those who raised cities on Erb before the first hut of Memphir squatted on tidal mud. Men forget knowledge in time. Even in Memphir the lords of the last days forgot the wisdom of their earlier sages—they fell before the barbarians easily enough."

"If ever men had wisdom to produce this—it was not of Asti's giving," she edged away from the glare. "Let us go."

But now they had to fight their way through jungle, and it was hard—until they reached a ridge of rock running out from the mountain as a tongue thrust into the blasted valley. And along this they picked their slow way.

"There is water near—" Lur's thought answered the girl's desire. She licked dry lips longingly. "This way—" her companion's sudden turn was to the left, and Varta was quick to follow him down a slide of rock.

Lur's instinct was right, as it ever was. There was water before them, a small lake. But even as he dipped his fanged muzzle toward that inviting surface, Lur's spined head jerked erect again. Varta snatched back the hand she had put out, staring at Lur's strange actions. His nostrils expanded to their widest, his long neck outstretched, he was swinging his head back and forth across the limpid shallows.

"What is it—?"

"This is no water such as we know," the scaled one answered flatly. "It has life within it."

Varta laughed. "Fish, water snakes, your own distant kin, Lur. It is the scent of them which you catch—"

"No. It is the water itself which lives—and yet does not live—" His thought trailed away from her as he struggled with some problem. No human brain could follow his unless he willed it.

Varta squatted back on her heels and began to look at the water and then at the banks with more care. For the first time she noted the odd patches of brilliant color which floated just below the surface of the liquid. Blue, green, yellow, crimson, they drifted slowly with the tiny waves which lapped the shore. But they were not alive, she was almost sure of that; they appeared more a part of the water itself.

Watching the voyage of one patch of green she caught sight of the branch. It was a drooping shoot of the turbi, the same tree vine which produced the fruit she had relished less than an hour before. Above the water dangled a cluster of the fruit, dead ripe with the sweet pulp stretching its skin. But below the surface of the water—

Varta's breath hissed between her teeth and Lur's head snapped around as he caught her thought.

The branch below the water bore a perfect circle of green flowers close to its tip, the flowers which the turbi had borne naturally seven months before and which should long ago have turned into just such sweetness as hung above.

With Lur at her heels the girl edged around to pull cautiously at the branch. It yielded at once to her touch, swinging its tip out of the lake. She sniffed—there was a languid perfume in the air, the perfume of the blooming turbi. She examined the flowers closely, to all appearances they were perfect and natural.

"It preserves." Lur settled back on his haunches and waved one front paw at the quiet water. "What goes into it remains as it was just at the moment of entrance."

"But if this is seven months old—"

"It may be seven years old," corrected Lur. "How can you tell when that branch first dipped into the lake? Yet the flowers do not fade even when withdrawn from the water. This is indeed a mystery!"

"Of which I would know more!" Varta dropped the turbi and started on around the edge of the lake.

Twice more they found similar evidence of preservation in flower or leaf, wherever it was covered by the opaline water.

The lake itself was a long and narrow slash with one end cutting into the desert of glass, while the other wet the foot of the mountain. And it was there, on the slope of the mountain, that they found the greatest wonder of all, Lur scenting it before they sighted the remains among the stones.

"Man made," he cautioned, "but very, very old."

And truly the wreckage they came upon must have been old, perhaps even older than Memphir. For the part which rested above the water was almost gone, rusty red stains on the rocks outlining where it had lain. But underwater was a smooth silver hull, shining and untouched by the years. Varta laid her hand upon a ruddy scrap between two rocks and it became a drift of powdery dust. And yet—there a few feet below was strong metal!

Lur padded along the scrap of shore surveying the thing.

"It was a machine in which men traveled," his thoughts arose to her. "But they were not as the men of Memphir. Perhaps not even as the sons of Erb—"

"Not as the sons of Erb!" her astonishment broke into open speech.

Lur's neck twisted as he looked up at her. "Did the men of Erb, even in the old chronicles, fight with weapons such as would make a desert of glass? There are other worlds than Erb, mayhap this strange thing was a sky ship from such a world. All things are possible by the Will of Asti."

Varta nodded. "All things are possible by the Will of Asti," she repeated. "But, Lur," her eyes were round with wonder, "perhaps it is Asti's Will which brought us here to find this marvel! Perhaps He has some use for us and it!"

"At least we may discover what lies within it," Lur had his own share of curiosity.

"How? The two of us cannot draw that out of the water!"

"No, but we can enter into it!"

Varta fingered the folds of the hood on her shoulders. She knew what Lur meant, the suit which had protected her in the underworld was impervious to everything outside its surface—or to every substance its makers knew— just as Lur's own hide made his flesh impenetrable. But the fashioners of her suit had probably never known of the living lake. And what if she had no defense against the strange properties of the water?

She leaned back against a rock. Overhead the worlds and sun of Asti still traveled their appointed paths. The worlds of Asti! If it was His Will which had brought them here, then Asti's power would wrap her 'round with safety. By His Will she had come out of Memphir over ways no human of Erb had ever trod before. Could she doubt that His Protection was with her now?

It took only a moment to make secure the webbed shoes, to pull on and fasten the hood, to tighten the buckles of her gloves. Then she crept forward, shuddering as the water rose about her ankles. But Lur pushed on before her, his head disappearing fearlessly under the surface as he crawled through the jagged opening in the ship below.

Smashed engines which had no meaning in her eyes occupied most of the broken section of the wreck. None of the metal showed any deterioration beyond that which had occurred at the time of the crash. Under her exploring hands it was firm and whole.

Lur was pulling at a small door half hidden by a mass of twisted wires and plates, and just as Varta crawled around this obstacle to join him, the barrier gave way allowing them to squeeze through into what had once been the living quarters of the ship.

Varta recognized seats, a table, and other bits of strictly utilitarian furniture. But of those who had once been at home there, there remained no trace. Lur, having given one glance to the furnishings, was prowling about the far end of the cabin uncertainly, and now he voiced his uneasiness.

"There is something beyond, something which once had life—"

Varta crowded up to him. To her eyes the wall seemed without line of an opening, and yet Lur was running his broad front paws over it carefully, now and then throwing his weight against the smooth surface.

"There is no door—" she pointed out doubtfully.

"No door—ah—here—" Lur unsheathed formidable fighting claws to their full length for perhaps the first time in his temple-sheltered life, and endeavored to work them into a small crevice. The muscles of his forelegs and quarters stood out in sharp relief under his scales, his fangs were bare as his lips snapped back with effort.

Something gave, a thin black line appeared to mark the edges of a door. Then time, or Lur's strength, broke the ancient locking mechanism. The door gave so suddenly that they were both sent hurtling backward and Lur's breath burst from him in a huge bubble.

The sealed compartment was hardly more than a cupboard, but it was full. Spread-eagled against the wall was a four-limbed creature whose form was so smothered in a bulky suit that Varta could only guess that it was akin in shape to her own. Hoops of metal locked it firmly to the wall, but the head had fallen forward so that the face plate in the helmet was hidden.

Slowly the girl breasted the water which filled the cabin and reached her hands toward the bowed helmet of the prisoner. Gingerly, her blunted talons scraping across metal, she pulled it up to her eye-level.

The eyes which stood within the suit were closed, as if in sleep, but there was a warm, healthy tint to the bronze skin, so different in shade to her own pallid coloring. For the rest, the prisoner had the two eyes, the centered nose, the properly shaped mouth common to the men of Erb. Hair grew on his head, black and thick, and there was a faint shadow of beard on his jaw line.

"This is a man—" her thought reached Lur.

"Why not? Did you expect a serpent? It is a pity he is dead—"

Varta felt a rich warm tide rising in her throat to answer that teasing half question. There were times when Lur's thought reading was annoying. He had risen to his hind legs so that he too could look into the shell which held their find.

"Yes, a pity," he repeated. "But—"

A vision of the turbi flowers swept through her mind. Had Lur suggested it, or had that wild thought been hers alone? Only this ship was so old—so very old!

Lur's red tongue flicked. "It can do no harm to try—" he suggested slyly and set his claws into the hoop holding the captive's right wrist, testing its strength.

"But the metal on the shore, it crumpled into powder at my touch—" she protested. "What if we carry him out only to have—to have—" Her mind shuddered away from the picture which followed.

"Did the turbi blossom fade when pulled out?" countered Lur. "There is a secret to these fastenings—" He pulled and pried impatiently.

Varta tried to help, but even their united strength was useless against the force which held the loops in place. Breathless, the girl slumped back against the wall of the cabin while Lur settled down on his haunches. One of the odd patches of color drifted by, its vivid scarlet like a jewel spiraling lazily upward. Varta's eyes followed its drift and so were guided to what she had forgotten, the worlds of Asti.

"Asti!"

Lur was looking up too.

"The power of Asti!"

Varta's hand went up, rested for a long moment under the sun and then

74

drew it down, carefully, slowly, as she had in Memphir's temple. Then she stepped toward the captive. Within her hood a beaded line of moisture outlined her lips, a pulse thundered on her temple. This was a fearsome thing to try.

She held the sun on a line with one of the wrist bonds. She must avoid the flesh it imprisoned, for Asti's power could kill.

From the sun there shot an orange-red beam to strike full upon the metal. A thin line of red crept across the smooth hoop, crept and widened. Varta raised her hand, sending the sun spinning up, and Lur's claws pulled on the metal. It broke like rotten wood in his grasp.

The girl gave a little gasp of half-terrified delight. Then the old legends were true! As Asti's priestess she controlled powers too great to guess. Swiftly she loosed the other hoops and restored the sun and worlds to their place over her head as the captive slumped across the threshold of his cell.

Tugging and straining, they brought him out of the broken ship into the sunlight of Erb. Varta threw back her hood and breathed deeply of the air which was not manufactured by the wizardry of the lizard skin. Lur sat panting, his nostril flaps open. It was he who spied the spring on the mountain side above, a spring of water uncontaminated by the strange life of the lake. They both dragged themselves there to drink deeply.

Varta returned to the lake shore reluctantly. Within her heart she believed that the man they had brought from the ship was truly dead. Lur might hold out the promise of the flowers, but this was a man, and he had lain in the water for countless ages—

So she went with lagging steps, to find Lur busy. He had solved the mystery of the spacesuit and had stripped it from the unknown. Now his clawed paw rested lightly on the bared chest and he turned to Varta eagerly.

"There is life—"

Hardly daring to believe that, she dropped down beside Lur and touched their prize. Lur was right, the flesh was warm and she had caught the faint rhythm of shallow breath. Half remembering old tales, she put her hands on the arch of the lower ribs and began to aid that rhythm. The breaths were deeper—

Then the man half turned, his arm moved. Varta and Lur drew back. For the first time the girl probed gently the sleeping mind before her—even as she had read the minds of those few of Memphir who had ascended to the temple precincts in the last days.

Much of what she read now was confused or so alien to Erb that it had no meaning for her. But she saw a great city plunged into flaming death in an instant and felt the horror and remorse of the man at her feet because of his own part in that act, the horror and remorse which had led him to open rebellion and so to his imprisonment. There was a last dark and frightening memory of a door closing on light and hope—

The spaceman moaned softly and hunched his shoulders as if he struggled vainly to tear loose from bonds.

"He thinks that he is still prisoner," observed Lur. "For him life begins at the very point it ended—even as it did for the turbi flowers. See—now he awakens."

The eyelids rose slowly, as if the man hated to see what he must look upon. Then, as he sighted Varta and Lur, his eyes went wide. He pulled himself up and looked dazedly around, striking out wildly with his fists. Catching sight of the clumsy suit Lur had taken from him he pulled at it, looking at the two before him as if he feared some attack.

Varta turned to Lur for help. She might read minds and use the wordless speech of Lur. But his people knew the art of such communication long before the first priest of Asti had stumbled upon their secret. Let Lur now quiet this outlander.

Delicately, Lur sought a way into the other's mind, twisting down paths of thought strange to him. Even Varta could not follow the subtle waves sent forth in the quick examination and reconnoitering, nor could she understand all of the conversation which resulted. For the man from the ancient ship answered in speech aloud, sharp harsh sounds of no meaning. It was only after repeated instruction from Lur that he began to frame his messages in his mind, clumsily and disconnectedly.

Pictures of another world, another solar system, began to grow clearer as the spaceman became more at home in the new way of communication. He was one of a race who had come to Erb from beyond the stars and discovered it a world without human life: So they had established colonies and built great cities—far different from Memphir—and had lived in peace for centuries of their own time.

Then on the faraway planet of their birth there had begun a great war, a war which brought flaming death to that world. The survivors of a last battle in space had fled to the colonies on Erb. But among this handful were men driven mad by the death of their world, and these had blasted the cities of Erb, saying that their kind must be wiped out.

The man they had rescued had turned against one such maddened leader and had been imprisoned just before an attack upon the largest of the colony's cities. After that he remembered nothing.

Varta stopped trying to follow the conversation—Lur was only explaining now how they had found the spaceman and brought him out of the wrecked ship. No human on Erb, this one had said, and yet were there not her own people . . . the ones who had built Memphir? And what of the barbarians, who, ruthless and cruel as they seemed by the standards of Memphir, were indeed men? Whence had they come then, the men of Memphir and the ancestors of the barbarian hordes? Her hands touched the scaled skin of the suit she still wore and then rubbed across her own smooth flesh. Could one have come from the other, was she of the blood and heritage of Lur?

"Not so!" Lur's mind, as quick as his flickering tongue, had caught that panic-born thought. "You are of the blood of this space wanderer. Men from the riven colonies must have escaped to safety. Look at this man, is he not like the men of Memphir—as they were in the olden days of the city's greatness?"

The stranger was tall, taller than the men of Memphir, and there was a certain hardness about him which those city dwellers in ease had never displayed. But Lur must be right; this was a man of her race. She smiled in sudden relief and he answered that smile. Lur's soft laughter rang in both their heads.

"Asti in His Infinite Wisdom can see through centuries. Memphir has fallen because of its softness and the evildoing of its people, and the barbarians will now have their way with the lands of the north. But to me it appears that Asti is not yet done with the pattern He was weaving there. To each of you He granted a second life. Do not disdain the Gifts of Asti, Daughter of Erb!"

Again Varta felt the warm tide of blood rise in her cheeks. But she no longer smiled. Instead she regarded the outlander speculatively.

Not even a Maiden of the Temple could withstand the commands of the All Highest. Gifts from the Hand of Asti dared not be thrown away.

Above the puzzlement of the stranger she heard the chuckling of Lur.

FALCON BLOOD
Amazons! (1979) DAW,
Wizards' Worlds (1989) TOR

Tanree sucked at the torn ends of her fingers, tasted the sea salt stinging in them. Her hair hung in sticky loops across her sand-abraded face, too heavy with sea water to stir in the wind.

For the moment it was enough that she had won out of the waves, was alive. Sea was life for the Sulcar, yes, but it could also be death. In spite of the trained resignation of her people, other forces within her had kept her fighting ashore.

Gulls screamed overhead, sharp, piercing cries. So frantic those cries Tanree looked up into the gray sky of the after-storm. The birds were under attack. Wider dark wings spread away from a body on the breast of which a white "V" of feathers set an unmistakable seal. A falcon soared, swooped, clutched in cruel talons one of the gulls, bearing its prey to the top of the cliff, where it perched still within sight.

It ate, tearing flesh with a vicious beak. Cords flailed from its feet, the sign of its service.

Falcon. The girl spat gritty sand from between her teeth, her hands resting on scraped knees barely covered by her undersmock. She had thrown aside kilt, all other clothing, when she had dived from the ship pounding against a foam-crowned reef.

The ship!

She got to her feet, stared seaward. Storm anger still drove waves high. Broken backed upon rock fangs hung the *Kast-Boar*. Her masts were but jaggered stumps. Even as Tanree watched, the waters raised the ship once more, to slam her down on the reef. She was breaking apart fast.

Tanree shuddered, looked along the scrap of narrow beach. Who else had won to shore? The Sulcar were sea born and bred; surely she could not be the only survivor.

Wedged between two rocks so that the retreating waves could not drag him back, a man lay face down. Tanree raised her broken-nailed, scraped fingers and made the Sign of Wottin, uttering the age-old plea:

"Wind and wave,

Mother Sea,

Lead us home.

Far the harbor,

Wild thy waves—Still, by thy Power,

Sulcar saved!"

Had the man moved then? Or was it only the water washing about him which had made it seem so?

He was—this was no Sulcar crewman! His body was covered from neck to mid-thigh by leather, dark breeches twisted with seaweed on his legs.

"Falconer!"

She spat again with salt-scoured lips. Though the Falconers had an old pact with her people, sailed on Sulcar ships as marines, they had always been a race apart—dour, silent men who kept to themselves. Good in battle, yes, so much one must grant them. But who really knew the thoughts in their heads, always hidden by their bird-shaped helms? Though this one appeared to have shucked all his fighting gear, to appear oddly naked.

There came a sharp scream. The falcon, full-fed, now beat its way down to the body. There the bird settled on the sand just beyond the reach of the waves, squatted crying as if to arouse its master.

Tanree sighed. She knew what she must do. Trudging across the sand, she started for the man. Now the falcon screamed again, its whole body expressing defiance. The girl halted, eyed the bird warily. These creatures were trained to attack in battle, to go for the eyes or the exposed face of an enemy. They were very much a part of the armament of their masters.

She spoke aloud as she might to one of her own kind: "No harm to your master, flying one." She held out sore hands in the oldest peace gesture.

Those bird eyes were small reddish coals, fast upon her. Tanree had an odd flash of feeling that this one had more understanding than other birds possessed. It ceased to scream, but the eyes continued to stare, sparks of menace, as she edged around it to stand beside the unconscious man.

Tanree was no weakling. As all her race she stood tall and strong, able to lift and carry, to haul on sail lines, or move cargo, should an extra hand be needed. Sulcarfolk lived aboard their ships and both sexes were trained alike to that service.

Now she stooped and set hands in the armpits of the mercenary, pulling him farther inland, and then rolling him over so he lay face up under the sky.

Though they had shipped a dozen Falconers on this last voyage (since the *Kast-Boar* intended to strike south into waters reputed to give sea room to the shark boats of outlaws), Tanree could not have told one of the bird fighters from another. They wore their masking helms constantly and kept to themselves, only their leader speaking when necessary to the ship people.

The face of the man was encrusted with sand, but he was breathing, as the slight rise and fall of his breast under the soaked leather testified. She brushed grit away from his nostrils, his thin-lipped mouth. There were deep frown lines between his sand-dusted brows, a masklike sternness in his face.

Tanree sat back on her heels. What did she know about this fellow survivor? First of all, the Falconers lived by harsh and narrow laws no other race would accept. Where their original home had been, no outsider knew. Generations ago something had set them wandering, and then the tie with her own people had been formed. For the Falconers had wanted passage out of the south from a land only Sulcar ships touched.

They had sought ship room for all of them, perhaps some two thousand— two-thirds of those fighting men, each with a trained hawk. But it was their custom which made them utterly strange. For, though they had women and children with them, yet there was no clan or family feeling. To Falconers, women were born for only one purpose: to bear children. They were made to live in villages apart, visited once a year by men selected by their officers. Such temporary unions were the only meetings between the sexes.

First they had gone to Estcarp, learning that the ancient land was hemmed in by enemies. But there had been an unbreachable barrier to their taking service there.

For in ancient Estcarp, the Witches ruled. And to them, a race that so degraded females was cursed. Thus the Falconers had made their way into the no-man's-land of the southern mountains, building there on the border between Estcarp and Karsten. They had fought shoulder to shoulder with the Borderers of Estcarp in the great war. But when, at last, a near exhausted Estcarp had faced the overpowering might of Karsten, and the Witches concentrated all their power (many of them dying from it) to change the earth itself. The Falconers, warned in time, had reluctantly returned to the lowlands.

Their numbers were few by then, and the men took service as fighters where they could. For at the end of the great war, chaos and anarchy followed. Some men, nurtured all their lives on fighting, became outlaws; though in Estcarp itself some measure of order prevailed, much of the rest of the continent was beset.

Tanree thought that this Falconer, lacking helm, mail shirt, weapons, resembled any man of the Old Race. His dark hair looked black beneath the clinging sand; his skin was paler than her own sun-browned flesh. He had a sharp nose, rather like the jutting beak of his bird, and his eyes were green. For now they had opened to stare at her. His frown grew more forbidding.

He tried to sit up, fell back, his mouth twisting in pain. Tanree was no reader of thoughts, but she was sure his weakness was like a lash laid across his face. Once more he attempted to lever himself up, away from her. Tanree saw one arm lay limp. She moved closer, sure of a broken bone.

"No! You—you female!" There was such a note of loathing in his voice that anger flared in her in answer.

"As you wish—" She stood up, deliberately turned her back on him, moving away along the narrow beach, half encircled by cliff and walls of water-torn, weed-festooned rocks.

Here was the usual storm bounty brought ashore, wood—some new torn from the *Kast-Boar*, some the wrack of earlier storms. She made herself concentrate on finding anything which might be of use.

Where they might now be in relation to the lands she knew, Tanree had no idea. They had been beaten so far south by the storm that surely they were no longer within the boundaries of Karsten. And the unknown, in these days, was enough to make one wary.

There was a glint in a half ball of weed. Tanree leaped to jerk that away just as the waves strove to carry it off. A knife—no, longer than just a knife— by some freak driven point deep into a hunk of splintered wood. She had to exert some strength to pull it out. No rust spotted the ten-inch blade yet.

Such a piece of good fortune! She sat her jaw firmly and faced around, striding back to the Falconer. He had flung his sound arm across his eyes as if to shut out the world. Beside him crouched the bird uttering small guttural cries. Tanree stood over them both, knife in hand.

"Listen," she said coldly. It was not in her to desert a helpless man no matter how he might spurn her aid. "Listen, Falconer, think of me as you will. I offer no friendship cup to you either. But the sea has spat us out. Therefore this is not our hour to seek the Final Gate. We cannot throw away our lives heedlessly. That being so—" she knelt by him, reaching out also for a straight piece of drift lying near, "you will accept from me the aid of what healcraft I know. Which," she admitted frankly, "is not much."

He did not move that arm hiding his eyes. But neither did he try now to evade as she slashed open the sleeve of his tunic and the padded lining beneath to bare his arm. There was no gentleness in this—to prolong handling would only cause greater pain. He uttered no sound as she set the break (thank the Power it was a simple one) and lashed his forearm against the wood with strips slashed from his own clothing. Only when she had finished did he look to her.

"How bad?"

"A clean break," she assured him. "But—" she frowned at the cliff, "how you can climb from here one-handed—" He struggled to sit up; she knew better than to offer support. With his good arm as a brace, he was high enough to gaze at the cliff and then the sea. He shrugged.

"No matter—"

"It matters!" Tanree flared. She could not yet see a way out of this pocket, not for them both. But she would not surrender to imprisonment by rock or wave.

She fingered the dagger-knife and turned once more to examine the cliffs. To venture back into the water would only sweep them against the reef. But the surface of the wall behind them was pitted and worn enough to offer toe- and handholds. She paced along the short beach, inspecting that surface. Sulcarfolk had good heads for heights, and the Falconers were mountaineers. It was a pity this one could not sprout wings like his comrade in arms.

Wings! She tapped her teeth with the point of the knife. An idea flitted to her mind and she pinned it fast.

Now she returned to the man quickly.

"This bird of yours—" she pointed to the red-eyed hawk at his shoulder, "what powers does it have?"

"Powers!" he repeated and for the first time showed surprise. "What do you mean?"

She was impatient. "They have powers; all know that. Are they not your eyes and ears, scouts for you? What else can they do besides that, and fight in battle?"

"What have you in mind?" he countered.

"There are spires of rock up there." Tanree indicated the top of the cliff. "Your bird has already been aloft. I saw him kill a gull and feast upon it while above."

"So there are rock spires and—"

"Just this, bird warrior," she dropped on her heels again. "No rope can be tougher than loops of some of this weed. If you had the aid of a rope to steady you, could you climb?"

He looked at her for an instant as if she had lost even that small store of wit his people credited to females. Then his eyes narrowed as he gazed once more at the cliff.

"I would not have to ask that of any of my clan," she told him deliberately. "Such a feat would be play as our children delight in." The red stain of anger arose on his pale face.

"How would you get the rope up there?" He had not lashed out in fury to answer her taunt as she had half expected.

"If your bird can carry up a finer strand, loop that about one of the spires there, then a thicker rope can be drawn in its wake and that double rope looped for your ladder. I would climb and do it myself, but we must go together since you have the use of but one hand."

She thought he might refuse. But instead he turned his head and uttered a crooning sound to the bird.

"We can but try," he said a moment later.

The seaweed yielded to her knife and, though he could use but the one hand, the Falconer helped twist and hold strands to her order as she fashioned her ropes. At last she had the first thin cord, one end safe-knotted to a heavier one, the other in her hands.

Again the Falconer made his bird sounds and the hawk seized upon the thin cord at near mid-point. With swift, sure beat of wings it soared up, as Tanree played out the cord swiftly hoping she had judged the length aright.

Now the bird spiraled down and the cord was suddenly loose. Slowly and steadily Tanree began to pull, bringing up from the sand the heavier strand to dangle along the cliff wall.

One moment at a time, think only that, Tanree warned herself as they began their ordeal. The heavier part of the rope was twisted around her companion, made as fast as she could set it. His right arm was splinted, but his fingers were as swift to seek out holds as hers. He had kicked off his boots and slung those about his neck, leaving his toes bare.

Tanree made her way beside him, within touching distance, one glance for the cliff face, a second for the man. They were aided unexpectedly when they came upon a ledge, not to be seen from below. There they crouched together, breathing heavily. Tanree estimated they had covered two thirds of their journey but the Falconer's face was wet with sweat which trickled down, to drip from his chin.

"Let us get to it!" He broke the silence between them, inching up to his feet again, his sound arm a brace against the wall.

"Wait!"Tanree drew away, was already climbing. "Let me get aloft now. And do you keep well hold of the rope."

He protested, but she did not listen, any more than she paid attention to the pain in her fingers. But, when she pulled herself over the lip of the height, she lay for a moment, her breath coming in deep, rib-shaking sobs. She got to her knees and crawled to that outcrop of higher rock around which the noose of the weed rope strained and frayed. She set her teeth grimly, laid hold of the taut strand they had woven. Then she called, her voice sounding in her own ears as high as the scream of the hawk that now hovered overhead.

"Come!"

She drew upon the rope with muscles tested and trained to handle ships' cordage, felt a responding jerk. He was indeed climbing. Bit by bit the rope passed between her torn palms.

Then she saw his hand rise, grope inward over the cliff edge. Tanree made a last great effort, heaving with a reviving force she had not believed she could summon, falling backward, but still keeping a grasp on the rope.

The girl was dizzy and spent, aware only for a moment or two that the rope was loose in her hands. Had—had he fallen? Tanree smeared the back of her fist across her eyes to clear them from a mist.

No, he lay head pointing toward her, though his feet still projected over the cliff. He must be drawn away from that, even as she had brought him earlier out of the grasp of the sea. Only now she could not summon up the strength to move.

Once more the falcon descended, to perch beside its master's head. Three times it screamed harshly. He was moving, drawing himself along on his belly away from the danger point.

Seeing that, Tanree clawed her way to her feet, leaning back against one of the rocky spires, needing its support. For it seemed that the rock under her feet was like the deck of the *Kast-Boar*, rising and falling, so she needs must summon sea-legs to deal with its swing.

On crawled the Falconer. Then he, too, used his good arm for a brace and raised himself, his head coming high enough to look around. That he was valiantly fighting to get to his feet she was sure. A second later his eyes went wide as they swept past her to rest upon something at her own back. Tanree's hand curved about the hilt of the dagger. She pushed against the rock which had supported her, but she could not stand away from it as yet.

Then she, too, saw—

These spires and outcrops of rock were not the work of nature after all. Stones were purposefully piled upon huge stones. There were archways, farther back and what looked like an intact wall—somber, without a break until, farther above her head than the cliff had earlier reached, there showed openings, thin and narrow as a giant axe might have cleft. They had climbed into some ruin.

A thrust of ice chill struck Tanree. The world she had known had many such ancient places and most were ill-omened, perilous for travelers. This was an old, old land, and there had been countless races rise to rule and disappear once more into dust. Not all of those peoples had been human, as Tanree reckoned it. The Sulcar knew many such remained, and wisely avoided them—unless fortified by some power spell set by a Wise One.

"Salzarat!"

The surprise on the Falconer's face had become something else as Tanree turned her head to stare. What was that faint expression? Awe—or fear? But that he knew this place, she had no doubt.

He made an effort, pulling himself up to his feet, though he clung for support to a jumble of blocks even as she did.

"Salzarat—" His voice was the hiss of a warning serpent, or that of a disturbed war bird.

Once more Tanree glanced from him to the ruins. Perhaps a lighting of the leaden clouds overhead was revealing. She saw—saw enough to make her gasp.

That farther wall, the one which appeared more intact, took on new contours. She could trace—

Was it illusion, or some cunning art practiced by the unknowns who had laid those stones? There was no wall; it was the head of a giant falcon, the fierce eyes marked by slitted holes above an outthrust beak.

While the beak—

That closed on a mass which was too worn to do more than hint that it might once have been intended to represent a man.

The more Tanree studied the stone head, the plainer it grew. It was reaching out—out—ready to drop the prey it had already taken, to snap at her.... "No!" Had she shouted that aloud or was the denial only in her mind? Those were stones (artfully fitted together, to be sure) but still only old, old stones. She shut her eyes, held them firmly shut, and then, after a few deep breaths, opened them again. No head, only stones.

But in those moments while she had fought to defeat illusion, her companion had lurched forward. He pulled himself from one outcrop of ruin to the next, and his Falcon had settled on his shoulder, though he did not appear aware of the weight of the bird. There was bemusement on his face, smoothing away his habitual frown. He was like a man ensorceled, and Tanree drew away from him as he staggered past her, his gaze only for the wall.

Stones only, she continued to tell herself firmly. There was no reason for her to remain here. Shelter, food (she realized then that hunger did bite at her), what they needed to keep life in them could only lie in this land. Purposefully she followed the Falconer, but she carried her blade ready in her hand.

He stumbled along until he was under the overhang of that giant beak. The shadow of whatever it held fell on him. Now he halted, drew himself up as a man might face his officer on some occasion of import—or—a priest might begin a rite.

His voice rang out hollowly among the ruins, repeating words—or sounds (for some held the tones of those he had used in addressing his hawk). They came as wild beating cadence. Tanree shivered. She had a queer feeling that he might just be answered—by whom—or what?

Up near to the range of a falcon's cry rose his voice. Now the bird on his shoulder took wing. It screamed its own challenge, or greeting—so that man-voice and bird-voice mingled until Tanree could not distinguish one from the other.

Both fell into silence; once more the Falconer was moving on. He walked more steadily, not reaching out for any support, as if new strength had filled him. Passing under the beak he was—gone!

Tanree pressed one fist against her teeth. There was no doorway there!

Her eyes could not deceive her that much. She wanted to run, anywhere, but as she looked wildly about her she perceived that the ruins funneled forward toward that one place, and there only led the path.

This was a path of the Old Ones; evil lurked here. She could feel the crawl of it as if a slug passed, befouling her skin. Only—Tanree's chin came up, her jaw set stubbornly.

She was Sulcar. If there was no other road, then this one she would take. Forward she went, forcing herself to walk with confidence, though she was ever alert. Now the shadow of the beak enveloped her, and, though there was no warmth of sunlight to be shut out, still she was chilled.

Also—there was a door. Some trick of the stone setting and the beak shadow had concealed it from sight until one was near touching distance. With a deep breath, which was more than half protest against her own action, Tanree advanced.

Through darkness within, she could see a gray of light. This wall must be thick enough to provide not just a door or gate but a tunnel way. And she could see movement between her and that light; the Falconer.

She quickened step so that she was only a little behind him when they came out in what was a mighty courtyard. Walls towered all about, but it was what was within the courtyard itself which stopped Tanree near in mid-step.

Men! Horses!

Then she saw the breakage, here a headless body, there only the shards of a mount. They had been painted once, and the color in some way had sunk far into the substance which formed them, for it remained, if faded.

The motionless company was drawn up in good order, all facing to her left. Men stood, the reins of their mounts in their hands, and on the forks of their saddles falcons perched. A regiment of fighting men awaiting orders.

Her companion skirted that array of the ancient soldiers, almost as if he had not seen them, or, if he had, they were of no matter. He headed in the direction toward which they faced.

There were two wide steps there, and beyond the cavern of another door, wide as a monster mouth ready to suck them in. Up one step he pulled, now the second . . . . He knew what lay beyond. Tanree could not remain behind. She studied the faces of the warriors as she passed by. They each held their masking helm upon one hip as if it was needful to bare their faces, as they did not generally do. So she noted that each of the company differed from his fellows in some degree, though they were all plainly of the same race. These had been modeled from life.

As she came also into the doorway, Tanree heard again the mingled call of bird and man. At least the two she followed were still unharmed, though her sense of lurking evil was strong.

What lay beyond the door was a dim twilight. She stood at the end of a great hall, stretching into shadows right and left. Nor was the chamber empty. Rather here were more statues; and some were robed and coiffed. Women! Women in an Eyrie? She studied the nearest to make sure.

The weathering which had eroded that company in the courtyard had not done any damage here. Dust lay heavy on the shoulders of the life-size image to be sure, but that was all. The face was frozen into immobility. But the expression. Sly exultation, an avid . . . hunger? Those eyes staring straight ahead, did they indeed hold a spark of knowledge deep within?

Tanree pushed aside imagination. These were not alive. But their faces— she looked to another, studied a third—all held that gloating, that hunger-about-to-be-assuaged; while the male images were blank of any emotion, as if they had never been meant to suggest life at all.

The Falconer had already reached the other end of the hall. Now he was silent, facing a dais on which were four figures. These were not in solemn array, rather frozen into a tableau of action. Deadly action, Tanree saw as she trotted forward, puffs of dust rising from the floor underfoot.

A man sat, or rather sprawled, in a throne-chair. His head had fallen forward, and both hands were clenched on the hilt of a dagger driven into him at heart level. Another and younger man, lunged, sword in his hand, aiming at the image of a woman who cowered away, such an expression of rage and hate intermingled on her features as made Tanree shiver.

But the fourth of that company stood a little apart, no fear to be read on her countenance. Her robe was plainer than that of the other woman, with no glint of jewels at wrist, throat, or waist. Her unbound hair fell over her shoulders, cascading down, to nearly sweep the floor.

In spite of the twilight here, that wealth of hair appeared to gleam. Her eyes—they, too, were dark red— unhuman, knowing, exulting, cruel—alive!

Tanree found she could not turn her gaze from those eyes.

Perhaps she cried out then, or perhaps only some inner defense quailed in answer to invasion. Snakelike, sluglike, it crawled, oozed into her mind, forging link between them.

This was no stone image, man-wrought. Tanree swayed against the pull of that which gnawed and plucked, seeking to control her.

"She-devil!" The Falconer spat, the bead of moisture striking the breast of the red-haired woman. Tanree almost expected to see the other turn her attention to the man whose face was twisted with half-insane rage. But his cry had weakened the spell laid upon her. She was now able to look away from the compelling eyes. The Falconer swung around. His good hand closed upon the sword which the image of the young man held. He jerked at that impotently. There was a curious wavering, as if the chamber and all in it were but part of a wind-riffled painted banner.

"Kill!"

Tanree herself wavered under that command in her mind. Kill this one who would dare threaten her, Jonkara, Opener of Gates, Commander of Shadows.

Rage took fire. Through the blaze she marched, knowing what must be done to this man who dared to challenge. She was the hand of Jonkara, a tool of force.

Deep within Tanree something else stirred, could not be totally battered into submission.

I am a weapon to serve. I am—

"I am Tanree!" cried that other part of her. "This is no quarrel of mine. I am Sulcar, of the seas—of another blood and breed!"

She blinked, and that insane rippling ceased for an instant of clear sight. The Falconer still struggled to gain the sword.

"Now!" Once more that wave of compulsion beat against her, heart high, as might a shore wave. "Now— slay! Blood—give me blood that I may live again. We are women. Nay, you shall be more than woman when this blood flows and my door is opened by it. Kill—strike behind the shoulder. Or better still, draw your steel across his throat. He is but a man! He is the enemy—kill!"

Tanree swayed, her body might be answering to the flow of a current. Without her will her hand arose, blade ready, the distance between her and the Falconer closed. She could easily do this, blood would indeed flow. Jonkara would be free of the bonds laid upon her by the meddling of fools.

"Strike!"

Tanree saw her hand move. Then that other will within her flared for a last valiant effort.

"I am Tanree!" A feeble cry against a potent spell. "There is no power here before whom Sulcar bows!"

The Falconer whirled, looked to her. No fear in his eyes, only cold hate. The bird on his shoulder spread wings, screamed. Tanree could not be sure—was there indeed a curl of red about its feet, anchoring it to its human perch?"She-devil!" he flung at her. Abandoning his fight for the sword, he raised his hand as if to strike Tanree across the face. Out of the air came a curl of tenuous red, to catch about his upraised wrist, so, even though he fought furiously, he was held prisoner.

"Strike quickly!" The demand came with mind-bruising force.

"I do not kill!" Finger by finger Tanree forced her hand to open. The blade fell, to clang on the stone floor. "Fool!" The power sent swift punishing pain into her head. Crying out, Tanree staggered. Her outflung hand fell upon that same sword the Falconer had sought to loosen. It came into her hold swiftly and easily.

"Kill!"

That current of hate and power filled her. Her flesh tingled, there was heat within her as if she blazed like an oil-dipped feast torch.

"Kill!"

She could not control the stone sword. Both of her hands closed about its cold hilt. She raised it. The man before her did not move, seek in any way to dodge the threat she offered. Only his eyes were alive now — no fear in them, only a hate as hot as what filled her.

Fight — she must fight as she had the waves of the storm-lashed sea. She was herself, Tanree — Sulcar — no tool for something evil which should long since have gone into the Middle Dark.

"Kill!"

With the greatest effort she made her body move, drawing upon that will within her which the other could not master. The sword fell.

Stone struck stone — or was that true? Once more the air rippled, life overrode ancient death for a fraction of time between two beats of the heart, two breaths. The sword had jarred against Jonkara.

"Fool —" a fading cry.

There was no sword hilt in her hands, only powder sifting between her fingers. And no sparks of life in those red eyes either. From where the stone sword had struck full on the image's shoulder cracks opened. The figure crumbled, fell. Nor did what Jonkara had been vanish alone. All those others were breaking too, becoming dust which set Tanree coughing, raising her hands to protect her eyes. Evil had ebbed. The chamber was cold, empty of what had waited here. A hand caught her shoulder, pulling at her.

"Out!" This voice was human. "Out—Salzarat falls!"

Rubbing at her smarting eyes, Tanree allowed him to lead her. There were crashing sounds, a rumbling. She cringed as a huge block landed nearby. They fled, dodging and twisting. Until at last they were under the open sky, still coughing, tears streaming from their eyes, their faces smeared with gray grit.

Fresh wind, carrying with it the clean savor of the sea, lapped about them. Tanree crouched on a mat of dead grass through which the first green spears of spring pushed.

So close to her that their shoulders touched was the Falconer. His bird was gone.

They shared a small rise Tanree did not remember climbing. What lay below, between them and the sea cliffs' edge, was a tumble of stone so shattered no one now could define wall or passage. Her companion turned his head to look directly into her face. His expression was one of wonder.

"It is all gone! The curse is gone. So she is beaten at last! But you are a woman, and Jonkara could always work her will through any woman—that was her power and our undoing. She held every woman within her grasp. Knowing that, we raised what defenses we could. For we could never trust those who might again open Jonkara's dread door. Why in truth did you not slay me? My blood would have freed her, and she would have given you a measure of her power—as always she had done."

"She was no one to command me!" Tanree's self-confidence returned with every breath she drew. "I am Sulcar, not one of your women. So—this Jonkara—she was why you hate and fear women?"

"Perhaps. She ruled us so. Her curse held us until the death of Langward, who dying, as you saw, from the steel of his own Queen, somehow freed a portion of us. He had been seeking long for a key to imprison Jonkara. He succeeded in part. Those of us still free fled, so our legends say, making sure no woman would ever again hold us in bond."

He rubbed his hands across his face, streaking the dust of vanished Salzarat.

"This is an old land. I think though that none walk it now. We must remain here—unless your people come seeking you. So upon us the shadow of another curse falls."

Tanree shrugged. "I am Sulcar, but there was none left to call me clan-sister. I worked on the *Kast-Boar* without kin-tie. There will be no one to come hunting because of me." She stood up, her hands resting on her hips, and turned her back deliberately upon the sea."Falconer, if we be cursed, then that we live with. And, while one lives, the future may still hold much, both good and ill. We need only face squarely what comes."

There was a scream from the sky above them. The .clouds parted, and, through weak sunlight, wheeled the falcon. Tanree threw back her head to watch it.

"This is your land, as the sea is mine. What make you of it, Falconer?"

He also got to his feet. "My name is Rivery. And your words have merit. It is a time for curses to slink back into shadows, allowing us to walk in the light, to see what lies ahead."

Shoulder to shoulder they went down from the hillock, the falcon swooping and soaring above their heads.

THE DOWRY OF
THE RAG PICKER'S DAUGHTER

Arabesques: More Tales of the Arabian Nights (1988) AvoNova, A Century of Fantasy 1980-1989 (1996) MJF Books

The Way of the Limping Camel was six houses long and one wide—if mounds of tumbled earthen bricks could still be termed houses. Yet they were indeed inhabited by the very least and lowest of those who vowed allegiance to Caliph Ras el Fada, whose own dwelling at the other side of the city proudly showed a blazing watchtower striped with gold leaf.

The least of the houses on the way had been claimed by the rag picker Muledowa. He was always careful to thank the Great One of the Many Names for his luck in finding it when his former roof had nearly landed on his head and had put an end to two ragged hens which were in the care of his daughter Zoradeh. Well had he used his cane on her, too, for not foreseeing such a catastrophe and being prepared against it.

He sighed as he slip-slapped along on his worn sandals, for no one looking upon Zoradeh's unveiled face would ever come brideseeking—nor could he ever put her up for sale in the Market of Slaves, for again her djinn-given face would put an end to any hope of sale.

Deliberately he pushed Zoradeh out of his mind as he wished he could pull the whole of her misbegotten face and skinny body out of his life as well. At least this day the Compassionate and All-Powerful had smiled in his direction. His grip about the edge of the collection bag tightened as he trudged along.

Caliph Ras el Fada might be the ruler of Nid and at least ten surrounding territories. But he was not the ruler of his own harem; and he frowned blackly every time he thought about that. He too had a daughter, a rose of a daughter, in whose person and face no man could find fault. The trouble was no longer hidden—and it was one often found among women—love of power and a hot temper. Better such a one be bagged and left in the waste to trouble mankind no more than introduced into the company of any foolish man. For Jalnar had a strong will and a sharp mind of her own. All smiling eyes and cooing lips could she be until she got her will—then, like some warrior female of the djinn, she became a force with whom no man could deal. Willing indeed was Caliph Ras ready to get rid of her. However, gossip was gossip and spread from the harem even into the marketplace. Since rumor had near a thousand tongues, he could not cut out every one of them. Also, there was the matter of the future rule of his town. Though he had taken four wives, and been served by a variety of eager and willing concubines, he had unaccountably no other child who had lived past the fifth year, save Jalnar. So he could not leave any heir save her husband—and he had yet to find one willing to accept, no matter how large a dowry he might offer; none for three years at least . . . until now. He ran his fingers through his beard, trying to put out of mind all else about this self-styled wizard Kamar, save the fact he had not only made an offer for Jalnar but had already gifted her with one of the dresses for her bridal viewing—all of silvery stuff, so sewn with pearls as to be worth a fortune.

The caliph clapped hands and summoned his favorite mamluk, sending him to the harem with a message for the head eunuch. But still he was too ill at ease to retire to his gold-embroidered cushions, and his hand gave such a hard tug to his beard that the tweak brought smarting tears to his eyes and words to his lips which were hardly those of a sublime ruler and respected Commander of the Faithful.

Down the Way of the Limping Camel came Muledowa. Zoradeh moved closer to the wall, waited to feel his digging stick laid hard about her shoulders, though she could remember no recent fault which would arouse her father's ire. To her great surprise he squirmed past the tall pile of broken mud bricks which served as a door without any greeting curse. To her even greater astonishment, he stooped to gather up the chunk of crumbling masonry which sealed the door and thumped it home, keeping his gathering bag still tight-pressed to him under his other arm. For the first time she could recall, there was an upturn to his lips within the thick beard which might be almost taken for a smile.

The shadow smile still lingered as he looked at her.

"Fortune sometimes aids the worthy man after all." With great care he placed the bag on the pavement between them. "I am at a turning of the road now, and soon I shall mount a fine she-mule and have a slave to run before me. Nor shall I grub among foul things for bread to fill the mouth."

She eyed him warily, afraid to ask any questions for fear he might well slide back into that other whom she had always known. But he had gone down on his knees and was tugging at the fastening of the bag. Still paying her no attention, he brought out something which caused her to cry out when she saw it.

Creased, and possessing a ragged tear down the front as if its last wearer had ripped it or had it torn from her body, was such a dress as she could not believe ever existed except in some tale. It was silver, shimmering, seeming to reflect the light here and there; and there were small and large pearls cunningly sewn in pattern on it.

Her father was holding it up to the light, turning it carefully. He lifted the torn portion and held it in its place. Then for the first time he spoke to her. "Loathsome thou art, but still there is some use for you. Bring out your needle and the right kind of thread and make this as perfect as can be done. And" —he looked to the bucket of water she had brought from the well in the street— "wash your hands twice—thrice, before you lay hand on this. A princess' ransom might be in your hold."

Zoradeh reached out a hand to the shimmering pile of beauty. Then she leaned far forward and kissed the dusty pavement at her father's feet.

"On my head and hands be this done," she said as she gathered the bag around the treasure. She had myriad questions but dared voice none of them. She could only fear in silence that her father had in some manner stolen the robe.

"Aye, on your head, your hands, and your eyes." He went back to the broken door before he turned with infinite malice in both the look he directed at her and in his voice as he answered, "Good fortune seldom pays two visits to a man, and this is mine!"

He looked back at the shimmering heap and then went out. Zoradeh listened to the slap of his worn sandals. He was going down the street toward the small inn where he would drink minted tea and strive to out-lie his two rivals for the rest of the afternoon.

She followed orders and washed her hands three times, daring to put in the rinse water of the last immersion a bit of well-shaved cinnamon bark, so that its fragrance warred against all the other, fouler odors in the wash that had once been a courtyard. Then, taking up the bag that was still half-wrapped about the wonder her father had brought home, she scrambled up to the part of the house which she had made her own, her father not choosing to follow her over the loose brick which often started sliding under one's feet. Once this must have been the harem of a noble house, for there were still fading pictures painted in flaring designs on the wall, or what was left of it. But now it was Zoradeh's own place of hiding. She spread out the bag as far as she could and stood up to shake free the robe.

Carefully the girl examined the tear across the front of the robe. It was a jagged opening apparently made by a knife, and, as she moved, pearls dripped from broken threads. Hastily she folded it tear-side-up and explored the bag and the floor until she had near a full palm of the gleaming gems. How many had been lost along the way, or still lay near to where her father had found it? Find it he must have done, for Muledowa was the last man in the city to put his right hand into jeopardy for theft.

Oft times before she had mended thrown-away things her father had found in the trash and done so well that he was able to sell them to a dealer in old clothes in the market. But she had never set fingers to such as this before. Bringing forth her packet of needles, she chose the smallest, and, using ravellings of the material itself, she set to work.

In the tree-shadowed court of the harem which formed nearly a third of the Caliph's palace, Jalnar lay soft and at ease on a pile of silken rugs while a slave rubbed her feet and ankles with sweet-smelling cream. She held up her silver hand mirror and studied her reflection in the polished surface critically. Nor did she turn her head as she spoke to the blowsy bundle of shawls and face-veil who squatted a few feet away.

"They say that there be only two lots for a woman—marriage or the grave. To me it seems that these be equal choices and there should be a third—a hidden rule, which we will find within the hour. You did as was told to you, Mirza? The thing will never again see the light of day?"

"Hearing was doing, Flower of All Flowers. The dress was thrust deep amid the foul refuse of the city—no one would go delving for profit there."

"In a way, Old One, it is a pity, for I have never seen its like. But then I have never been courted by a wizard before, and who knows what tricks of magic he bound around it—what tricks he might use against me when I went among his womenfolk. Wizards claim great powers, and they may be right. Better not yield to such a one.

"It is the duty of the caliph to provide me with at least seven bride dresses so that when I am shown to my lord, he sees me in full beauty. Why should this Kamar present one, thus breaking custom? Perhaps he would so bind me to some ifrit who would be ever with me that I may not in anything have my will."

The bundle of shawls shook. "Precious as Water in the Desert, speak not of such horrors. It is said that some may be summoned merely by thinking on them. It could well be that the wizard wishes only to do you honor, and that such affairs are arranged differently in his country. I have heard it ever said that foreigners have queer customs."

Jalnar slapped the fan on her knee and kicked out at one of the girls soothing her feet. "Be gone, it is done as well as your awkward hands can do so. And you, Mirza, forget such foolishness. Has not the mighty Orban himself laid upon this castle and all it contains a protecting shell? All have heard of Orban—who has raised a voice to cry aloud the deeds of Kamar? Only by his own words do we know that he claims to be a wizard at all.

"If he is one, and has striven to burden me with some fate of his own devising—well, we have taken care of that, have we not, Old One?"

"Hearing and obeying, Great Lady," came her servant's answer, so softly that Jalnar had to strain to hear it, and her ears were the keenest ever known in Nid.

"Go now, all of you, I would sleep away the hot hours that I may appear at my best at the second showing—"

There was a grunt from the shawls and Jalnar laughed.

"So it has been said that Kamar wanted his gift shown tonight. Now you will whisper in the halls and kitchen that he misjudged my size—that my workers of needlecraft need to make some changes in it. Since he cannot come into the harem to search and ask, he needs must accept my words for that if he ask outright. You may tell all your old gossips that I shall wear it on the seventh night when the contract is to be signed, which will make me one to answer his slightest whim. That will bring us time and we can plan—" Her voice slid down into a hissing whisper as she waved all those with her away.

Zoradeh had feared the task her father had set her, for the stuff of its making was so fragile she thought that even handling might bring more destruction. Yet her needle slipped through the gauzy material as if there were holes there already awaiting it. She made fast each pearl with interweaving. It would seem that the rent was less than it looked at first, and she finished well before sundown. Standing up on the scrap of wall left to the house she allowed the faint breeze tug it out to the full. Truly a robe for a princess. How had her father come upon such a thing?

She held it close to her and wondered how it would feel to go so bravely clad through the days with maids aplenty, eunuchs and mamluks to obey and guard her. Now she looked carefully down along the street, and then it was but a moment's work to undo her trousers which were patch upon patch, and her faded, much-mended shirt. Over her head went the robe; and it settled down about her, seeming to cling to her as might another, fairer skin. Zoradeh drew a deep breath and brought forward the water pail, waiting for the slopping of its contents to end so that she could use it as a mirror. Then she whipped the end of the veil worn modestly about the lower part of her djinn-given face and looked.

Ah! With her face thus covered she looked like someone out of a fair dream, and she straightened her back, aching from many hours of being bent above a task, giving her head a proud little toss... princess! So did clothes make the woman. Were she to venture forth with some guards and a bevy of maids, would her passage not have them talking about a princess very quickly indeed?

"Pearl among Pearls!" The voice startled her so that she nearly lost her precarious footing and fell down into the courtyard. There was a man in the outer lane, mounted on a fine black horse which seemed to dance with eagerness under his hand. And he wore the red scarf of the caliph's own guard looped about the rim of his helm.

"Fortune's Own Daughter!" He smiled gaily and raised his spear in salute. "Foolish is your lord to allow such a treasure to be seen. How came you here to glow like a lily under the full moon, but set in a marsh of muck so hard to reach and pluck forth—"

She must rid herself of this stranger before the return of her father, and what better way to do so than to prove to him what ugliness could be seen as a woman's face? Deliberately she jerked the wedge of the shawl from the veiling of her face, and waited for him to show distaste and dislike of the tooth-gnashing wrinkled mask as all the rest had done. Yet he did not turn away his head, spit out some charm against ifrit or demon. Instead he brought his horse closer to the crumbling wall and called up to her.

"Are you wed, Pearl of Great Price? If this be so I shall search out your husband and ask him to try blade against blade with me—and I am counted a mighty swordsman. If the Uniter of Souls has decreed that you are not so tied to another, tell me then your name and that of your father that I may make him an offer—"

She had backed away from the edge of the wall. Now sure that she spoke with a man whose wits were awry, she answered: "Master, why do you make me the butt of your cruel pleasure? You see me clearly—and so seeing you view what no man would bargain for." Then she scrambled down the rude pile of bricks that led from her perch, not listening to aught he called after her, rubbing the tears from her eyes. So she stayed in hiding until she heard him ride away, and was able to reach for her own clothing and fold away the mended pearl dress in the bag.

She could hope that he might forget his foolishness and that he could not indeed set forth on a hunt for Muledowa, for the latter would indeed deem the guard mad—as would any in this quarter hearing him speak so of the rag picker's daughter, easily the most foul of countenance of any who drew water from the public well and went openly unveiled. She wrapped the dress carefully in her father's collection bag and hid it under his sleep mat, hoping he would take it away soon. For within her, long-buried hope awakened; and she would not be so hurt again.

In the palace of the caliph there was much to do, for the seventh-day bride feast had yet three nights to go. Jalnar bathed and then had her smooth, pale skin anointed with a scent made of many herbs, so that it would seem that a whole garden had broken into the bathing chamber. Her dark hair was smoothed until there was the look of fine satin to its length; and the maid had just finished with that when Mirza scurried into the room and bent her shoulder the more so that she might kiss the ground before her mistress's feet.

There was such a look on her much-wrinkled face as made Jalnar wave her attendants away and lean toward her with a whisper for a voice.

"Old One, what trouble does Fate or ifrit lay upon us? You look like one on the way to the beheading block, with no chance of any mercy at the end of that journey."

"Well, my lady, do you choose such a description." Plainly there was both fear and anger to make her voice like the croak of carrion crown. "Our caliph, the great lord, the Prophet-descended one, has given an order—already he must be close to the guarded doorway—and he said with all men hearing him that this night you shall do proper honor to Kamar after the fashion of his own people, and wear for his viewing the robe which he brought—"

"It is too tight, too small, it was damaged in the chest in which it came to me—I would do him greater honor if I wear it on the final night after it is repaired."

Mirza began to shake her head—first slowly, and then with greater vigor. "Lady, the Companion of djinn will see through such excuses, even if it is you who speak them."

Jalnar caught a lock of her hair and held it between her teeth. The plan she had thought was so simple—how could she have hoped to use it against a wizard?

"What shall I do then, Mother of Maids?"

"You have the robe brought forth, and then perhaps it may be repaired in time. For those at the banquet sit long over such delicacies as your honored father has set before him. He is, thank the Compassionate, one who is not easily disturbed from any meal."

"There is wisdom in your speech, Old One. Go and have out that rag, and my best sewing maid, to whom the All-Seeing has given a great gift with the needle, shall see what she can do. It might be well that I wear the robe from the far eastern nation which was gifted to me three years ago, and then have the wizard's rag brought in to show and say that I would keep the honor of its wearing to the last night of all, when my father gives me to this hunter of stars and teller of strange tales, despite all his present urging."

"To hear is to obey," mumbled Mirza. She once more padded away. But when she sought the hole into which she had thrust the robe there was nothing there—save a number of date seeds, and the rind of a melon. For a moment or two she looked about her wildly, thinking surely she must have been mistaken. Only, she remembered so well other points of reference to that hidey-hole and they were still about.

"Grub you for the kitchen leavings, Old One?" A boy who wore only a ragged loincloth and who was gray with the grime of the dump looked down upon her from a neighboring mound of refuse. "There will be naught worth the having there, for old Muledowa has already been here. Though his bones may be so old he cannot scramble around well, he has never lost what may bring him any sort of a bargain. Even the ifrit would welcome such skill as he has."

"Muledowa?" Mirza raised her voice a little. "He is known to you, quick one, and he has been here today?"

"As the sun weighs upon us with its heat, so it is true. Also his find here must have been a fine one, for he turned and went toward his home, looking no more this day. I strove to see what he held, but he rolled it so quickly into his collecting bag that I got no sight of it, and when I asked him a question he spat at me as if we were strange cats made foes over a choice morsel of baked camel."

Jalnar twisted the lock of hair fiercely between her hands upon Mirza's return, as she said, "Go you to Raschman of the guard and say to him that one of my maids stole out at night and buried something among the rubbish where it was later found by this Muledowa and taken away—that it must be a plot between the two of them, and" — she hesitated a moment and then added — "say that it was Dalikah who did this—for all know that I have had her beaten for breaking my bottle of scent and she has good reason to have ill thoughts against me. Tell the guardsman that you have heard of this rag picker who lives in the refuse of the town, and to send there to obtain the bag. Only warn him not to open it or look upon its contents, for it is doubtless true that it has been magicked by the djinn."

"And Muledowa and those who live under his roof, who may have already seen what lies within that bag, my lady? What do we with them?"

"I do not think," Jalnar replied with a small cruel smile, "that he will have shared such a secret with many—they would be on him as a hawk upon a desert snake if he had. But if he does have other of his own blood—let that one or all others be brought also." Mirza struck her head three times against the floor at the princess's feet. "Hearing is doing, lady."

So she left Jalnar to be swathed in the green gown of her choice and slipped away through the gates, for all the guards knew her well and she often ran errands for this or that of the ladies of the inner rooms.

She went to the outer palace, where she huddled by the door of the guards' room, trying to catch the eye of the man who was making swooping motions in the air and talking loudly.

"—fair as the moon in full glory, she moves like swallows a-wing, her skin like the softest satin such as those in the forbidden palace lie upon for sleeping. Ah, I have seen beauties a-many in my day—"

Two of the listeners laughed and the man's hand went to his sword hilt, his face frowning in warning.

"Brother by the sword," one of the listeners spoke. "Is it not true that many times you have seen maids of surpassing beauty, only later to find some irredeemable flaw in them? Let us go then to the ruin by the outer wall and test whether your story be right or whether some djinni has ensorcelled your eyes—"

But the young man had already seen Mirza, and now he came to her with some relief in his expression. "Why do you seek us out, Mother?" he asked with some respect and a tone of courtesy.

"My lady has been grievously despoiled of a treasure." She told her story quickly. "One of the slave girls took ill her punishment for a fault and stole a robe of great price. She hid this in the mound of refuse beyond the palace, and there it was picked up by one Muledowa, a picker of rags, and carried home. My lady would have back her belongings and with them the rag picker and all else under his roof who might have seen this thing—for she fears it all be a piece of sport by those ifrits who dislike all mankind. Of this she wishes to be sure before she tells her father of it—lest he, too, be drawn into some devilish sorcery."

He touched his turban-wreathed helm with both hands and said, "Having heard, it is as done."

Zoradeh was kneeling in the ruined courtyard of her home, washing her father's feet and listening with growing fear to his mumbling speech, for he was talking, if not to her, then to some djinni who had accompanied him.

"Orbasan will pay me much for this treasure." He stretched out an arm so he could finger the bag which held the robe. "Then I shall buy a donkey and, with the aid of that creature, be able to carry twice as much from the refuse heaps. For I am an old man and now it hurts my back to stretch and strain, to kneel and stand erect again all for some bit I may take. There is much greater profit to be made with things I cannot carry. Eh, girl," for the first time he looked directly at her with a cruel snarl twisting his lips, "how then has the work gone? Let me look upon your handiwork. If you have erred then you shall taste of my stick until each breath shall cost you sore—"

Zoradeh brought the bag quickly and spread it out before him, taking care that she not touch the wondrous thing with her own hands, damp and dusty as they were. For a long moment her father stared down at the fine silk and the moonlike pearls. His hand went out as if to touch and then he drew it back quickly with a deep-drawn breath.

"Aye, worth a wazir's ransom at least, that must be. We shall get but a third, a fifth, nearly an eighth portion of its price in gain. Yet I know no one else—" His hand went to his beard as he ran his nails through the crisp, age-sullied gray of it. "No," he added as one who had just made a decision of great import, "not yet shall I go to Orbasan with this. We shall put it away in secret and think more of the matter—"

But even as he spoke, they heard the clatter of horse hooves on the uneven pavement without, and Zoradeh clasped the robe tightly; while her father lost all his sly, cunning look in a rush of fear—for no one rode horses within the city save the guard of the caliph or that protector of the city himself. Her father got swiftly to his feet and hissed at her:

"Get you inside with that and put it upon you; they will think it is some foreign trash discarded by a trader. Best stay in open sight and not try to conceal it lest it show that we believe ourselves at fault!"

She hurried into the single of the lower rooms, which was walled and ceilinged and so might be considered a home. There she tore hurriedly out of her own rags, wondering the while if her father had lost his wits—or was pulled into some djinni's plot and did as his master bade him. The robe slid easily across her body and she had just given the last fastening to a breast buckle when her father's voice, raised high, reached her ears.

"Come, my daughter, and show this brave rider what manner of luck I did have this morning—"

She pulled the throat scarf up about her chin, though that would in no way hide better her devil face, and made herself walk out into the wrecked courtyard of the building.

There her father stood in company with three of the guard—one of those being the young officer who had so teased her earlier in the day. All three stood silent, facing her as if she were some evil ifrit ready to suck the flesh from their bones.

"Lady—where got you this robe of great beauty?" The captain found his tongue first and she, believing only the truth might save them from whatever vengeance might strike now, dared to say in return:

"Lord, my father brought it, and it was torn and of no value to any. See— do you see here the stitches I, myself, set to make it whole again?"

Hurriedly she gathered up a portion of the skirt and held it out—though so perfect had been her repairs that none might see the work and swear an oath that it was indeed secondhand goods, thrown away because it was damaged.

"That is my lady's robe," grated a sour voice from the door as Mirza pushed through the opening to join them. She was panting and red-faced from her effort to join them.

"These are thieves whom that misbegotten she-ass of my lady's following got to come to her aid."

Muledowa had fallen to his knees, and now he gathered up a palmful of sand to throw over his dirty headcloth.

"Lord of Many, Commander of Archers, I have made no pact with any— woman or ifrit or djinni. It is my way of life to sift out that which others have thrown away—things which can be resold in the Second Market which our great lord, the caliph himself, has decreed be established for those of lean purses. This I found torn asunder and thrust into the pile of refuse before the Gate of the Nine-Headed Naga at the palace."

Mirza came forward a step or two, thrusting her face close to Muledowa, and spat forth her words as might a cat who finds another within its hunting place. "Find it you did, provider of filth and evil. But first you had notice of the place from Dalikah, who has already tasted of my lady's justice." She turned to the guardsmen. "Take you this fool of a thief and also his ugly daughter to the left wing of the palace where lies the screen through which my peerless lady views the world. Since this crime was committed against her, she would have the judging of it."

Thus with a rope around his throat, fastened to the saddle of a guardsman, Muledowa was pulled at a pace hard for his old bones to make. Mirza took off the topmost of her swathing of grimy and too-well-worn shawls, which she tugged around Zoradeh, forcing the girl's arms against her body as tightly as if they were bound, and keeping the veil well over her head.

So they set off across the city, while behind them gathered a crowd of idlers and lesser merchants and craftsmen who were all agog to see and hear what must be the story behind such a sight.

They came into the courtyard that Mirza had described, but to Mirza's discomfort she found there the caliph himself and the wizard Kamar who had come to see the fair white pigeons which were one of the joys of the caliph's heart.

Seeing the caliph and thinking that perhaps one fate might be better than another, for the Lord of Many Towers was reputed to discern truth from lies when spoken before him, the rag picker jerked on the rope about his neck and fell upon his knees, giving forth that wail with which the honest meet with misfortune. The caliph made a gesture with his hand so that the guards left Muledowa alone.

"Wretched man," he said, "what misfortune or ill wish by an ifrit brought you to this place, and in such a sorry state?"

"Only the lawful enterprise of my business, Great One." Muledowa upon his knees reached forward to touch the pavement before the caliph three times with his dust covered lips. "I have no evil within me which wishes danger to you or any under this roof. It was this way—" and with one word tumbling over the other in his eagerness he told his story.

"Now that be a marvelous tale," the caliph commented when he was done. "Child"—he beckoned to Zoradeh—" stand forth and let us see this treasure which your father found."

Trembling, and with shaking hands, Zoradeh dropped the shawl from her shoulders and stood in the bright sunlight of the courtyard, her head hanging and her hands knotted together before her.

"Where is this tear over which so much has been made?" asked the caliph.

Timidly she passed her hand over that part which she had so laboriously stitched and rewoven. Then Kamar, who had stood silent all the while, looking first to those gathered in the courtyard and then at the pierced marble screen as if he knew who sheltered behind that, spoke:

"You have a deft needle, girl," he commented. "She who is to wear this will thank you. My lord," he turned to the Caliph then and said: "My lord, as you know this robe was gifted to me by the Fira Flowers. Let her who lightens this city now put it on and I shall pronounce on both robe and the enhanced beauty of she who rightly wears it such a spell as will never more part them."

The Caliph considered for a moment and then answered: "Let it be as you will, Kamar. It seems that by odd chance alone it has been returned to us. You" — he pointed to Mirza — "do you take this maiden behind the screen and let her change garments again—this time with that flower of my house—Jalnar."

The tall lady wearing the shimmering green was not the only one waiting behind the screen. There was also a gaggle of maids reaching into the shadows behind her, and it seemed to Zoradeh that every time one of those moved, if only for so little, there followed a breeze of the finest scent set wandering. She gasped, but Mirza had already dragged the face-veil from her, and now she waited to see the disgust of the princess and the loathing of her maidens rise. Yet, and she marveled at this, they had gathered around her at a distance and none of them showed the old loathing her djinn-like face had always roused in all she met.

Two of the maids hurried to disrobe the princess while Mirza's dry and leathery hands were busied about her own body. The shimmering robe of moonlike pearls was handled by the old hag, while in turn she took a dull gray slave robe and threw it to Zoradeh, leaving her to fasten it about her as best she could.

But the princess!

Zoradeh gasped and heard a cry of fright from one of the maids, while another knelt before the princess holding up a mirror of burnished silver so that she might look at herself. The robe covered her skin as tightly as it had Zoradeh, but she had not yet raised the face-veil. And— "Djinn-face— now she bears such—the teeth which are tusks— the skin of old leather," whispered Zoradeh under her breath, glancing quickly about to make sure none had heard her. For if Jalnar was in truth not a djinna, her features were twisted in the same ugliness Zoradeh's had shown all her life long.

The princess screamed and, putting her hands to her face, rubbed hard as if to tear loose a close-fitting mask. At the sound of her cry two armed eunuchs burst in upon them, but seeing the princess they both shivered and drew back, like wise men not daring to question those who have other powers.

But that cry not only brought the eunuchs. For the first time there were visitors to the inner harem which custom and law denied them. The caliph, his curved sword in his hands, was well in the fore of that invasion, but close indeed to his very heels came the guardsmen, one of them still dragging Muledowa on his restraining rope with him. And they halted, too, even as the eunuch guards had done.

For the princess stood a little apart from them all, shaking her misshapen head from side to side and moaning piteously.

"My daughter!" The caliph looked to Kamar, who was the only one who had not drawn a weapon. "Wizard—what has happened to my daughter, who was as the full moon in all its glory and now wears the face of a djinna—even of an ifrit. There is weighty magic here, and to my eyes, it is evil." Without warning he swung his sword at the wizard, but before the blade touched Kamar, it seemed to melt, as if it had passed through some fire, and the blade dripped down to form a hook.

"My Lord." Kamar wore no armament which could be seen, yet he appeared totally unaware of the swords now pointed at him.

Zoradeh thought that surely they would attack him, yet he had no fear at all. "My Lord, this robe was my gift and it has powers of its own. It draws the inner soul into the light."

He came a little more forward then and looked to the princess, instead of the men who stood ready to deliver his death.

"What," Kamar asked then as if speaking to all of them, "what does a man wish the most in a bride? Fairness of face sometimes fades quickly, and also it makes its owner proud, vain, and thoughtless of those who serve her. You—" He made a pounce forward and caught at the mirror which the maid had left on the floor. Turning, he held that before Zoradeh and she cried out a plea to save herself from looking at what hung here.

Only she did not see a djinna's twisted face above the gray garment they had given her. Instead—she drew a deep breath of wonder and glanced shyly at the wizard for some answer to this.

"You are also a maid marriageable by age, but none came to seek you out. Is that not so?"

"I was—I had the face of a djinna," she said in a voice hardly above a whisper. "My father is too poor to find me a dowry—thus even a humpbacked beggar did not desire me under his roof. But" — she rubbed her hands down the smooth flesh of her face — "what has happened to me, lord?"

"You have met with truth and it has set you free. Lord of Many Towers," he spoke to the caliph now, "I came hither to have me a wife. I have found the one that fate, which is the great weapon of the All-Compassionate, intended should rule my inner household—"

He held out his hand to Zoradeh, and she, greatly daring, for the first time in her life, allowed her fingers to lie on the rein-callused palm of a man.

"But, my daughter—" The caliph looked at Jalnar.

"In time," answered Kamar, "the Compassionate may bring to her will and desire, but they must be by her earning, and not because she dwelt before her own mirror in admiration for what she sees therein."

Jalnar let out a wail as deep with feeling as that of a newly-made widow, and then, her hands covering her face, she rushed from the room of the screen, her maids following in disorder.

Kamar went now to Muledowa who sat staring as if he did not believe what he had seen. Kamar took a heavy purse from his sash and dropped it before the bound man.

"Let this one go free, Lord of many mercies," he said to the caliph. "For he shall live under my protection from this day forth and what troubles him also troubles me. Now, my lady, we shall go—"

She flung her neck scarf over her head and shoulders, veiling a face which even now she could not believe was hers, and followed Kamar from the room.

It is said among the tellers of tales that they lived long past the lifetimes of others, and that the Divider of Souls and the Archer of the Dark did not come to them in any of the years that those living have tale of. But of Jalnar— ah, there lies another tale.

ALL CATS ARE GRAY

Fantastic Universe Science Fiction, August–September (1953)

Steena of the Spaceways—that sounds just like a corny title for one of the Stellar-Vedo spreads. I ought to know, I've tried my hand at writing enough of them. Only this Steena was no glamour babe. She was as colorless as a lunar plant—even the hair netted down to her skull had a sort of grayish cast, and I never saw her but once draped in anything but a shapeless and baggy gray space-all.

Steena was strictly background stuff and that is where she mostly spent her free hours—in the smelly smoky background corners of any stellar-port dive frequented by free spacers. If you really looked for her you could spot her—just sitting there listening to the talk—listening and remembering. She didn't open her own mouth often. But when she did spacers had learned to listen. And the lucky few who heard her rare spoken words—these will never forget Steena.

She drifted from port to port. Being an expert operator on the big calculators, she found jobs wherever she cared to stay for a time. And she came to be something like the master-minded machines she tended—smooth, gray, without much personality of her own.

But it was Steena who told Bub Nelson about the Jovan moon-rites—and her warning saved Bub's life six months later. It was Steena who identified the piece of stone Keene Clark was passing around a table one night, rightly calling it unworked Slitite. That started a rush which made ten fortunes overnight for men who were down to their last jets. And, last of all, she cracked the case of the *Empress of Mars*.

All the boys who had profited by her queer store of knowledge and her photographic memory tried at one time or another to balance the scales. But she wouldn't take so much as a cup of canal water at their expense, let alone the credits they tried to push on her. Bub Nelson was the only one who got around her refusal. It was he who brought her Bat.

About a year after the Jovan affair he walked into the Free Fall one night and dumped Bat down on her table. Bat looked at Steena and growled. She looked calmly back at him and nodded once. From then on they traveled together—the thin gray woman and the big gray tom-cat. Bat learned to know the inside of more stellar bars than even most spacers visit in their lifetimes. He developed a liking for Vernal juice, drank it neat and quick, right out of a glass. And he was always at home on any table where Steena elected to drop him.

This is really the story of Steena, Bat, Cliff Moran and the *Empress of Mars*, a story which is already a legend of the spaceways. And it's a damn good story too. I ought to know, having framed the first version of it myself.

For I was there, right in the Rigel Royal, when it all began on the night that Cliff Moran blew in, looking lower than an antman's belly and twice as nasty. He'd had a spell of luck foul enough to twist a man into a slug-snake, and we all knew that there was an attachment out for his ship. Cliff had fought his way up from the back courts of Venaport. Lose his ship and he'd slip back there—to rot. He was at the snarling stage that night when he picked out a table for himself and set out to drink away his troubles.

However, just as the first bottle arrived, so did a visitor. Steena came out of her corner, Bat curled around her shoulders stole-wise, his favorite mode of travel. She crossed over and dropped down without invitation at Cliff's side. That shook him out of his sulks. Because Steena never chose company when she could be alone. If one of the man-stones on Ganymede had come stumping in, it wouldn't have made more of us look out of the corners of our eyes.

She stretched out one long-fingered hand and set aside the bottle he had ordered and said only one thing, "It's about time for the *Empress of Mars* to appear again."

Cliff scowled and bit his lip. He was tough, tough as jet lining—you have to be granite inside and out to struggle up from Venaport to a ship command. But we could guess what was running through his mind at that moment. The *Empress of Mars* was just about the biggest prize a spacer could aim for. But in the fifty years she had been following her queer derelict orbit through space many men had tried to bring her in—and none had succeeded.

A pleasure-ship carrying untold wealth, she had been mysteriously abandoned in space by passengers and crew, none of whom had ever been seen or heard of again. At intervals thereafter she had been sighted, even boarded. Those who ventured into her either vanished or returned swiftly without any believable explanation of what they had seen—wanting only to get away from her as quickly as possible. But the man who could bring her in—or even strip her clean in space—that man would win the jackpot.

"All right!" Cliff slammed his fist down on the table. "I'll try even that!"

Steena looked at him, much as she must have looked at Bat the day Bub Nelson brought him to her, and nodded. That was all I saw. The rest of the story came to me in pieces, months later and in another port half the system away.

Cliff took off that night. He was afraid to risk waiting—with a writ out that could pull the ship from under him. And it wasn't until he was in space that he discovered his passengers—Steena and Bat. We'll never know what happened then. I'm betting that Steena made no explanation at all. She wouldn't.

It was the first time she had decided to cash in on her own tip, and she was there—that was all. Maybe that point weighed with Cliff, maybe he just didn't care. Anyway the three were together when they sighted the *Empress* riding, her dead-lights gleaming, a ghost ship in night space.

She must have been an eerie sight because her other lights were on too, in addition to the red warnings at her nose. She seemed alive, a Flying Dutchman of space. Cliff worked his ship skillfully alongside and had no trouble in snapping magnetic lines to her lock. Some minutes later the three of them passed into her. There was still air in her cabins and corridors. Air that bore a faint corrupt taint which set Bat to sniffing greedily and could be picked up even by the less sensitive human nostrils.

Cliff headed straight for the control cabin, but Steena and Bat went prowling. Closed doors were a challenge to both of them, and Steena opened each as she passed, taking a quick look at what lay within. The fifth door opened on a room which no woman could leave without further investigation.

I don't know who had been housed there when the *Empress* left port on her last lengthy cruise. Anyone really curious can check back on the old photo-reg cards. But there was a lavish display of silks trailing out of two travel kits on the floor, a dressing table crowded with crystal and jeweled containers, along with other lures for the female which drew Steena in. She was standing in front of the dressing table when she glanced into the mirror—glanced into it and froze.

Over her right shoulder she could see the spider-silk cover on the bed. Right in the middle of that sheer, gossamer expanse was a sparkling heap of gems, the dumped contents of some jewel case. Bat had jumped to the foot of the bed and flattened out as cats will, watching those gems, watching them and—something else!

Steena put out her hand blindly and caught up the nearest bottle. As she unstoppered it she watched the mirrored bed. A gemmed bracelet rose from the pile, rose in the air and tinkled its siren song. It was as if an idle hand played…. Bat spat almost noiselessly. But he did not retreat. Bat had not yet decided his course.

She put down the bottle. Then she did something which perhaps few of the men she had listened to through the years could have done. She moved without hurry or sign of disturbance on a tour about the room. And, although she approached the bed, she did not touch the jewels. She could not force herself to that. It took her five minutes to play out her innocence and unconcern. Then it was Bat who decided the issue.

He leaped from the bed and escorted something to the door, remaining a careful distance behind. Then he mewed loudly twice. Steena followed him and opened the door wider.

Bat went straight on down the corridor, as intent as a hound on the warmest of scents. Steena strolled behind him, holding her pace to the unhurried gait of an explorer. What sped before them both was invisible to her, but Bat was never baffled by it.

They must have gone into the control cabin almost on the heels of the unseen—if the unseen had heels, which there was good reason to doubt—for Bat crouched just within the doorway and refused to move on. Steena looked down the length of the instrument panels and officers' station-seats to where Cliff Moran worked. On the heavy carpet her boots made no sound, and he did not glance up but sat humming through set teeth as he tested the tardy and reluctant responses to buttons which had not been pushed in years.

To human eyes they were alone in the cabin. But Bat still followed a moving something with his gaze. And it was something which he had at last made up his mind to distrust and dislike. For now he took a step or two forward and spat—his loathing made plain by every raised hair along his spine. And in that same moment Steena saw a flicker—a flicker of vague outline against Cliff's hunched shoulders as if the invisible one had crossed the space between them.

But why had it been revealed against Cliff and not against the back of one of the seats or against the panels, the walls of the corridor or the cover of the bed where it had reclined and played with its loot? What could Bat see?

The storehouse memory that had served Steena so well through the years clicked open a half-forgotten door. With one swift motion she tore loose her spaceall and flung the baggy garment across the back of the nearest seat.

Bat was snarling now, emitting the throaty rising cry that was his hunting song. But he was edging back, back toward Steena's feet, shrinking from something he could not fight but which he faced defiantly. If he could draw it after him, past that dangling spaceall…. He had to—it was their only chance.

"What the…." Cliff had come out of his seat and was staring at them.

What he saw must have been weird enough. Steena, bare-armed and shouldered, her usually stiffly-netted hair falling wildly down her back, Steena watching empty space with narrowed eyes and set mouth, calculating a single wild chance. Bat, crouched on his belly, retreating from thin air step by step and wailing like a demon.

"Toss me your blaster." Steena gave the order calmly—as if they still sat at their table in the Rigel Royal.

And as quietly, Cliff obeyed. She caught the small weapon out of the air with a steady hand—caught and leveled it.

"Stay just where you are!" she warned. "Back, Bat, bring it back!"

With a last throat-splitting screech of rage and hate, Bat twisted to safety between her boots. She pressed with thumb and forefinger, firing at the spacealls. The material turned to powdery flakes of ash—except for certain bits which still flapped from the scorched seat—as if something had protected them from the force of the blast. Bat sprang straight up in the air with a scream that tore their ears.

"What…?" began Cliff again.

Steena made a warning motion with her left hand. "*Wait!*"

She was still tense, still watching Bat. The cat dashed madly around the cabin twice, running crazily with white-ringed eyes and flecks of foam on his muzzle. Then he stopped abruptly in the doorway, stopped and looked back over his shoulder for a long silent moment. He sniffed delicately.

Steena and Cliff could smell it too now, a thick oily stench which was not the usual odor left by an exploding blaster-shell.

Bat came back, treading daintily across the carpet, almost on the tips of his paws. He raised his head as he passed Steena and then he went confidently beyond to sniff, to sniff and spit twice at the unburned strips of the spaceall. Having thus paid his respects to the late enemy he sat down calmly and set to washing his fur with deliberation. Steena sighed once and dropped into the navigator's seat.

"Maybe now you'll tell me what in the hell's happened?" Cliff exploded as he took the blaster out of her hand.

"Gray," she said dazedly, "it must have been gray—or I couldn't have seen it like that. I'm colorblind, you see. I can see only shades of gray—my whole world is gray. Like Bat's—his world is gray too—all gray. But he's been compensated, for he can see above and below our range of color vibrations and—apparently—so can I!"

Her voice quavered and she raised her chin with a new air Cliff had never seen before—a sort of proud acceptance. She pushed back her wandering hair, but she made no move to imprison it under the heavy net again.

"That is why I saw the thing when it crossed between us. Against your spaceall it was another shade of gray—an outline. So I put out mine and waited for it to show against that—it was our only chance, Cliff.

"It was curious at first, I think, and it knew we couldn't see it—which is why it waited to attack. But when Bat's actions gave it away, it moved. So I waited to see that flicker against the spaceall and then I let him have it. It's really very simple...."

Cliff laughed a bit shakily. "But what *was* this gray thing? I don't get it."

"I think it was what made the *Empress* a derelict. Something out of space, maybe, or from another world somewhere." She waved her hands. "It's invisible because it's a color beyond our range of sight. It must have stayed in here all these years. And it kills—it must—when its curiosity is satisfied." Swiftly she described the scene in the cabin and the strange behavior of the gem pile which had betrayed the creature to her.

Cliff did not return his blaster to its holder. "Any more of them on board, d'you think?" He didn't look pleased at the prospect.

Steena turned to Bat. He was paying particular attention to the space between two front toes in the process of a complete bath. "I don't think so. But Bat will tell us if there are. He can see them clearly, I believe."

But there weren't any more, and two weeks later Cliff, Steena, and Bat brought the *Empress* into the lunar quarantine station. And that is the end of Steena's story because, as we have been told, happy marriages need no chronicles. And Steena had found someone who knew of her gray world and did not find it too hard to share with her—someone besides Bat. It turned out to be a real love match.

The last time I saw her she was wrapped in a flame-red cloak from the looms of Rigel and wore a fortune in Jovan rubies blazing on her wrists. Cliff was flipping a three-figure credit bill to a waiter. And Bat had a row of Vernal juice glasses set up before him. Just a little family party out on the town.

THE WAY WIND
Sisters in Fantasy Vol. 1 (1995) Roc

The crumbling walled fortress and the dreary, ragged town, which had woven a ragged skirt about it during long years, stood at the end of the Way Pass. It was named l'Estal, which in a language older than legend, had a double meaning—First and Last.

For it was the first dwelling of men at the end of Way Pass along which any traffic from the west must come. And it was also the end of a long, coiling snake of a road stretching eastward and downward to Klem, which long ago it had been designed to guard.

There could have been another name for that straggle of drear buildings also—End of Hope.

For generations now it had been a place of exile. Those sent from Klem had been men and women outlawed for one reason or another. The scribe whose pen had been a key used too freely, the officer who was too ambitious—or at times, too conscientious, the rebel, the misfit, those sometimes fleeing the law or ruler's whim, they came hither.

There was no returning, for a geas had been set on the coil road, and those of lowland blood coming up might only travel one way—never to return. There had been countless attempts, of course. But whatever mage had set that barrier had indeed been one of power, for the spell did not dwindle with the years as magic often did.

Through the Way Pass there came only a trickle of travelers, sometimes not more than three or four in a season. None of them lingered in l'Estal; there was that about the place which was like a dank cloud, and its people were grim of face, meager of livelihood.

During the years they had managed to scrape a living, tilling small scraps of fields they terraced along the slopes, raising lean goats and small runtish sheep, hunting, burrowing into the rock of the heights to bring out stores of ore.

The latter was transported once a year to a certain bend in the descending road, and there traded for supplies they could not otherwise raise—salt, pigs of iron, a few items of what was luxury to them. Then it was also that the Castellan of the fort would receive the pouch bearing the royal arms containing, ever the same, orders. And now and again there would be another exile to be sent aloft.

The trickle of travelers from the west included mostly merchants, dealers in a small way, too poor to make the long journey by sea to the port of Klem itself.

They were hunters with pelts, drovers of straggles of lean mountain cattle or sheep, small, dark people who grunted rasping words in trade language, kept to themselves, and finished their business as soon as possible.

Of the Klemish exiles, none took the westward road. If there was a geas set upon that also, no one spoke of such. It was simply accepted that for them there was only one place to be longed for, dreamed of, hopelessly remembered—that that lay always eastward.

There had been many generations of exiles, and their children had known no other place; yet to them l'Estal was not a home but a prison of sorts, and the tales told of the eastern land made of that a paradise forbidden, changed out of all knowledge of what it had been or was.

Still there was always one point of interest that stirred the western gate sentries each year—and that was the Way Wind. At the very beginning of spring, which came slowly and harshly in these gaunt uplands, a wind blew strongly from west to east, souring the pass, carrying with it strange scents. It might last a single day; it might blow so for three or four.

And by chance, it always brought with it someone of the western travelers, as if it pulled them on into the line of the pass and drew them forward. Thus, in a place where there was so little of the new and strange, the Way Wind farers were a matter of wager, and often time not only the armsmen at the gate but their officers and their women gathered, along with townspeople, when they heard the outer horn blast, which signaled that the wind herded a traveler to them.

This day there were four who stood on the parapet of the inner wall, not closely together as if they were united in their company, but rather each a little apart. The oldest of that company, a man who had allowed the hood of his cloak to fall back so the wind lifted tuffs of steel gray hair, had the paler face of one who kept much indoors. Yet there was strength in his features, a gleam of eye which that about him had not defeated, nor ever would. At the throat of his cloak was the harp badge of a bard. Osono he had named himself ten years before when he had accompanied the east traders back from their rendezvous. And by that name he was accepted, eagerly by the Castellan and those of his household.

Next to him, holding her own thick cloak tightly about her as if she feared the wind might divest her of it, was the Lady Almadis, she who had been born to the Castellan's lady after their arrival here. Her clothing was as coarse as that of any townswoman on the streets below, and the hands that held to that cloak were sun-browned. There was a steady look to her, as if she had fitted herself to the grim husk housing her.

At pace or so behind her was a second man. Unlike the other two he had no cloak, but rather dressed in mail and leather, sword-armed. But his head was bare also as he cradled a pitted helm on one hip. His features were gaunt, thinned, bitter, his mouth a mere line above a stubborn jaw—Urgell, who had once been a mercenary and now served as swordsmaster in the fortress.

The fourth was strange even in that company, for she was a broad-girthed woman, red of face, thick of shoulder. Her cloak was a matter of patched strips, as if she had been forced to sew together the remains of several such in order to cover her. A fringe of yellow-white hair showed under the edge of a cap covering her head. For all the poverty of her appearance, Forina had a good position in the town, for she was the keeper of the only inn, and any of the Way Wind brought would come to her for shelter.

"What is your wager, my lady?" Osono's trained bard's voice easily overreached the whistle of the wind.

Almadis laughed, a hard-edged sound which lacked any softening of humor.

"I, sir bard? Since my last two wind wagers were so speedily proved wrong, I have learned caution. This year I make no speculation; thus I shall not be disappointed again. Think me over-timid of my purse if you will."

Osono glanced at her. She was not looking toward him but rather down the road. "Lady," he returned, "I think you are over-timid in nothing."

After a moment she laughed again. "Bard, life in l'Estal makes for dull acceptance—perhaps that gives root to timidity."

"There is the priest." The observation from the mercenary cut through their exchange. He had moved forward, as if drawn by some force beyond his own understanding, to look down at the cluster of townspeople and guards by the gate.

"Thunur," Osono nodded. "Yes, that crow is well on the hop. Though if he tries to deliver his message to either herdsman or trader, he will not get the better of them. Shut-mouthed they are, and to all of them I think we are Dark-shadowed—they would listen no more to one of us than to the bark of a chained hound."

Urgell had put his hand to the edge of the parapet wall, and now his mail and leather gauntlet grated on the stone there. Chained hound, Almadis thought, proper term not only for such as this man, but perhaps for all of them. But then a Bard was trained in apt word choice.

"That is one as makes trouble—" Forina had come forward also on the other side of the soldier. "He has a tongue as bitter as var, and he uses it to dip into many pots. T'would be well to keep an eye on him."

Urgell turned his head quickly. "What stir has he tried to set, Goodwife?"

"More than one. Ask Vill Blacksmith what a pother made his sister sharp-tongue him. Ask of Tatwin why three of those snot-nosed brats he strives to beat learning into no longer come to his bidding, and ask Solasten why she was pelted with market dung. Ask me why the doors of the Hafted Stone are now barred to him. A troublemaker he is, and this is a place where we need no one to heat old quarrels and pot new ones!"

"If he is a brawler, speak to the guard," Osono suggested. "But I think he is perhaps something even more to be watched—"

"What may that be?" The bard had all their attention now, but it was Almadis who asked that question.

"A fanatic, my lady. One so obsessed with his own beliefs that he is like a smoldering torch ready to be put to a straw heap. We have not an easy life here; there were many old hatreds, despairs, and these can be gathered up to fuel a new fire. Ten years ago, one of his nature arose in Salanika—there was such a bloodletting thereafter as the plains had not seen since the days of Black Gorn. It took full two seasons to quench that fire, and some brands still smoldering may have been scattered to blaze again—"

"Such a one as Thunur, you think?" Almadis demanded. "L'Estal has answers to such—have we not?" The bitterness in her voice was plain. "What are we all but outlaws, and we can exist only as we hold together." She did not turn her head, but she loosed one hand from her cloak hold and motioned to that dark, ill-fortuned spread of age-hardened timbers which surmounted the wall of the shorter tower. "That has borne fruit many times over."

"He has a following," Urgell said, "but he and they are under eye. If he tries aught with the western travelers, he will be in a cell within an hour. We want no trouble with them."

Certainly they could afford no trouble with the few who came the western road. Such wayfarers were their only real link with a world which was not overshadowed by the walls about them and the past which had brought them here.

The gray-robed priest had indeed been roughly jostled away from the gate. He was making small hops, for he was a short man, trying to see over the crowd the nature of the wayfarer who was now well within sight.

"It—it is a child!" Almadis was shaken out of her composure and came with a single step to stand beside the mercenary. "A child—! But what fate has brought her here?"

The wayfarer was slight, her bundle of travel cloak huddled about her as if it were intended for a much larger and stouter wearer. Hood folds had fallen back on her shoulders, and they saw hair that the wind had pulled from braids to fly in wisps about her face. She was remarkably fair of skin for a wilderness traveler, and her hair was very fair, though streaked here and there by a darker strand closer to the gleam of red-gold.

There was no mistaking, however, the youth of that slight body and those composed features. She walked confidently, and at her shoulder bobbed the head of a hill pony, still so thick with winter hair that it was like an ambling mound of fur.

Bulging panniers rode on either side of a packsaddle. And that was surrounded in the middle by what looked to be a basket half covered by a lid.

Contrary to all who made this perilous way through the high mountains, the girl carried no visible weapons except a stout staff which had been crudely hacked from some sapling, stubs of branches yet to be marked along its length. This was topped, however, with a bunch of flowers and leaves, massed together. Nor did any of them look wilted; rather it would seem they had just been plucked, though there were yet no flowers to be found in the upper reaches where reluctant patches of snow could be sighted.

"Who—what—" Almadis was snapped out of her boredom, of that

weariness which overshadowed her days and nights.

As the girl came to the gate, there was a sudden change. The Way Wind died, there was an odd kind of silence as if they all waited for something; they did not know what.

So complete was that silence that the sound Osono uttered startled them all.

"Who—what—?" Almadis turned upon the bard almost fiercely.

He shook his head slowly. "Lady, I have seen many things in my time, and have heard of countless more. There is said to be—somewhere in the western lands—those who are one with the land in a way that none of our blood can ever hope to be—"

The sentries at the gate seemed disinclined to ask any questions. In fact they had fallen back, and with them the townspeople withdrew to allow her a way path. In their doing so, Thunur won to the front rank and stood, his head stretched a little forward on his lank neck, staring at her, his teeth showing a little.

Almadis turned swiftly, but Osono matched her, even extending his wrist in a courtly fashion to give her dignity. Forina, closest to the stairway, was already lumbering down, and behind them Urgell seemed as eager to catch a closer sight of this most unusual wayfarer.

They gained the portion of street just in time to witness Thunur's upflung arm, hear his speech delivered with such force as to send spittle flying.

"Witchery! Here comes witchery! See the demon who is riding in such state!"

The crowd shrunk back even more as there was a stir to that half-covered basket on the top of the pony pack.

"Fool!" Forina's voice arose in the kind of roar she used to subdue a taproom scuffle. For so large a woman she moved very fast, and now she was halfway between the slavering priest and the girl, who watched them both serenely as if she had no cause to suspect that she was unwelcome.

"Fool! That is but a cat—"

The rust-yellow head with pricked ears had arisen yet farther from within its traveling basket, and green eyes surveyed them all with the same unconcern as that of the girl.

But such a cat. One of those pricked ears was black, and as the cat arose higher in its riding basket, they could see that there was a black patch on its chest. There was such a certain cockiness about it, an air of vast self-confidence, that Almadis laughed; and that was a laugh that had no edge of harshness.

Her laugh was quickly swallowed up by a chuckle from Osono, and a moment later there sounded no less than a full-lunged bellow from Vill Blacksmith.

The girl was smiling openly at them all as if they were greeting her with the best of goodwill.

"I am Meg, dealing in herbs and seeds, good folk. These traveling companions of mine are Kaska and Mors—"

The hair-concealed head of the pony nodded as if it perfectly understood the formalities of introduction, but Kaska merely opened a well-fanged mouth in a bored yawn.

Now the sergeant of the guard appeared to have recovered from the surprise that had gripped them all. He dropped his pike in a form of barrier and looked at the girl.

"You are from—, mistress?" he demanded gruffly.

"From Westlea, guardsman. And I am one who trades—herbs—seeds."

Almadis blinked. The girl had moved her staff a fraction. That bouquet of tightly packed flowers, which had looked so fresh from above, now presented another aspect. The color was still there, but faded—these were dried flowers surely, yet they preserved more of their once life than any she had ever seen.

"There be toll," the pike had lowered in the sergeant's hold. "A matter of four coppers, and there be a second taking for a market stall."

Meg nodded briskly. Her hand groped beneath her cloak and came forth again to spill out four dulled rounds of metal into his hand.

Those who had gathered there had begun to shift away. Since this stranger the wind had brought was going to set up in the marketplace, there would be plenty of time to inspect her—though she was indeed something new. None of her kind of merchant had entered l'Estal before in the memories of all.

Only Thunur held his place until the sergeant, seemingly unaware that he was close behind him, swung back the pike, and the priest had to skip quickly aside to escape a thud from that weapon. He was scowling at the girl, and his mouth opened as if to deliver some other accusation when Urgell took a hand in the matter.

"Off with you, crow—you stand in the lady's way!"

Now the priest swung around with a snarl, and his narrowed eyes surveyed Almadis and the bard. There was a glint of red rage in that stare. But he turned indeed and pushed through the last of the thinning crowd, to vanish down one of the more narrow alleys.

"Mistress," the mercenary spoke directly to the young traveler. "If that fluttering carrion eater makes you trouble, speak up—his voice is not one we have a liking for."

Meg surveyed him as one who wished to set a face in memory. "Armsman," she inclined her head, "I think that here I have little to fear, but for your courtesy I give you thanks."

To Almadis's surprise, she saw Urgell flush and then he moved swiftly, leaving as abruptly as the priest had done.

"You'll be wantin' shelter," Forina said. "I keep the Halfed Stone—it be the trade inn."

Again Meg favored the speaker with one of those long looks, and then she smiled. "Goodwife, what you have to offer we shall gladly accept. It has been a long road, and Mors is wearied. Our greatest burden has been his—sure foot and clever trail head that he has."

She reached out to lace fingers in the puff of long hair on the pony's neck. He gave another vigorous nod and snorted.

"If you have spices—or meadowsweet for linens—" Almadis had an odd feeling that she did not want this girl to disappear. A new face in l'Estal was always to be hoped for, and this wayfarer was so different. She had kept stealing glances at the bouquet on the staff. It seemed so real, as if, at times, it had the power of taking on the freshness it had when each of those blossoms had been plunked.

"Your flowers, Herbgatherer, what art gives the dried the seeming of life?"

"It is an art, my lady, an ancient one of my own people. In here"—Meg drew her hand down the side of one of those bulging panniers, "I have others. They be part of my trade stock. Also scents such as your meadowsweet—"

"Then surely I shall be seeing you again, Herbgatherer," Almadis said. "A good rest to you and your companions."

"My lady, such wishes are seeds for greater things—"

"As are ill wishes!" Osono said. "Do some of your wares come perhaps from Farlea?"

Meg turned now that measuring look to the bard.

"Farlea is sung of, sir bard. If it ever existed, that was many times ago. No, I do not aspire to the arts of the Fair Ones, only to such knowledge as any herbwife can know, if she seeks always to learn more."

Now it was her turn to move away, following Forina. Kaska had settled down again in her basket until only those mismatched tips of ears showed. But there were those who had been in the crowd at the gate who trailed the girl at a distance as if they did not want to lose sight of her for some reason.

"Farlea, Osono? I think with that question you may have displeased our herbwife," Almadis said slowly. "You are a storer of legends; which do you touch on now?"

He was frowning. "On the veriest wisp of an old one, my lady. There was a tale of a youth who followed my own calling, though he was of a roving bent. He vanished for a time, and then he returned hollow-eyed and wasted, saying that he sought something he had lost, or rather had thrown away through some foolishness, and that his fate was harsh because of that. He had been offered a way into a land of peace and rare beauty, and thereafter he sang always of Farlea. But he withered and died before the year was done, eaten up by his sorrow."

"But what makes you think of Farlea when you look upon this herbwife?" Almadis persisted.

"Those flowers on her staff—fresh plucked." His frown grew deeper.

"So I, too, thought when first I saw them. But no, they are rather very cleverly dried so that they are preserved with all their color, and I think their scent. Surely I smelled roses when she held them out a little. That is an art worth the knowing. We have no gardens here—the rose walk gives but a handful of blooms, and those are quickly gone. To have a bouquet of such ever to hand"— her voice trailed off wistfully and then she added—" yes, such could even fight the grim aging of these walls. I must go to the market when she sets up her stall."

Meg did set up her stall on the following day. From the market mistress she rented the three stools and a board to balance on two of them, to form the humblest of the displays. Mathe, who oversaw the trading place, watched the girl's sure moves in adjusting the plank to show her wares. He lingered even a fraction longer, though it was a busy day, to see her unpack bundles of dried herbs, their fragrance even able to be scented over the mixed odors, few of them pleasant, which were a part of market day.

There were packets also of yellowish, fine-woven cloth which gave forth even more intensified perfumes, and small, corner wrapped, bits of thin parchment such as were for the keeping of seeds. While in the very middle of that board was given honored place to that same bunch of flowers as had crowned Meg's trail staff.

Kaska's basket was set on the pavement behind the rude table. And Mors stood behind. The cat made no attempt to get out of her basket, but she was sitting well up in it surveying all about her with manifest interest.

Two small figures moved cautiously toward the stall. Beneath the grimed skin and the much-patched clothing, one face was the exact match of the other. Between them strutted a goat, each of his proud curl of horns clasped by a little, rough-skinned hand.

They proceeded slowly, darting glances to either side as if they were scouts in enemy territory. Only the goat was at ease, apparently confident in his ability to handle any situation which might arise.

"You—Tay—Tod—take that four-legged abomination out of here!" A man arose from the stoop behind one of the neighboring stalls and waved his arms.

The goat gave voice in a way which suggested that he was making a profane answer to that, and refused to answer to the force dragging at him from either side. The boys cowered, but it was apparent they had no idea of deserting their four-legged companion to run for cover.

Meg was on her feet also, smiling as if the two small herds and their beast were the most promising of customers. When her neighbor came from behind his own stall table, a thick stick in his hand, she waved him back.

"No harm, goodman," she said. "This beast but seeks what is a delicacy for his kind. Which he shall be freely given." She selected a stalk wrapped loosely around with its own withered leaves and held it out to the goat. For a moment he regarded her and then, with the neat dexterity of one who had done this many times before, he tongued the proffered bit of dried stuff and drew it into his mouth, nodding his head up and down, as if to signify his approval, with a vigor to near shake free the grip of his two companions.

The other tradesman stared, his upraised club falling slowly to his side. But there was a wariness in his look when he shifted his glance toward Meg. Then he withdrew behind his own table, as if he wished some barrier against a threat he did not truly understand.

However, Meg paid no attention to him. Rather now, she reached behind her and brought out a coarse napkin from which she unrolled thick slices of bread with green-veined cheese between—the food she had brought for her nooning.

Two pairs of small eyes fastened upon that, as she broke the larger of the portion in half, holding it out to the boys. Though they did not entirely loose their hold on the goat's horns, their other hands shot out to snatch what she held, cramming it into their mouths as if they feared that it might be demanded back.

"Tay—Tod." She spoke the names the man had spoken.

The one to her right gave a gulp that left him choking, but his twin was the quicker to answer. "I be Tod, lady—this be Tay."

"And your friend—" Meg nodded gravely to the goat, as if indeed the beast were a person of two-legged consequence.

"He be Nid!" There was pride in that answer such as a liege man might show in naming his lord.

"Well met, Tod, Tay, and Nid," Meg nodded gravely. "I am Meg, and here are my friends, Kaska and Mors." The cat only stared, but the pony uttered a soft neigh.

A valiant swallow had carried the food down, and Tay was able to speak:

"Lacy-lorn"— he gestured toward the bouquet of dried flowers— "But too cold now—" He shook his head.

"Lacy-lorn," Meg repeated with a note of approval in her voice, "and hearts-ease, serenity, and love-light, Kings-silver, Red-rose, Gold-for-luck, Sorrows end, Hope-in-the-sun—maiden's love, and knight's honor, yes." The old country names came singingly from her as if she voiced some bard's verse.

"Bright—" Tod said before he stuffed his mouth with another huge bit.

"You see them bright?" Meg's head was cocked a little to one side. "That is well, very well. Now, younglings, would you give me some service? My good Mors needs some hay for his nooning, and we had too much to carry from the inn to bear that also. Can you bring me such? Here is the copper for Mistress Forina."

"Nid—" began Tod hesitantly.

"Nid will bide here, and there will be no trouble." There was complete assurance in her answer.

Tod took the proffered coin and with his twin shot off across the marketplace. Meg turned to the man who had warned off the boys and the goat.

"Of whose household are those two, if you please, goodman?"

He snorted. "Household? None would own such as those two. Oh, they make themselves useful as herds. They be the only ones as can handle beast Nid," he shot a baneful glance at the goat. "Three of a kind they be, stealing from stalls and making trouble."

"But they are but children."

The man flushed, there was that he could read in her voice and eyes which he did not like.

"There are a number such. We had the green-sick here three seasons agone. Many died, and there were tireless hearths left. Mistress Forina, she gives them leftovers and lets them sleep in the hay at the stable. More fool she; they are a plaguey lot." He turned away abruptly as a woman approached his stall, glad to have done with Meg's questions.

The goat had shifted to one side and touched noses with Mors. Kasha gave a fastidious warn-off hiss just as a thin man in a shabby cloak paused before Meg's narrow table.

He was eyeing the flowers.

"I thought them real." He spoke as if to himself.

"Real, they are, good sir. But this is what you wish—for your daughter." Meg's hand was already on a small packet. "Steep it in apple ale, and let her have it each morning before she breaks her fast."

"But—herbwife—you did not ask me—I did not tell—"

"You saw," Meg answered slowly and firmly, as one might speak to a child learning its letters, "and I am a healer. We all have gifts, good sir. Even as you have yours. Out of love of learning, you have striven hard and given much—"

Never taking his eyes from hers, he fumbled in the pouch at his belt and brought out a coin.

"Herbwife, I know not what you are—but there is good in what you do, of that I am sure. Just as"—his eyes had dropped as if against his will to the flowers and he gave a start—" just as those are real! Yet it is out of season, and some I have not seen for long. For such grew once in a garden eastward where I can no longer go. I thank you."

Meg was busy with the bouquet, freeing from its tight swathering a spike of flower violet-red. As she held it up, it did in truth seem to be fresh plucked.

"This for your hearth-home, scholar. May it bring you some ease of heart for not all memories are ill ones."

He seemed unable for a moment or two to realize that she meant it. And when he took it between two fingers, he was smiling.

"Lady, how can one thank—"

Meg shook her head. "Thanks are worth the more when passed along. You had one who has given much, scholar—therefore to you shall be given in turn. Remember this well"—and there was force in those words.

It was almost as if he were so bemused by the flowers that he did not hear her. For he did not say one word in farewell as he turned away from her stall.

Those shadows awakened in the afternoon from the walls about the market square were growing longer when Almadis came. As usual Osono was at her side, and behind her Urgell. Though she had been free of l'Estal since childhood, taking no maids with her, it was insisted that she ever have some guard. And usually the armsmaster took that duty upon himself.

There were feuds brought into l'Estal, for men of power arose and fell in the lowlands, and sometimes a triumphant enemy suffered the same fate as his former victim. Lord Jules had been a mighty ruler of a quarter of Klem before his enemies had brought him down. His lordship became this single mountain hold, instead of leading armies he rode with patrols to keep the boundaries against the outlaws of the western heights; his palace was this maze of ancient cold and crooked walls, and warrens of rooms. But he was still remembered and feared, and there were those who would reach him even if they must do so through his only child.

So Urgell went armed, and Almadis carried in her sleeve a knife with which she was well trained. There was a sword also sheathed by Osono's side, though as a bard he supposedly had safe conduct wherever he might go. Might go—that was no longer true—there was only l'Estal. No man or woman asked of another what had brought one to exile here, so Almadis did not know the past tale of either of the men pacing with her now, but that they were of honor and trust she was sure, and she welcomed their company accordingly.

Meg's stall had been a popular one this day. Most of those coming to buy had been dealt with briskly, but there were some with whom she spoke with authority, and twice more she had drawn flowers from that bouquet and given them to the amazement of those with whom she dealt. So it had been with Vill Blacksmith, who had come seeking herbs known to be helpful against a burn such as his young apprentice had suffered. He went off with not only his purchase, but a sprig of knight's honor, gold bright in the hand of his bonnet. And there was Brydan the embroideress, who wished a wash for aching eyes, and received also a full-blown heart's-ease, purple and gold as a fine lady's gem when she fastened it to the breast of her worn gray gown.

Oddly enough it seemed that, though Meg plundered her bouquet so from time to time, it did not appear to shrink in size. Her neighbor began to watch her more closely, and his frown became a sharp crease between his eyes. Now and again his own hand arose to caress a certain dark-holed stone which hung from a dingy string about his throat, and once he muttered under his breath while he fingered that.

He was the first to sight Almadis and her companions, and his frown became a sickly kind of smile, though there was no reason to believe the Castellan's daughter would be interested in his withered roots of vegetables, the last remaining from the winter stores.

Indeed she crossed the market as one with a definite mission in mind, heading straight to Meg's stand.

"Goodwill to you," she said. "I trust that trade has been brisk for you. We have but very few here who follow such a calling."

Meg did not curtsey, but smiled as one who greets an old friend.

"Indeed, lady, this is a fair market, and I have been well-suited in bargaining. We spoke of meadowsweet for the freshening before times—"

"Lad's Love—dove's wings"— Osono paid no attention to the women, his was all for the bouquet— "Star fast—"

"Falcon feather!" Urgell's much harsher voice cut across the smooth tones of the bard.

"You are well learned, good sirs," Meg returned, and her hand hovered over the bouquet. "Those are names not common in these parts."

Osono's gaze might be aimed at the flowers, but yet it was as if he saw beyond them something else—as might grow in a meadow under that full, warm sun, which never even in summer seemed to reach into these stark heights.

Meg's fingers plucked and brought forth a stem on which swung two white blooms, star-pointed. She held that out to the bard, and he accepted it as one in a dream. Then she snapped thumb and forefinger together with more vigor and freed a narrow leaf, oddly colored so that it indeed resembled a feather.

"For you also, warrior." And her words held something of an order, as if to make sure he would not refuse. Then she spoke to Almadis:

"Meadowsweet, yes." She swept up a bundle of leaves and wrapped them expertly in a small cloth. "But something else also, is it not so?"

"Red-rose," Almadis said slowly. "My mother strove to grow a bush, but this land is too sere to nurture it. Red-rose—"

The flower Meg handed her was not full opened yet, and when Almadis held it close to her, she could smell a perfume so delicate that she could hardly believe such could come into the grayness that was l'Estal.

"Herbwife," she leaned a little forward, "who are you?"

"Meg, my lady, a dealer—a friend—"

Almadis nodded. "Yes, of a certainty that."

She brought out her purse. "For the meadowsweet"—she laid down one of the coins.

"Just so," Meg agreed. "For the meadowsweet."

Osono was fumbling at his own purse with one hand, the other carefully cupping the starflower. Then he caught Meg's eye, and flushed. Instead he bowed as he might to the lady of some great hall where he had been night's singer.

"My thanks to you—herbwife."

Urgell's bow was not so low or polished, but there was a lightening of his harsh features. "And mine also, mistress—your gifts have a value beyond price."

There were others who sought the herb dealer after the castle's lady had departed. But few of them were favored with a gift of bloom. Perhaps six in all bore away a leaf or flower, but still the bouquet appeared to grow no smaller. When Meg, in the beginning twilight, gathered up her wares and repacked them, two small figures appeared.

Behind them still ambled their horned and bewiskered companion. For the second time Nid touched noses with Mors, who was hardly taller than he. And Kaska voiced a small hiss.

"Help you, mistress?" Tay shuffled a bare foot back and forth in the straw which strewed the market square in marketing days.

"But of course. Many hands make light of work." Meg swung one of her cord-tied bundles to the boy, and he hurried to fit it into the panniers, which his brother had already placed on Mors.

"You are not out with the herds, youngling?" she added as she picked up as the last of her supplies, that bouquet.

Tod hung his head. "They will not have Nid now—he fought with Whrit, and they say he has too bad a temper—that any of his get are not wanted. They—set the dogs on us and Nid savaged two, so—so they talk now of—" He gulped and his brother continued:

"They talk of killing him, mistress."

"But he is yours?"

Both small faces turned toward hers, and there was a fierce determination in the chorus of their answer.

"Before times, he was herd leader, mistress. When Lan, our brother, was herder. But"—now their voices faltered—" Lan died of the green-sick. And the herd went to Finus—they said as how Lan had told him so—that we were too young. And Finus—he said as how there was much owed him by Lan, and that he had the rights. Only Nid would come with us, and he stayed. But—" Tod stopped as if to catch breath, however Tad's words gushed on:

"They won't let us to the pasture anymore. Finus, he lives in our house and says it is his."

"What have you then as shelter?" asked Meg quietly. She was holding the flowers close to her, beneath her chin, as if she breathed in for some purpose the faint scents.

"Inn mistress Forina—she lets us in the stable—but they say that Nid is bad for the horses."

"Not for this one," Meg nodded to Mors. "Let he and Nid bed down together, and we shall see what can be done."

They made a small procession of their own out of the marketplace. Meg carried the flowers and humped Kaska's basket up on one hip with the familiar gesture of a countrywoman bearing burdens. Mors trotted after her, no leading rein to draw him on, and he was matched by the goat, the two forming a guard, one to each side.

There were those who watched them go, narrow-eyed and sour of face. It would seem that just as there were those who had been drawn to the stall during that day, so also there were those who shunned it. Now a darker shadow moved forward to stand beside the stall which had neighbored Meg's.

"You have kept eye on her, goodman?" it hissed a question.

"I have, priest. There is that about her which is not natural, right enough. She is weaving spells, even as a noxious spider weaves a web. Already she has touched some here—"

"Those being?" The voice was hot, near exulting.

Now the stall keeper spoke names, and those names were oddly companioned—lady, bard, soldier, smith, scholar, needlewoman, a laborer in from one of the scanty hill farms, a gate sentry off duty, a washerwoman, the wife of a merchant and her daughter—

And with the speaking of each name, Thunur nodded his head. "You have done well, Danler, very well. Continue to watch here, and I shall search elsewhere. We shall bring down this slut who deals with the Dark yet! You are a worthy son of Gort, the Ever-Mighty."

Within the keep the ways were dark and damp as always. Though in some of the halls there were dank and moldy tapestries on the walls, no one had made any attempt to renew them, to bring any hint of color into those somber quarters. Even candles seemed here to have their halos of dim light circumscribed so that they could not reveal too much.

Almadis tugged at her heavy trained skirt with an impatient hand. She had but little time, and this was a way which had not been trodden for long. She could remember well her last visit here, when rage at all the world had seemed to heat her, she had felt none of the chill thrown off by the walls. The loss of her mother had weighed both heart and spirit.

Now the pallid light of her candle picked out the outline of the door she sought. But she had to set that on the floor and use both hands in order to force open the barrier, which damp had near sealed beyond her efforts.

Then she was in, candle aloft, looking about. No one had cared—there had probably been no one here since last she left. Yet the mustiness was still tinged with a hint of incense. The room was small, its floor covered with the rotting remnants of what had once been whortle reeds, which trodden upon, gave back sweet scent.

There was a single window, shuttered tight, a bar dropped firmly in place to hold it so. Beneath that stood a boxlike fixture which might be an altar.

That was shrouded with thick dust, a dust which clouded the round of once-polished mirror set there, gathered about the bases of three candlesticks.

For a long moment Almadis merely stood and looked at that altar and its furnishings. She had turned her back on what this stood for, told herself that there was nothing here beyond what she could see, touch, that to believe in more was folly—a child's folly. Yet her mother—

Slowly Almadis moved forward. There were still half-consumed candles in those sticks, grimed, a little lopsided. She used the one she carried to touch the wicks of those into life. Then, suddenly, she jerked her long scarf from about her shoulders, and, in spite of its fine embroidery, she used it to dust the mirror, dropping its grime-clogged stuff to the floor when she had done.

Lastly she turned to that window. Straining, she worked free the bar, threw back the shutter, and opened the room to the night, in spite of the wind which wove about this small side tower.

For so long it had not mattered what rode the sky; this night it did. And what was rising now was the full moon in all its brilliance and glory. Almadis returned to the altar. She could not remember the forms. Those other times she had merely repeated words her mother had uttered without regard for their meaning. There were only scraps which she could assemble now.

But she stationed herself before that mirror, leaning forward a little, her hands placed flat on either side. On its tarnished surface she could see reflected the light of the three candles—but nothing else. There was no representation of her own face—the once-burnished plate was too dim.

Nor had she that learning which could bring it alive. Yet she had been drawn here and knew that this had meaning, a meaning she dared not deny.

Tucked in the lacing of her bodice was that rose Meg had given her. Dried it might be—with great skill—yet it seemed to have just been plucked from a bush such as her mother had striven to keep alive.

The girl moistened her lips.

"One In Three," she began falteringly. "She who rules the skies, She who is maiden, wife, and elder in turn, She who answers the cries of her daughters in distress, who reaches to touch a land and bring it into fruitfulness, She who knows what truly lies within the heart—"

Almadis's voice trailed into silence. What right had she to ask for anything in this forsaken place, return to a faith she had said held no meaning?

There was certainly another shadow of something on the mirror—growing stronger. It was—the rose!

Almadis gasped, for a moment she felt light-headed, that only her hold on the altar kept her upright.

"Lady" — her voice was the thinnest of whispers — "Lady who was, and always will be—give me forgiveness. Your messenger—she must be one of your heart held— Lady, I am not fit—"

She raised her hands to that flower caught in her lacing. Yet something would not let her loosen it as she wished, to leave it as an offering here.

Instead there was the sweetness of the rose about her, as if each candle breathed forth its fragrance. She looked down—that flower which had been yet half a bud was now open.

Quickly, almost feverishly in her haste, Almadis reached again for the altar. There had been something else left there long ago. The dust had concealed it, but she found it. Her fingers caught the coil of a chain, and she held it up, from it swung that pendant—the flat oval of silver (but the silver was not tarnished black as it should have been) on it, in small, raised, milky white gems, the three symbols of the Lady in Her waxing, Her full life, Her waning.

It seemed to Almadis that the candlelight no longer was the illumination of that chamber, rather the moon itself shown within, brighter than she could remember it. She raised the chain, bowed her head a fraction, slipped those links over it, allowing the moon gem-set pendant to fall upon her breast. Then she did as she remembered her mother had always done, tucked it into hiding beneath her bodice, so that now the pendant rested between her breasts just under the rose. Though it did not carry the chill of metal to her flesh, it was rather warm, as if it had but been passed from one who had the right to wear it to another.

Now she gathered courage to speak again.

"Lady, you know what will be asked of me, and what is in me. I cannot walk my father's way—and he will be angry. Give me the strength and courage to remain myself in the face of such anger—though I know that by his beliefs he means me only well."

She leaned forward then, a kind of resolution manifest in her movements, to blow out the three candles. But she made no move to bar away the moonlight before she picked up her journey candle to leave the room.

✢

Though it was day without, the guardroom was grimly dusk within.

"Three of them we took," a brawny man in a rust-marked mail coat said to one of his fellows. He jerked a thumb at a rolled ball of hide. "Over the gate to the west he says."

The older man he addressed grunted. "We do things here by my Lord Jules's ordering."

"Don't be so free with words like that hereabouts, Ruddy," cautioned the other. "Our Knight-Captain has long ears—"

"Or more than one pair of them," retorted Ruddy. "We've got us more trouble than just a bunch of lousy sheep raiders, Jonas. While you've been out a-ridin', there's a stew boilin' here."

The bigger man leaned on the edge of the table. "Thunur, I'm thinkin'. That one came at dawn light a-brayin' somethin' about a witch. He's a big mouth, always yapping."

"To some purpose, Jonas, there's more n'more listen to him. An' you know well what happened below when those yelling 'Gort, come down' broke loose."

"Gods," snorted the city sergeant. "We be those all gods have forgot. Perhaps just as well, there was always a pother o' trouble below when priests stuck their claws into affairs. There are those here who are like to stir if the right spoon is thrust into the pot, too. Thunur is gettin' him a followin'— let him get enough to listen an' we'll be out with pikes, an' you'll remember outlaw hunting as somethin' as a day's good ramble."

"Well, I could do with a ramble—over to the Hafted Stone to wet m' 'gullet an' then to barracks an' m'bunk. His Honor is late—"

"Right good reason." A younger man turned from the group of his fellows by the door and leered. "Hear as how it was all to be fixed up for our Knight-Captain—wed and bed the lord's daughter—make sure that he is firm in the saddle for the time when m'lord don't take to ridin' anymore. They have a big feastin' tonight just to settle the matter, don't they?"

There was no time for an answer. Those by the door parted swiftly to allow another to enter. He was unhelmed, but wore mail, and over that a surcoat patterned with a snarling wolf head. His dark hair was cropped after the fashion of one who wore a helm often, and it was sleeked above a high forehead. The seam of a scar twisted one corner of his mouth, so that he seemed to sneer at the world around.

He was young for all of that, and once must have been handsome. His narrow beak of a nose gave him now the look of some bird of prey, an impression his sharp yellowish eyes did nothing to lighten. Otger, Knight-Captain under the Castellan, was no man to be taken lightly either in war or council. Now he stalked past the men who crowded back to give him room, as if they were invisible. Even Jonas pulled away quickly as his commander fronted Ruddy face-to-face.

"There is trouble, Town Sergeant?"

Ruddy had straightened. His face was as impassive as that of a puppet soldier.

"Sir, no more than ever. Th' priest of Gort is brayin' again. Some are beginnin' to listen. This mornin' he came here—"

"So!" Otger turned his head but a fraction. "Dismissed to the courtyard."

They were quick to go. Only Jonas and Ruddy remained. The knight regarded them with the hooded eyes of a predator biding time.

"He is still here?"

"Sir, he spilled forth such blather that I thought it best you hear. He speaks of those above him in a manner which is not fit."

Otger moved past him, seated himself on the single chair behind that table, as a giver of justice might install himself in court. His hand went to his cheek, the fingers tracing that scar. Jonas edged backward another step. That was always a trouble sign. Young as Otger was, he had gained such influence here as to be served swiftly.

It was the Castellan who had advanced him swiftly—and in a way, who could blame Lord Jules? The years spun by only too swiftly, and a man aged with them. The lord had no son—but there was a daughter. One wedding her would surely rule here. Those of the east plains would take no notice, if all was done properly, and there had been no exile of high blood now since Otger himself had ridden in as a gold-eyed youth five seasons back.

"Bring the priest," he ordered now. And Jonas went to fetch Thunur.

The man did not cringe as he came. Instead, he was bold at this fronting, his head up, and eyes blazing with the fire of the rage that always burned in him.

"I hear you wish to see me," Otger's gaze swept the fellow from head to foot and back again. Just so had he looked two days before at that wounded outlaw they had taken.

"Witchery, Sir. Foul witchery has come by the Way Wind into l'Estal. It must be routed out. Already it has ensorcelled many—many, Sir Knight. Among them"— Thunur paused for a moment to make his next statement

135

more portentous, "The Lady Almadis—"

"And who is this dealer in witchery?" Otger's voice was very calm. Ruddy hitched one shoulder. This priest would soon learn his lesson by all the signs.

Thus encouraged, Thunur spoke his tale, so swiftly that spittle accompanied the words he spewed forth. He ended with the listing of those who had borne away tokens of Meg's giving. And at the saying of some of those names, Otger's eyes narrowed a fraction.

"It is laid upon all true men and women to deal with witches as Gort has deemed right—with fire. This—this sluttish whore, and those brutes she brought with her—they must be slain. And those whom she has entoiled must be reasoned with 'less they too are tainted past cleansing."

"You name some who are above you, priest.

Tongues that wag too freely can be cut from jaws. I would advise you to take heed of the need of silence for now—"

"For now?" Thunur repeated slowly.

"For now." Otger arose. "You seem to have an eye for such matters. Out with you to use that eye, but not the tongue, mind you!"

Thunur blinked. And then he turned and went. But Otger spoke to Ruddy. "Have the patrol keep an eye to that one. I have seen his like before—they can be well used if they are handled rightly, but if they are not under rein, they are useless and must be removed."

The market was alive. Though some of the sellers noted that there were more men at arms making their ways leisurely among the booths. However, since the border patrol had just returned, that might be expected.

Again Meg had taken her place, Mors behind her and Kaska's basket carefully out of the way. Her bouquet centered her table board. But those who came to look over her stock this day did not seem to note it particularly, nor did she all the morning lose any bloom from it for gifting.

Tod and Tay came by just before the nooning bell and brought her a basket Forina had promised. This time Nid walked behind them, his heavy-horned head swinging from side to side, as if he wished to keep a close eye on all about.

Just as he stepped up to exchange polite nose taps with Mors, one of the guards halted before Meg's display. He had the weather-roughened and darkened skin of a man who had spent many years around and about, and there was a small emblem caught fast in the mail shirt he wore that marked his rank.

"Fair day to you, herbwife." He studied her, and then his eyes dropped to her wares. "You have Ill- bane, I see."

"You see and you wonder, Guard Sergeant? Why?"

She took up the bundle of leaves. "It stands against evil, does it not—ill of body, ill of mind. What do they say of it? That if those of dark purpose strive to touch it, they are like to find a brand laid across their rash fingers."

"You know what they say of you, then?"

Meg smiled. "They say many things of me, Guard Sergeant Ruddy. It depends upon who says it. I have already been called witch—"

"And that does not alarm you?"

"Guard Sergeant Ruddy, when you are summoned to some duty, would any words from those not your officers turn you aside?"

"Duty—" he repeated. "Herbwife, I tell you that you may well have a right to fear."

"Fear and duty often ride comrades. But fear is the shadow and duty the substance. Look you"—she had laid down the bundle of leaves, turned her hand palm-up to show the unmarked flesh, and carried that gesture on so that as his eyes followed they touched the bouquet.

"Rowan leaf and berry," he said.

"Such as grow in hedgerows elsewhere." Meg pulled out the stem to show a pair of prick defended leaves, a trefoil of berries.

Slowly he reached out and took it from her.

"Watch with care, herbwife." He did not tuck her gift into full sight as had the others who had taken such, but rather closed his fist tightly upon it and thrust that into his belt pouch.

Almadis stood by the window. One could catch a small sight of the market square from this vista. But she could not sight Meg's stall. She was stiff with anger, and yet she must watch her speech. It might be that she was caught at last, yet she could not bring herself to believe that.

"He rode in," she tried to keep her words even in tone, not make them such as could be used against her. "And with him he brought *heads*—heads of men! He would plant those as warnings! Warnings!"

"Against raiders, outlaws. They only understand such." That answering voice held weariness. "Their raids grow bolder—oftener. The land we hold, which supplies us with food, with that very robe you are wearing, cannot yield what we need when it is constantly under raid. Now, with the upper snows fast-going, we shall have them down upon us more and more. I know not what presses them these past few seasons, but they have grown bolder and bolder. We lost a farm to fire and sword—Otger collected payment. They deal in blood, thus we must also."

Almadis turned. "He is a man of blood," she said flatly.

"He holds the peace. You call him man of blood—well, and that he is in another way also. We are of ancient family, daughter—thrown aside though we may be. Rank weds with rank. Otger is the son of a House near equal to our own. Whom you wed will rule here afterward; he must be one born to such heritage. There is no one else."

She came to stand before her father where he sat in his high-back chair. And she was suddenly startled, then afraid. Somehow—somehow he had aged—and she had not seen it happening! He had always remained to her, until this hour, the strong leader l'Estal needed. He was old and to the old came death.

So for the moment she temporized. "Father, grant me a little more time. I cannot find it in me to like Otger—give me a little time." Her fingers were at her breast pressing against the hidden pendant, caressing the rose which still held both color and fragrance.

"Where got you that flower, Almadis?" There was a sharpness in his tone now.

Swiftly she told him of Meg, brought by the Way Wind, and of her stall in the market.

"I have heard a tale of witchery," he returned.

"Witchery? Do some then listen to that mad priest?" Almadis was disturbed. "She came with the Way Wind—from the west—she brings herbs such as we cannot grow—for the soothing of minds and bodies. She is but a girl, hardly more than a child. There is no evil in her!"

"Daughter, we are a people shunned, broken from our roots. There is shame, pain, anger eating at many of us. Such feelings are not easily put aside. And in some they take another form, seeking one upon whom blame may be thrown, one who may be made, after a fashion, to pay for all that which has caused us ill. Eyes have seen, ears have heard, lips reported—there are those who cry, witchery, yes. And very quickly such rumors can turn to action. This Meg may be a harmless trader—she may be the cause of an uprising. There is the ancient law for the westerners, one which we seldom invoke but which I turn to now—not only for the sake of town peace but for her safety also. This is the third day in the market—by sundown—"

Almadis swallowed back the protest she would have cried out. That her father spoke so seriously meant that indeed there might be forces brewing who take fire in l'Estal. But on sudden impulse, she did say:

"Let me be the one to tell her so. I would not have her think that I have been unmindful of her gift." Once more she touched the rose.

"So be it. Also let it be that you think carefully on what else I have said to you. Time does not wait. I would have matters settled for your own good and for my duty."

So once more Almadis went down to the market and with her, without her asking, but rather as if they understood her unhappiness about this matter, there came Osono and Urgell. She noted in surprise that the bard had his harp case riding on his shoulder, as if he were on the way to some feast, and that Urgell went full armed.

It was midday, and Almadis looked about her somewhat puzzled for the usual crowd of those in the market, whether they came to buy and sell, or merely to spend time, was a small one. The man whose stall had neighbored Meg's was gone, and there were other empty spaces. Also there was a strange feeling which she could not quite put name to.

Ruddy, the guard sergeant, backed by two of his men, were pacing slowly along the rows of stalls. Now Urgell came a step forward so that he was at Almadis's right hand. His head was up, and he glanced right and left. Osono shifted the harp case a little, pulling loose his cloak so that the girl caught sight of his weapon, a span of tempered blade between a dagger and a sword in length.

If there had been a falling away of the crowd, that was not so apparent about the stall where Meg was busied as she had been since she first came into l'Estal. But those who had drifted toward her were a very mixed lot. Almadis recognized the tall bulk of the smith, and near shoulder to him was Tatwin, the scholar, his arm about the shoulders of a slight girl whose pale face suggested illness not yet past, while by her skirts trotted a small shaggy dog with purpose which seemed even more sustained than that of the two it accompanied.

There was also, somewhat to Almadis's surprise, Forina of the inn, and behind her wide bulk of body came Tod and Tay, once more grasping the horns of Nid with the suggestion about them that they were not going to lose touch with that four-footed warrior.

Others, too, a shambling-footed laborer from the farmlands, with one hand to the rope halter of a drooping-headed horse that might have drawn far too many carts or plows through weary seasons.

Just as they gathered, so did others in the marketplace draw apart. That feeling of menace which had been but a faint touch when Almadis trod out on this cobbled square grew.

There was movement in the alleyways, the streets, which led into that square. Others were appearing there who did not venture out into the sunlight.

Urgell's hand was at sword hilt. Almadis quickened pace to reach Meg's stall.

"Go! Oh, go quickly!" she burst out. "I do not know what comes, but there is evil rising here. Go while you can!"

Meg had not spread out her bundles of herbs. Now she looked to the Castellan's daughter and nodded. She picked up her staff and set to the crown of it the bouquet of flowers. The twins suddenly loosed their hold on Nid and pushed behind the board of the stall, shifting the panniers to Mors's back. Meg stooped and caught up the basket in which Kaska rode, settled it firmly within her arm crook.

"Witch—get the witch!" The scream arose from one of the alley mouths.

In a moment, Vill was beside Urgell, and Almadis saw that he carried with him his great hammer. Osono had shifted his harp well back on his shoulder to give him room for weapon play. There were others, too, who moved to join that line between Meg and the sulkers in the streets and alleys.

"To the gate," Almadis said. "If you bide with me, they will not dare to touch you!" She hoped that was true. But to make sure that these who threatened knew who and what she was and the protection she could offer, she pushed back her cloak hood that her face might be readily seen.

"To the gate," Ruddy appeared with his armsmen, added the authority of his own to the would-be defenders.

They retreated, all of them, bard, mercenary, smith, sergeant forming a rear guard. Only before the gate there were others—

A line of men drawn up, men who had been hardened by the riding of the borders, Otger's chosen. Before them stood the Knight-Captain himself.

"My lady," he said as they halted in confusion. "This is no place for you."

Almadis's hand went to Meg's arm. "Sir, if you come to give protection, that is well. But this much I shall do for myself, see an innocent woman free of any wrong—"

"You give me no choice then—" He snapped his fingers, and his men moved in, he a stride ahead plainly aiming to reach Almadis himself.

"Sir Knight," Almadis's hand was on her breast, and under it the moon token was warm. "I come not at your demand or that of any man, thank the *Lady*, save at a wish which is my own."

Otger's twisted mouth was a grimace of hate, and he lunged.

Only—

From the staff Meg held, there blazed a burst of rainbow-hued light. Otger and those with him cried out, raising their hands to their eyes and stumbled back. From behind Almadis and Meg moved Mors and Nid, the ancient horse, whose head was now raised, and those three pushed in among the guard, shouldering aside men who wavered and flailed out blindly.

Then Almadis was at the gate, and her hands were raised to the bar there. Beside her was the scholar, and with more force than either of them came Forina. And they came out into the crisp wind without the walls, the very momentum of their efforts carrying them into the mouth of the Way Wind road.

There were cries behind them, and the screeching of voices, harsh and hurting. Almadis looked behind. All their strangely constituted party had won through the gates, the rear guard walking backward. Urgell and Osono had both drawn steel, and the smith held his hammer at ready. There were improvised clubs, a dagger or two, Ruddy's pike, but none were bloodied. Urgell and Ruddy, the smith beside them, slammed the gates fast.

Almadis could still hear the shouting of Otger, knew that they had perhaps only moments before they would be overwhelmed by those who were ready for a hunt.

Meg swung up her staff. There was no wide burst of light this time—rather a ray as straight as a sword blade. It crisscrossed the air before them, leaving behind a shimmer of light the width of the road, near as high as the wall behind them.

As she lowered her staff, she raised her other hand in salute to that shimmer, as if there waited behind it someone or thing she held in honor.

Then she spoke, and, though she did not shout, her words cried easily over the clamor behind them.

"Here is the Gate of Touching. The choice now lies with you all. There will be no hindrance for those going forward. And if you would go back, you shall find those behind will accept you again as you are.

"Those who come four-footed are comrades—the choice being theirs also. For what lies beyond accepts all life of equal worth. The comradeship of heart is enough.

"The choice is yours, so mote it be!"

She stood a little aside to give room, and Tod and Tay, laying hands once more to Nid's horns, went into the light. Behind them, his hand on the old horse's neck, the laborer trod, head up and firmly. Almadis stood beside Meg and watched them pass. None of them looked to her or Meg, it was as if they were drawn to something so great they had no longer only any knowledge of themselves, only of it.

At last there were those of the rear guard. Osono and Vill did not glance toward her. But Urgell, whose sword was once more within its sheath, dropped behind. Somehow her gaze was willed to meet his. The leaf Meg had given him was set in his battered helm as a plume, the plume that a leader might wear to some victory.

Almadis stirred. She stepped forward, to lay her hand on the one he held out to her, as if they would tread some formal pattern which was long woven into being.

Meg steadied Kaska's basket on her hip and looked up to the glimmer as Castellan's daughter and mercenary disappeared.

"Is it well-done, *Lady?*"

"It is well-done, dear daughter. So mote it be!"

With staff and basket held steady, Meg went forward, and when she passed the gate of light it vanished. The Way lay open once again to the scouring of the wind.

BLACK IRISH
From The Boys' World, Vol. 38, No. 51,
(December 17, 1939)

As one man the students were on their feet. Cheek against the ice sprawled
Charteris, Junior Academy's ace defense man. Looming above him another
skater wearing academy colors attempted to swerve, but, as if that body
huddled on the rink were a magnet, he stumbled and went down with a crash
over Charteris' outflung arm.

"You meant that, Mohun!"

Dazedly Neil Mohun watched the thick scarlet stream dribble from the
ragged tear in Charteris' hockey glove. He shook his head, trying to clear it
of the mist between his eyes and the slashed leather.

"No, I didn't," he denied slowly. But then the rest of the team was upon
them and Mohun found himself on the edge of the solicitous group about
Charteris. No one had listened to him.

Back in the dressing room Neil tugged his sweater over his head. He
winced as the fabric scraped across a swelling lump. Somewhere behind his
eyes there was a dull ache.

Surely Charteris wouldn't believe that Neil had deliberately taken that
spill. Why, their feud was a sort of class joke. Only yesterday Anderson had

made some fool remark about Neil's "fixing" Charteris before they entered the fencing finals. Just because they had been rivals in sport and classroom since their first days at Junior Academy, they were supposed to be deadly enemies. But, of course, they weren't!

Neil paused, his shirt half on. If Charteris stuck to that absurd story of his there might be trouble. Charteris was popular, more popular than the reserved Mohun could ever be.

With his dark head held high Neil strode back to the dormitory. From certain Down County ancestors he had inherited a liking for meeting trouble head on.

The halls were unusually empty. A single freshman pelted up the stairs at the required double, casting a somewhat awed glance at the upper classman as he passed. Athlete Mohun moved in exalted heights a frosh hardly dared to dream about.

Neil entered his room. The bleak severity of its regulation furnishings seemed even more angular in the light he snapped on. He crossed the room to change the entry on his absence card. A place for every man, and every man in that place, thought Neil, might well be the academy's private motto. Sleeping, waking, working, playing, the authorities knew where every student was every minute of the day. There was no such thing as privacy. He leaned his aching head against the cool pane of the window. It would be nice to have a little uninterrupted peace and quite right now.

"Neil, what happened down at the rink? It's all over the school that you lost your temper and half murdered Charteris!" Jimmie Doran stormed into the room, demanding the attention of his roommate.

Mohun grinned crookedly. "Even allowing for the romantic additions of amateur news-gatherers, that is a bit steep," he commented. "We had an accident. Charteris tripped, I tried to avoid him, was clumsy and ended by falling myself. I slashed one of his hands with my skate. He chose to believe that I did it purposely."

Jimmie's round face was grave. "Is that what Charteris said?"

"Yes. Pleasant, isn't it?"

"He's crazy!" stated Jimmie with conviction. "No one would do a thing like that—"

"Apparently they"—Neil made a comprehensive gesture which included the quarters—" think that I could."

"But why didn't you tell them—"

"I tried. They wouldn't listen to me. I'll see Charteris at the hospital tonight. He may change his story."

"And if he doesn't?"

"It may be—nasty."

Jimmie shook his head. "I don't like it. Anderson is hot-headed."

"He's been talking?" asked Neil quietly. The pain in his head was pounding again. It was difficult to understand what Jimmie was saying.

"Too much. Watch out, Neil. The council has a way of making it unpleasant for a man."

Mohun stiffened. There was a pinched look about his nostrils, a line about his firm mouth. "You mean they would 'silence' me, refuse to speak to me except officially?"

"Men have been 'silenced,'" Jimmie met Neil's level gaze.

"Until they broke. I know." There was something grim about the set of Neil's square jaw. "But I'm not guilty, and neither am I very breakable—as they shall discover if they try that. But they wouldn't dare. I'm going to see Charteris."

He was breathing rather fast when he reached the hospital—less from his walk than from the uncomfortable feeling that perhaps Jimmie's apprehensions were well founded and there was something to fear. To fear! Neil's shoulders went back as he unconsciously braced himself to face what might come.

"Dr. Harnett," he caught sight of the senior physician, "how is Charteris, sir?"

"He'll do. Took five stitches in that hand of his. Nasty cut and he'll have to watch it: liable to tear it open before it's healed if he uses it. Odd, never saw a skate cut like that before, clean as if it had been done with a knife."

"May I see Charteris, sir?" asked Neil impatiently.

The doctor shook his head. "He's had something to make him forget hockey for awhile. That's a bad bump you have there yourself. Better let me see it."

In spite of Neil's protests he was borne off to be treated. And it wasn't until after mess that he reached the haven of his room again.

"See Charteris?" demanded Jimmie almost before Neil was across the threshold.

"Couldn't. Doc wouldn't let me in."

"Anderson is talking," began Jimmie.

"He seems to make a habit of it," replied Neil wearily, and reached for a book. He was very tired of Charteris, Anderson, and the whole mess. His head ached and he wanted nothing so much as to crawl into bed and forget everything.

"Mohun!"

Neil looked up. Just within the door stood Anderson. Behind him were his usual companions, Crawford and Hendriks.

"Well?" Neil was not cordial.

"We want to see you." They were already in the room. Hendriks closed the door, standing with his back against its panels. As if, thought Neil for one amused second, I might try to escape.

"We have something to say to you," began Anderson. His flat mouth was really too wide for his narrow jaw, decided Neil critically. And why did he keep moistening his lips that way?

"Why don't you say it?" prompted Mohun.

"The students," Anderson complied, "want an explanation of what happened on the rink."

"The students," prodded Jimmie, "or just you and your friends?"

Again Anderson's tongue flickered over his thin lips. "I speak for the students," he retorted.

"Ha, a distinguished guest," Jimmie waved him toward one of the cots. "In your official capacity have a seat."

"Anderson!" A core of steel sounded in Neil's voice. "I have no explanation to make to you or your friends. What happened today is my business and Charteris'. We'll settle it without outside interference."

"You're making a mistake, Mohun," warned the other.

"Not interested."

"You may be in the future!" Anderson's long face was pale and he could not conceal the angry tremble in his tone.

Neil arose leisurely and came around the table, his six feet topping Anderson by a good two inches.

"I prefer to handle my private affairs privately. Do you understand English, Anderson? Or do you want to meet me at the gym and take a lesson in language—and manners?"

Anderson's smile was three-quarters sneer. "You're a fool, Mohun, if you think anyone would accept a challenge from you—now."

Neil stared at him. And then he moved. As Anderson's head snapped back from his blow, Neil Mohun laughed.

As Anderson stumbled away between two supporters, Jimmie turned upon Mohun.

"You've done it," he accused. "They've got you just where they want you."

"It's my business," flared Neil, "and I'll handle it!"

"Do!" snapped Jimmie. "How long do you think it will take Anderson to spread his tale—with additions of his own? Remember that crack he made about your 'fixing' Charteris before the fencing finals? Suppose he repeats that now?"

"I like a fight—"

"You've got one," Jimmie told him morosely.

"There will be a meeting of the class at four o'clock today." The announcement rang in Neil's ears long after the speaker had finished. He marched to mess still thinking about it.

"What, Mr. Dumbjohn," Upperclassman Kimberly inquired of the humblest frosh at the table, "is the most important athletic event of the coming week?"

"The fencing finals, sir."

Kimberly coughed as Neil looked up.

"Why?" asked Mohun.

"I—I do not know, sir," the frosh suddenly lost his nerve and glanced appealingly at Kimberly.

"Surely, Mr. Durcourt, after that prompt reply you have some idea upon the subject?"

The freshman did not answer. Neil smiled pleasantly. "One might almost believe," he suggested, "that Mr. Durcourt's recitation was coached."

"I don't care for your attitude, Mohun," said Kimberly as they arose from the table. "But I think I shall leave the council to deal with you."

"I have heard that the black Irish hold grudges but to do what Mohun did—"

Neil stepped well within the room where Anderson was holding forth. "As the black Irishman under discussion," he interrupted, "perhaps I may be allowed a few words."

"You had your chance for an explanation, Mohun," Shaffer, the class president, frowned at him, "and you chose to refuse. We don't like your attitude, and we don't like the whole affair. What have you to say for yourself?"

Neil's jaws set squarely. Shaffer's irritated impatience added to the affair of the mess hall only confirmed his stubbornness. "I say that the matter is a private one."

"I'm afraid we can't accept that—"

"Then don't!" Neil's fists clenched. "Do as you please, I am not answerable to the class." He walked out of the room.

"Well?" he demanded when Jimmie joined him.

"What could you expect, you stupid fool? They've voted to 'silence' you."

Mohun laughed harshly. "Good enough." He shrugged and went on his way.

"Charteris came back from the hospital today," Jimmie ventured one evening. "And I don't think he was any too pleased with Anderson's efforts on his behalf. He tried to talk to some of the fellows—"

"I'm not interested in Charteris," Neil returned curtly.

The days slid swiftly into weeks as the lines between Neil's eyes grew deeper and his sullen stubbornness became more and more a part of him.

Students who had qualified in riding and were on the selected list might explore the reservation bridle paths. Neil, since his trouble, had taken full advantage of this. Once away from the academy he could forget a little of what had happened to him since that disastrous spill on the rink.

He drew reign as he glanced down the valley. Just how had the present state of affairs come about anyway? His dislike of Anderson, Charteris' story, his loss of temper—they all added up. But why—

With a snort of pain Neil's horse reared, pawing the air with its front hoofs.

Mohun clung with knee and thigh, using sheer wrist strength to bring the frantic animal under control. As the horse obeyed, a snicker of laughter came from behind. Neil crashed through the thin underbrush in the direction of the sound. Two small boys scuttled away.

"Johnny Carruthers!" Neil recognized the tow-headed youngster known in the district as "the worst boy in the countryside." Nor did he miss the bean shooter in Johnny's fist. But Johnny and his companion escaped.

Furious at the thought of what might have been—horse and rider over the cliff—Neil started back down trail. That Carruthers kid needed a talking to.

Halfway down, Neil met another rider. Charteris drew to the side of the path. As Mohun cantered by, Charteris leaned forward in the saddle as if to speak. But when Neil's eyes flicked over him with no sign of recognition, he settled back again.

Mohun rode on at a slower pace, allowing the horse to choose its own gait. Why was Charteris riding? If what the doc had said was true, he had little practical use of his left hand and that roan brute he was on needed both hands and the full attention of any rider fool enough to bestride him.

Neil made a quick decision and urged his reluctant mount back up the slope. If Johnny Carruthers was still in action … At a shout from above Mohun used his spurs. Under their tormenting prick the black bounded on, its hoofs drumming on the path.

"Hold on!" the Irishman shouted. In the clearing a whirling, maddened horse neared the edge of the cliff, his rider tugging fruitlessly at the reins. Neil eased his feet out of the stirrups.

Then he lunged, his hands closing about the reins of the roan. He gritted his teeth as a pawing hoof scraped his knee, ripping cloth and drawing blood. But a hundred and seventy-eight pounds of dead weight at its head brought the horse to terms.

Neil sprawled on his back, the sweating animal almost on him. Then Charteris slid out of the saddle.

"Hurt?"

"Not seriously," Neil panted. "But I'd like to break Johnny Carruthers' neck. The little beast is back in the woods shooting beans at the horses."

"What!" Charteris started for the trees, a purposeful look about him.

"No use, he's gone by now," Neil called. "He tried the same trick on me."

Charteris turned. "Is that why you followed me?"

Neil hesitated and then nodded. "Yes, I knew you couldn't use your hand."

Charteris stooped to pick up Neil's hat. "I am beginning to think that there are other fools besides Johnny Carruthers around here," he announced.

Neil puzzled that out, and then, in spite of the throbbing of his bruised knee, he laughed. "Is this a pipe of peace, Charteris?"

The other grinned. "Would I dare offer you one? Seriously, Mohun, I never honestly thought that you slashed me on purpose, not after I had time to cool down. But by then the damage was done. When I tried to tell the truth, the others thought I was just being a good sport!" he spat out the last two words as if they hurt him. "I wanted to see you, but Doran warned me off—said you were too bitter. I had Anderson to thank for that. I shall have something to say to Anderson. But at least I've learned to hold my tongue."

"I've had a few lessons too," Neil accepted Charteris' help to get to his feet. "I may be black Irish but I think I shall disappoint Anderson—and others—by refusing to hold a grudge."

Charteris led up their horses. "Shall we join the others?" He pointed with his chin toward the valley.

For the first time in many long weeks, sparks of mischief shone in Neil's eyes. "I would," he said with slow satisfaction, "like nothing better."

THE BOY AND THE OGRE

Golden Magazine for Boys and Girls Volume 3 No. 9
(September 1966)

A folktale based on original sources.

In the old days when one could still find ogres living here and there about the countryside—and very disagreeable creatures they were, too, I can assure you, with their eating people and suchlike deeds—a boy and his mother lived in a tumbledown cottage not far from just such an ogre.

Now the ogre had a very fine house, but the boy and his mother were very poor. Often there was not even a dried crust of bread or a rind of cheese to be found in their cupboard. And no mouse ever thought of coming inside their door.

But the ogre was so rich that if he began to count the gold pieces in his moneybags on one Saturday and he did not leave off counting until the next, he would still have some left lying about unnumbered. And in his house there was no lack of good things to eat—that I can tell you. An ox roasted whole, or half a dozen turkeys baked together in a pie–that was only a trifle for the ogre, to say nothing of cakes by the half-hundred and tarts by the thousands!

The fine smells of all these good things would float across the fields to the cottage until the boy could not stand it any longer. One day, when there was nothing at all in *his* cupboard, and the ogre had a regiment of mince pies set out on the window ledge to cool, the boy said to his mother:

"The ogre has more gold than he knows what to do with. Surely if I went to him and asked humbly and honestly for a loan of some of it, he would give it to me."

But his mother was very much alarmed by such an idea.

"Remember, no ogre has any liking for mankind. Indeed many dark tales have been told of what has happened to those unfortunate enough to fall into an ogre's power. Do not go near his house, or evil will come of it."

But the boy was sure that he was quicker of wit than an ogre and was determined to try his plan. Accordingly, the next morning he crossed the fields to the door of the ogre's fine house.

The house was large, and the stones of its walls were dark and old. For the first time the boy began to wonder if he were as clever as he thought himself. But before he had time to be off again, the door opened and the ogre stood there grinning—and not a very pleasant grin either.

"Aha, my brave lad! And why have you come this way? You must indeed have more courage than the rest of your kind, for you are the first human being I have had seek me out in many a year."

Since he could not escape now, the boy put as bold a face as possible upon the matter and replied:

"I am a poor lad, unfavored by fortune. With you, things have gone very well. So I have come to ask a loan from you."

Now the ogre began to laugh, and his laugh was even less pleasant than his tooth-studded grin had been.

"You are honest enough, that I must say. So I shall be as straight with you. Come in."

It was not without a shiver or two up his back and a cold feeling in his middle that the boy entered the ogre's house and followed the monster upstairs and along a dark hall to a room where fat bags of gold were piled up all along the walls. There was even more of the shining stuff lying about higgle-ti-pigglety, in no order at all.

The ogre reached out a long arm and picked up a small wooden tub. Into this he threw round yellow pieces until it was not only full but had a mound of gold above the edge.

"Now this I can spare you for a year," he said grandly.

"And when the year is done?" asked the boy anxiously.

The ogre pulled at the straggly beard on his chin. "I shall not be too hard with you. Return this tub only level full and we shall be quits."

"And if I cannot return it?"

"Why, then—" the ogre laughed again— "I shall find a use for you, never fear."

The boy looked at the tub and thought for a long moment. Then he drew his hand across the heap of gold pieces in it, leaving it level full and taking only those which had been swept to the floor.

"Here." With his foot he pushed back the tub. "I repay your loan at once, friend. And as you have said, we are now quits."

The ogre scowled and scratched his head, but he could not see anything left for him to do but accept. And the boy went back to his mother with two pockets full of good yellow gold. But when he told her how he had gotten it, she was very much frightened for her son.

"Once you have outwitted the ogre, but luck may not be with you a second time. Do not, I beg of you, try him again."

"The same trick would not serve twice," returned her son. "As for visiting the ogre, about that we shall see."

With the gold he was able to put a new roof on the cottage and buy seeds for the garden, as well as some hens and a cock. But one day he said to his mother:

"If we had a pig or two and a cow we should be very well off. Now that ogre over there could certainly spare a few pieces from those he has in his moneybags, and he would never miss them at all!"

His mother begged him not to go to the ogre's house. But early the next morning he set out.

As he came near to the big stone house, his eye lit on a tall tree which stood beside the ogre's front door. The fall winds were beginning to blow, and its leaves were already fluttering down to the ground. The boy watched these fall and then, as quickly as he could, he climbed up into the topmost branches and, pulling some hairs from his head, he so twisted and wound them about the stems of two leaves that he was sure even the hardest blasts of the winter storms could not tear them out of the tree. Having done this to his satisfaction, he slid down and knocked loudly on the front door.

When the ogre saw who was standing on his doorstep, his eyes widened and he puffed out his lips in surprise.

"And what do you want now, little man?" he demanded.

"We have fared very well with your gift to us," returned the boy politely. "But life would be even easier for us if we had a couple of pigs and a cow to give us milk and butter."

"Is that so? But I am thinking," said the ogre, "that our bargain must be slightly different this time."

"I shall agree to whatever you wish," said the boy, and then he pointed to the falling leaves. "I shall not need such a loan for long. Let us say that I shall repay the whole amount when all the leaves are off your tree here!"

The ogre blinked as a breeze came through the branches carrying a huge handful of leaves away with it.

"That seems a fair bar gain, little man. But you may find it a hard one. Remember when you lose it that it was of your own suggesting."

"Be sure, sir, that if I lose I shall have no complaints to make," answered the boy.

So, for the second time, he returned from the ogre's house with well-lined pockets. Two pigs and a cow were bought in the market town and the boy was very happy.

The ogre kept a sharp eye on the leaves in his tree as by tens and then by hundreds they fell—except for two on a topmost bough. He would have climbed up to see what kept those leaves so stubbornly in place but the branches there were too small to support his weight. He could only fuss and fume. And those two never fell, even when the worst of the winter storms tore at them.

When spring came again, the boy looked out of the cottage window and thought what a fine thing it would be to own the rich field which lay beyond the edge of his tiny garden. Since this belonged to the ogre, he began to make plans for getting it. But this time he was sure that any bargain between them would be of the ogre's choosing. At last he decided that if twice his wits had saved him, surely they would do so a third time, and he went off to the ogre's house.

"Aha!" The ogre opened the door even before the boy knocked. "And have you come to pay back the gold you owe me, little man?"

The boy glanced up at the two brown leaves. "As you have said, a bargain is a bargain. Your tree is not yet bare, as you can see, Master Ogre."

"Then why do you come?" exploded the ogre in anger.

"You have a fine rich field which borders my garden patch," began the boy, when the ogre interrupted him.

"And I suppose you think I should give it to you?"

"Give it to me? Oh, no, sir. Only lend it to me for a short time, and I shall make any bargain you wish."

The ogre combed his beard with his nails and thought for a long time. And then he laughed.

"Very well, little man. This bargain is of my choosing, and, mind you, I shall hold you to it. You shall give me whatever I ask of you when your crop has grown and stands tall along the fence there—tall and ripe and ready to harvest."

"I agree," said the boy and went home to get his seed. But even as the sound of the monster's laughter came booming over the fields behind him, he was choosing two kinds of seed.

In the field he sowed his two crops. In a short time the green of young wheat showed over most of the field. The ogre came from time to time to watch it ripen. At last, when the wheat was yellow and the boy had come to harvest it, he said:

"Well, our bargain is now at an end, is it not, little man?"

"Not yet," answered the boy. "For I planted two crops in this field and the one along yonder fence is not yet nearly ready to harvest."

"And what did you plant there?" demanded the ogre.

"Acorns," replied the boy.

The ogre gave a howl of rage. "Wait until the next time you try to deal with me, you trickster!" he screamed over his shoulder as he made his way home.

But the boy shook his head. "It does not pay to be greedy," he said to himself, "and three times at any bargaining is enough."

THROUGH THE NEEDLE'S EYE
High Sorcery (1970) ACE

It was not her strange reputation which attracted me to old Miss Ruthevan, though there were stories to excite a solitary child's morbid taste. Rather it was what she was able to create, opening a whole new world to the crippled girl I was thirty years ago.

Two years before I made that momentous visit to Cousin Althea, I suffered an attack of what was then known as infantile paralysis. In those days, before Salk, there was no cure. I was fourteen when I met Miss Ruthevan, and I had been told for weary months that I was lucky to be able to walk at all, even though I must do so with a heavy brace on my right leg. I might accept that verdict outwardly, but the "me" imprisoned in the thin adolescent's body was a rebel.

Cousin Althea's house was small, and on the wrong side of the wrong street to claim gentility. (Cramwell did not have a railroad to separate the comfortable, smug sheep from the aspiring goats.) But her straggling back garden ran to a wall of mellow, red brick patterned by green moss, and in one place a section of this barrier had broken down so one could hitch up to look into the tangled mat of vine and brier which now covered most of the Ruthevan domain.

Three-fourths of that garden had reverted to the wild, but around the bulk of the house it was kept in some order. The fat, totally deaf old woman who ruled Miss Ruthevan's domestic concerns could often be seen poking about, snipping off flowers or leaves after examining each with the care of a cautious shopper, or filling a pan with wizened berries. Birds loved the Ruthevan garden and built whole colonies of nests in its unpruned trees. Bees and butterflies were thick in the undisturbed peace. Though I longed to explore, I never quite dared, until the day of the quilt.

That had been a day of disappointment. There was a Sunday school picnic to which Ruth, Cousin Althea's daughter, and I were invited. I knew that it was not for one unable to play ball, race, or swim. Proudly I refused to go, giving the mendacious excuse that my leg ached. Filled with bitter envy, I watched Ruth leave. I refused Cousin Althea's offer to let me make candy, marching off, lurch-push to perch on the wall.

There was something new in the garden beyond. An expanse of color flapped languidly from a clothesline, giving tantalizing glimpses of it. Before I knew it, I tumbled over the wall, acquiring a goodly number of scrapes and bruises on the way, and struggled through a straggle of briers to see better.

It was worth my struggle. Cousin Althea had quilts in plenty, mostly made by Grandma Moss, who was considered by the family to be an artist at needlework. But what I viewed now was as clearly above the best efforts of Grandma as a Rembrandt above an inn sign.

This was appliqué work, each block of a different pattern; though, after some study, I became aware that the whole was to be a panorama of autumn. There were flowers, fruits, berries, and nuts, each with their attendant clusters of leaves, while the border was an interwoven wreath of maple and oak foliage in the richest coloring. Not only was the appliqué so perfect one could not detect a single stitch, but the quilting over-pattern was as delicate as lace. It was old; its once white background had been time-dyed cream; and it was the most beautiful thing I had ever seen.

"Well, what do you think of it?"

I lurched as I tried to turn quickly, catching for support at the trunk of a gnarled apple tree. On the brick wall from the house stood old Miss Ruthevan. She was tall and held herself stiffly straight, the masses of her thick, white hair built into a formal coil which, by rights, should have supported a tiara. From throat to instep she was covered by a loose robe in a neutral shade of blue-gray which fully concealed her body.

Ruth had reported Miss Ruthevan to be a terrifying person; her nickname among the children was "old witch." But after my first flash of panic, I was not alarmed, being too bemused by the quilt.

"I think it's wonderful. All fall things—"

"It's a bride quilt," she replied shortly, "made for a September bride."

She moved and lost all her majesty of person, for she limped in an even more ungainly fashion than I, weaving from side to side as if about to lose her balance at any moment. When she halted and put her hand on the quilt, she was once more an uncrowned queen. Her face was paper white, her lips blue lines. But her sunken, very alive eyes probed me.

"Who are you?"

"Ernestine Williams. I'm staying with Cousin Althea." I pointed to the wall.

Her thin brows, as white as her hair, drew into a small frown. Then she nodded. "Catherine Moss's granddaughter, yes. Do you sew, Ernestine?"

I shook my head, oddly ashamed. There was a vast importance to that question, I felt. Maybe that gave me the courage to add, "I wish I could—like that." I pointed a finger at the quilt. I surprised myself, for never before had I wished to use a needle.

Miss Ruthevan's clawlike hand fell heavily on my shoulder. She swung her body around awkwardly, using me as a pivot, and then drew me along with her. I strove to match my limp to her wider lurch, up three worn steps into a hallway, which was very dark and cool out of the sun.

Shut doors flanked us, but the one at the far end stood open, and there she brought me, still captive in her strong grasp. Once we were inside she released me, to make her own crab's way to a tall-backed chair standing in the full light of a side window. There she sat enthroned, as was right and proper.

An embroidery frame stood before the chair, covered with a throw of white cloth. At her right hand was a low table bearing a rack of innumerable small spindles, each wound with colorful thread.

"Look around," she commanded. "You are a Moss. Catherine Moss had some skill; maybe you have inherited it."

I was ready to disclaim any of my grandmother's talent; but Miss Ruthevan, drawing off the shield cloth and folding it with small flicks, ignored me. So I began to edge nervously about the room, staring wide-eyed at the display there.

The walls were covered with framed, glass-protected needle-work. Those pieces to my left were very old, the colors long faded, the exquisite stitchery almost too dim to see. But, as I made my slow progress, each succeeding picture became brighter and more distinct. Some were the conventional samplers, but the majority were portraits or true pictures. As I skirted needle-work chairs and dodged a fire screen, I saw that the art was in use everywhere. I was in a shrine to needle creations which had been brought to the highest peak of perfection and beauty. As I made that journey of discovery, Miss Ruthevan stitched away the minutes, pausing now and then to study a single half-open white rose in a small vase on her table.

"Did you make all these, Miss Ruthevan?" I blurted out at last.

She took two careful stitches before she answered. "No. There have always been Ruthevan women so talented, for three hundred years. It began" — her blue lips curved in a very small shadow of a smile, though she did not turn her attention from her work—" with Grizel Ruthevan, of a family a king chose to outlaw—which was, perhaps, hardly wise of him." She raised her hand and pointed with the needle she held to the first of the old frames. It seemed to me that a sparkle of sunlight gathered on the needle and lanced through the shadows about the picture she so indicated. "Grizel Ruthevan, aged seventeen —she was the first of us. But there were enough to follow. I am the last."

"You mean your—your ancestors—did all this."

Again she smiled that curious smile. "Not all of them, my dear. Our art requires a certain cast of mind, a talent you may certainly call it. My own aunt, for example, did not have it; and, of course, my mother, not being born a Ruthevan, did not. But my great-aunt Vannessa was very able."

I do not know how it came about, but when I left, I was committed to the study of needlework under Miss Ruthevan's teaching; though she gave me to understand from the first that the perfection I saw about me was not the result of amateur work, and that here, as in all other arts, patience and practice as well as aptitude were needed.

I went home full of the wonders of what I had seen; and when I cut single-mindedly across Ruth's account of her day, she roused to counterattack.

"She's a witch, you know!" She teetered back and forth on the boards of the small front porch. "She makes people disappear; maybe she'll do that to you if you hang around over there."

"Ruthie!" Cousin Althea, her face flushed from baking, stood behind the patched screen. Her daughter was apprehensively quiet as she came out. But I was more interested in what Ruthie had said than any impending scolding.

"Makes people disappear—how?"

"That's an untruth, Ruthie," my cousin said firmly. True to her upbringing, Cousin Althea thought the word "lie" coarse. "Never let me hear you say a thing like that about Miss Ruthevan again. She has had a very sad life—"

"Because she's lame?" I challenged.

Cousin Althea hesitated; truth won over tact. "Partly. You'd never think it to look at her now, but when she was just a little older than you girls she was a real beauty. Why, I remember mother telling about how people would go to their windows just to watch her drive by with her father, the Colonel. He had a team of matched grays and a carriage he'd bought in New York.

"She went away to school, too, Anne Ruthevan did. And that's where she met her sweetheart. He was the older brother of one of her schoolmates."

"But Miss Ruthevan's an old maid!" Ruth protested. "She didn't ever marry."

"No." Cousin Althea sat down in the old, wooden porch rocker and picked up a palm leaf fan to cool her face, "No, she didn't ever marry. All her good fortune turned bad almost overnight, you might say. She and her father went out driving. It was late August and she was planning to be married in September. There was a bad storm came up very sudden. It frightened those grays and they ran away down on the river road. They didn't make the turn there, and the carriage was smashed up. The Colonel was killed. Miss Anne— well, for days everybody thought she'd die, too.

"Her sweetheart came up from New York. My mother said he was the handsomest man: tall, with black hair waving down a little over his forehead. He stayed with the Chambers family. Mr. Chambers was Miss Anne's uncle on her mother's side. He tried every day to see Miss Anne, only she would never have him in—she must have known by then—"

"That she was always going to be lame," I said flatly.

Cousin Althea did not look at me when she nodded agreement.

"He went away, finally. But he kept coming back. After a while people guessed what was really going on. It wasn't Miss Anne he was coming to see now; it was her cousin, Rita Chambers.

"By then Miss Anne had found out some other pretty unhappy things. The Colonel had died sudden, and he left his business in a big tangle. Soon, most of the money was gone. Here was Miss Anne, brought up to have most of what she had a mind for; and now she had nothing. Losing her sweetheart to Rita, and then losing her money; it changed her. She shut herself away from most folks. She was awful young—only twenty.

"Pretty soon Rita was planning *her* wedding—they were going to be married in August, just about a year after that ride which changed Miss Anne's life. Her fiancé came up from New York a couple of days ahead of time; he was staying at Doc Bernard's. Well, the wedding day came, and Doc was to drive the groom to the church. He waited a good long time and finally went up to his room to hurry him along a little, but he wasn't there. His clothes were all laid out, nice and neat. I remember hearing Mrs. Bernard, she was awfully old then, telling as how it gave her a turn to see the white rose he was to wear in his buttonhole still sitting in a glass of water on the chest of drawers. But he was gone—didn't take his clothes nor nothing—just went. Nobody saw hide nor hair of him afterwards."

"But what could have happened to him, Cousin Althea?" I asked.

"They did some hunting around, but never found anyone who saw him after breakfast that morning. Most people finally decided he was ashamed of it all, that he felt it about Miss Anne. 'Course, that didn't explain why he left his clothes all lying there. Mother always said she thought both Anne and Rita were well rid of him. It was a ten days' wonder all right, but people forgot in time. The Chamberses took Rita away to a watering place for a while; she was pretty peaked. Two years later she married John Ford; he'd always been sweet on her. Then they moved out west someplace. I heard as how she'd taken a dislike to this whole town and told John she'd say 'yes' to him provided he moved.

"Since then—well, Miss Anne, she began to do a little better. She was able to get out of bed that winter and took to sewing—not making clothes and such, but embroidery. Real important people have bought some of her fancy pictures; I heard tell a couple are even in museums. And you're a very lucky girl, Ernestine, if she'll teach you like you said."

It was not until I was in bed that night, going over my meeting with Miss Ruthevan and Cousin Althea's story, that something gave me a queer start: the thought of that unclaimed white rose.

Most of the time I had spent with Miss Ruthevan she had been at work. But I had never seen the picture she was stitching, only her hands holding the needle dipping in and out, or bringing a thread into the best light as she matched it against the petals of the rose on her table.

That had been a perfect rose; it might have been carved from ivory. Miss Ruthevan had not taken it out of the glass; she had not moved out of her chair when I left. But now I was sure that, when I had looked back from the door, the rose had been gone. Where? It was a puzzle. But, of course, Miss Ruthevan must have done something with it when I went to look at some one of the pictures she had called to my attention.

Cousin Althea was flattered that Miss Ruthevan had shown interest in me; I know my retelling of the comment about Grandma Moss had pleased her greatly. She carefully supervised my dress before my departure for the Ruthevan house the next day, and she would not let me take the shortcut through the garden. I must limp around the block and approach properly through the front door. I did, uncomfortable in the fresh folds of skirt, so ill looking I believed, above the ugliness of the brace.

Today Miss Ruthevan had put aside the covered frame and was busied instead with a delicate length of old lace, matching thread with extra care. It was a repair job for a museum, she told me.

She put me to work helping her with the thread. Texture, color, shading—I must have an eye for all, she told me crisply. She spun some of her thread herself and dyed much of it, using formulas which the Ruthevan women had developed over the years.

So through the days and weeks which followed I found cool refuge in that high-walled room where I was allowed to handle precious fabrics and take some part in her work. I learned to spin on a wheel older than much of the town, and I worked in the small shed-like summer kitchen skimming dye pots and watching Miss Ruthevan measure bark and dried leaves and roots in careful quantities.

It was only rarely that she worked on the piece in the standing frame, which she never allowed me to see. She did not forbid that in words, merely arranged it so that I did not. But from time to time, when she had a perfectly formed fern, a flower, and once in the early morning when a dew-beaded spider web cornered the window without, she would stitch away. I never saw what she did with her models when she had finished. I only knew that when the last stitch was set to her liking, the vase was empty, the web had vanished.

She had a special needle for this work. It was kept in a small brass box, and she made a kind of ceremony of opening the box, holding it tightly to her breast, with her eyes closed; she also took a great while to thread the needle itself, running the thread back and forth through it. But when Miss Ruthevan did not choose to explain, there was that about her which kept one from asking questions.

I learned, slowly and painfully, with pricked fingers and sick frustration each time I saw how far below my goals my finished work was. But there was a great teacher in Miss Ruthevan. She had patience, and her criticism inspired instead of blighted. Once I brought her a shell I had found. She turned it over, putting it on her model table. When I came the next day it still lay there, but on a square of fabric, the outline of the shell sketched upon the cloth.

"Select your threads," she told me.

It took me a long time to match and rematch. She examined my choice and made no changes.

"You have the eye. If you can also learn the skill . . ."

I tried to reproduce the shell; but the painful difference between my work and the model exasperated me, until the thread knotted and snarled and I was close to tears. She took it out of my hand.

"You try too hard. You think of the stitches instead of the whole. It must be done here as well as with your fingers." She touched one of her cool, dry fingers to my forehead.

So I learned patience as well as skill, and as she worked Miss Ruthevan spoke of art and artists, of the days when she had gone out of Cramwell into a world long lost. I went back to Cousin Althea's each afternoon with my head full of far places and the beauty men and women could create. Sometimes she had me leaf through books of prints, or spend afternoons sorting out patterns inscribed on strips of parchment older than my own country.

The change in Miss Ruthevan herself came so slowly during those weeks that I did not note it at first. When she began to refuse commissions, I was not troubled, but rather pleased, for she spent more time with me, only busy with that on the standing frame. I did regret her refusing to embroider a wedding dress; it was so beautiful. It was that denial which made me aware that now she seldom came out of her chair; there were no more mornings with the dye pots.

One day when I came there were no sounds from the kitchen, a curious silence in the house. My uneasiness grew as I entered the workroom to see Miss Ruthevan sitting with folded hands, no needle at work. She turned her head to watch as I limped across the carpet. I spoke the first thing in my mind.

"Miss Applebee's gone." I had never seen much of the deaf housekeeper, but the muted sounds of her presence had always been with us. I missed them now.

"Yes, Lucy is gone. Our time has almost run out. Sit down, Ernestine. No, do not reach for your work, I have something to say to you."

That sounded a little like a scolding to come. I searched my conscience as she continued.

"Someday very soon now, Ernestine, I too, shall go."

I stared at her, frightened. For the first time I was aware of just how old Miss Ruthevan must be, how skeleton thin were her quiet hands.

She laughed. "Don't grow so big-eyed, child. I have no intention of being coffined, none at all. It is just that I have earned a vacation of sorts, one of my own choosing. Remember this, Ernestine, nothing in this world comes to us unpaid for; and when I speak of pay, I do not talk of money. Things which may be bought with money are the easy things. No, the great desires of our hearts are paid for in other coin; I have paid for what I want most, with fifty years of labor. Now the end is in sight—see for yourself!"

She pushed at the frame so for the first time I could see what it held.

It was a picture, a vivid one. Somehow I felt that I looked through a window to see reality. In the background to the left, tall trees arched, wearing the brilliant livery of fall. In the foreground was a riot of flowers.

Against a flaming oak stood a man, a shaft of light illuminating his high-held, dark head. His thin face was keenly alive and welcoming. His hair waved down a little over his forehead.

Surrounded by the flowers was the figure of a woman. By the grace and slenderness of her body she was young. But her face was still but blank canvas.

I went closer, fascinated by form and color, seeing more details the longer I studied it. There was a rabbit crouched beneath a clump of fern, and at the feet of the girl a cat, eyeing the hunter with the enigmatic scrutiny of its kind. Its striped, gray and black coat was so real I longed to touch—to see if it were truly fur.

"That was Timothy," Miss Ruthevan said suddenly. "I did quite well with him. He was so old, so old and tired. Now he will be forever young."

"But, you haven't done the lady's face." I 'ventured.

"Not yet, child, but soon now." She suddenly tossed the cover over the frame to hide it all.

"There is this." She picked up the brass needle-case and opened it fully for the first time, to display a strip of threadbare velvet into which was thrust two needles. They were not the ordinary steel ones, such as I had learned to use, but bright yellow slivers of fire in the sun.

"Once," she told me, "there were six of these—now only two. This one is mine. And this," her finger did not quite touch the last, "shall be yours, if you wish, only if you wish, Ernestine. Always remember one pays a price for power. If tomorrow, or the day after, you come and find me gone, you shall also find this box waiting for you. Take it and use the needle if and when you will—but carefully. Grizel Ruthevan bought this box for a very high price indeed. I do not know whether we should bless or curse her. . . ." Her voice trailed away and I knew without any formal dismissal I was to go. But at the door I hesitated, to look back.

Miss Ruthevan had pulled the frame back into working distance before her. As I watched she made a careful selection of thread, set it in the needle's waiting eye. She took one stitch and then another. I went into the dark silence of the hall. Miss Ruthevan was finishing the picture.

I said nothing to Cousin Althea of that curious interview. The next day I went almost secretly into the Ruthevan house by the way I had first entered it, over the garden wall. The silence was even deeper than it had been the afternoon before. There was a curious deadness to it, like the silence of a house left unoccupied. I crept to the workroom; there was no one in the chair by the window. I had not really expected to find her there.

When I reached the chair, something seemed to sap my strength so I sat in it as all those days I had seen her sit. The picture stood in its frame facing me—uncovered. As I had expected, it was complete. The imperiously beautiful face of the lady was there in detail. I recognized those wing brows, though now they were dark, the eyes, the mouth with its shadow smile; recognized them with a shiver. Now I knew where the rose, the fern, the web and all the other models had gone. I also knew, without being told, the meaning of the gold needles and why the maiden in the picture wore Anne Ruthevan's face and the hunter had black hair.

I ran, and I was climbing over the back wall before I was truly aware of what I did. But weighting down the pocket of my sewing apron was the brass needle-box. I have never opened it. I am not Miss Ruthevan; I have not the determination, nor perhaps the courage, to pay the price such skill demands. With whom—or *what*—Grizel Ruthevan dealt to acquire those needles, I do not like to think at all.

THE TOYMAKER'S SNUFFBOX

Golden Magazine for Boys and Girls
Volume 3 No. 8 (August 1966)

A folktale based on original sources

Once upon a time when the world of magic was much closer to our world than it is today, there lived in the city of Kammerstadt a toymaker who had his shop at the very end of the Street of Carpenters. So perfect were the toys he made and so well had he learned his trade, that all the kingdom found their way to that shop to buy. No child's Christmas or birthday was complete unless among the gifts was a doll or a box of soldiers, a talking bear or a galloping horse made by Master Franz.

It was often Master Franz's custom to work late in his shop to finish some toy. And one night while he was painting the last red spoke in the wheel of a cart, he heard a sound which was made neither by the wind whistling around the crooked old roofs in the Street of Carpenters nor by a mouse nibbling within the walls. He put down his brush and got up to hunt for the source of that sound.

On the shelves around the room were arranged all the finished toys. Soldiers marched in regiments and armies; animals stood in herds and families. Rows of tiny chairs fit for doll queens' palaces were placed beside tables, chests, and curtained beds. And it was from the last and largest of these that the sound was coming.

With his paint-stained finger Master Franz looped aside the bed curtain. And there, lying on the embroidered coverlet, her hooded head half-buried in the tiny pillows, was a little lady hardly taller than the finger which disturbed her hiding place. The sound he had heard was her sobbing.

"What is this? By St. Nick himself, I must be dreaming!" burst out Master Franz, his eyes wide as he stared at the creature.

The sobs ended in a frightened gasp as the tiny head was raised, and eyes as blue as the satin of the doll queen's best court robe met his.

"I am surely dreaming! How did you get out of your box now?" He looked up at the row of fine lady dolls, each neat and tidy in her own lace-paper-edged box.

"I'm not one of your dolls, man!" answered the little thing indignantly.

"No? But then you are not a child either. You are much too small to be one of them. Just what are you, and why should you hide in the best bed to cry?"

"I am an elf. And why am I crying?" Her little voice became a wail. "Because of this, man!" With her two hands she pulled off her hood. And there was the round ball of her head, as smooth and polished as fine ivory. There was not a single hair on it!

"So-o-o? Is that the way of it now?" Master Franz, thumb to chin, considered her thoughtfully. "Lost your wig, have you? Well, that should be a lesson to you to stay comfortably in your proper box and not stray about in this giddy way."

But at this the elf leaped down from the bed and stamped her foot.

"I tell you, man, I am NOT one of your sawdust-stuffed puppets!"

But Master Franz was no longer listening to her. Instead he pulled open a narrow drawer where, each in a compartment all its own, lay tresses of hair, hair in all colors and shades from glowing red-gold to shadeless black.

"Blue eyes," he muttered to himself. "Not brown, then, nor this yellow. Yes, we shall use black."

The elf who had been leaning over the edge of the shelf in a most perilous manner drew a deep breath.

"Why not?" she asked herself. "That old witch's spell may have wiped the hair from my head, but wearing a wig I could still go to the ball tonight. Let him continue to believe me a doll until after he has done that for me."

So she allowed Master Franz to lift her down to his worktable, to measure and fit until she could stand it no longer, but wriggled out of his fingers to run and stare at herself in the mirror of a doll's toilet set.

"One of my best jobs, I think," said Master Franz with some pride. "Now you are even prettier than Her Majesty up yonder." He pointed to the doll queen seated haughtily on her throne on the very top shelf.

"I should think that I am!" retorted the elf. "Prettier than a puppet, indeed! But I like your work very much, toymaker, so I shall make you a gift in return. What do you want most in the world?"

"What do I want? This is a queer dream indeed. Well, I shall answer the truth to that. I wish for nothing that I do not now have in my two hands. I am very content with this shop and my work here. No, there is nothing at all for me to wish for," laughed Master Franz.

The elf frowned. "That is not a proper answer at all, man. But since you will not tell me, I shall choose for you. And now I must be off or I shall be late for the ball. Goodnight, toymaker, and see what you shall find on this table tomorrow!"

With that she disappeared and Master Franz sat blinking. He rubbed his eyes sleepily. To be sure, there were two long black hairs caught in a drop of glue on the boards before him. But of course he had been dreaming.

"Bed is the place for me. I'm too sleepy to be of use here."

He blew out his candles and went off to his bed.

When he came into the shop the next morning something lay glittering in a patch of sunlight on the worktable. It was a snuffbox of gold with a quaint design of dancing elves scrolled around its edge.

"Was I dreaming last night or not?" marveled Master Franz. He turned the box over. "But I'm no fine gentleman to be using snuff. I do not need this." He dropped the snuffbox into one of the table drawers, and before the hour was past he had forgotten all about it.

But the happy days in the Street of Carpenters did not last. One day the King's trumpeters rode into the marketplace to proclaim war, and the men of Kammerstadt were called upon to serve in the army. Master Franz gave away the rest of the toys, laid aside his tools, and locked his shop, to put on a red coat and march away with the rest.

One cold winter's night he came home again. But there were no bright lights in the crooked-roofed houses to welcome him, only dark shadows and the driving cold of winter to bite through his worn coat and freeze the tears on his cheeks.

Only in the baker's shop was there the gleam of a candle. And Master

Franz turned in there to spend his last coin for a bit of bread.

"These are hard times for us now, Master Franz. The good days are gone from Kammerstadt," the baker's wife told him. "And if you are wise, you will try your fortune elsewhere. Here the King's treasurer has sent tax gatherers to sweep up all our money, and no one has aught to spare for the buying of silly toys. A man must labor from daylight to candlelight for bare bread alone."

Franz went on to his shop. But all the magic which had once filled it was gone. Cobwebs, heavy with dust, hung from the empty shelves and he could hardly remember now how it had once looked. He crouched down beside the worktable with his aching head in his hands, and there he spent the night. In the morning he opened the drawers to look for his tools, but they had all been stolen long ago.

However, as he pulled open the last drawer something within it rattled. And so again he found the snuffbox. Franz could hardly believe his good fortune. Such a trinket would certainly be worth a pocketful of gold to him now. But should he, dared he, offer it for sale in Kammerstadt? Who would believe that one as ragged and poor as he had come by it honestly? He might be thrown into prison if he showed it.

It would be better to take the advice of the baker's wife. If no one in Kammerstadt would now buy toys, there were other cities where his skill might again earn his living. He had no ties to keep him fast in these ruins of his old life.

So, with the snuffbox safely hidden, Franz went out through the gates of Kammerstadt and followed the highway eastward to a new life.

He wandered from city to city, village to village. And he did not sell the snuffbox, for it seemed to him that his luck had changed from the moment he had found it. Now he was able to find work, and for some weeks he was a carpenter's helper. When he left that shop he had a new coat on his back, whole shoes on his feet, and a knapsack of supplies.

But in all his wanderings he found no city or village in which he wished to settle, or where he thought that the toymaker's craft would be truly welcomed.

After many months he came through the pass in the Gorgen Mountains and looked down upon a green and smiling land below wherein was set a fair city of many towers.

"Now I believe," said Franz to the tumbled rocks about him," that this is the place for which I have been searching all these weary days. Here lies the city where I wish to stay."

And he set off down the mountain road at a good pace. But the city was farther off than it had appeared from the pass. At nightfall he found himself still in the wilderness, so he built a fire and grubbed in his knapsack for any bits of food he might have overlooked. His fingers found only the snuffbox. He brought it out into the firelight, turning it over and over.

"There is good gold in you," he observed. "Mayhap it will buy me proper tools and a roof to use them under. But tonight I could almost wish that you would give me food and drink."

No sooner had those words passed his lips than the snuffbox squeezed between his fingers and flew open on the moss at his feet. Before he could pick it up, a square of cloth floated out to grow and grow and spread itself with smoking dishes fit for a king's table.

At first Franz was almost afraid to eat the mysterious feast. But his hunger was greater than his caution, and he ate and drank to the last crumb. When he had done, the cloth and the dishes shrank back into the snuffbox, which then snapped shut with a click. Franz picked it up and stowed it away in his money belt.

"It would seem that I have an even greater treasure than I thought," he mused. "Will it obey my every wish or only three? That is a point I must think about, for many such gifts in past legends have been limited that way. And if that is true, I must take care as to how I spend the two still remaining."

He began to dream of all a man might wish for: wealth, a throne, the hand of the loveliest princess in the world. But none of these seemed very real to Franz. He decided that he had lived too long by the skill of his hands to care for any of them.

By noon of the next day he came to the gates of the city. But now its grim gray walls and the many angry-red and somber-black banners hanging over them did not seem inviting. The spiked gates were closed, and to enter he had to pass through a small postern and answer the many sharp questions of the sentries on duty there.

Within, the city was no pleasanter. There were many merchants' booths in the market, but the men who kept them had white, worried faces, and they all glanced back now and again over their shoulders as if an enemy might creep upon them. To Franz it was plain that this was a city where some terror ruled.

He found an inn, but when he sat down and called for ale, the little serving maid came reluctantly to bring it. As she put down his tankard she lingered a moment, scrubbing the table with her stained apron.

"Get you gone, stranger," she whispered.

"Why?"

Her face was twisted with fear as she answered. "They will be after you. No stranger enters the gates that *she* does not hear of it. And with strangers she has her sport."

"And who is she?"

"The Lady Carola, she whom the Princess Katha set over us in rule. Go quickly now, if you can, stranger. But perhaps it is already too late. And if that is so, no man or woman within these walls will raise a hand to aid you."

Franz sipped his ale. Fear he had known many times before, and never did it profit a man to turn his back upon it.

Some minutes later a file of men-at-arms tramped into the inn and ordered him to come with them. So was Franz brought to the tall keep in the very heart of the city to meet the ruler of that place.

She was neither young nor old, and he could not have said whether she had beauty or was plain. But in her face and her clutching hands there were both power and evil, and Franz straightway hated her as he had never known hatred before.

"A strong man," she said harshly. "Now if you but have wits to match your strength, it shall make our contest the more interesting for both of us."

"Our contest, Lady?"

"Aye. Since the Princess Katha thought it wise to retire from the world, I have ruled this doltish city and its teeming fools. Contests of wit and will are my only amusement. Thus shall I set you three tasks, and if you cannot accomplish them—then you shall take your place among these!"

At her gesture one of the guards swept back a curtain of tapestry, and Franz saw in the wall a row of niches. In each, except for one, was a man of stone.

"Witch," returned the toymaker, "the contest you propose is an old one. There are legends in my homeland of such. But in the fullness of time there was always the same end to them."

"And that?" she prompted him.

"The witch lost."

She laughed. "If I lose, stranger, your reward shall be all the greater. But time is passing. I must set the first task before daylight is gone.

"On the top of this keep there is an eagle's nest which has been there this hundred years. And in that nest—so men say—is the crown of an earlier ruler of this land. I have a fancy to wear that crown. Fetch it down for me, stranger!"

The guards marched Franz out into the courtyard.

"You have two hours," the captain told him sharply.

The walls of the keep were smooth stone without even hold enough for a fingernail of one who would climb. Franz slipped his hand beneath his coat and brought out the snuffbox. Now, if never again, he needed its aid.

"I wish for a way to climb the keep," he said slowly.

The box clicked open, and a thin golden vine hitched out of it. Up to the wall of the keep it crept and plastered itself against the stone, clinging as an ivy vine, growing steadily higher and higher. On this ladder Franz began to climb, not daring to look down. Up and up he followed the golden vine until at last, with aching arms, he pulled himself over the top and half tumbled, half jumped into a great mass of sticks and the bones of the eagles' prey.

Through this evil-smelling mess he combed until he found a circlet which flashed with jeweled fire. Then he trusted himself again to the vine. As he climbed down it, it shrank with his passing, so that when the stones of the courtyard were once more under his feet, the vine flowed back into the snuffbox.

But the Lady Carola had no pleasure in the crown when he offered it to her. Instead, flames of anger danced in her eyes.

"You are very clever, stranger!" Her voice was the hiss of a serpent. "Once you have won, but not twice, I think. Listen to the second task I set you:

"In the stable stands a roan mare which it is my will to ride. But since the beast is mad and attacks all who would approach it, it has never been saddled. Bring it hither gentled, stranger, and I shall believe that you have powers greater than mine!"

"So be it," replied Franz calmly.

Now Franz was city bred and knew but little of horses. However, it was plain to the most ignorant that the roan that the guards showed him was not only mad, but in its madness it was driven by a hate against all mankind. It reared and beat its hoofs against the wall, baring teeth at those who would come near it, restrained only by the heavy chains at its bridle.

"Within the hour, fool," laughed the captain, "we shall return to carry hence what is left of you."

"A most courteous act," returned Franz quietly. He waited until they had left the stable before he brought out the snuffbox.

"Give me now what will best master this demon," he asked of it.

Over the rim of the snuffbox fell a ball of rosy light which grew larger as it rolled across the floor until it lay quiet before the mare. The tall horse stood still, its eyes fixed upon the light. Franz ventured to lay a hand on a quivering flank. The horse did not move.

So did it continue to stand statue-still while Franz, with many fumblings, saddled it. Then it allowed the toymaker to lead it out, while the ball rolled before them. Thus Franz brought the mare through the crowd of awestricken men into the great hall.

At the sight of the mare, the Lady Carola shrank back in her seat. But the flames in her eyes grew, and her mouth was straight and grim.

"Twice you have won, stranger!" Her voice arose in a harsh scream of rage. "But for you there shall be no third victory. Ten years upon ten years ago the Princess Katha went from among us, leaving this city in my hands. And no man knows whither she went. Bring her back to this high seat! That I ask of you now, little man who would match wits with me!"

For the last time Franz touched the snuffbox and muttered his wish. But nothing happened. And he knew, with a sinking heart, that three wishes only had that box held, and he had used them all. As he stood there defenseless, the Lady Carola laughed.

"So do I win! Seize him, guards!"

But Franz was desperate, and he turned to the nearest man-at-arms, snatching the spear from his hands. He hurled it swiftly, not at any who moved upon him, but at that ball of light which held the wild horse captive.

There was the tinkling of breaking crystal, and fast upon it came the scream of the mare released from the thrall the ball had laid upon her, ready to turn on them all. The Lady Carola cowered in the high seat.

"No!" she screamed. "Be as you were! Be as you were!"

And the mare was gone. In its place stood a girl with a banner of red-gold hair flying about her shoulders and a high, proud look about her such as a queen might wear.

"At last!" Her voice carried through the hall. "At last your spell is broken, Carola, and we two come to an accounting!"

To that the Lady Carola made no answer. She crouched, babbling; nor did she ever again speak a word of sense. Thus did the Princess Katha return to her city. And with her coming, the dark cloud which had held its towers in thrall was whirled away and the sun shone brightly once more in its streets and squares.

To Franz, the Princess Katha offered a place at court and what honors it was in her power to bestow. But he returned a straight and honest answer.

"Liege Lady, in my hands is my fortune. I want only to be left to use my skill as best I may."

So did there appear in that city a toy shop. And, since peace and plenty were there also, Franz indeed found the home of his dreams. By the princess' will he served upon her council, and it was often noted that when a matter of import was to be decided, Master Franz fingered a golden snuffbox until he gave his word upon the matter. It was his luck, he sometimes said.

ULLY THE PIPER
High Sorcery (1970) ACE,
Fantasy Stories (2003) Kingfisher

The dales of High Hallack are many and some are even forgotten, save by those who live in them. During the great war with the invaders from overseas, when the lords of the dales and their armsmen fought, skulked, prospered, or sank in defeat, there were small places left to a kind of slumber, overlooked by warriors. There, life went on as it always had, the dalesmen content in their islands of safety, letting the rest of the world roar on as it would.

In such a dale lay Coomb Brackett, a straggle of houses and farms with no right to the title of village, though so the indwellers called it. So tall were the ridges guarding it that few but the wild shepherds of the crags knew what lay beyond them, and many of their tales were discounted by the dalesmen. But there were also ill legends about those heights that had come down from the elder days when humankind first pushed this far north and west. For men were not the first to settle here, though story said that their predecessors had worn the outward seeming of men for convenience, their real aspect being such that no dalesman would care to look upon them by morn light.

While those elder ones had withdrawn, seeking a refuge in the Beyond Wilderness, yet at times they returned on strange pilgrimages. Did not the dalesmen keep certain feast days—or nights—when they took offerings up to rocks which bore queer markings that had not been chiseled there by wind and weather? The reason for those offerings no man now living could tell, but that luck followed their giving was an established fact.

But the dale was good enough for the men of Coomb Brackett. Its fields were rich, a shallow river winding through them. Orchards of fruit flourished, and small woodland copses held nut trees, which also bore crops in season. Fat sheep fed placidly in the uplands, cattle ambled to the river to drink and went then to graze once more. Men sowed in spring, harvested in early autumn, and lay snug in their homesteads in winter. As they often said to one another, who wanted more in this life?

They were as plump as their cattle and almost as slow moving at times. There was little to plague them, for even the Lord of Fartherdale, to whom they owed loyalty, had not sent his tithemen for a tale of years. There was a rumor that the lord was dead in the far-off war. Some of the prudent put aside a folding of woolen or a bolting of linen, well sprinkled with herbs to keep it fresh, against the day when the tithes might be asked again. But for the most part they spun their flax and wool, wove it into stout cloth for their own backs, ate their beef and mutton, drank ale brewed from their barley and wine from their fruit, and thought that trouble was something which struck at others far beyond their protecting heights.

There was only one among them who was not satisfied with things as they comfortably were, because for him there was no comfort. Ully of the hands was not the smallest, nor the youngest of the lads of Coomb Brackett— he was the different one. Longing to be as the rest filled him sometimes with a pain he could hardly bear.

He sat on his small cart and watched the rest off to the feasting on May Day and Harvest Home; and he watched them dance Rings Around following the smoking great roast at Yule—his clever hands folded in upon themselves until the nails bit sorely into the flesh of his palms.

There had been a tree to climb when he was so young he could not rightly recollect what life had been like before that hour. After he fell he had learned what it meant to go hunched of back and useless of leg, able to get from one place to another only by huddling on his cart and pushing it along the ground with two sticks.

He was mender-in-chief for the dale, though he could never mend himself. Aught that was broken was brought to him so that his widowed mother could sort out the pieces, and then Ully worked patiently hour by hour to make it whole again. Sometimes he thought that more than his body had been broken in that fall, and that slowly pieces of his spirit were flaking away within him. For Ully, being chained to his cart, was active in his mind and had many strange ideas he never shared with the world.

Only on a night such as this, when it was midsummer and the youth of the village were streaming up into the hills to set out first fruit, new bread, a flagon of milk, and another of wine on the offering rock. . . . He did not want to sit and think his life away! He was young in spirit, torn by such longings as sometimes made him want to howl and beat with his fists upon the ground, or pound the body which imprisoned him. But for the sake of his mother he never gave way so, for she would believe him mad, and he was not that—yet.

He listened to the singing as the company climbed, giving the rallying call to the all-night dancing:

"High Dilly, High Dally,
Come Lilly, Come Lally!
Dance for the Ribbons—
Dance for new Shoes!"

Who would dance so well this night that he would return by morn's light wearing the new shoes, she the snood of bright ribbons?

Not Stephen of the mill; he was as heavy-footed in such frolicking as if he carried one of the filled flour sacks across his ox-strong shoulders. Not Gretta of the inn, who so wanted to be graceful. (Ully had seen her in the goose meadow by the river practicing steps in secret. She was a kind maid, and he wished her well.)

No, this year, as always, it would be Matt of High Ridge Garth, and Morgana, the smith's daughter. Ully frowned at the hedge which hid the upper road from him, crouched low as he was.

Morgana he knew little of, save that she saw only what she wished to see and did only what it pleased her to do. But Matt he disliked, for Matt was rough of hand and tongue, caring little what he left broken or torn behind his heavily tramped way—whether it was something which could be mended, or the feelings of others, which could not. Ully had had to deal with both kinds of Matt's destruction, and some he had never been able to put right.

They were still singing.

Ully set his teeth hard upon his lower lip. He might be small and crooked of body, but he was a man; and a man did not wail over his hurts. It was so fine a night he could not bear as yet to go back to the cottage. The scent of his mother's garden arose about him, seeming even stronger in the twilight.

He reached within his shirt and brought out his greatest triumph of mending, twisted it in his clever fingers, and then raised it to his lips.

The winter before, one of the rare strangers who ever came over the almost obliterated ridge road had stopped at the inn. He had brought news of battles and lords they had never heard of. Most of Coomb Brackett, even men from the high garths, had come to listen, though to them it was more tale than reality.

At last the stranger had pulled out his pipe of polished wood and had blown sweet notes on it. Then he had laid it aside as Morgana came to share his bench; she took it as her just due that the first smiles of any man were for her. Matt, jealous of the outsider, had slammed down his tankard so hard that he had jarred the pipe on the floor and broken it.

There had been hot words then, and Matt had sullenly paid the stranger a silver piece. But Gretta had picked up the pieces and brought them to Ully, saying wistfully that the music the stranger had made on it was so sweet she longed to hear its like again.

Ully had worked hard to put it together, and when it was complete once again he had taken to blowing an odd note or two. Then he tried even more, imitating a bird's song, the sleepy murmur of the river, the wind in the trees. Now he played the song he had so put together note by note, combining the many voices of the dale itself. Hesitatingly he began, and then grew more confident. Suddenly he was startled by a clapping of hands and jerked his head painfully around to see Gretta by the hedge.

"Play—oh, please play more, Ully! A body could dance as light as a wind-driven cloud to music like that."

She took up her full skirt in her hands and pointed her toes. But then Ully saw her smile fade, and he knew well her sorrow, the clumsy body which would not obey the lightness of mind. In a moment she was smiling again and ran to him, holding out her work-calloused hand.

"Such music we have never had, Ully. You must come along and play for us tonight!"

He shrank back, shaking his head, but Gretta coaxed. Then she called over her shoulder.

"Stephen, Will! Come help me with Ully, he can pipe sweeter than any bird in the bush. Let him play for our dancing tonight, and we shall be as well served as they say the old ones were with their golden pipes!"

Somehow Ully could not refuse them, and Stephen and Will pushed the cart up to the highest meadow where the token feast had been already spread on the offering rock and the fire flamed high. There Ully set pipe to lips and played.

But there were some not so well pleased at his coming. Morgana, having halted in the dance not far away, saw him and cried out so that Matt stepped protectively before her.

"Ah, it's only crooked Ully," she cried spitefully. "I had thought it some one of the monsters out of the old tales crawled up from the woods to spy on us." And she gave an exaggerated shiver, clinging to Matt's arm.

"Ully?" Matt laughed. "Why does Ully crawl here, having no feet to dance upon? Why stare at his betters? And where did you get that pipe, little man?" He snatched at the pipe in Ully's hands. "It looks to me like the one I had to pay a round piece for when it was broken. Give it here now; for if it is the same, it belongs to me!"

Ully tried to hold onto the pipe, but Matt's strength was by far the greater. The resting dancers had gathered close to the offering rock where they were opening their own baskets and bags to share the midnight feast. There was none to see what chanced here in the shadow. Matt held up the pipe in triumph.

"Good as new, and worth surely a silver piece again. Samkin the peddler will give me that and I shall not be out of pocket at all."

"My pipe!" Ully struggled to get it, but Matt held it well out of his reach.

"*My* pipe, crooked man! I had to pay for it, didn't I? Mine to do with as I will."

Helpless anger worked in Ully as he tried to raise himself higher, but his movements only set the wheels of the cart moving, and he began to roll down the slope of the meadow backward. Morgana cried out and moved as if to stop him. But Matt, laughing, caught her back.

"Let him go, he will come to no harm. And he has no place here now, has he? Did he not even frighten you?"

He put the pipe into his tunic and threw an arm about her waist, leading her back to the feast. Halfway they met Gretta.

"Where is Ully?"

Matt shrugged. "He is gone."

"Gone? But it is a long way back to the village and he—" She began to run down the slope of the hill calling, "Ully, Ully!"

The runaway cart had not gone that way, but in another direction, bumping and bouncing toward the small wood which encircled half the high meadow, its green arms held out to embrace the open land.

Ully crouched low, afraid to move, afraid to try to catch at any of the shrubs or low hanging branches as he swept by, lest he be pulled off to lie helpless on the ground.

In and out among the trees spun the cart, and Ully began to wonder why it had not upset, or run against a trunk or caught in some vine. It was almost as if it were being guided. When he tried to turn and look to the fore, he could see nothing but the dark wood.

Then with a rush, the cart burst once more into the open. No fire blazed here, but the moon seemed to hang oddly bright and full just above, as if it were a fixed lamp. Heartened somehow, Ully dared to reach out and catch at a tuft of thick grass, a vine runner, and pulled the cart around so that he no longer faced the wood through which he had come, but rather an open glade where the grass grew short and thick as if it were mown. Around was a wall of flowers and bushes, while in the middle was a ring of stones, each taller than Ully, and so blazingly white in the moonlight that they might have been upright torches.

Ully's heart ceased to pound so hard. The peace and beauty of the place soothed him as if soft fingers stroked his damp face and ordered his tousled hair. His hands resting on his shrunken knees twitched, he so wanted his pipe.

But there was no pipe. Softly Ully began to hum his tune of the dale: bird song, water ripple, wind. Then his hum became a whistle. It seemed to him that all the beauty he had ever dreamed of was gathered here, just as he had fit together broken bits with his hands.

Great silvery moths came out of nowhere and sailed in and out among the candle pillars, as if they were weaving some unseen fabric, netting a spell. Hesitatingly, Ully held out one hand, and one of the moths broke from the rest and lit fearlessly on his wrist, fanning wings which might have been tipped with stardust for the many points of glitter there. It was so light he was hardly aware that it rested so, save that he saw it. Then it took to the air again.

Ully wiped the hand across his forehead, sweeping back a loose lock of hair, and as he did so . . .

The moths were gone; beside each pillar stood a woman. Small and slight indeed they were, hardly taller than a young child of Ully's kin, but these were truly women, for they were dressed only in their long hair. The bodies revealed as they moved were so perfectly formed that Ully knew he had never seen real beauty before. They did not look at him, but glided on their small bare feet in and out among the pillars, weaving their spell even as the moths had done. At times they paused, gathering up their hair with their two hands, to hold it well away from their bodies and shake it. It seemed to Ully that when they did so there was a shifting of glittering motes carried along in a small cloud moving away from the glade, though he did not turn his eyes to follow it.

Though none of them spoke, he knew what they wanted of him, and he whistled his song of the dale. He must truly be asleep and dreaming, or else in that wild dash downslope he had fallen from the cart and suffered a knock from which this vision was born. But dream or hurt, he would hold to it as long as he could. This—this was such happiness as he had never known.

At last their dance grew slower and slower, until they halted, each standing with one hand upon a pillar side. Then they were gone; only the moths fluttered once again in the dimming light.

Ully was aware that his body ached, that his lips and mouth were dry, and that all the weight of fatigue had suddenly fallen on him. But still he cried out against its ending.

There was movement by the pillar directly facing him, and someone came farther into the pale light of new dawn. She stood before him, and for the last time she gathered up her hair in both hands, holding it out shoulder high. Once, twice, thrice, she shook it. But this time there were no glittering motes. Rather he was struck in the face by a blast of icy air, knocked from his cart so his head rapped against the ground, dazing him.

He did not know how long it was before he tried to move. But he did struggle up, braced on his forearms. Struggle—he writhed and fought for balance.

Ully who could not move his shriveled legs, nor straighten his back—why—he was straight! He was as straight as Stephen, as Matt! If this were a dream . . .

He arched up, looked for the woman to babble questions, thanks, he knew not what. But there was no one by the pillar. Hardly daring to trust the fact that he was no longer bowed into a broken thing, he crawled, feeling strength flow into him with every move, to the foot of the pillar. He used that to draw himself to his feet, to stand again!

His clothes were too confining for his new body. He tore them away. Then he was erect, the pillar at his back and the dawn wind fresh on his body. Still keeping his hold on the white stone, he took small cautious steps, circling his support. His feet moved and were firm under him; he did not fall.

Ully threw back his head and cried his joy aloud. Then he saw the glint of something lying in the center of the pillar circle and he edged forward. A sod of green turf was half uprooted, and protruding from it was a pipe. But such a pipe! He had thought the one he mended was fine; this was such as a high lord might treasure!

He picked it loose of the earth, fearing it might well disappear out of his very fingers. Then he put it to his lips and played his thanks to what, or who, had been there in the night; he played with all the joy in him.

So playing he went home, walking with care at first because it was so new to him. He went by back ways until he reached the cottage and his mother. She, poor woman, was weeping. They had feared him lost when he had vanished from the meadow and Gretta had aroused the others to search for him without result. When she first looked at this new Ully his mother judged him a spirit from the dead, until he reassured her.

All Coomb Brackett marveled at his story. Some of the oldest nodded knowingly, spoke of ancient legends of the old ones who had once dwelt in the dales, and how it was that they could grant blessings on those they favored. They pointed out symbols on the pipe which were not unlike those of the tribute rock. Then the younger men spoke of going to the pillar glade to hunt for treasure. But Ully grew wroth and they respected him as one set apart by what had happened, and agreed it was best not to trouble those they knew so little of.

It would seem that Ully had brought back more than straight legs and a pipe. For that was a good year in the dale. The harvest was the richest in memory, and there were no ill happenings. Ully, now on his two feet, traveled to the farthest homestead to mend and play, for the pipe never left him. And it was true that when they listened to it the feet of all grew lighter, as did their hearts, and any dancer more skillful.

But inside Matt there was no rest. Now he was no longer first among the youth; Ully was more listened to. He began to talk to himself, hinting dire things about gifts from unknown sources, and a few listened, those who are always discontent to see another prosper. Among them was Morgana, for she was no longer so courted. Even Gretta nowadays was sometimes partnered before her. And one day she broke through Matt's grumbling shortly.

"What one man can do, surely another can also. Why do you keep muttering about Ully's fortune? Harvest Eve comes soon and those old ones are supposed then to come again to view the wealth of the fields and take their due. Go to Ully's pillars and play; they may be grateful again!"

Matt had been practicing on the pipe he had taken from Ully, and he did well enough with the rounds and the lays the villagers had once liked; though the few times he had tried to play Ully's own song the notes had come sourly, off-key.

The more Matt considered Morgana's suggestion, the better it seemed, and the old thought of treasure clung in his mind. There could be deals with the old ones if a man were shrewd. Ully was a simple fellow who had not known how to handle such. His thoughts grew ambitious.

So when the feast came Matt lagged behind the rest and turned aside to take a brambly way he judged would bring him to Ully's oft-described ring of pillars. Leaving much of his shirt hanging in tatters on the briers and his skin red-striped by thorns, he came at last into the glade.

There were the pillars right enough, but they were not bright and white and torchlike. Instead, each seemed to squat direfully in a mass of shadow which flowed about their bases as if something unpleasant undulated there. But Matt dropped down beneath one of the trees to wait. He saw no moths, though there were vague flutterings about the crowns of the pillars. At last, thinking Ully fashioned out of his own imagination much of his story, Matt decided to try one experiment before going back to the feasting villages to proclaim just how much a lie his rival was.

But the notes he blew on his pipe were shrill squeaks; and when he would have left, he found to his horror and dismay that he could not move, his legs were locked to the ground as Ully's had once been. Nor could he lower the pipe from his lips, but was compelled by a will outside his own to keep up that doleful, sorry wailing. His body ached, his mouth was dry, and fear was laid as a lash upon him. He saw things around those pillars.

He would close his eyes! But again he could not, but must pipe and watch, until he was close to the brink of madness. Then his leaden arms fell, the pipe spun away from his lax fingers, and he was dimly aware the dawn had come.

From the pillar before him sped a great bloated thing with an angry buzzing—such a fly as he had seen gather to drink the blood spilled at a butchering—yet this was greater than six of those put into one.

It flew straight into his face, stinging him. He tried to beat it away, but could only manage to crawl on his hands and knees; the fly continued to buzz about him as a sheepdog might herd a straggler.

Somehow Matt finally struggled to his feet, but it was long before he could walk erect. For many days his face was so swollen that he would not show it in the village, nor would he ever tell what happened to him.

But for many a year thereafter Ully's pipe led the people of Coomb Bracket to their feasting and played for their dancing. Sometimes, it was known, he slipped away by himself to the place of pillars and there played for other ears, such as did not side mortal heads.

DREAM SMITH
Spell of the Witch World (1972) DAW

There are many tales which the songsmiths beat out in burnished telling, some old and some new. And the truth of this one or that—who knows? Yet at the heart of the most improbable tale may be a kernel of truth. So it was with the tale of the Dream Smith—though for any man now living to prove it—he might as well try to empty Fos Tern with a kitchen ladle!

Broson was smith in Ghyll, having both the greater and the smaller mysteries of that craft. Which is to say that he wrought in bronze and iron and also in precious metals. Though the times he could use tools on the latter were few and far between.

He had two sons, Arnar and Collard. Both were, in boyhood, deemed likely youths. So Broson was looked upon, not only in Ghyll (which lies at river-fork in Ithondale), but as far off as Sym and Boldre, as a man well fortuned. Twice a year he traveled by river to Twyford with small wear of his own making, wrought hinges and sword blades, and sometimes brooches and necklets of hill silver.

This was in the days before the invaders came and High Hallack was at peace, save with outlaws, woods-runners, and the like, who raided now and then from the wastes. Thus it was needful that men in the upper dales have weapons to hand.

Vescys was lord in Ithondale. But the dalesmen saw little of him since he had heired, through his mother, holdings in the shorelands and there married a wife with more. So only a handful of elderly men and a wash-wife or two were at the keep, and much of it was closed from winter's midfeast to the next.

It was in the third year after Vescys' second marriage (the dalesmen having that proclaimed to them by a messenger) that something of more import to Ghyll itself occurred.

A trader came down from the hills, one of his ponies heavily laden with lumps of what seemed pure metal, yet none Broson could lay name to. It had a sheen, even unworked, which fascinated the smith. And, having tried a small portion by fire and hammer, he enthusiastically bargained for the whole of the load. Though the peddler was evasive when asked to name the source, Broson decided that the man was trying to keep secret something which might well bring him profit again. Since the pony was lame, the man consented with visible (or so it appeared) reluctance to sell, leaving in one of Broson's metal bins two sacks of what was more melted scrap than ore.

Broson did not try to work it at once. Rather he spent time studying, thinking out how best he might use it. His final decision was to try first a sword. It was rumored that Lord Vescys might visit this most western of his holdings, and to present his lord with such an example of smith work could only lead to future favor.

The smelting Broson gave over to Collard, since the boy was well able to handle such a matter. He had determined that each of his sons in turn would learn to work with this stuff, always supposing that the peddler would return, as Broson was sure he would, with a second load.

And in that he gave his son death-in-life, even as he had once given him life.

For, though no man could ever learn what had gone wrong in the doing, for all those standing by, including Broson himself, had detected no carelessness on Collard's part (he was known to be steady and painstaking), there was an explosion which nigh burst the smithy to bits.

There were burns and hurts, but Collard had taken the worst of both. It would have been better had he died in that moment. For when he dragged back into half-life after weary months of torment and despair, he was no longer a man.

Sharvana, Wise Woman and healer, took the broken body into her keeping. What crawled out of her house was no Collard, a straight, upstanding son for any man to eye with pride, but a thing such as you see sometimes carved (luckily much weathered away) on the ruins left by the Old Ones.

Not only was his body so twisted that he walked bent over like a man on whom hundreds of seasons weighed, but his face was a mask such as might leer at the night from between trees of a haunted forest. Sharvana had an answer to that, but it was not enough to shield him entirely from the eyes of his fellows—though all were quick to avert their gaze when he shambled by.

She took supple bark and made a mask to hide his riven face. And that he wore at all times. But still he kept well out of the sight of all.

Nor did he return to his father's house, but rather took an old hut at the foot of the garden. This he worked upon at night, never coming forth by day lest his old comrades might sight him. And he rebuilt it into a snug enough shelter. For, while the accident seemed to have blasted all else, it had not destroyed his clever hands, nor the mind behind the ruined face.

He would work at the forge at night, but at last Broson said no to that. For there was objection to the sound of hammers, and the people of Ghyll wanted no reminding of who used them. So Collard came no more to the smithy.

What he did no man knew, and he came to be almost forgotten. The next summer, when his brother married Nicala of the Mill, he never appeared at the wedding, nor ventured out in those parts of the yard and garden where those of the household might see him.

It was in the third year after his accident that Collard did come forward, and only because another peddler came into the forge. While the trader was dickering with Broson, Collard stood in the shadows. But when the bargain for a set of belt knives was settled, the smith's son lurched forward to touch the trader's arm.

He did not speak, but motioned to a side table where-on he had spread out a square of cloth and set up a series of small figures. They were fantastical in form, some animals, some men, but such men as might be heroes from the old tales, so perfect were their bodies. As if poor Collard, doomed to go crooked for as long as he lived, had put into these all his longing to be one with his fellows.

Some were of wood, but the greater number of metal. Broson, astounded at viewing such, noted the sheen of the metal. It was the strange stuff he had thrown aside, fearing to handle again after the accident.

The trader saw their value at once and made an offer. But Collard, with harsh croaks of voice, brought about what even Broson thought a fair bargain.

When the man had gone, Broson turned eagerly to his son. He even forgot the strangeness of that blank mask which had only eyes to give it the semblance of a living man.

"Collard, how made you these? I have never seen such work. Even in Twyford, in the booths of merchants from overseas—before—before you never fashioned such." Looking at that mask his words began to falter. It was as if he spoke not to his son, but to some-thing as alien and strange as those beings reputed to dance about certain stones at seasons of the year, stones prudent men did not approach.

"I do not know—" came the grating voice, hardly above an animal's throaty growl. "They come into my head—then I make them."

He was turning away when his father caught at his arm. "Your trade—"

There were coins from overseas, good for exchange or for metal, a length of crimson cloth, two knife handles of carven horn.

"Keep it." Collard might be trying to shrug but his convulsive movement sent him off balance, so he must clutch at the tabletop. "What need has such as I to lay up treasure? I have no bride price to bargain for."

But if you wanted not what the trader had to offer—why this?" Arnar, who had been watching, demanded. He was a little irked that his brother, who was younger and, in the old days had no great promise, could suddenly produce such marketable wares.

"I do not know." Again Collard slewed around, this time turning his bark mask in his brother's direction. "I think I wished to know if they had value enough to attract a shrewd dealer. But, yes, father, you have reminded me of another debt." He took up the length of fine cloth, a small gold coin which had been looped so that one might wear it on a neck chain. "The Wise Woman served me as best she could."

He then added: "For the rest—let it be for my share of the household, since I cannot earn my bread at the forge."

At dusk he carried his offering to Sharvana. She watched as he laid coin and cloth on the table in her small house, so aromatic of drying herbs and the brews from them. An owl with a wing in splints perched on a shelf above his head, and other small wild things, here tame, had scuttled into cover at his coming.

"I have it ready—" She went to the cupboard, bringing out another mask. This was even more supple. He fingered it wonderingly.

"Well-worked parchment," she told him, "weather-treated, too. I have been searching for something to suit your purpose. Try it. You have been at work?"

He took from the safe pocket of his jerkin the last thing he had brought her. If the trader had coveted what he had seen that morn, how much more he would have wanted this. It was a figure of a winged woman, her arms wide and up as if she were about to take to the skies in search of something there seen and greatly desired. For this was to the figures he had sold as a finished sword blade is to the first rough casting.

"You have seen—*her?*" Sharvana put out her hand as if to gather up the figure, but she did not quite touch it.

"As the rest," he grated. "The dreams—then I awaken. And I find that, after a fashion, I can make the dream people. Wise Woman, if you were truly friend to me, you would give me from your stores that which would make me dream and never wake again!"

"That I cannot do, as you know. The virtue of my healing would then pour away, like running water, through my fingers. But you know not why you dream, or of what places?" Her voice became eager, as if she had some need to learn this.

"I know only that the land I see is not the dales—at least the dales as they now are. Can a man dream of the far past?"

"A man dreams of his own past. Why not, were the gift given, of a past beyond his own reckoning?"

"Gift!" Collard caught up that one word and made it an oath. "What *gift—?*'

She looked from him to the winged figure. "Collard, were you ever able to make such before?"

"You know not. But to see my hands so—I Would trade all for a straight back and a face which would not afright a woman into screaming!"

"You have never let me foresee for you—"

"No! Nor shall I!" he burst out. "Who would want that if he were as I am now? As to why this—this dreaming and the aftermaking of my dream people has come upon me—well, that which I was handling in the smithy was no common metal. There must have been some dire ensorcelment in it. That trader never returned so we could ask about it."

"It is my belief," said Sharvana, "that it came from some stronghold of the Old Ones. They had their wars once, only the weapons used were no swords, nor spears, no crossbow darts, but greater. It could be that trader ventured into some old stronghold and brought forth the remains of such weapons."

"What matter?" asked Collard.

"Only this—things which a man uses with emotion, fashions with his hands, carries with him, draw into themselves a kind of—I can only call it 'life.' This holds though many seasons may pass. And if that remnant of emotion, that life, is suddenly released—it could well pass in turn into one unwary, open—"

"I see." Collard ran fingertips across the well-scrubbed surface of the table. "Then as I lay hurt I was so open—and there entered into me perhaps the memories of other men?"

She nodded eagerly. "Just so! Perhaps you see in dreams the dales as they were before the coming of our people."

"And what good is that to me?"

"I do not know. But use it, Collard, use it! For if a gift goes unused it withers and the world is the poorer for it."

"The world?" his croak was far from laughter. "Well enough, I can trade these. And if I earn my bread so, then no man need trouble me. It is young to learn that all one's life must be spent walking a dark road, turning never into any welcoming door along the way."

Sharvana was silent. Suddenly she put out her hand, caught his before he could draw back, turning it palm up in the lamplight.

He would have jerked free if he could, but in that moment her strength was as great as that of any laboring smith, and she had him pinned. Now she leaned forward to study the lines on the flesh so exposed.

"No foreseeing!" He cried that. The owl stirred and lifted its sound wing.

"Am I telling you?" she asked. "Have it as you wish, Collard. I have said naught." She released his wrist.

He was uneasy, drawing back his hand quickly, rubbing the fingers of the other about that wrist as if he would erase some mark she had left there.

"I must be going." He caught up the parchment mask—that he would try on only in his own hut where none could see his face between the taking off of one covering and the putting on of another.

"Go with the good will of the house." Sharvana used the farewell of their people. But somehow those words eased his spirit a little.

Time passed. All avoided Collard's hut, he invited no visitors, not even his father. Nor did another trader come. Instead there was news from the greater world outside the Dale, a world which seemed to those of Ghyll that of a songsmith.

When the Lord Vescys had wedded, his second wife had had already a daughter, though few had heard of her. But now the story spread throughout all of Ghyll and to the out-farms and steads beyond.

For a party had ridden to the keep, and thereafter there was much cleaning and ordering of the rooms in the mid-tower. It was that Vescys was sending his daughter, the Lady Jacinda, to the country, for she sickened in the town.

"Sickened!" Collard, on his way to the well, paused in the dark, for the voice of his sister-in-law Nicala was sharp and ringing in the soft dusk. "This is no new thing. When Dame Matild had me come into the rooms to see how much new herb rushing was needed for the undercarpeting, she spoke freely enough. The young lady has never been better than she is now—a small, twisted thing, looking like a child, not a maid of years like to wed. Not that our lord will ever find one to bed with her unless he sweetens the bargain with such dowry as even a High Lord's daughter could bring!

"The truth of it is, as Dame Matild said—the new Lady Gwennan, she wants not this daughter near her. Very delicate she is, and says she cannot bear my lord a fine son if she sees even in bower and at table such a twisted, crooked body."

Collard set his pail noiselessly down and moved a step or two nearer the window. For the first time in seasons curiosity stirred in him. He willed Nicala to continue.

Which she did, though he gained little more facts. Until Broson growled he wanted his mulled ale, and she went to clatter at the hearth. Collard, once more in his hut, did not reach for his tools, but looked into the flames in the fireplace. He had laid aside his mask, and now he rubbed his hands slowly together while he considered word by word what he had overheard.

This Lady Jacinda—so she was to be thrust out of sight, into a country keep where her kin need not look at her? Oh, he knew the old belief that a woman carrying dared not see anything or anyone misshapen, lest it mark the babe in her womb. And Lord Vescys would certainly do all he could to assure the coming of a son. There would be no considering the Lady Jacinda. Did she care? Or would she be glad, as he had, to find a place away from sight of those who saw her not like them?

Had she longed to be free of that and would be pleased to come to Ghyll? And was it harder for her, a maid, to be so, than it was for him? For the first time Collard was pulled out of his dreams and his bitterness, to think of someone living, breathing, walking this world.

He arose and picked up the lamp. With it in hand, he went to a wall shelf and held the light to fully illumine the figures there. There were a goodly company of them, beasts and humanoid together. Looking upon them critically, something stirred in his mind, not quite a dream memory.

Collard picked several up, turned them about. Though he did not really look at them closely now, he was thinking. In the end he chose one which seemed right for his purpose.

Bringing the figure back to the table he laid out his tools. What he had was a small beast of horselike form. It was posed rearing, not as in battle but as if it gamboled in joyous freedom. But it was not a horse, for from between its delicate ears sprang a single horn.

Laying it on its side, Collard went to work on the base. It was cockcrow when he was done. And now the dancing unicorn had become a seal, its base graven to print a "J" with a small vine tracery about it.

Collard pushed back from the table. The need which had set him to work was gone. Why had he done this? He was tempted almost to sweep the piece into the melting pot so he could not see it again. But he did not, only pushed it away, determined to forget his folly.

He did not witness the entrance of the Lord Vescys and his daughter, though all the rest of Ghyll gathered. But he heard later that the Lady Jacinda came in a horse litter, and that she was so muffled by cloaks and covers that only her face could be seen. It was true that she was small and her face very pale and thin.

"Not make old bones, that one won't," he heard Nicala affirm. "I heard that Dame Matild has already sent for Sharvana. The lady brought only her old nurse and she is ailing, too. There will be no feasting at Ghyll Keep." There was regret in her voice, not, Collard believed, for the plight of the Lady Jacinda, but rather that the stir at the keep would be soon over, with none of the coming and going which the villagers might enjoy as a change in their lives.

Collard ran fingers along the side of his mask. For all his care it was wearing thin. He might visit Sharvana soon. But why, his hard honesty made him face the truth, practice such excuses? He wanted to hear of the lady and how she did in a body which imprisoned her as his did him. So with the coming of dark he went. But at the last moment he took the seal, still two-minded over it.

There was a light in Sharvana's window. He gave his own private knock and slipped in at her call. To his surprise she sat on her stool by the fireplace, her journey cloak still about her shoulders, though its hood had slipped back. Her hands lay in her lap, and there was a kind of fatigue about her he had never seen before.

Collard went to her quickly, took her limp hands in his.

"What is it?"

"That poor little one, Collard, cruel—cruel—"

"The Lady Jacinda?"

"Cruel," she repeated. "Yet she is so brave, speaking me fair and gentle even when I needs must hurt her poor body. Her nurse, ah, she is old and for all her love of her lady can do little to ease her. They traveled at a pace which must have wracked her. Yet I would judge she made no word of complaint. Just as she has never spoken out against her banishment, or so her nurse told me privately after I had given a soothing draught and seen her asleep. But it is a cruel thing to bring her here—"

Collard squatted on his heels, listening. It was plain that the Lady Jacinda had won Sharvana's support. But at length she talked herself quiet and drank of the herb tea he brewed for her. Nor did she ask why he had come, seemed only grateful that he was there. At last, to shake her out of bleak thoughts, he took the seal out of his belt wallet and set it in the lamplight.

It had been fashioned of that same strange metal which had been his bane. He was drawing on that more and more, for it seemed to him that those pieces he fashioned of that were his best and came the closest to matching his dream memories. Now it glowed in the light.

Sharvana drew a deep breath, taking it up. When she looked upon the seal in the base she nodded.

"Well done, Collard. I shall see this gets to her hand—"

"Not so!" Now he wanted to snatch it back, but somehow his hand would not obey his wish.

"Yes." She was firm. "And, Collard, if she asks—you will bring others. If for even the short space of the fall of a drop of water you can make her forget what her life is, then you have done a great thing. Bring to me the happy ones, those which will enchant her—perhaps even make her smile."

So Collard culled his collection, startled to find how few he had which were "happy." Thus he set to work, and oddly enough now his dream people he remembered as beautiful or with an amusing oddness.

Twice had he made visits to Sharvana with his offerings. He was working only with the strange metal now and found it easy to shape. But the third time she came to him, which was so unusual he was startled.

"The Lady Jacinda wants to see you, to thank you face to face."

"Face to face!" Collard interrupted her. His hands went up to cover even that mask in a double veiling of his "face."

Then Sharvana's eyes flashed anger. "You are—or you were—no coward, Collard. Do you so fear a poor, sick maid who wants only to give you her thanks? She has fretted about this until it weighs on her mind. You have given her pleasure, do not spoil it. She knows how it is with you, and she has arranged for you to come by night, through the old posten gate, I with you. Do you now say 'no'?"

He wanted to, but found he could not. For there had grown in him the desire to see the Lady Jacinda. He had been, he thought, very subtle in his questioning of Sharvana, perhaps too subtle for the bits he had learned he had not been able to fit into any mind picture. Now he found himself agreeing.

Thus, with Sharvana as his guide, Collard came to the bower of the Lady Jacinda, trying to walk as straight as his crooked body would allow, his mask tightly fastened against all eyes, most of all hers.

She was very small, even as they said, propped with cushions and well covered with furred robes, as she sat in a chair which so overtopped her with its tall back that she seemed even smaller. Her hair was long and the color of dark honey, and it lay across her hunched shoulders in braids bound with bell-hung ribbons. But for the rest she was only a pale, thin face and two white hands resting on the edge of a board laid across her lap for a table. On that board marched all the people and beasts he had sent to her. Now and then she caressed one with a fingertip.

Afterward he could not really remember their greeting to one another. It was rather as if two old friends, long parted, came together after many seasons of unhappiness, to sit in the sun and just enjoy warmth and their encounter. She asked him of his work, and he told her of the dreams. And then she said something which did linger in his mind:

"You are blessed, Collard-of-the-magic-fingers, that you can make your dreams live. And I am blessed that you share them with me. Now—name these—"

Somehow he began to give names to each. And she nodded and said:

"That is just right! You have named it aright!"

It was a dream itself, he afterward thought, as he stumbled back to the village beside Sharvana, saying nothing as he wavered along, for he was reliving all he could remember, minute by minute.

With the morn he awoke after short hours of sleep with the urgency to be at work again. And he labored throughout the day with the feeling that this was a task which must be done, and he had little time in which to do it.

What he wrought now was not any small figure but a hall in miniature—such a hall as would be found, not in the small Keep of Ghyll, but perhaps in the hold of a High Lord. Scented wood for paneling, metal—the strange metal wherever it could be used.

Exhausted, he slept. He ate at times when hunger pinched him hard, but time he did not count—nor how long before he had it done.

He sat studying it carefully, marking the furnishing. There were two high seats upon a dais. Those were empty—and that was not right. Collard rubbed his hand across his face, the rough scar tissue there for the first time meant nothing to him. There was something lacking—and he was so tired. He could not think.

He staggered away from the table, dropped upon his bed. And there he slept so deeply he believed he did not dream. Yet when he woke he knew what it was he must do. Again came that feeling of time's pressure, so he begrudged the moments it took to find food to eat.

Once more he wrought and worked with infinite care. When he had done, with that passing of time he did not mark, he had the two who must sit on those high seats and he placed them therein.

She—no twisted, humped body, but straight and beautiful, free to ride, to walk, to run as she never had been. Yet her face, it was Jacinda and none could deny it.

The man—Collard turned him around, surveying him carefully. No, this was no face he knew, but it had come to him as the right one. And when he put them both into the high hall, he looked about the hut with new eyes.

He rose and washed and dressed in his poor best, for to him for some years now clothing was merely to cover the body, not for pleasure. Then he put away all his tools, those he had made himself. Afterward he gathered up all the figures, those which were too grotesque or frightening, the first he had made. These he threw one by one into the melting pot.

Putting a wrapping of cloth about the hall he picked it up. It was heavy to carry and he must go slowly. But when he went outside the village was astir, lights of street torches such as were used only on great occasions were out. And the Keep was also strung with such torches.

A cold finger of fear touched Collard, and he hobbled by the back way to Sharvana's cottage. When he knocked upon her door he was sweating, though the wind of night was chill enough to bring shivers to those it nipped.

When she did not call, Collard was moved to do what he had never done before; his hand sought the latch and he entered unbidden. Strange scents filled the air and the light of two candles set one at either end of the table burned blue as he had never seen. Between those candles lay certain things he guessed were of the Wise Craft: a roll of parchment spread open with two strange-colored rocks to hold it so, a basin of liquid which shimmered and gave off small sparks, a knife crossed with a rune-carved wand.

Sharvana stood there, looking at him. He feared she might be angry at his coming, but it seemed more as if she had been waiting for him, for she beckoned him on. And though heretofore he had been shy of her secrets, this time he went to her, with the feeling that something was amiss and time grew shorter with each breath.

He did not set down his burden on the table until Sharvana, again without speaking, waved him to do so. She pulled free the cloth, and in the blue candle flame the small hall—Collard gasped. For a moment or two it was as if he had stood at a distance and looked into room which was full-sized—real.

"So—that is the answer." Sharvana spoke slowly. She leaned closer, studying it all, as if she must make sure it was fit for some purpose of her own. She straightened again, her eyes now on Collard.

"Much has happened, you have not heard?"

"Heard what? I have been busied with this. The Lady Jacinda—?"

"Yes. The Lord Vescys died of a fever. It seems that his new lady was disappointed in those hopes which made it necessary to send the Lady Jacinda here. His only heir is his daughter. She is no longer forgotten, and by those who mean her no good. The Lady Gwennan has sent to fetch her— she is to be married forthwith to the Lady's brother Huthart, that they may keep the lands and riches. No true marriage, and how long may she live thereafter—with them wishing what she brings—not her?"

Collard's hands tightened on the edge of the table as he listened. Sharvana's words were a rain of blows, hurting more than any pain of body.

"She—she must not go!"

"No? Who is to stop her, to stand in the path of those who would fetch her? She has bought a little time by claiming illness, lying in bed. Her nurse and I together have afrighted the ladies of the household sent to fetch her by foreseeing death on the road. And that they fear—*before* she is wedded. Now they speak of the Lord Huthart riding here, wedding her on her deathbed if this be it."

"What—"

Sharvana swept on. "This night I called on powers which I have never dared to trouble before, as they can be summoned only once or twice by a Wise Woman. They have given me an answer—if you will aid—"

"How?"

"There is a shrine of the Old Ones—high in the northern craigs. That power which once dwelt there—perhaps it can be summoned again. But it must have a focus point to work through. You have that—" she pointed to the hall. "There sits the Lady Jacinda as she should be, wrought of metal once worked by the Old Ones themselves. How better can power be summoned? But this must be taken to the shrine, and the time is very short."

Collard once more looped the cloth about the hall. He was sure of nothing now save that Sharvana herself believed in the truth of what she said. And if she was right—if she was wrong, what could he do? Try to strike down those who would take the lady away or wed her by force? He—the monster one?

Better believe that Sharvana was right. No one could deny that the Old Ones could still show power if they would; there were too many tales of such happenings. Sharvana had caught up a bag, pushed into it two unlit candles, a packet of herbs.

"Set what you carry on mid-stone," she told him, "light a candle on either side of it, even as you see them here. Give a pinch of herb powder to each flame when it is lit. Call then three times upon Talann. I shall go back to the keep, do what I can to delay matters there. But hurry!"

"Yes." He was already on his way to the door.

Run he could not. The best he could produce was a shambling trot and that was hard to keep over rough ground. But at least he was near the craigs. Doubtless the house of the Wise Woman had always been there for a reason to be close to the shrine of the Old Ones.

Crossing the fields was not too hard, but the climb which followed taxed all his strength and wit. There was a path—perhaps in fairer weather was it easier to follow. But now it proved hard in the dark. Until Collard saw that there was a faint glow of light from what he carried, and he twitched off part of the cloth so that there was radiance from the metal showing.

Twice he slipped and fell, both times rising bruised and bloody, yet he kept on doggedly, more careful of what he carried than his own warped body. He was so tired that he must force himself on inch by painful inch. Now and again overlying that nightmare way he could see the white face of the Lady Jacinda, and there was that in her eyes which kept him struggling.

So he came to the ancient shrine. It was a cleft in the rock, smoothed by the arts of men—or whatever creatures once gathered here—and there was a band of badly eroded carving. Collard thought he could make out in that hints of his dream creatures. But he focused his attention to the stone set directly before the cleft. It was shaped like the crescent moon, its horns pointing outward so Collard stood between them as he set the hall on the altar and took away the covering.

With shaking hands he put up the candles, drew out his tinderbox to light them. Then the pinch of herb for each. His hand shook so he had to steady it with the other as he followed Sharvana's orders.

There was a puff of scented smoke. Collard leaned against the moon altar as he cried out in the best voice he could summon—no louder than the hoarse croak of a fen frog:

Talann, Talann, Talann!"

Collard did not know what he expected. The Old Power was fearsome—he might be blasted where he stood. But when nothing came, he fell to the ground, not only overcome by weariness, but in black despair of mind. Old Power—perhaps too old and long since gone!

Then—was it in his mind?—or did it echo from the rocks about him, tolled in some deep voice as if the ridge itself gave tongue?

"What would you?"

Collard did not try to answer in words; he was too dazed, too awed. He made of his feelings a plea for the Lady Jacinda.

From where he crouched on the frost-chilled rock his eyes were on a level with the hall. It shone in splendor, more and more as if a hundred, a thousand lamps were lit within. He thought he could hear a distant murmur of voices, a sound of lute-playing—warmth—sweet odors—and life—swelling life!

For Jacinda—life for her! Like this—as it should have been! No words—just the knowledge that this was what should have been had matters not gone fearfully astray in another time and place.

Warmth—light—around him! He was not crouched in the cold, he was sitting—looking down a hall—around him—no! For a moment he remembered what must be the truth—he was dreaming again!

But this dream—he pushed aside all doubts. This dream he could claim, it was his to keep, to hold forever! His dream—and hers!

Collard toned his head. She was watching him, a small smile on her lips, welcoming— And in her eyes—what glory in her eyes! He put forth his hand and hers came quickly to meet it.

"My lord—"

For a moment he was troubled. "We dream—"

"Do we? Then let us claim this dream together, and claiming it, make it real!"

He did not quite understand, but she answered his uncertainty somehow.

He began to forget, as she had already resolutely forgotten.

There was a shining pool of strange metal on the altar. It began to flow, to cascade to the ground, to sink into the waiting earth which would safe-hide it forever.

In the Keep Sharvana and the nurse each snuffed a candle by a curtained bed, nodded thankfully to one another.

But in the hall wrought by Collard there was high-feasting and an everlasting dream.

ONE SPELL WIZARD
Garan the Eternal (1972) Fantasy, Moon Mirror (1988) TOR

In all professions there are not only the inspiring great successes and the forgotten failures, but also those who seem unable to climb the tallest peaks, yet do not tumble hopelessly into the pits in between. There were magicians in High Hallack of whom nobles were quick to speak with reverence when in company; what they said in private remained private if they were lucky. One could never be quite sure of the substance of shadows, nor even of the pedigree of a web-weaving spider. Such uncertainty can be nerve-racking at times.

Near the other end of the scale there were warlocks and wizards, who barely made livings in tumbledown cottages surrounded by unpleasant bogs, or found themselves reduced to caves where water dripped unendingly and bats provided a litter they could well do without. Their clients were landsmen who came to get a cure for an ailing cow or for a stumbling horse. Cow—horse—when a man of magic should be rightfully dealing with the fate of dales, raking in treasure from lords, living in a keep properly patrolled at night by things which snuffled at the doors to keep all unhappy visitors within their chambers from dusk to dawn—or the reverse, depending upon the habits of the visitor. Magicians have a very wide range of guests, willing and unwilling.

Wizards have no age, save in wizardry. And to live for long in a bat- and water-haunted cave sours men. Though even in the beginning, wizards are never of a lightsome temperament. A certain acid view of life accompanies the profession.

And Saystrap considered he had been far too long in a cave. It was far past the time when he should have been raised to at least a minor hill keep with a few grisly servitors, if not to the castle of his dreams. There was certainly no treasure in his cave, but he refused to face the fact that there never would be.

The great difficulty was the length of Saystrap's spells—they were a hindrance to his ambition. They worked very well for as much as twenty-four hours—if he expended top effort in their concoction. He was truly a master of some fine effects with those; he was labeled a dismal failure because they did not last.

Finally he accepted his limitations to the point of working out a method whereby a short-lived spell could be put to good account. To do this, he must have an assistant. But, while a magician of note could pick and choose apprentices, a half-failure such as Saystrap had to take what he might find in a very limited labor market.

Not too far from his cave lived a landsman with two sons. The eldest was a credit to his thrifty upbringing, a noble young man who was upright enough to infuriate all his contemporaries in the neighborhood to who he was constantly cited as an example. He worked from sunrise to early dusk and never spent silver when copper would do—in all ways an irritating youth.

But his brother was as useless a lad as any father wanted to curse out of house and field. With the mowing hardly begun he could be found lying on his back watching clouds—*clouds*, mind you! Put to any task, he either broke the tools by some stupid misuse or ruined what he was supposed to be working on. And he could not even talk plain, but gobbled away in so thick a voice that no decent man could understand him—not that any wanted to.

It was the latter misfortune that attracted Saystrap's attention. A wizard's power lies in spells, and most of these must be chanted aloud in order to get the proper effect—even a short-time effect. An assistant who was as good as dumb—who would not learn a few tag ends of magic and then have the audacity to set up in business for himself—was the best to employ.

So one morning Saystrap arrived via a satisfactory puff of smoke in the middle of the cornfield where the landsman was berating his son for breaking a hoe. The smoke curled very impressively into the sky as Saystrap stepped out of its curtain. And the landsman jumped back a step or two, looking just as amazed as he should.

"Greetings," said Saystrap briskly. He had long ago learned that any long build-up was not for a short-spelled wizard. It was best to forego the supposedly awed mumbles and get right to the point.

But he did not overlook the staging, of course. A pass or two in the air produced two apple trees about shoulder height. And, as an additional nice touch, a small dragon winked into existence and out again before the landsman found his voice. "It is a fair morning for field work," Saystrap continued.

"It was," the landsman returned a bit uncertainly. Magic in the woods or a cave now—that was one thing. But magic right out in the middle of your best cornfield was a different matter. The dragon was gone, and he could not really swear it had been here. But those trees were still standing where they would be a pesky nuisance around which to get the plow. "How—how can I serve you, Master—Master—?"

"Saystrap," supplied the wizard graciously. "I am your near neighbor, Master Ladizwell. Though busy as you have been on your very fruitful land you may not be aware of that."

Master Ladizwell looked from the trees to the wizard. There was a hint of a frown on his face. Wizards, like the lord's taxmen, were too apt to take more than they gave in return. He did not relish the thought of living cheek by jowl, as it were, with one. And he certainly had not invited this meeting.

"No, you have not," said Saystrap answering his thought. This was the time to begin to bear down a little and let the fellow know just whom and what he was dealing with. "I have come now to ask your assistance in a small matter. I need a pair of younger feet, stronger arms, and a stout back to aid me. Now this lad" —for the first time he glanced at the younger son— "has he ever thought of going into service?"

"Him?" The landsman snorted. "Why, what fool would—" Then he stopped in mid-word. If this wizard did not know of his stupid son's uselessness, why tell the family shame abroad? "For what length of service?" he demanded quickly. If a long bond could be agreed upon, he might get the lout out from underfoot and make a profit into the bargain.

"Oh, the usual—a year and a day."

"And his wages, Master Saystrap?"

"Well, now, at this season another pair of knowledgeable hands—" Ladizwell hurriedly kicked at the broken hoe, hoping the wizard had not seen that nor heard his hot words to his son.

"Will this suffice?" Saystrap waved a hand in a grand, wide gesture, and in the field stood a fine horse.

Ladizwell blinked. "Yes, right enough!" he agreed hurriedly and held out his hand. Saystrap slapped his into it, thus binding the bargain.

Then the wizard gestured again and smoke arose to wreathe both him and his newly engaged servant. When that cleared, they had vanished; and Ladizwell went to put a halter on the horse.

At dawn the next day Ladizwell was far from pleased when he went to the stable to inspect his new prize and found a rabbit instead of a horse nibbling the straw in the stall. At least he did not have to feed and clothe that slip-fingered lout for a year and a day, so perhaps he was still better off than he had been yesterday.

Saystrap, back in his cave, was already making use of his new servant. To him, Joachim was a tool with neither wit nor will of his own. But the sooner he began to give what aid he could, the better. There were brews boiled and drunk—by Joachim. And he had to be led, or pushed and pulled, through patterns drawn in red and black on the rough floor. But in the end Saystrap was satisfied with the preliminaries and went wearily to his hammock, leaving Joachim to huddle on a bed of bracken.

At dawn the wizard was up and busy again. He allowed Joachim a hasty—and to the lad very untasty—meal of dried roots and berries, hurrying him until Joachim was almost choking on the last bite. Then they took to the traveling cloud again and emerged from it not too far from the Market Cross of Hill Dallow. That is—there strode out of the cloud a man in a gray wool tunic leading a fine frisky two-year-old colt, as promising an animal as anyone would want to lay eye on. And this was sold at the first calling in the horse fair for a bag of silver pieces heavy enough to weight a man's belt in a satisfying manner.

The colt was led home by the buyer and shown off as being an enviable bargain. But when the moon rose, Joachim stole out of the barn, dropping stall and door latch into place behind him. He shambled off to the far side of the pasture where Saystrap waited impatiently.

This was a game they played several times over, always with a good gain thereby. Saystrap treated Joachim well enough, though more as if he were really a horse than any man. And this was a mistake on Saystrap's part. Joachim might seem stupid and be too thick of speech to talk with his fellows, but he was not slow-witted. He learned from all he heard and saw his master do. Deep in him a small spark of ambition flared. There had not been anything about his father's land that had ever brought that spark into being. There, no matter how hard he tried, his brother could outdo him without seeming to put forth any great effort. But this was another world.

Then, by chance, he learned something that even Saystrap did not know: spells were not always wedded to the spoken word.

His master had sent him to gather herbs in a wild country where men seldom traveled. But furred and four-footed hunters had their own well-trodden trails.

For all the barrenness of the wild land, Joachim was glad enough to be alone in the open. He missed the fields more than he would have believed possible. It seemed a very long time since he had had a chance to lie and watch the slow passing of clouds overhead and to dream of what he might do if he had a magician's treasure now or had been born into a lord's family.

But this day he found himself mulling over Saystrap's doings rather than paying attention to clouds and his one-time dreams. In his mind he repeated the words he had heard the wizard use in spells. By now the change spell, at least, was as familiar to him as his own name. Then he heard a sound and looked around—into the yellow-green eyes of a snow cat. It hissed a challenge, and Joachim knew that here stalked death on four paws. So, he concentrated—without being sure of how or on what.

The snow cat vanished! On the rock crouched a barn rat.

Joachim shivered. He put out his hand to test the reality of what he saw, and the rat scuttled away squealing. Was this by any chance some ploy of Saystrap's, meant to frighten him into his work? But—there was another way of testing. Joachim looked down at his own body. Did he dare? He thought again.

Soft fur, paws with claws—he was a snow cat! Not quite believing, he leaped up to bound along the ridge. Then he stopped beneath a rock spur and thought himself a man again, more than a little frightened at his own act.

Then that fear became pride, the first time in his life he had cause to feel that. He was a wizard! But only in part. One spell alone could not make him a real one. He must learn more and more and at the same time try to keep his secret from Saystrap if he could. Doubts about that gnawed at him all the way back to the cave.

The only trouble was that Saystrap no longer tried other spells. And the few scraps Joachim assembled from his master's absent-minded mutterings were no help at all. Saystrap was concentrating on what he intended to be his greatest coup in shape-changing.

"The harvest fair at Garth Haigis is the chance to make a good profit," he told Joachim, mainly because he had to tell someone of his cleverness. "We must have something eye-catching to offer. A pity I cannot change you into a coffer of jewels; I could sell you to more than one buyer. Only then, when the spell faded" —he laughed a little, evilly, and poked Joachim in the ribs with his staff-of-office— "you would be too widely scattered between one keep and the next ever to be put together again." He was deep in thought now, running his long forenail back and forth across his teeth.

"I wonder." He eyed Joachim appraisingly. "A cow is bait only for a landsman. And we have dealt too often in horses; there might be someone with a long memory there." He tapped the end of his staff on the rock. "Ah! A trained hunting falcon—one such as brings a gleam of avarice to any lord's eye!"

Joachim was uneasy. True enough, all Saystrap's tricks had always worked smoothly. He had had no trouble freeing himself from barns and stables when the spell lifted. But keeps were better guarded, and it might not be easy to flee out of those. Then he thought of his own secret. He might in the allotted time cease to be Saystrap's falcon, but that did not mean he had to become an easily recognized man.

The fair at Garth Haigis was an important one. Joachim, wearing falcon shape, gazed about eagerly from his perch on Saystrap's saddle horn. Men in booths remarked on the fine bird and asked its price. But the wizard set such a high one that all shook their heads, though one or two went so far as to count the silver in their belt purses.

Before noon a man wearing the Cross-Key badge of Lord Tanheff rode up to Saystrap.

"A fine bird that—fit for a lord's mews. My lord would like to look at it, Master Falconer."

So Saystrap rode behind the servant to an upper field where tents were set up for the comfort of the nobly born. They summoned to them merchants with such wares as they found interesting.

Lord Tanheff was a man of middle years, and he had no son to lift shield after him. But his daughter, the Lady Juluya, sat at his right hand. Since she was a great heiress, she was the center of a goodly gathering of young lords, each striving to win her attention. It was her way to be fair and show no one favor over his fellows.

She was small and thin. Had she not been an heiress, none perhaps would have found her a beauty. But she had a smile that could warm a man's heart (even if he forgot the gold and lands behind it) and eyes that were interested in all they saw. Once Joachim looked upon her, he could not see anything else.

Neither could Saystrap. It suddenly flashed into his mind as a great illuminating truth that there were other ways of gaining a keep than through difficult spells. One such way was marriage. He did not doubt that, could he gain access to the lady, he would win her. Was he not a wizard and so master of such subtleties that these clods sighing around her now could not imagine?

His planned trickery might also be turned to account. For if he sold Joachim to her father, and the bird apparently escaped and returned to him, then he could enter the lady's own hall to bring it back. He could use the pretense of the strayed bird to open all doors.

"Father—that falcon! It is a lordly bird," the Lady Juluya cried as she saw Joachim.

He felt the warmth of pride. Though she saw him as a bird, he was admired. Then he lost that pride. If she could see him as he really was, she would speedily turn away.

Lord Tanheff was as pleased as his daughter and quickly struck a bargain with Saystrap. But the wizard whispered into the bird's ear before he placed it on the gloved hand of the lord's falconer, "Return swiftly tonight!"

Joachim, still watching the Lady Juluya, did not really heed that order. For he was wondering why, at the moment of change, he could not wish himself into some new guise that would bring him close to the lady. He did not have long to watch her, however, for the falconer took him to the keep. Joachim stood on a perch in the mews, hooded now and seeing nothing, left in the dark to get the feel of his new home as was the way with a bird in a strange place. He could hear other hawks moving restlessly and, beyond, the noises of the keep. He wondered how Saystrap thought he could get out of this place in man's shape. Had the wizard some magic plan ready to cover that?

Joachim guessed right. The wizard knew that his falcon-turned-man could not leave the mews as easily as a landsman's barn. He did not trust his assistant to have wits enough to work out any reasonable escape. He himself would move cautiously to gain Joachim's release and not allow magic to be suspected, not when he planned to enchant the Lady Juluya. So Saystrap sat down in a copse near the keep to wait moonrise.

At sunset, however, the clouds gathered, and it was plain that no moon would show. Saystrap could not summon moon magic now, but perhaps he could put the coming storm to account. If he could only be sure when

Joachim's change would occur, a matter with which he had never concerned himself before. Had it not been for his new plan to win Lady Juluya, the wizard would not have cared what happened to Joachim. Stupid lads could always be found, but a wizard was entitled to keep his own skin safe. Lord Tanheff, if he did suspect spells, would be just the sort to appeal to some major sorcerer for protection. Saystrap, for all his self-esteem, was not blinded to his own peril from an encounter of that kind.

He could not sit still, but paced back and forth, trying to measure time. To be too early would be as fatal as being too late. The cloud-traveling spell could not be held long. If Joachim could not take to its cover at once, Saystrap could not summon it again that night. He bit his thumbnail, cursing the rain now beginning to fall.

At the keep that same rain drove men to take cover indoors. Joachim heard footsteps in the mews and the voices of the falconer and his assistant. His time for change was close. He shifted on the perch, and the bells fastened to his jesses rang. The footsteps were closing in, and the change was now!

Suddenly he was standing on his own two feet, blinking into the light of a lantern the falconer held. The man's mouth opened for a shout of alarm. Joachim thought his mind spell.

A snow cat crouched snarling. The falconer, with some presence of mind, threw his lantern at that fearsome beast before he took to his heels, Joachim in great bounds behind. But as the shouting falconer broke one way out of the door, Joachim streaked in the other, trying to reach the outer wall.

That wall was far too high to leap over, but he sped up the stairs leading to the narrow defense walk along its top. Men shouted, and a torch was thrown, nearly striking him. Joachim leaped at a guard aiming a spear, knocked the man down, and was over him and on. Just ahead more men were gathering, bending bows. He thought—

There was no cat on the wall—nothing! The men-at-arms hurried forward, thudding spear heads into every patch of shadow. They were unable to believe that the animal had vanished.

"Wizardry! Tell my lord quickly. There is wizardry here!"

Some stayed to patrol by twos and threes, no man wanting to walk alone in the dark with wizardry loose. The storm struck harder; water rushed over the wall. It washed with such force that it swept away a small gold ring no man had seen in that dusk, carrying it along a gutter, tumbling it out and down, to fall to the muddy earth of the inner garden where the Lady Juluya and her maids grew sweet herbs and flowers. There it lay under the drooping branches of a rain-heavy rose bush.

When the Lord Tanheff heard the report of the falconer and the wall guards, he agreed that it was plain the falcon had been enchanted and was some stroke of wizardry aimed at the keep. He then dispatched one of his heralds to ride night and day to demand help from the nearest reputable sorcerer, one to whom he already paid a retaining fee as insurance against just such happenings. In the meantime he cautioned all to keep within the walls; the gates were not to be opened for any cause until the herald returned.

Saystrap heard the morning rumors at the fair where men now looked suspiciously at their neighbors, bundling their goods away to be on the road again even though the fair was not officially over. With magic loose, who knew where it would strike next? Better be safe, if flatter of purse. The lord had sent for a sorcerer—and with magic opposed to magic anything might happen to innocent bystanders. Magic was no respecter of persons.

The wizard did not give up his plan, however, for the Lady Juluya; it was such a good one. Common sense did not even now baffle his hopes. So he lurked in hiding and made this new plan and that, only to be forced to discard each after some study.

The Lady Juluya, walking in her garden, stooped to raise a rain-soaked rose and saw a glint in the mud. Curious, she dug and uncovered a ring that seemed to slip on her finger almost of its own accord.

"Wherever did you come from?" She held her hand into the watery sunshine of the morning, admiring the ring. She was more than a little pleased at her luck in finding it. Since all her maids denied its loss, she finally decided that it must have lain buried for years until the heavy rain washed it free. She would claim it for her own.

Two days passed; and then three. Still the herald did not return. The Lord Tanheff did not permit the keep gates to be opened. The fairground was deserted now. Saystrap, driven to a rough hiding place in the woods, gnawed his nails down to the quick. Only a fanatical stubbornness kept him lurking there.

None in the lady's tower knew that the ring grew loose and slipped from her finger when she took to her bed at night. It became a mouse feasting on crumbs from her table. Joachim realized that this was a highly dangerous game he played. It would be much wiser to assume wings and feathers once more and be out of the castle with three or four good flaps of his wings. Yet he could not bring himself to leave.

The Lady Juluya was courted and flattered much; yet she was a girl of wit and good humor, wise enough to keep her head. She was both kind and courteous. Time and time again Joachim was tempted to take his true form and tell her his story. But she was seldom alone; when she was, he could not bring himself to do it. Who was he? A loutish clod, so stupid and clumsy he could not even work in the fields nor speak plainly. At his mere appearance he was sure she would summon a guard immediately. And talk! He could not tell anything they would understand.

After the first night he did not remain a mouse, but went out onto the balcony and became a man, squatting in the deepest pool of shadow. He thought about speech and how hard it was for him to shape words to sound like those of others. He practiced saying in whispers the strange sounds he had heard Saystrap mumble, tongue twisters though they were. He did not use them for the binding of spells, but merely to listen to his own voice. By daybreak of the third day he was certain, to his great joy, that he did speak more clearly than he ever had before.

In the woods Saystrap had at last fastened upon a plan he thought would get him into the keep. If he could be private with the lady only for a short space, he was certain that he could bind her to his will and that all would be as he wished. He had seen the herald ride forth and knew that it might not be too long before he would return with aid.

Though the gates were shut, birds flew over the wall. And pigeons made their nests in the towers and along the roofs. On the fourth day Saystrap assumed a feathered form to join them.

They wheeled and circled, cooed, fluttered, peered in windows, preened on balconies and windowsills. In her garden the Lady Juluya shook out grain for them, and Saystrap was quick to take advantage to such a summons, coming to earth before her.

There is this about wizardry: if you have dabbled even the nail tip of one finger in it, then you have gained knowledge beyond that of ordinary men. The ring that was Joachim recognized the pigeon that was Saystrap. At first he thought his master had come seeking him. Then he noted the wizard-pigeon ran a little this way, back that, and so was pacing out a spell pattern about the feet of Lady Juluya.

Joachim did not know what would happen if Saystrap completed that magic, but he feared the worst. So he loosed his grip on the lady's finger and spun out, to land across one of the lines the pigeon's feet were marking so exactly.

Saystrap looked at the ring and knew it. He wanted none of Joachim, though he was shaken at meeting his stupid apprentice in such a guise. One thing, however, at a time. If this spell were now spoiled or hindered, he might not have another chance. He could settle with Joachim later, after accomplishing his purpose. So with a sharp peck of bill, he sent the ring flying.

Joachim spun behind the rose bush. Then he crept forth again—this time a velvet-footed tom cat. He pounced, and the wildly fluttering pigeon was between his jaws.

"Drop it—you cruel thing!" Lady Juluya struck at the cat. Still gripping the pigeon, Joachim dodged and ran into the courtyard.

Then he found he held no pigeon, but a snarling dog twice his size broke from his grip. He leaped away from Saystrap to the top of a barrel and there grew wings, beak, and talons. Once more a falcon, Joachim was able to soar above the leaping, slavering hound, so eager to reach him.

There was no dog, but a thing straight out of a nightmare—half scaled, with leathery wings more powerful than Joachim's and a lashing tail with a wicked spiked end. The creature spiraled up after the falcon into the sky.

He could perhaps outfly it if he headed for the open country. But he sensed that Saystrap was not intent upon herding an unwilling apprentice back to servitude. He was after the Lady Juluya; therefore there must be fight not flight.

From the monster came such a force of gathered power that Joachim weakened. His poor feat of wizardry was feeble opposed to Saystrap's. With a last despairing beat of wings, he landed on the roof of Lady Juluya's tower and found himself sliding down it, once more a man. While above him circled the griffin, seemingly well content to let him fall to his death on the pavement below.

Joachim summoned power for one last thought.

He fell through the air a gray pebble. So small and so dark a thing escaped Saystrap's eyes. The pebble struck the pavement and rolled into a crack.

Saystrap meanwhile turned to bring victory out of defeat. He alighted in the courtyard and seized upon the Lady Juluya to bear her away. The pebble rolled from hiding, and Joachim stood there. Bare-handed, he threw himself at the monster. This time he shouted words clear and loud, the counterspell which returned Saystrap to his own proper form. Grappling with the wizard, he bore him to the ground, trying to gag him with one hand over his mouth so that he might not utter any more spells.

At that moment the herald rode in upon them as they struggled, ringed around (at a safe distance) by such of the keep folk who were not afraid to be caught in the backlash of any spells from the tangle.

Lord Tanheff shouted an order from the door of the hall to where he had swept his daughter. The herald tossed at the fighters the contents of a box he had brought back with him (one ruby, two medium-sized topazes). These caused a burst of light and a clap of thunder. Joachim stumbled out of a puff of smoke, groping his way blindly. A fat black spider sped in the opposite direction, only to be gobbled up by a rooster.

Well pleased now that they had someone reasonably normal in appearance to blame for all the commotion, the men-at-arms seized Joachim. When he tried to use his spell, he found it did not work. Then the Lady Juluya called imperiously:

"Let him alone!" she ordered. "It was he who attacked the monster on my behalf. Let him tell us who and what he is—"

Let him tell, thought Joachim in despair, *but I cannot do that.* He looked at the Lady Juluya and knew that he must at least try. As he ran his tongue over his lips, she prompted him encouragingly, "Tell us first who you are."

"Joachim," he croaked miserably.

"You are a wizard?"

He shook his head. "Never more than a very small part of one, my lady." So eager was he to let her know the truth of it all that he forgot his stumbling tongue and all else but the tale he had to tell. He told it in a flow of words all could understand.

When he was done, she clapped her hands together and cried, "A fine, brave tale. I claim you equal to such acts. Wizard, half-wizard, third or fourth part of a wizard that you may be reckoned, Joachim, I would like to know you better."

He smiled a little timidly. Though he might be finished with wizardry, anyone the Lady Juluya claimed to be a man had a right to pride. Fortune had served him well this time. If he meddled in magic concerns again, it might not continue to do so.

In that he was a wise man—as he later had chance to prove on numerous occasions. Joachim, his foot firmly planted on the road to success in that hour, never turned back nor faltered.

But the rooster had a severe pain in its middle and was forced to let the spider go. How damaged it was by that abrupt meeting with the irony of fate no man knew thereafter, for Saystrap disappeared.

LONDON BRIDGE
Magazine of Fantasy and Science Fiction, October (1973)

"Just another deader—" Sim squatted to do a search.

Me, I don't dig deaders much. No need to. There're plenty of den-ins and stores to rummage if you need a pricker or some cover-ups. Of course, I took that stunner I found by what was left of the dead Fuzz's hand. But that was different, he wasn't *wearing* it. Good shooter too; I got more'n a dozen con-rats before it burned out on me. Now I didn't want to waste any time over a deader, and I said so, loud and clear.

Sim told me to cool the air. He came back with a little tube in his hand. I took one look at that and gave him a sidesweep, took his wrist at just the right angle. The tube flew as straight as a beam across the stalled wiggle-walk and into a blow duct.

"Now what in blue boxes did you want to do that for?" Sim demanded. Not that he squared up to me over it. By now he knows he can't take me and it's no use to try. "I could have traded that to an Up—real red crowns and about ten of them!"

"What trade? Those hazeheads haven't got anything we want and can't get for ourselves."

"Sure, sure. But it's kinda fun showing them a haul like that and seeing 'em get all hot."

"Try it once too often and you'll take a pricker where it won't do you any good. Anyway, we're not here to scrounge."

The city's big. I don't know anybody who's ever gotten all over it. You could walk your feet raw trying since all the wiggle-walks cut out. And some of it is deathtraps—what with Ups who have lost any thinking stuff which ever was between their dirty ears, or con-rats. Those get bigger and bolder every time we have a roundup to kill them off. The arcs have shut off in a lot of places, and we use flashes. But those don't show much and they die awfully quick. So we don't go off the regular paths much. Except because of this matter of the Rhyming Man, which was why Sim and I were trailing now. I didn't much like the look ahead. A lot of arcs were gone, and the shadows were thick between those which were left. Anything could hide in a doorway or window to jump us.

We're immune, of course, or we wouldn't be kicking around at all. When the last plague hit, it carried off most of the cits. All the oldies went. I must have been nine—ten—I don't know. You forget about time where the ticks can tell you the hour but not the day or year. I had a good tick on my wrist right now, but it couldn't tell me what day it was, or how many years had gone by. I grew a lot, and sometimes when I got a fit to do something different, I went to the lib and cut into one of the teachers. Most of the T-casts there didn't make much sense. But I'd found a couple in the histro-division on primitives (whatever those were) which had some use. There was Fanna— she got excited about some casts which taught you about how to take care of someone who got hurt. Because of that Sim was walking beside me today. But, as I say, most of the stuff on the tapes was useless to us now.

There are twenty of us, or were 'til the Rhyming Man came around. Some don't remember how it was before the plague. They were too young then. And none of us remember back to before the pollut-die-off. Some of us have paired off for den-in—Lacy and Norse, Bet and Tim. But me, I'm not taking to den-in with some fem yet. There's too much to see and do, and a guy wants to be free to take off when he feels like it. Course I have to keep an eye on Marsie. She's my sister—she was just a baby in the plague days—and she's still young enough to be a nuisance—like believing in the Rhyming Man. Like he's something out of a tape, I mean—that he's going to take good children Outside.

Maybe there was an Outside once. There's so much about it in the tapes, and why would anyone want to spend good time making up a lot of lies and taping them? But to go Outside—no one has for longer than I've been around.

Marsie, she's like me, she digs the tapes. I can take her with me, and she'll sit quiet, not getting up and running out like most littles just when I get interested. No, she'll sit quiet with a teacher. I found some tapes of made-up stories—they showed the Outside and animals moving on their own and making noises before you squeezed them. Marsie, she had a fur cat I found and she lugged it everywhere. She wanted it to come alive and kept thinking she could find a way to make it. Kept asking Fanna how you could do that. Littles get awfully set on things sometimes and near burn your ears out asking why—why—why—

That was before the Rhyming Man. We heard about him later. Our territory runs to the double wiggle-walk on Balor, and there we touch on Bart's crowd's hangout. They're like us—not Ups. Once in a while we have a rap-sing with them. We get together for con-rat roundups and things like that. But we don't live cheek by cheek. Well, some time back Bart came over on a mission—a real important search. He had this weirdo story about a couple of their littles going off with the Rhyming Man.

Seems like one of his fems saw part of it. She must have been solid clear through between the ears not to guess it was trouble. She heard his singing first, and she thought someone was running a tape, only it didn't sound right. Said the littles were poking around down in the streets—she could see them through a window. All of a sudden they stood up and stopped what they were doing, and then went running off. She didn't think of it again—because Bart's crowd's like us, they don't have any Ups in their territory. He keeps scouts out to make sure of that.

But when it came feed time, those two didn't show. Then the fem shoots out what she saw and heard. So they send out a mission, armed. Though Bart couldn't see how Ups could have got through.

Those littles, they never did find them. And the next day two more were gone. Bart rounded them up, kept them under cover. But three more went, and with them the fem he had set with a stunner on guard. So now he wanted to know what gives, and if we had anything to tell him. He was really sky climbing and shadow watching by the time he got to us. Said now a couple more fems were missing. But he had two guys who had seen the Rhyming Man.

What Bart told us sounded like an Up was loose. But for an Up to do the same thing all the time, that wasn't in curve at all. Seems he wore this bright suit—all sparkling—and danced along singing and waving. Bart's boys took straight shots at him (with burners). And they swore that the rays just bounced off him, didn't even shake him.

We organized for a roundup quick and combed as much as you can comb with all the den-ins up and down. There was nothing at all. Only, when we came back—two more littles were gone. So Bart's crowd packed up and moved over to our side of the double wiggle-path and settled in a block front, downside from our place. But he was tearing mad, and now he spent most of his time over in his old territory hunting. He was like an Up with a new tube of pills, thinking only of one thing, getting the Rhyming Man.

Though right now I could understand it, how he felt, I mean, because Marsie was gone. We'd warned all our littles and fems good after Bart told us the score. They weren't to go on any search—not without a guy with them. But Marsie had gone to the tape lib this morning with Kath and Don. Don came back by him-self saying they had heard some funny singing and that the girls had run away so he could not find them.

We rounded up all the littles and fems and posted a guard like an Up raid was on. Jak and Tim took out one way, Sim and I the other. The lib was empty. We searched there first. And whoever had been there couldn't have doubled back toward us. Too many had the path in good sight. So we went the other way and that took us into deep territory. Only I knew we were going right by what I found just a little while ago and had tucked in my belt now—Marsie's cat.

And if she'd dropped *that*—! I kept my hand on my pricker. Maybe you couldn't finish this Rhyming Man with a burner, but let me get close enough, and I'd use a pricker and my own two hands!

The deep territories are places to make a guy keep watching over his shoulder. They're always so quiet, and you keep coming across deaders from the old days, mostly just bones and such—but still they're deaders. And all those windows—you get an itchy feeling between your shoulders that someone just looked at you and ducked away when you turned around. With a hundred million places for a loony Up to hide out we had no chance at all of finding him. Only I wasn't going to give up as long as I could keep walking—knowing he had Marsie.

Sim had been marking our way. It's been done—getting lost—even keeping to paths we know. But we were coming into a place I'd never seen, big buildings with straight walls, no windows in them. There were a couple of wide doors—and one was open.

"Listen!" Sim pawed my arm. But he needn't have, I heard it too.

London Bridge is broken down.

Broken down, broken down,

My fair lady.

How shall we built it up again?

Up again, up again?

My fair lady.

Built it up with silver and gold.

Silver and gold, silver and gold.

My fair lady.

I had it now, pointed with my pricker— "In there." Sim nodded and we went through the open door.

Silver and gold will be stole away,

Stole away, stole away,

My fair lady.

Odd, the sound didn't seem to get any louder, but it wasn't fading away either, just about the same. We were in a big wide hall with a lot of openings off on either side. There were lights here, but so dim you had to take a chance on your path.

Build it up with iron and steel,

Iron and steel, iron and steel.

My fair lady.

Still ahead as far as I could tell.

Iron and steel will rust away,

Rust away, rust away,

My fair lady.

Build it up with wood and clay,

Wood and clay, wood and clay.

My fair lady.

All at once the singing was loud and clear. We came out on a balcony above a place so big that most of the den-ins I knew could be packed into it with room to spare. There was light below, but it shone up from the floor in a way I had never seen before.

"There he is!" Again I didn't need Sim to point him out. I saw the blazing figure. Blaze he did, blue and gold, like he was a fire, but the wrong color. And he was dancing back and forth as he sang:

Wood and clay will wash away,

Wash away, wash away,

My fair lady.

Build it up with stone so strong,

Stone so strong, stone so strong.

My fair lady.

Hurrah, it will hold for ages long,

Ages long, ages long.

My fair lady.

At the end of each verse he would bend forward in a jerky little bow, and those listening would clap their hands and laugh.

Because Marsie and Kath were not the only littles down there. There were four others I had never seen before. And none of them were Up brats.

The Rhyming Man jigged around. When he stopped and they all yelled for more, he shook his head and waved his hands as if he couldn't talk but could make motions they could understand. They all got up and formed a line and began to hop and skip after him. The floor was all laid out in squares of different colors. And, as those were stepped on, lights flashed underneath. It was as if the littles were playing a game. But I couldn't understand it.

Then the Rhyming Man began that singing again:

Erry, Orrey, Ickery Ann

Fillison, follison, Nicholas John

Queevy, quavey, English Navy

One, two, three, out goes—

She, he, she, he, she, she, he!

Like he was shooting off a burner, he pointed his finger at each little in line. And, as he did so (it was like an Up dream), they just weren't there anymore!

Marsie! I couldn't jump over that balcony. I'd go splat down there, and that wouldn't do Marsie any good, if she was still alive. But I began running along, trying to find some way down, and there was no way down. Only what would I do when I got there, because now the Rhyming Man was gone also.

Sim pounded along behind me. We were about halfway around that place—still no way down. Then I saw it ahead, and I guess I more fell than footed it down those inner stairs. When I came charging out on the empty floor—nothing, nothing at all!

I even got down and felt the squares where they had been standing, pounded on those, thinking those might be doors which opened to drop them through. But the blocks were tight. Then I began to wonder if I had tripped out like an Up—without any pills. I just sat there holding my head, trying to think.

"I saw them, they were here—then they weren't." Sim kicked at one of the squares. "Where did they go?"

If he saw it, too, then I hadn't tripped. But there had to be an answer. I made myself try to remember everything I had seen—that crazy song, them marching, and then another crazy song—

I stood. "They got out somehow. And if there's a door it can be opened." I couldn't just be wild mad, I had to think, and straight now. No use of just wanting to grab the Rhyming Man and pound his head up and down on the floor.

"Listen here, Sim. We've got to find out what happened. I'm staying here to look around. You cut back and get the rest of the guys, bring them here. When he comes out, I want that Rhyming Man!"

"Staying here by yourself mightn't be too good an idea, Lew."

"I can take cover. But I don't want to miss him when he comes back. Then I can trail him until you catch up." It might not be too bright, but it was the best plan I had. And I intended going over that flooring until something did happen and we could find the way in to wherever Marsie and the rest of the littles were.

Sim went off. I knew he was glad to get out of that place, but he'd be back. Sim had never back-footed yet on any mission. Meanwhile, I'd better get busy.

I closed my eyes. Sometimes if you think about a thing hard enough you see it like a picture in your mind. Now—the six littles—and then, in front of them, the Rhyming Man jiggling back and forth, his suit all bright and shining—singing about London Bridge—

Opening my eyes again I studied the blocks. The littles had been sitting, or squatting, there, there, and there. And he had been over there. I raised my hand to point as if I were showing it all to someone else.

London Bridge? London was another city—somewhere—not near here. When the cities were all sealed against the bad air—well, for a while they talked to each other with T-casts. Then it wasn't any use—everyone had it all just as bad.

Cities died when their breathers broke—those that had been the worst off in the beginning. In others—who knows what happened? Maybe we were lucky here, maybe we weren't. But our breathers had kept on going—only the plagues hit and people died. After all the oldies died, there was a lot more air.

But London was a city once. London Bridge? A bridge to another city? But how could one step off a block onto a bridge you couldn't see, nor feel? Silver and gold—we wore silver and gold things—got them out of the old stores. My tick was gold.

The whole song made a kind of sense, not that that helped any. But that other thing he had sung, after they had moved around on the blocks—I closed my eyes trying to see that march, and I moved to the square Marsie had stood on right at the last, following the different-colored blocks just as I had seen her do.

Yeah, and I nearly lost my second skin there. Because those blocks lit up under my feet. I jumped off—no lights. So the lights had meaning. Maybe the song also—

I was almost to the block where the Rhyming Man had been, but before I reached it, he was back! He was flashing blue and gold in a way to hurt your eyes, and he just stood there looking at me. He had no stunner, nor burner, not even a pricker. I could have cut him down like a con-rat. Only if I did that, I'd never get to Marsie, I had to have what was in his mind to do that.

Then he gave me one of those bows and said something, which made no more sense than you'd get out an Up high on red:

Higgity, piggity, my black hen—
She lays eggs for gentlemen.

I left my pricker in my belt, but that didn't mean I couldn't take him. I'm light but I'm fast, and I can take any guy in our crowd. It's mostly thinking, getting the jump on the other. He was still spouting when I dived at him.

It was like throwing myself head first into a wall. I never laid a finger on him, just bounced back and hit the floor with a bang which knocked a lot of wind out of me. There he was, standing as cool as drip ice, shaking his head a little as if he couldn't believe any guy would be so dumb as to rush him. I wanted a burner then—in the worst way. Only I haven't had one of those for a long time.

One, two, three, four,
Five, six, seven.
All good children
Go to Heaven.
One, two, three, four,
Five, six, seven, eight,
All bad children
Have to wait.

I didn't have to have it pounded into my head twice. There was no getting at him—at least not with my hands. Sitting up, I looked at him. Then I saw he was an oldie—*real* oldie. His face was all wrinkled, and on his head there was only a fringe of white hair, he was bald on top. The rest of him was all covered up with those shining clothes. I had never seen such an oldie except on a tape—it was like seeing a story walking around.

"Where's Marsie?" If the oldie was an Up, maybe he could be startled into answering me. You can do that with Ups sometimes.

One color, two color,
Three color, four,
Five color, six color,
Seven color more.
What color is *yours*?

He pointed to me. And he seemed to be expecting some answer. Did he mean the block I was sitting on? If he did—that was red, as he could see for himself. Unless he was on pills—then it sure could be any color as far as he was concerned.

"Red," I played along. Maybe I could keep him talking until the guys got here. Not that there was much chance in that; Sim had a good ways to go.

You 're too tall,
The door's too small.

Again he was shaking his head as if he were really sorry for me for some reason.

"Listen," I tried to be patient, like with an Up you just *had* to learn something from, "Marsie was here. You pointed at her—she was gone. Now just where did she go?"

He took to singing again:
Build it up with stone so strong,
Stone so strong, stone so strong.
Hurrah, it will last ages long—
Ages long, ages long—

Somehow he impressed me that behind all his queer singing there was a meaning, if I could only find it. That bit about my being too tall now—

"Why am I too tall?" I asked.

A.B.C.D.
Tell your age to me.

Age? Marsie was a little—small, young. That fitted. He wanted littles. I was too big, too old.

"I don't know—maybe I'm about sixteen, I guess. But I want Marsie—"

He had been jiggling from one foot to the other as if he wanted to dance right out of the hall. But still he faced me and watched me with that queer "I'm-sorry-for-you" look of his.

Seeing's believing—no, no, no!
Seeing's believing, you can't go!

Believing, that is best,

Believing's seeing, that's the test.

Seeing's believing, believing's seeing—I tried to sort that out.

"You mean—the littles—they can believe in something, even though they don't see it? But me, I can't believe unless I see?"

He was nodding now. There was an eager look about him. Like one of the littles playing some trick and waiting for you to be caught. Not a mean trick, a funny, surprise one.

"And I'm too old?"

He was watching me, his head a little on one side.

One, two, sky blue.

All out but you.

Sky blue—Outside! But the sky hadn't been blue for years—it was dirty, poisoned. The whole world Outside was poisoned. We'd heard the warnings from the speakers every time we got close to the old sealed gates. No blue sky—ever again. And if Marsie was Outside—dying!

I pointed to him just as he had to the littles. I didn't know his game, but I could try to play it, if that was the only way of reaching Marsie now—I had to play it!

"I'm too big, maybe, and I'm too old, maybe. But I can try this believing-seeing thing. And I'm going to keep on trying until I make it work! Either that, or I turn into an oldie like you doing it. So—"

I turned my back on him and went right back to that line of blocks up which they had gone and I started along those with him watching, his head still a little to one side as if he were listening, but not to me. Under my feet those lights flashed. All the time he watched. I was determined to show him that I meant just what I said—I was going to keep on marching up and down there—maybe till I wore a hole through the floor.

Once I went up and nothing happened. So I just turned around, went back, ready to start again.

"This time," I told him, "you say it—loud and clear—you say it just like you did the other time—when the littles went."

At first he shook his head, backed away, making motions with his hands for me to go away. But I stood right there. I was most afraid he would go himself, that I would be left in that big, bare hall with no one to open the gate for me. But so far he hadn't done that vanishing bit.

" 'Orrey,' " I prompted.

Finally, he shrugged. I could see he thought I was heading into trouble.

Well, now it was up to me. Believing was seeing, was it? I had to keep thinking that this was going to work for me as well as it had for the littles. I walked up those flashing blocks.

The Rhyming Man pointed his finger at me.

"Erry, Orrey, Ickery Ann."

I closed my eyes. This was going to take me to Marsie; I had to believe that was true, I hung on to that—hard.

Fillison, follison, Nicholas John.

Queeuy, quavey, English Navy

One, two, three—

This was it! Marsie—I'm coming!

"Out goes he!"

It was awful, a twisting and turning, not outside me, but in. I kept my eyes shut and thought of Marsie and that I must get to her. Then I fell, down flat. When I opened my eyes—this—this wasn't the city!

There was a *blue* sky over me and things I had seen in the T-casts—grass that was still green and not sere and brown like in the last recordings made before they sealed the city forever. There were flowers and a bird—a real live *bird*—flying overhead.

"Amazing!"

I was still on my knees, but I moved around to face him. The Rhyming Man stood there, but that glow which hung around him back in the hall was gone. He just looked like an ordinary oldie, a real tired oldie. But he smiled and waved his hand to me.

"You give me new hopes, boy. You're the first of your age and sex. Several girls have made it, but they were more imaginative by nature."

"Where are we? And where's Marsie?"

"You're Outside. Look over there."

He pointed and I looked. There was a big gray blot—ugly looking, spoiling the brightness of the grass, the blue of the sky. You didn't want to keep looking at it.

"There's your city, the last hope of mankind, they thought, those poor stubborn fools who had befouled their world. Silver and gold, iron and steel, mud and clay—cities they've been building and rebuilding for thousands of years. Their bridge cities broke and took them along in the destruction. As for Marsie, and those you call the littles, they'll know about real stone, how to really build. You'll find them over that hill."

"And where are you going?"

He sighed and looked even more tired. "Back to play some more games, to hunt for more builders."

"Listen here," I stood up. "Just let me see Marsie, and then I'll go back, too. They'll listen to me. Why, we can bring the whole crowd, Bart's, too, out—"

But he'd started shaking his head even before I was through.

"Ibbity, bibbity, sibbity, Sam.

Ibbity, bibbity, as I am—" he repeated and then added, "No going back once you're out."

"You do."

He sighed. "I am programmed to do just that. And I can only bring those ready to believe in seeing—"

"You mean, Sim, Jak, the others can't get out here—ever?"

"Not unless they believe to see. That separates the builders, those ready to begin again, from the city blind men."

Then he was gone, just like an old arc winking out for the last time.

I started walking, down over the hill. Marsie saw me coming. She had flowers stuck in her hair, and there was a soft furry thing in her arms. She put it down to hop away before she came running.

Now we wait for those the Rhyming Man brings. (Sim and Fanna came together two days ago.) I don't know who he is, or how he works his tricks. If we see him, he never stays long, and he won't answer questions. We call him Nicholas John, and we live in London Bridge, though it's not London, nor a bridge—just a beginning.

CPSIA information can be obtained at www.ICGtesting.com
Printed in the USA
BVOW08s1835211213

339337BV00005B/7/P